THE CYPRESSES BELIEVE IN GOD

· *Volume Two* ·

CLUNY CLASSICS

RICCARDO BACCHELLI
The Mill on the Po: God Save You (BOOK ONE)
The Mill on the Po: Misery (BOOK TWO)
The Mill on the Po: Nothing New Under the Sun (BOOK THREE)

ROBERT HUGH BENSON
Come Rack, Come Rope
Dawn of All
The Light Invisible
No Other Gods

GEORGES BERNANOS
A Bad Dream
Joy
Under the Sun of Satan

ORESTES BROWNSON
Like a Roaring Lion

MALACHY G. CARROLL
The Stranger

G. K. CHESTERTON
A Chesterton Reader

MYLES CONNOLLY
The Bump on Brannigan's Head
Dan England and the Noonday Devil
Mr. Blue
The Reason for Ann & Other Stories
Three Who Ventured

ALICE CURTAYNE
House of Cards

GERTRUD VON LE FORT
The Veil of Veronica

JOSÉ MARÍA GIRONELLA
The Cypresses Believe in God (VOLUME ONE)
The Cypresses Believe in God (VOLUME TWO)

CAROLINE GORDON
The Life and Passion of Aleck Maury
The Malefactors

NATHANIEL HAWTHORNE
The Shattered Fountain: Selected Tales

ELISABETH LANGGÄSSER
The Quest

FRANÇOIS MAURIAC
The Dark Angels
The Desert of Love
Genetrix
A Kiss for the Leper
The Lamb
The River of Fire
The Unknown Sea
Vipers' Tangle
What Was Lost

DOROTHY L. SAYERS
Whose Body?

IGNAZIO SILONE
Fontamara
Bread and Wine
The Seed Beneath the Snow

SIGRID UNDSET
The Burning Bush
The Wild Orchid
Four Stories
Images in a Mirror
Madame Dorthea

LEO L. WARD
Men in the Field: Eighteen Short Stories

The Cypresses Believe in God

· *Volume Two* ·

José María Gironella

Translated from the Spanish
LOS CIPRESES CREEN EN DIOS
by Harriet de Onís

CLUNY
Providence, Rhode Island

Cluny Media edition, 2020

This Cluny edition is a republication of *The Cypressess Believe in God*,
Volume Two,
originally published by Alfred A. Knopf in 1955.

This edition is published under license of Preservation Books,
a non-profit corporation dedicated to promoting
the fair use, appreciation, and preservation of great works.

For more information regarding this title,
please write to info@clunymedia.com, or to
Cluny Media, P.O. Box 1664, Providence, RI 02901

• • • • •

VISIT US ONLINE AT WWW.CLUNYMEDIA.COM

ISBN: 978-1952826412

Cover design by Clarke & Clarke
Cover image: Vincent van Gogh, *Cypresses* (detail), oil on canvas, 1889
(Courtesy of The Metropolitan Museum of Art, New York)

CONTENTS

The Cypresses Believe in God

VOLUME TWO

From whence are wars and contentions among you?
Are they not hence, from your concupiscences,
which war in your members?

THE CATHOLIC EPISTLE
OF ST. JAMES THE APOSTLE (4:1)

NOTE FOR THE AMERICAN EDITION

SPAIN is an unknown country. Experience proves that it is hard to view my country impartially. Even writers of high order succumb to the temptation to adulterate the truth, to treat our customs and our psychology as though everything about them were of a piece, of a single color. Legends and labels pile up: black Spain, inquisitorial Spain, beautiful Spain, tragic Spain, folkloric Spain, unhappy Spain, a projection of Africa into the map of Europe.

I defend the complexity of Spain. If this book attempts to demonstrate anything it is this: that there are in this land thousands of possible ways of life. Through a Spanish family of the middle class—the Alvears—and the day-by-day living of a provincial capital—Gerona—I have tried to capture the everyday traits, the mentality, the inner ambiance of my compatriots in all their pettiness and all their grandeur. In Spain the reaction to this novel has been that it is "implacable." Nothing could satisfy me more.

This book spans a period of five years, five years in the private and public life of the nation: those which preceded the last civil war, which speeded its inevitable coming. The explosion of that war, its scope, and its significance are described in minute detail.

A single warning to the American reader: Spain is a peculiar country and its institutions therefore take on unique coloration. Certain constants of the Spanish temperament operate under any circumstance. A Spanish Freemason is not an international Freemason. A Spanish Communist is not even an orthodox Communist. In every instance what is characteristic is a tendency toward the instinctive, toward the individualistic, and toward the anarchic. Spaniards follow men better than they follow ideas, which are judged not by their content, but by the men who embody them. This accounts for the inclemency of personal relationships, the small respect for laws; this, too, is what causes our periodic civil wars.

To bear all this in mind is important in understanding this book. When the narrative deals with a priest, a policeman, a Socialist, a bootblack, it is essential to remember that it is dealing with a Spanish priest, a Spanish policeman, a Spanish Socialist, a Spanish bootblack, not with generic types. This warning is doubly necessary with reference to Freemasonry, Communism, and Catholicism, the interpretation of which will undoubtedly clash with the American reader's concept of these doctrines.

The book's protagonist—Ignacio Alvear—is a type of young man who abounds in present-day Spain.

José Marïa Gironella
Palma de Mallorca, Spain,
August 1954

PART III
(CONTINUED)

October 6, 1934 to February 16, 1936

CHAPTER FORTY-THREE

IGNACIO'S terror at the sight of the pus stain on the sheet was so great that he was sure he was lost. Venereal disease! The image of Canela hit his mind like a blow.

His shame was so great that, stupefied, he turned out the light; but then he felt the gnawing evil even more forcibly.

He hesitated a minute before turning on the light again. "Dear Lord, if all this were only a nightmare..." He promised a thousand things at the same time; he promised to climb barefoot to the nearby Hermitage of the Angels....

He flicked on the light anew and carefully pulled his legs out from under the bedclothes and stood up on the rug. He felt a sharp pain. He tried to walk, but could move only with difficulty. It was evident that he would get worse every minute. Then, motionless in the middle of the room, he looked up. The mirror reflected his image, hair disheveled, in pajamas, and in the background the eyes of St. Ignatius fixed on him.

With sudden decision he examined himself. He remembered half-glimpsed illustrations in hygiene pamphlets. Then he examined the sheet. How could he get rid of that spot so his mother and Pilar wouldn't find out? The first thing they did each morning, his mother and Pilar, was to come into his room and make the bed.

He lay down again, thought about Canela again, and remembered his father's warning. He sobbed, clutching the pillow.

Suddenly there was a knock at the door. Good God! It was striking eight; he had to get up. The door half-opened, and Carmen Elgazu entered.

"Mamma—" he stammered.

Carmen Elgazu came to his bedside.

"What's the matter, son?"

Ignacio looked at her with unusual intensity. Carmen Elgazu, frightened, reached out her hand and touched his forehead. "Why, you have fever!"

"I think so."

"Have you any pain? When did you begin to feel bad?"

"Last night."

The thermometer was eloquent. Matías Alvear entered his room, and Pilar. They all surrounded his bed, never suspecting what the blanket concealed. They all loved him. "Don't worry, we'll let the bank know you're not coming in." "I'll get you another blanket." "It's just a touch of grippe."

The new blanket definitively hid his secret. The blinds were drawn, and he was left alone with his darkness. He heard the careful steps of his family in the hall. He recognized the familiar sounds in the dining room. He was overcome by a feeling of complete hopelessness.

On waking, he sensed immediately that his illness was advancing relentlessly. He had to make a decision. Something that had to be avoided at all costs was a visit from the doctor. Unfortunately for him, he was very inexperienced; he had to act quickly, and he had to have advice.

Ignacio thought: "The best thing would be to tell my father the truth." But he didn't feel up to it. What a shame, and what a shock it would be for him! He thought of all the people who might be able to help him: Julio, David, Tower of Babel... Any of the fellows at the bank should know the way to... Oh, if his cousin José, of Madrid, were only there!

He remembered that José had told him: "I've got bit three or four times. But now they can take care of it in no time."

That—but suppose he had something serious.

Then he thought about Mateo. Yes, he was the one. And he'd keep the secret. But what if he was as inexperienced as himself? Mateo had always told him: "I manage to control myself. Chastity is very important."

The clock at the City Hall kept striking the hours. His mother came in to see him. "How do you feel? Do you want anything?" The thermometer registered even higher. Carmen Elgazu sat down on the edge of the bed for a minute. Ignacio saw her silhouetted against the slightly opened blinds. "It's probably nothing. A touch of grippe."

It was about noon when he made up his mind. He would tell his father. The stain on the sheet could not be effaced, and eventually it would all come out. His father might find a way to hide the truth from the rest of the family.

Matías Alvear arrived home from the Telegraph office earlier than usual. He was impatient to see how Ignacio was. He hung his hat on the rack, shed his coat, and told his wife it was so cold you could hardly stand it. Then he went into Ignacio's room. "How's everything, son? How do you feel?"

"The same."

Matías stood over him and put his hand on his forehead. Ignacio thought: "Now." But an uncontrollable fear clutched at his throat.

Suddenly a sob broke from him. He couldn't contain it. The silhouette of his father against the half-light, the warm and affectionate silhouette of his father, had disarmed him.

"But what's the matter, Ignacio? Why are you crying?"

Ignacio felt an urge to turn on the light, throw back the sheets, and shout: "Look!" But he controlled himself. He cried, instead, weeping without stopping.

"But what's the matter? Tell me. Careful, your mother is going to hear you."

Ignacio steeled himself. "Papa, I have to give you some bad news. I'm sorry."

"What bad news?"

"I didn't listen to you and—I've got something."

Matías stood up and turned on the light. "What do you mean, you have something?"

"Yes," Ignacio said, and added: "Canela."

Matías looked perplexed. Suddenly he saw the whole thing. He clenched his fists and his teeth. He looked at his son. "So!" Without being able to control himself, he raised his arm and struck Ignacio a terrific slap.

The boy broke into inconsolable sobbing, and at that moment Carmen Elgazu appeared in the door. Ignacio buried himself in the bedclothes.

"But—what's going on?"

Matías replied: "Nothing, woman. Nothing at all."

LATER Matías told his wife the whole story. It was impossible to conceal it, no matter how hard it might be to know. The doctor had to be called, and Ignacio had to be cured.

It hit Carmen Elgazu like a bolt of lightning. She didn't know what to say. She took off her apron and went into the kitchen.

Matías Alvear followed her, saying: "I forgive him everything except having been a hypocrite."

Carmen Elgazu couldn't understand it. She drew close to Matías. She looked into his eyes. "You and I must have done something very bad to deserve this punishment." She had no thought of going in to see her son. And it would be the first time she ever hid anything from Mosén Alberto.

The doctor said: "It's not serious."

ONE of their greatest concerns was Pilar. At all costs Pilar must be kept from knowing. This forced them into mysterious double talk and sudden silences.

Even so, Pilar would ask: "What's the matter with you? Has Ignacio got something serious?"

Ignacio had discovered one consolation: Pilar. He had never loved her as he did during those days. When she was away, working in the shop, he was absolutely alone. His parents never came into his room except when the doctor called or they were carrying out his instructions; but even then they did not speak to him. Pilar, on the other hand, had found the opportunity to demonstrate her affection for him. She did not leave his side. She would chatter away, smooth the bedclothes, and bring him bowls of milk, making the spoon tinkle on the way. Ignacio, in order not to cry with gratitude, pretended to be asleep. Then Pilar would sigh, and sit on César's bed, watching him without moving.

As for the boy, he found the situation very difficult to bear. He was haunted by a feeling of fear. The doctor's visits were torture, he was dying of shame. Every gesture, every word of his parents seemed an allusion to him. There were times when he was sure that they would never forgive him. The doctor was stern. Ignacio would have preferred Dr. Rosselló...

Sometimes he thought that he would never be able to give blood again at the hospital.... There were his law books, untouched in the bookcase.

There was one thing that he both desired and dreaded: visitors. Tower of Babel, the cashier, and Outstanding Drafts had come to see him. "Just a little grippe, that's all."

To Outstanding Drafts, Ignacio had said: "I'm sorry because of the work."

"Don't worry about it," he had replied. "We manage between us, though there is plenty to do." The teller wore a black band on his coat sleeve, and always spoke about Paco, his adopted son.

Julio García had suggested: "Do you want a book? Do you want the phonograph?"

Mosén Alberto had joked. Seeing Ignacio's growth of beard, he said: "You know I can handle the razor, too." But Ignacio, catching the expression on his mother's face, felt such shame that he couldn't come up with an answer.

Don Emilio Santos visited him the first day. And then he never failed to call Matías every morning at the Telegraph office to ask about Ignacio.

As for Mateo, he said: "I have talked with the professor. We won't start the classes again until you are back on your feet."'

Not a day went by that Mateo did not visit him before supper. If it seemed to him that Ignacio did not tire, he would stay an hour; otherwise, he would go right away.

Ignacio's burden of solitude was so great, his heart felt such a wrench each time Matías Alvear, after opening the front door, walked past his room without stopping, that one day, Epiphany, on seeing Mateo enter, all smiles with an armful of magazines, he said: "You think I have the grippe, right?"

"Of course."

"Well—that's not true. I have a venereal disease."

Mateo was rocked back on his heels. He pulled out his blue handkerchief. "But—how did that happen? I don't get it. Is it something serious?"

"No. A few years ago it would have been. Now they can cure it."

"But—will you be all right?"

"Completely."

Mateo did not know what to say.

"Don't preach," said Ignacio abruptly. "I know it is my fault. I am an imbecile."

Mateo was moved. After a silence he said: "Did you know the woman?"

"Yes. The affair had been going on for six months."

"That makes it worse."

"I know." Then Ignacio added: "My parents are about ready to give me up."

Mateo had pulled himself together. "Bah!" he said. "Your mother will forgive you soon." Then he added: "Of course, for your father—it will take a little longer."

Ignacio said: "Thank God, Pilar—"

"What?"

"She is always here keeping me company and telling me things."

Then he said that what he saw as the most difficult thing in the whole business was to forgive himself.

Mateo replied: "If I were you, as soon as I was cured, I'd go and make a confession."

MATEO had read his mind. Make a confession! How long he had gone without doing it! As soon as he was cured, as soon as he was able to leave his bed for good and could walk like other men, he would go and take a bath, to wash away all his sweat and impurities; then he would go to confession. It would be just like the days when he and César used to run along the walls and Montjuich. He would enter any church and kneel before a man who would bless him with the sign of the cross. Actually, that had been the idea in his head at the moment of the great terror when he promised to climb barefoot to the Hermitage of the Angels if he were cured; now Mateo reminded him of it, and he was right. The idea of a silent, dimly lighted temple with an understanding hand resting on his shoulder comforted him.

It was Epiphany. Mateo, in addition to the magazines, had brought a box of candy for Pilar. Pilar was so overcome with emotion that she hardly dared touch the cellophane in which it was wrapped. It was the first box of candy she had received in her life. Pilar had no idea that Marta, the daughter of Major Martínez de Soria, had received a similar box from Mateo.

Matías and Carmen Elgazu were grateful to Mateo for his visits and those thoughtful attentions. On seeing him so healthy and with such an expression of youth on his face, they could not help comparing him with Ignacio, sunken and sweaty in his bed.

Five days were too short a time for them to reach the point of forgiveness, though they never stopped thinking about their son alone in his room with the light out. But except for his silence and prostration, neither did Ignacio do anything to bring the situation to a head.

On the eighth day something unexpected occurred. Carmen Elgazu was alone in the dining room, looking over the laundry. It was midafternoon, and the door to Ignacio's room suddenly opened. Out of the corner of her eye she saw him come out in his pajamas, a scarf around his neck, his shoulders slumped. Ignacio advanced toward the dining room, dragging his slippers, weak, but walking without difficulty. Carmen Elgazu did not lift her head; nevertheless, she felt that her son had stopped and was looking at her. The muffler around his neck and the slump of his shoulders had wrung her heart. She saw him alone, utterly alone. Something in her heart was at the breaking point. Between her, seated next to the window, and him, in the hall, stood the stove and the table. What could she do to keep from raising her head? Suddenly she realized that Ignacio had started moving again. The slippers had crossed the entrance to the dining room, and it was evident that they were coming around the table. Perhaps he was going to the kitchen, for a glass of water. The smell of her son—a smell of sickbed, fever, unaired room—reached her. The slippers stopped again. She realized that her son was standing behind her. Perhaps he was looking at the river. But no, she felt a hand on her bowed neck. And then another hand, clumsily, on her head. Carmen Elgazu did not move; and she could feel Ignacio's breath. Suddenly Ignacio hugged her tight, pressing his cheek against her hair; and then Carmen Elgazu's eyes filled with tears and she endured the shower of kisses without complaint. Soon their moist cheeks found one another, and no one could say which of the two cried the most. Nor which of the two would succeed in articulating the first word.

Neither one. Ignacio turned away and went back, dragging his slippers. He crossed the threshold to the hall, exhausted. Carmen Elgazu did not follow him with her eyes, but she could see him. She could have described every wrinkle in his pajamas, each lock of his hair. The silhouette of her son was fixed in her entrails.

Ignacio buried himself in his room again. He had not gone out with the intention of doing what he did, but that was the way it happened. Neither had Carmen Elgazu sat down to sew thinking about it; nevertheless, now she realized that she was darning one of Ignacio's socks. Now everything had a different color, the ebbing afternoon a new sweetness. There was the sound of the secret, monotonous, crackling life of the lighted stove. A great silence reigned in the house. Carmen Elgazu's features had become immobile as though carved in wood; but she had the feeling that she had just finished separating the good beans from the bad.

She had only one desire: for Matías Alvear to get home. How would she tell him? Matías was stubborn; he did not want to hear one word about Ignacio. Crystal set, newspaper, dominoes. But Carmen Elgazu knew that ever since the first days of January he had been losing every game at the Neutral.

The next day Matías Alvear, seated at the dining room table, was eating breakfast in preparation for setting off to work at the Telegraph office. Suddenly he looked up and saw Ignacio standing before him, shaved and dressed. Matías's graying temples trembled, as did the hand that held the cup. But he kept on drinking as though nothing had happened.

The night before, he had said to Carmen Elgazu: "Don't pay any attention to him. He is a hypocrite." Nevertheless, now, as he tried to get up on the side opposite to where Ignacio stood, his legs got tangled up in the chair and he couldn't rise. Then he heard the voice of his son: "Father, forgive me."

The little wrinkles between Matías's eyes and temples stood out as never before. He hardly breathed. He managed to stand up and look at Ignacio. Pilar had come to the door of her room. Ignacio said it again: "Father, forgive me," while he read the signs of Matías's struggle in his eyes. Then, lowering his head, he threw his arms around his father's neck and embraced him; and Matías Alvear found himself pounding his son on the back.

Camren Elgazu had gone out shopping. Pilar didn't know if she should join the two. On seeing them draw apart, she hit on the idea of shouting: "Colds?" But she waited in vain for one of them to answer: "Michelin tires." Matías Alvear and Ignacio had lumps in their throats that made it impossible for either to speak.

In the presence of that scene, Pilar kept asking herself, without finding the answer, what sin her brother could have committed.

FORTY-FOUR

A great joy entered the family, a joy that restored Ignacio's strength and allowed him to go out on the balcony to take advantage of the thin noon sun. The next day he went downstairs. His knees wobbled, and he walked like an old man. The day after that he said to his mother: "Today, if you will go with me, we will go to confession."

Little by little he felt the sap of youth rising in him again.

Sunday afternoon David and Olga had come to see him. They thought he looked very bad. "We'll have to go back to San Felíu." The teachers told him they had succeeded in getting back almost all their pupils. Classes would soon start again. The memory of jail was still very much with them, but all that was now the past.

"Everything passes. You can see it yourself—imprisonment, sickness."

Matías Alvear had begun to speak of his son again in the Telegraph office. "He's started going out on the balcony to take the sun." And in the Neutral he said over the dominoes: "It looks as though my luck has changed." And sure enough, teamed up with Don Emilio Santos, he was constantly scribbling points in his favor on the marble-topped table. Julio García and Dr. Rosselló had to pick up the check for all four of them.

As for Ignacio, he kept his promise. Arm in arm with Carmen Elgazu, he went out in midafternoon to go to confession.

"Where do you want to go?"

"To Mosén Francisco."

Carmen Elgazu was pleased with the choice. And they turned their steps in the direction of the parish of San Félix, crossing the Calle de las Ballesterías.

The choice of priest had been deliberate. Ignacio wanted someone who would understand and console him, who would give him courage to begin a new life. César had spoken to him so often of the priest that he did not hesitate.

They entered the church and found it empty. Ignacio knelt down, and Carmen Elgazu herself went to the sacristy. There was Mosén Francisco, just back from a burial. Two men were waiting for him, it wasn't clear for what. "I am César's mother. My oldest son, Ignacio, is here. He wants to make his confession with you."

Mosén Francisco opened his big eyes with enthusiasm. "So you are César's mother!" He took her hand in both of his. He looked at her with great curiosity and affection. "I'll be right there. Let me take care of this pair of scalawags." The two men smiled. Every time they saw him go out to a burial they would wait for him afterwards in the sacristy and touch him for a couple of pesetas.

Ignacio prepared himself as best he could, with his face buried in his hands. He was ready to make a general confession. His mother told him: "He'll be with you in a minute." When the boy saw the priest come out of the sacristy, kneel for an instant to pray, and then enter the confessional, his heart began to thud. He got up and walked forward. Then it was Carmen Elgazu who covered her face with her hands.

What a confession! It was something perfect. To be sure, the priest eased his way, seeming to read his spirit. It was his great experience as a confessor. He dredged up the last particle of truth without Ignacio's being aware of it. He kept coming back to the circumstances. The confessional was in a corner; a purple curtain fell over Ignacio's back, hiding his head.

As soon as the boy had said all he had to say and concluded: "That is all," the priest adopted a familiar tone, which established a current of optimism.

"Good, there you are. You are a little rebellious. But don't get discouraged. We all do foolish things: I just let myself be touched for a peseta by a couple of beggars. It will be hard for you to conquer yourself; as hard as it is for me. But don't get discouraged. It is a question of bringing a little order into your life, of not giving up on yourself. The terrible thing is the habit of sin. You can get into the habit of sin just as one gets into any other habit.

"I am very young to be giving you advice. Nevertheless, I am going to tell you what I think, since you have had the goodness to come, since Christ has touched your heart. First, be done with women. Try to hold off a month or two. It will be hard, and one day you will say: 'I can't hold out anymore!' When that happens, try to resist a few hours, even a few minutes more. Perhaps in those moments the miracle will take place. And if it doesn't, well—what we said: confession as soon as possible, with me or with another. The memory of the sickness may help you; but not much, depend on it. We humans don't learn much from experience. I don't put much stock in fear; I have a lot more faith in manliness.

"And then manage to put your life in order. I don't think it would be a bad idea—and don't be surprised at what I am going to say—for you to do some strenuous exercise. Take up some sport, or gymnastics. And, of course, shower frequently. Cleanliness seems essential to me. From what you have told me I would say that you have everything you need to put your life in order. You work mornings and afternoons, then you go to class; after supper you study. What more do you want? You will see that it is all a question of making the most of your obligations. I would advise you to do one thing that may seem to you irrelevant: a silence cure. Try it, and tell me how it works out. Manage to go a few days, a couple of weeks, talking as little as possible. Work silently at the bank, study in silence, and economize on words as much as possible. You will see the effects. Almost immediately you will feel a greater serenity. You will find that you pay attention and see things much more clearly. Words distract a great deal, you can't imagine. You come across men who, to hear them talk, you would say were enemies. And basically they are in agreement without knowing it. Others, on the contrary, talk, thinking that they understand one another, and basically they continue poles apart.

"Above all, remember this that I tell you: pay attention. Give your full attention to everything you do, everything you hear. You will discover new worlds. The most humble employees will teach you something. Pay attention to the objects in your house, the things that happen at the bank, what you see along the street, everything that surrounds you. There is no thing or person that cannot teach you something. The same thing is happening to you now that happens to most people: they don't fix their attention. We move like automatons. That is a mistake. There must be reflection. When you hear some new theory, don't say: False! Think that there are thousands who have thought about it before you. But, at the same time, don't say: the Gospel! There is only one gospel: love God and your neighbor.

"If you pay attention—and don't think that all these theories are mine: they are St. Augustine's—you will without fail discover something very important: harmony. You will realize that there is harmony in everything, that everything forms part of a harmonious whole. Those very events that at first sight seem startling, you will come to understand as logical, as contributing to something harmonious and great. You will find harmony in the smallest details. This will assist you no end in ordering your daily life. Your spirit will feel itself strengthened by forming part of that harmonious whole.

"As for other practical advice—I don't know what to tell you. I think we have covered about everything. Actually, perhaps you should honor the family God has given you. That is to say—well, no example comes to me, but unite with your family, without that meaning that you should mortgage your liberty. For instance, it is not going to put you out to play a game of dominoes with your father, or even to go for a walk with your mother occasionally. Accompany her sometimes. You don't know the happiness it will give her. It is something of which we have no idea. Besides that, set a good example for your sister. I don't know her, but I have the impression that like most fellows you don't take her too seriously. There is no justification for this. In moments of difficulty sisters often give us big surprises. I know this from experience.

"You have talked to me about friends. Son, I am not the one to go into that. You know them, and will know how best to choose and what to do with them. I would only suggest to you that among all of them you at least choose one with Christian ideas. This notion of keeping a good distance between oneself and bad company has something unpleasant and cowardly about it. What does it imply, after all? If all the world followed that advice, many of us would find ourselves alone and abandoned. The thing to do is set an example for everyone around us. You have the opportunity to do it; you will not lack for strength if you are willing.

"As for political ideas, not one word. It is even less my place to get involved in that. I know very little about politics. I would only refer back to what we said before: in the presence of any doctrine there is an infallible touchstone by which to appraise its value: harmony. You will know the worth of doctrines by their harmony.

"Good, I think that is enough. If you want, come and see me when you like. You will always find me here, any time. And say at least three Hail Mary's every night; that is essential.

"Now, as penance, you will say one, only one, Hail Mary. But by way of starting off in keeping with what has been said, manage to give it your full attention. You will see how by this simple act you will feel much better."

AN hour and a half. It took him exactly an hour and a half to make his confession. When he rose from the confessional, his legs trembled much more than before and his knees hurt him as though they were incrusted with grains of sand.

He knelt at the high altar in the darkness and said the Hail Mary with bowed head. Then his eyes sought his mother. Carmen Elgazu hid her happiness. During the hour and a half she had been thinking: "Thank you, Lord." With each minute that passed she thought: "Let it last, let it last...."

They went out together. He took her by the arm. As they began to walk, they felt themselves enfolded in a mutual and solemn happiness. It was beginning to get dark, and it was cold. Ignacio squeezed his mother's forearm with his right hand. Carmen Elgazu's high heels resounded against the paving stones—crac, crac-crac.

FORTY-FIVE

DURING those Christmas holidays only a few of the professors and the servants remained at Collell. César had passed the whole night of December 31 practically in vigil, kneeling in his cell. The idea of the passing of the year affected him very deeply, and he wanted to remain awake for the moment when the bells in the monastery struck twelve. But the intensity with which he was sunk in his meditations at that moment was so great that something extraordinary happened to him: not only did he not remember Ignacio and his birthday, but he did not even hear the bells. When he came to himself, it was dawn. He found himself in 1935.

For several nights his Latin professor had been intently watching César's vigils, which on that occasion reached their high point. This professor was an expert in problems of asceticism and mysticism. He planned to compile an anthology of Spanish ascetic-mystic writers, and he had discovered that their works numbered more than three thousand during the golden age alone! Franciscans, Dominicans, Augustinians, Carmelites, Jesuits, even writers who did not belong to any religious order, like Servetus. Heading the list of ascetics were Fray Luis de Granada and Fray Luis de León; first among the mystics were St. Teresa and St. John of the Cross. The professor thought to see in César signs of mysticism, and he told himself that possibly in his prayers, of growing intensity, César was approaching the ecstatic state without realizing it. He thought that any of the bodily phenomena exhibited by those in ecstasy—levitation, the luminous aureole, emission of perfumes, or the appearance of stigmata—was possible in the case of the seminarian. He could not forget that César, when he first came to Collell, had seemed to spring as he walked.

In any case, that New Year's Eve the professor spent the whole night with his eye at the keyhole of César's cell, enduring the bitter cold of the corridor. But César remained kneeling and motionless. He did not rest for even a minute, and when he heard the bell he left his cell to wash.

In the sacristy, after the Mass, the professor approached him and pointedly questioned him. The boy, astonished and scared, opened his eyes wide: "Have I broken the rules?" he asked.

The professor replied that that did not matter. "What I am interested in knowing is if you felt fatigued."

"No—actually—no."

"What were you meditating?"

"Well—I was asking forgiveness."

"Did you—experience any special comfort?"

César ran his hand over his shorn head. "Well—I don't know, Father. There was a moment—a great peace."

The professor pulled his ear and advised him not to overdo it. "You have to get your sleep. Don't forget that you are not strong."

A great peace. The man decided that César was walking in the paths of asceticism, but that for the moment he had not received any mystical manifestation of spiritual espousal. But he was sure that he would some day. And then, fortunate those who had been at his side!

César had been greatly upset by the questions: he was in the infirmary until Epiphany. On that day the nuns placed a bag of caramels in his shoe, and a book on the stigmata of Teresa Neumann. "The Black King left it for you." The nuns knew that César had a special fondness for the Black King, who symbolized to him the fact that Christianity makes no distinctions of color or race. The boy took his gifts to his cell and spent the day reading the book from cover to cover and eating caramels.

The next day he sent Pilar the caramels that still remained in the bag, and Ignacio the book. "Read it," he wrote to his brother. "You will see what wonders. And Teresa Neumann still lives in Konnersreuth! Now one of my projects is to go and see her some day."

THE holidays were coming to an end for everyone, in Collell and in the city.

The sons of Major Martínez de Soria had left on the eve of Epiphany. Mateo had been their inseparable companion, as well as Marta's. Together they had visited Octavio Sánchez, who, as they had heard, was in sympathy with the Falange. The Treasury Department employee—an Andalusian whose lisping "s's" gave his speech an amusing note—listened to the three boys with close attention. When they had concluded, he had turned to Mateo and said in a straightforward, promising tone: "You can count on me."

Then—the city resumed its life and death. The truce had ended.

One fact came clearly to the forefront: unemployment was gnawing like a cancer at the vitals of many families. Metallurgy, construction, the great Soler factory—machine belts and rubber products—Chemical and Tartaric Industries, printing establishments, all displayed the same sign: three-workday week, two-workday week. Many workers received a slip of paper: "Until further notice." The soft drink factories were dormant with the cold; the rope-soled sandals were stacked up in the factories, unsalable because of the bad weather. The perfumeries contemplated their immense bottles, filled to the brim. Even the old women who sold chestnuts—ice cream in the summer—complained! Portugal was dealing mortal blows to the cork industry of the province. David and Olga had not lied about conditions in the rest of the nation: there were seven hundred thousand unemployed.

The Cataluña was crowded with somber-looking men, the same as the Gran Via Café. Some had invaded the back room of the Neutral. Nobody was in any hurry at the barbershops. Workers who had been in the habit of rising with the dawn stayed in bed until eleven o'clock. Then they would go into the kitchen, giving their wives a shove.

The Costas were the only ones who did anything to remedy the situation. Not only did they not let any workers go, but, utilizing the energies stored up in jail, they opened marble works right beside the quarry and began turning out gravestones. They took on three men: a very timid boy named Pedro, who had asked them for work; a fat fellow—Salvio by name—who turned out to be Orencia's boy friend; and Bernat, the maker of religious images.

Bernat was one of those directly affected by the great crisis. It had become impossible for him to stay in business. When he saw that the torch was not put to the churches with the October Revolution, he felt that the jig was up. His credit was canceled at the banks. "Maybe the next revolution," they told him. Now Bernat cut headstones like an ordinary day-laborer beside Salvio and Pedro, both of them clients of the Communist barbershop. If he felt sorry about the closing of the shop, it was most of all for César.

The Costas took still another step: they decided to build a seven-story building to relieve the unemployment in the construction industry. They put the project in the hands of the architects Massana and Ribas, who always, worked in collaboration.

When their sister Laura asked them for information, they answered: "There is a reason that we hope will convince you: we are going to be married."

"What?"

"That's right. We are going to be married."

It was true. Not one, but both of them together, to two sisters, daughters of an important rice merchant of the town of Pals. Laura was astounded. To the many friends who congratulated them and then asked them to reserve an apartment for them in the building under construction, the industrialists would answer: "Any one you want, except the main floor and mezzanine, which are for us. And the first floor for Laura if she wants it."

To round out their beneficent program, all the Costas lacked was permission to reopen the political headquarters. They thought of installing a series of comforts and conveniences in Izquierda Republicana headquarters which would serve to draw the members back into the ranks. For the time being, however, permission to reopen was not forthcoming.

The closing of the political centers made the layoffs seem more spectacular, and increased the defenseless feeling of those affected. According to official figures, there were 343 workers without jobs. That was a lot for a city like Gerona. What could they do to pass the time?

One man came forward prepared to alleviate the situation: Colonel Muñoz. Colonel Muñoz, seeing the unemployed standing around bored on street corners and in cafés, told himself that it was necessary to think up something. Something that would entertain them and at the same time permit them to make some use of their time and instruct them.

A born promoter, he hit on the solution. To instruct them, he introduced free showings of documentaries at the Albéniz; to entertain them, daily sessions of boxing and wrestling at popular prices.

The workers turned out en masse for both spectacles, and their reaction to both was enthusiastic. The documentaries impressed them greatly. César's three sandwichmen went up and down the Rambla at noontime displaying the titles of the films. Most of the titles seemed to have to do, in general, with subjects dealing with nature's mysteries. The documentary that served as the finale for the first session showed the life, at the bottom of the ocean, of a carnivorous monster with a thousand mouths and tentacles devouring without pause dozens of defenseless crustaceans. The workers developed such a hatred for that monster that some of them shook their fists at the screen.

As for the boxing and wrestling, the response exceeded Colonel Muñoz's wildest expectations. The Albéniz, converted into a ring, was packed every afternoon. The men sneaked from their wives' purses the two reales it cost to get in. The boxing excited them in proportion to the blood the contestants drew from one another, except for a few who understood the footwork, sparring, and fine points. But what really went over was the wrestling. Wrestling was practically unknown in Gerona. It was a great revelation. The rivals entered the ring wearing flashy cloaks with *Panther*, *The Ogre*, or *The Pirate* lettered on the back. They were great human tanks, who suddenly stripped and hurled themselves at one another.

Everything was allowed except punching, biting, choking, and hair-pulling. Everything else—butting, kicking, stomping, twisting of limbs, and back-snapping—was not only permitted, but highly recommended. The public would howl because a strange thing was taking place: in the ring—as on the floor of the ocean—one always found the Good and the Bad, as selected by Colonel Muñoz. A Panther who dismembered his opponent by using foul tactics was always pitted against a noble, gritty adversary who fought in silence, observing the rules and without complaint. The workers took an immediate dislike to the Panther; many threatened him, too, with their fists, as the spectators were allowed to do. If in the end the Panther managed to pin down the Good One, the crowd trudged out—Blasco at their head—disconsolate; but if, at the last moment, the Good One carried the day, the movie house went wild.

Matías Alvear on coming out of the Telegraph office would often see the multitude waiting in line to get into the theater. He was more than a little surprised to discover that there were plenty of women in the line, and people who he never would have believed would attend such a spectacle. Lieutenant Martín, for example, and Julio García were there, and sometimes Salvio, the boy friend of Don Emilio Santos's maid.

Some people went to police headquarters to protest against these spectacles: Don Pedro Oriol, Mosén Alberto. The Commissioner gave them to understand that he did not have the authority to interfere. Raimundo said in the barbershop: "At least in bullfighting there is art." Mateo, who always went there now for his shave, nodded assent.

But the diversion of those minds was superficial. Deep down, a great dissatisfaction gnawed away at them. All day long they disgustedly came across one another on the street. The United States cropped up in their conversations all the time as the place where they knew for a fact that the unemployed went in their automobiles to pick up their relief checks.

There was one place where the crisis made itself apparent in its most terrible aspects: the bank where Ignacio worked. When the boy went back to work, he found that the collection department had taken on two more persons than usual. "Nobody pays, everyone returns the drafts." Even firms in the black asked the bank: "Hold the drafts five days, eight days." The manager asked: "What are we heading for?" Cosme Vila read constantly. In his drawer he kept a picture of Vasiliev. Every time he opened the drawer to write a letter to another bank or to some bourgeois firm, he saw Vasiliev with his powerful head. Cosme Vila and his "companion" did not miss a wrestling match.

None of the employees seemed to suspect what had really been wrong with Ignacio. If they had, what a ribbing he would have taken! He had decided to take to the bank the book on Teresa Neumann that César had sent him, and the boys had quite a laugh over it.

The frontispiece showed the girl with tears of blood welling from her eyes.

"What's this? Who is it?"

"It's an Austrian woman who has visions."

"Visions? Those guys standing around on the corners without work have visions, too."

"Don't laugh. It is a scientifically proved fact. She has scarcely had a bite to eat since 1923."

"The workers in Spain haven't eaten since Philip II!"

"Bah! You fellows are hopeless. Dozens of doctors have examined her. Anybody can go see for himself."

The only one who listened to him with attention was the assistant manager. The book had made a strong impression on Ignacio. He said to the assistant manager: "I am going to specialize in this stigmata business, the way you specialize in the Masons. We can talk about it some time, if you are interested."

The assistant manager replied: "Of course it interests me." Then he added, looking at him hard: "What's happened to you? It looks to me as though you're becoming your old self again."

Ignacio was silent. The fact was that he himself didn't know. On entering the bank he had had the impression that it was the first time he had ever set foot there. With Mosén Francisco's counsels grafted on his mind and, above all, mingled in his blood, he saw everything in a different light. He reflected that it had been imprudent to bring in the book on Teresa Neumann, and still more imprudent to talk about her. For a moment he had forgotten that he was to keep quiet.

At any rate, he did not make the same mistake again. During the days that followed he carried out his purpose to the letter: he observed a strict silence. He didn't talk any more than was absolutely necessary and he began to get used to it. "What's the matter? Cat got your tongue?" He held his peace with conviction, for he saw for a fact that the results of the cure were striking. At home and with Professor Civil, on the days when there were classes, he said as little as possible. The result was just as had been foreseen: he found himself a different person, serene, with an inner life, and progressively able to see things more clearly. It seemed as though he learned respect for the world and for himself. He saw the unemployed standing about in the streets, and he kept silent. He thought: "Lord, there is something out of joint here. Help me to find the cause!" He no longer thought—as he would have before—of fascism or Warning Voice or the Moors that entered Oviedo. He knew that the problem went much deeper. He reflected that Spain had not found its center and that all over the peninsula people were terrified, seeking partial solutions, and that for dozens of years not one voice had been raised clear and ringing to say: "The cancer lies here. We must do this and we must do that." Then he became frightened because it seemed to him that these conclusions verged on those of Mateo, and he became more silent than ever to see if he could grasp the truth. But finding himself incapable, for the moment, of grasping the truth about Spain, he became humble and asked that he might at least grasp the truth about himself, which he supposed was less difficult because he was only twenty years old and his body measured only five feet nine and a half inches.

The truth about himself was circumscribed by his experiences in the bank; it was his first contact with the world, about which he knew nothing. Mosén Francisco was right. Or St. Augustine. Talking, one was deceived by the world; keeping silent, one paid attention. Simply because one was paying attention every minute, every second, every glance or change of light took on a value impossible to foresee. For example, he had discovered that though he had made the trip a thousand times, he had no idea of the stores between his home and the bank. He found that he had never understood as then to what degree each voice had a spiritual resonance that might be the measure of its owner. He had not noticed Pilar's nose, with its charming upward tilt, or the fact that the manager wore three rings on one finger, or that David and Olga always walked with their arms around each other's waist, not arm in arm, or that Doña Amparo Campo had a scar on her chin, or the variety of skies one could see in Gerona of a winter. Now each second held some surprise for him, as though he had been reborn. He looked at people full-face, and at the total surface and contour of things. And of course he looked at the sky. It was the first thing he looked at on leaving the house. The sky was different every day, sometimes distant, sometimes close, always immense, always the purest blue, never to be taken for granted, presiding over everyone's life. A great discovery, this paying attention! New colors, new shapes, new sounds offered themselves to his spirit in multiple display. The house-fronts created lights and shadows, the chairs took on human forms, the trees managed to interpret every sentiment from joy to desperation, along the rim of a plate there were a thousand reflections, a thousand faces in the concavity of a spoon, shoes did not squeak without a reason, time seemed to come to a stop on the spine of a book; men suddenly looked old, nature suddenly broke into a dance. And the colors! Purples, yellows, reds. Colors in the windowpanes, in the depths of eyes, in fingernails, in the rooms. How was it possible that he had not been aware of that multiplicity? "Every blade of grass is a miracle," as César had glimpsed.

And the world of forms. How beautiful the belfries of the city! It was very difficult to think up images. Everybody used to say the spire of San Félix looked like an arrow pointed at the sky, or a prayer in stone, or Heaven knows what. Or the Cathedral towered aloft, powerful as a gigantic shepherd's staff. Sheer nonsense. Mosén Francisco was right: words did not serve to give the exact measure of things. Ignacio confined himself therefore to observing them constantly. Depending on where he sat, sometimes the tower of the Cathedral seemed to him the taller of the two; then he would change to a new position and that of San Félix seemed taller. But they always rose, the two of them together. As inseparable as David and Olga, as the cypresses and the bones, as the revolution and blood.

And then there were the sounds. The endearing everyday sounds, which began with the dawn, succeeded each other one by one throughout the day, and died with sleep. Sometimes all the sounds seemed to drown in the river. An automobile would pass by, and the blare of its horn would fall in the water and stop there suspended, absorbed, immersed. Other times it was just the contrary, and all the sounds seemed to emerge from the water: the throbbing of the motors in the factories, the weeping of children!

Then there were the tick-tock of the clocks, people's footsteps, and the bells.

What a marvelous world! And what a man, Mosén Francisco, even though he covered his head with that preposterous hat. For if silence led to attention, as Mosén Francisco had said, it also was true that this led to harmony, as the priest had predicted. Better said, harmony was revealed—the gift of the Magi—to those who paid attention. Colors, forms, and sounds formed a combination both one and multiple, which was always in its place; a harmonic unity whose parts complemented each other. Men and chairs complemented each other, books and time, hands and fingernails, trees and wind, fathers and sons, the good and the bad. Things resembled one another in themselves or in their effects, or their divergences converged toward one outcry or into a common supplication. For that reason the bells did not interfere with one another even when they all rang at once; for that reason the Oñar, which now descended swollen with the rains, seemed to Ignacio the image of his heart.

And everything seemed to him to tend toward one goal: beauty. Nothing was disproportionate, excessive, or beyond proper bounds. Perhaps the cold! But no; thanks to the cold, the stove, with Matías Alvear and Carmen Elgazu and Pilar seated around it, acquired a deep secret personality, as of a source of life. Even the storms had their law. Each lightning flash illuminated the exact area to create grandeur, and the thunder penetrated the bowels of the world, reminding it of its origin. A cactus that the blast blew into the middle of the Rambla remained rooted, green and shiny, in a tree, as if to tell it that the spring would once again cause beautiful leaves to burgeon.

FORTY-SIX

JULIO García—also among the unemployed—spent all his afternoons in the Neutral, delivering short lectures to any who cared to listen. He had now gone in for statistics. Generally he talked from memory; if this failed him, he would pull a slip of paper out of his wallet.

"Take a good look at what we have come to after so many centuries of excellent administration. Ramón! Another cognac. Spain has: 5,000 miles of coastline and an embryonic merchant marine, even smaller than that which it had in 1929. The reason? The disaster the Armada suffered in 1588. The shipyards often located far from the sea. Now you will say: but we have plenty of trains! That is a mistake. We have two miles of track for every one hundred square kilometers. Mountainous country? Switzerland is more so, and it has nine miles of track for the equivalent area. Let us take comfort in our roads! Impossible; they don't exist. Yes, there are some; but rutted and rough, which explains why the buggy is on the increase in some regions. That gives you an idea of transportation, which is essential to a nation.

"As for heavy industry, we seem to be going from bad to worse, despite the Costa Brothers' efforts. Iron output was 5,000 tons in 1924, 2,000 tons last year. Coal, 9,000 tons in 1913, 6,000 last year. There are miners out of work—some of them in jail—so what are you going to do! There are foreign geologists who think that production could be tripled; Gil Robles is not a geologist, so you can't blame him. Good, let us go on to steel: twenty-four times less than Germany, which is logical; three times less than Luxemburg, which stops being quite so logical.... We don't have petroleum or gasoline; lots of soft coal, but poorly distributed; the Pyrenees filled—so they say—with precious minerals that nobody looks for. On the other hand—it must be acknowledged—this cognac is excellent. Though, of course, I would prefer a Napoleon.

"Let us look at the figures on agriculture. Where the devil is that paper? Here. Yes, the land—I've already said it here not long ago: the land is magnificent. One has only to read the end of Book Eight of the *Iliad.* Spain, here we are: 195,504 square miles surface area. Of all that, only one quarter can be cultivated. The rest consists of the deserts of Aragón, of La Mancha, of Almeria, and so on—in a word, poverty. As for the methods of cultivation—and if there are any here who till the soil, I would ask their indulgence—they are antediluvian. Working conditions—these, fortunately, are better. Take Seville, for example. In the province of Seville there is a town—Valodatosa—where the women who harvest the chick peas are paid one peseta a day. Of course, maybe they get away with a chick pea or two in their blouses. In the province of Avila there is another village—Narros del Puerto—which belongs lock, stock, and barrel to one lady; a well-to-do lady, to be sure. She is not one of the grandees of Spain—let's be fair. The lady bought Narros del Puerto—including the church and the cemetery—for 80,000 pesetas. The whole thing is hers. The title says, among other things: 'The owner may dispossess inhabitants who are foul-mouthed.' Here, on the other hand, we are luckier. Here Don Jorge tells his tenants: 'Let me know when someone in the family dies so one of us can go to the funeral.' Does the topic bore you? No? Well, let us proceed then. Transportation, industry, agriculture—now I will turn to the banking system.

"It would appear that there is one institution that works miracles: the Bank of Spain. It has 15,000 stockholders, who split up 125,000,000 pesetas a year. There is one consolation to be sure: some of those pesetas reach Gerona. Ask the notary Noguer and Don Pedro Oriol. Perhaps that is the reason they picked the notary Noguer as Mayor. Let's get down to cases! The year of the military disaster in Morocco—1921—was the most profitable: that year the bank declared a fifty-four percent dividend. No, no, the Republic cannot be blamed for everything, as certain malcontents, as I myself, sometimes think. The manager of the Arús Bank was telling me the other day that the monarchy, it would seem, left a debt of either 20,000 or 22,000 million pesetas, I can't remember which. Of course, the increase in the bureaucracy was responsible for that, not to mention the army, the Civil Guard, and the police. What are you laughing at? Here I am, dismissed from the force since the October Revolution. I have a right to criticize, don't you think?"

Julio always sat in the same corner of the café, which had an air of intimacy in spite of all its mirrors. Because of these, he always felt that he was addressing a huge audience. At times he really was, but not always. Nobody argued with him. The majority of his listeners got a kick out of his ironies when he began, but as the statistics piled up, a look of sadness replaced the smiles on their lips. Some thought he exaggerated, but how could they disprove him? Nobody had counter-statistics in his wallet.

Every now and then a stranger would show up who would finally break in: "All right, all right, so we're a bunch of slobs. But we're very witty, aren't we?"

Then Julio García would push his hat back on his head and say: "Welcome to the Neutral, friend! Can I buy you a drink?"

Don Emilio Santos suffered when the policeman touched on those topics. He usually made an excuse to leave the café. If he remained, he would interrupt in his own manner: "Agreed, agreed. Spanish institutions work very badly. It's that way now, and it was that way before. But the people are worth a great deal."

Julio García would look about him with an expression of dismay. "You see what I mean," he would reply. "The gentleman confesses that the institutions work badly, and he is the manager of the *Tabacalera*."

Matías Alvear was quicker on his toes than Don Emilio Santos. He had heard it all before at the Telegraph office. They all said: "We ought to turn the country over to North America."

Matías would say to Julio: "What's needed here is less criticism and more patriotism. Criticism only isolates us. All of us here have an overcoat and a scarf, right? And in Barcelona one can still get a decent meal for a peseta. No one denies that there is a lack of boats and trains. There is also a lack of schools and airplanes. But there are a lot of families that love each other and when the Three Kings come, there is no one who goes without a little present, even if at times it's not bought with money. As for the other countries, what you gain in the length you lose in the breadth. You won't get any argument about people living better in England, the United States, or France. Nevertheless, our women are prettier than theirs; and I'll go even farther than that: none of those countries have people from Andalusia or Madrid. Not all of us are alike, Julio. It seems that you can't live without great tons of steel. I, on the other hand—and no offense intended—can't live without Andalusians and Madrileños."

Julio would smile and stick to his guns. And the discussion would continue, back and forth, for Matías wouldn't give an inch. Ever since his reconciliation with Ignacio, Matías refused to see everything as hopeless. Nevertheless, the faces that the mirrors of the café multiplied were generally on Julio's side. Many left the café gripped by a feeling of discouragement. If anyone took Matías's part, it was always someone of the middle class, a merchant or small manufacturer, fed up with so much instability and the October Revolution, who wanted only to be able to work.

Julio García usually left the café late, only a little before supper time. He ate supper quickly—which offended Doña Amparo Campo—and went out again. "You're never home any more even for a minute. What's the matter with you?" his wife complained.

He would give her a kiss on the neck and go downstairs smiling. "I have things to do." His "things to do" consisted in going to the hospital to see Dr. Rosselló, sometimes to the Lodge, and often to the school of David and Olga.

As a matter of fact, he and the teacher had struck up quite a friendship in jail, and he liked Olga a lot. He liked her enormously. Sometimes he asked himself if he didn't like her better than Doña Amparo Campo.

Moreover, David listened with satisfaction to Julio's statistics.

"It is evident that the whole situation is a mess," he would say. "Less steel than Luxemburg!"

Then they would talk about their personal concerns with great familiarity. The teachers were preoccupied now because Santi, the pupil who went around with his shirt unbuttoned, had stolen a bicycle from the parking ground at the Soler factory. He had had to appear in children's court. And the presiding judge was Don Santiago Estrada!

At the same time they were happy because the aquarium in the classroom was at last a reality. It was a glass enclosure containing more than twenty multicolored specimens finning about among artificial rock formations and streams of bubbles. Hie pupils were forbidden to turn around to look at them; on the other hand, the fish could contemplate the students to their hearts' content. Olga, the day after attending the documentary put on at the Albéniz by Colonel Muñoz, said to the pupils: "Don't believe the entire submarine world is as beautiful as this. At the bottom of the ocean there are voracious and hideous monsters of indescribable ugliness." The teachers had managed to buy the aquarium with the profits of the summer's work at San Felíu.

The conversations at the Neutral and with David and Olga took place during the afternoon or evening. Julio spent the mornings reading and keeping his suicide file up to date. The last one to take place in the province had been that of a doctor, the third member of the family to take that step. He also gathered bits of information on Spanish intellectuals who had committed suicide: Ganivet throwing himself into the waters of the Dvina; Lara firing his pistol into his temple before the mirror; Bartrina...

Julio's interest in this matter had nothing to do with his police work. It was something psychological, a matter of temperament. Julio loved life with a passion. He could not understand how anyone would surrender it voluntarily. When he thumbed through the file—three hundred and seventy photographs of suicides blown up to postcard size—these faces looked at him fixedly and sometimes sent shivers up and down his back, but he maintained that they told him many things. The faces all had something in common, according to Julio: "deep-set eyes, or just the opposite, eyes almost popping out of their sockets."

Olga belonged to the first type, David to the second. Julio examined himself to make sure that his eyes were normal.

Doña Amparo Campo criticized him for devoting his time to this. It annoyed her. "It would be better if you took me for a walk now and then. I still have never been to La Molina."

Julio would answer her with a disconsolate air. "In the first place, I am forbidden to leave the city. And in the second, in Spain we lack means of transportation."

THE Rightists in Gerona slept soundly. It seemed that the three hundred and forty-three unemployed in the city did not weigh too heavily on their minds. "The government says it plans public works, that they will be put on relief."

The headquarters of the CEDA had been refurbished. Its magnificence was impressive—a doorman with gold buttons, and all the rest.

Attracted by the center and the prestige of the party, an avalanche of students had joined the CEDA, as had many young ladies. Their motto was honesty; their method of action, the spectacular; their common bond, religion.

At Liga Catalana it was a different story. They were concerned with the problem of the workers. Don Jorge, the notary Noguer, and the economists had got together to talk it over. Something had to be done. It was felt that if the mayoralty were in the hands of a member of the party it might help greatly, and so the notary Noguer was named Mayor pro tem until the municipal elections.

Nevertheless, all of them were somewhat frightened. The streets were not exactly an edifying sight. Filth seemed to be the order of the day. If the trend was not curbed, the moment would come when wearing a hat would be considered an affront to poverty. That was going too far. Something had to be done, but the right to wear a hat had to be defended.

For that reason the notary Noguer prepared with great care the speech he delivered when he took office as Mayor. He addressed himself first to the needy, and guaranteed that everything possible would be done to remedy their situation and find them work. He spoke with a tone of sincerity and confidence which gave many persons a certain measure of hope, envisioning some important program of municipal works. But then he added, addressing the population as a whole:

"Nevertheless, City Hall feels that one thing has nothing to do with the other. We will give our attention to all those things, to be sure, and to the water and sewerage systems. But at the same time we will fight to prevent an avalanche of crassness from smothering the aristocratic traditions of our beloved Gerona. There is something that really shocks me more than the failings and shootings: I mean the constant hammering away at everything that stands for well-being, culture, breeding, minority values. When someone spits on this sidewalk, I feel that not only as Mayor and notary, but simply as a man who loves cleanliness, I have a perfect right to cross the street and walk on the other side, without that constituting grounds for calling me an enemy of the people. Therefore, as long as I am Mayor, the municipal officers will dress neatly, garbage will be collected, blasphemy will be punished, disturbers of the peace will be fined, drunkards will be removed from circulation whether they belong to Liga Catalana or CNT, and a lawyer or architect will be considered as respectable a citizen as a mechanic or slaughterhouse worker. The cooperation of all is needed for the city government to function properly. We will put an end to all abuses and special privilege; but we will also cut short any attempt to convert our thrice immortal Gerona into a neighborhood sinkhole."

This was the big surprise. Nobody would have imagined that the notary Noguer, at the age of fifty-five, had such energies in reserve. Only his wife, it seemed, found it all very natural. "It doesn't surprise me at all," she said. "I know him."

The members of the CEDA agreed that the notary Noguer was right. Warning Voice published the speech in full. Everybody was pleased, especially Mosén Alberto. Mosén Alberto knew that the Diocesan Museum would have the unconditional support of Gerona's City Hall.

When they read at the Neutral: "Blasphemy will be punished," someone said: "Between this and the ideas of the Lady of Narros del Puerto there is about the width of a cigarette paper."

Major Martínez de Soria was happy. He felt upheld, supported. It was a great thing to have a mayor like that. Lieutenant Martín pointed out to him jokingly: "What I am afraid of are the measures against the lovers of the vine." The major smiled. True, he drank too much; but that was a part of his being, like the red blotches on his face. Major Martínez de Soria, contrary to Julio, seemed to attach little importance to life. He carried out every task in his daily life with an absolute disregard of danger, of possible adverse circumstances, just as when he had commanded a company in Africa. He would set off on horseback at a gallop, flex his foil in the fencing room, lift his glass, roll out the dice, and look at the wives of his friends, always with the same boldness, smiling, twisting his graying mustache, and shrugging his left shoulder in a characteristic gesture. He was an army man, through and through. Then again, at times he was suddenly another man. If he fancied any remote slur against the honor of the uniform, the nation, or his wife or daughter, then instead of twisting his mustache one would have said that he was prepared to tear that of his adversary directly from his lip. Nevertheless, as a rule, his character generally aroused a great sympathy in those who dealt with him. Someone said that to hate him one would have to do it at a distance. Possibly some of the soldiers in the garrison thought differently. But Major Martínez de Soria never allowed himself to be taken by surprise. Not even by the impeccable Commissioner Don Julian Cervera.

Major Martínez de Soria was happy—and down deep so were all the others of the Right, for they had the reins in their hands. The only exception was Warning Voice.

For if Professor Civil was convinced that the enemies of humanity were the Jews and technology—and to a lesser degree the Masons—Warning Voice was equally sure the enemies were the Socialists and their union, the UGT, the Communists and their barbershop, and the anarchists and their gymnasium. And he felt that they not only posed the problem of garbage in the streets, but went far beyond that. He felt that the failings had done nothing by way of stamping out the danger, but that, on the contrary, this was just beginning.

Warning Voice was of the opinion that the notary Noguer, despite his speech, the distinguished head of the CEDA despite his success with the ladies, Don Pedro Oriol for all his kindness, and Major Martínez de Soria lived in limbo. They had not grasped the significance of the 6th of October. Neither did they seem to recognize now the significance of those evenings of wrestling and the relentless spadework the enemy forces had resumed.

"Gil Robles refused to make a *coup d'état*; sooner or later *they* will make one again, and this time it will be for keeps." The fact was that the only one who listened to him was his maid, Dolores.

The dentist was more cultured than people gave him credit for. He had his own theories, his personal point of view. "When the bourgeoisie lets the opportunity to make its revolution slip through its fingers, it means that it is disintegrating. Nevertheless, it can still, with the help of a couple of generals, put down a poorly organized popular uprising; but the force of the popular ideas will eventually lop off its head." Warning Voice grasped the fact that, on a nation-wide level, the day the peasants of the south of Spain joined forces with the industrial workers of the Basque Provinces and Catalonia, these forces would fall upon the center—Madrid—throwing down from the seats of government all the Gil Robleses unto the fourth generation; on the provincial level—Gerona in particular—he felt that the hitherto inept skirmishes of unions and parties, naturally lacking in maturity, would soon be a thing of the past, as in many other provinces. What had happened in the cities having a revolutionary tradition and in the great peasant and proletarian areas had opened their eyes, and the press had helped. There was no community without its Cosme Vila studying, its Casal knowing by heart the workers' revolutions, successful and unsuccessful, and its Future—the young head of the FAI—who had come in a liaison capacity, with all of Bakunin at his fingertips. And, above all, the Communists, thanks to their unbroken international connections, were steeped in theory.

What had kept the fat out of the fire—according to the dentist—was that so far these groups had not been able to get together. The anarchists—individualism—were the declared enemies of the Socialists—control—and of the Communists—collectivization. Therefore, with a little shrewdness, one of the three fronts could always be turned against the other two, as had happened in the elections of 1933, without their even realizing it. Nevertheless, there were straws in the wind to show that the union that the Asturian revolutionaries had virtually achieved—Alianza Obrera had been a political reality in Asturias—was the goal pursued by the leaders who secretly manipulated the Red wires of the nation. Warning Voice still gambled on the traditional Spanish incapacity to reach an agreement on anything and the profound differences within the Communist Party itself between the followers of Moscow and those who thought that Stalin had completely betrayed the doctrines of Marx and Lenin. Notwithstanding, he sounded the alarm in the officers' café and at the Casino, calling special attention to the fact that the linotypist Casal had been named local head of the Socialist Party and of the UGT—a shrewd choice—and that the Commissioner would soon permit the reopening of the political headquarters.

His maid, Dolores, said to him: "In my opinion, sir, the women are worse than the men."

FORTY-SEVEN

THE dentist had been right in his prediction that the headquarters of the political parties would soon reopen: the order permitting them to resume activities arrived, and the city seemed shaken from top to bottom. No sooner had the order arrived than the three men he had spoken of—Cosme Vila of the Communist Party, Future of the CNT-FAI, and Antonio Casal of the Socialists—surged on to the first plane of importance. Their personalities gave substance to those parties, imbuing them with a spirit of action and efficiency.

The three men had only one thing in common: faith. Cosme Vila was the oldest, Future the youngest. Casal was the one who talked least, Cosme Vila the one who paid the closest attention, Future the one who destroyed all harmony.

Seeing them on the street, deep in their thoughts and followed by legions of fanatics, Mateo said to his father: "Oh, if only all those energies could be channeled in one direction!"

Matías looked at Future and predicted: "That one's going to stir up a lot of trouble."

COSME Vila was named the local head of the Communist Party in place of Victor, and he was on the point of quitting the bank, for his wife had said: "Why not? We'll make out. You know I can weave baskets."

Cosme Vila realized that the members of the party had joined it by instinct, but were completely ignorant of what Communism stood for and of its true situation in Spain. He was sure it would have a bad effect if he let them in on too much at once, for they would all want to express an opinion; but a few general ideas were indispensable. Therefore he announced at the barbershop that there would be a "short introductory course in Marxism," which had the shop bursting its seams. For the first time in Gerona, Communism was presented in a scientific manner.

The Communists of Gerona, thanks to their leader, learned that Marx was the theorist of the doctrine, Lenin its principal interpreter, and Stalin its perpetuator. That in Spain the first cells were formed in 1920 in Madrid and Barcelona. That what those cells sought then was the same thing they all sought now: union with Portugal to form a Union of Socialist Republics, nationalization of the land, of the railways, of the navy, of industry (including the Costas), of the dental clinics (including that of Warning Voice), of the banks (including the Arús Bank), a six-hour day, and a rifle for every worker...until not one capitalist was left in the world. Immediate plans in Gerona called for finding suitable headquarters, publishing a newspaper, and appointing a committee. Individually, each member had to carry a hammer and sickle stamped on his heart.

Listening to Cosme Vila and seeing him, Ignacio would have realized how much the light that seemed to stream from his head resembled that of César's. So many years of pondering over his typewriter, so much accumulated enthusiasm, so much solitude and austerity in that unfurnished flat with the bare walls.... Just as in César's presence the owner of the Crocodile Bar felt himself closer to the heavenly kingdom than to his bar, in Cosme Vila's presence his listeners felt that Russia was much closer to their sorrows than the nation in which they had been born. Gorki the perfumer, with his little potbelly, always said that he no longer lived in Gerona, that for many years he had practically been living in Moscow.

Only one or two members—Salvio and Pedro, both stonecutters—said to themselves on hearing Cosme Vila that he would wind up turning Communism into a bureaucracy.

When El Responsable got wind that Cosme Vila was lecturing with such success, he had a fit and immediately called a new general assembly in the gymnasium. It was on this occasion that Future revealed his full stature, achieving a triumph that was nothing short of an apotheosis.

The young anarchist was the living image of José of Madrid, but he had more personal force and had suffered more. He was twenty. He was born of unknown parents in the port of Barcelona in 1915, with the World War in full swing.

A second-hand bookdealer of Atarazanas, near the port, taught him to read during odd moments. A bearded old man who let spectators look through a telescope and see the moon for one peseta taught him tricks of palmistry and sleight of hand. One day Future thrust out his left arm horizontally and said to the book dealer: "Grab on there"—and held him aloft for a minute. Another day he thrust out his right arm and said to the old man of the telescope: "Now you," and held him aloft for a minute. The day when, by the statue of Columbus, he managed to hold both of them aloft simultaneously, one on each arm, the girls were ready to die for him.

He met El Responsable at the FAI in Barcelona. They hit it off, for Future, who had taken some lessons in jujitsu from a Japanese sailor, on telling El Responsable that he could make him turn two somersaults across the room by simply grabbing his wrist in a certain manner, received a most curious reply: "I could make you take your pants off right in the middle of Cataluña Square at high noon, and make you kiss a photographer as though he were Greta Garbo." Future realized that El Responsable was referring to hypnotism, and that carried him away. He called together his friends of the FAI of Barcelona and, flipping a coin in the air, he said: "Heads, I stay; tails, I'm going with him to Gerona." It came up tails, and he went with El Responsable.

He took a fancy to Gerona immediately because he moved right in as top dog. He dazzled Blasco telling him stories of the bootblacks of Barcelona, El Cojo with his sleight-of-hand tricks, and the daughters of El Responsable with his muscles, the brilliantine on his hair, and his palmistry. Above all, the older daughter, whose future he told first: "You'll lose your head over me." She smiled.

The speech Future made at that meeting of the general assembly was to go down as one of the most glorious pages in the anarchist annals of the city. He said that in 1814, in a Russian village named Torzhok, the first anarchist was born, Miguel Bakunin—whose father had had twelve hundred slaves. That "a fellow named Max tried to do him a bad turn, without succeeding..." That one of his spiritual heirs, the Italian Malatesta, had launched the principle of "direct action." That Spain had assimilated immediately the theories of Bakunin and Malatesta, and that now, after what had happened in Asturias and the assassination of Joaquin Santaló, the hour had come to go even beyond what they had counseled:

"Comrades, we are a million and a half strong. Catalonia leads the way; then comes the countryside of Andalusia. Our enemies are the bourgeoisie and the Communists. What do we care! We've had what it takes to give the kings the boot—let Alfonso XIII tell you—and to mutiny against Christopher Columbus. Forward, then! The hour has come to set up anarchism in Spain. Out with all the bureaucrats and all the cassocks here in Gerona. Even to get married you have to sign your name five times. We preach natural law. And down with banks and money! I'll do tricks and Blasco will shine my shoes. Someone will give you a ride in his car and El Cojo will fry him an egg. Comradeship raised to the third degree! Every day will be a holiday in Gerona. In the summer everyone will go to the Dehesa and pitch a tent. We won't have to support the Bishop, so we'll be all set. When we die, no fuss—off to the cemetery. Now we're going to hear El Responsable. I have said my piece. I'm not trying to pass myself off as a hot shot or anything else. I can dish it out, and I can take it. If anyone is looking for trouble, he knows where to find me. This is anarchism. Long live the CNT! Long live the FAI!"

The ovation was earsplitting. Blasco waved his black brush and his red brush at the same time. The gymnasium glowed with happiness and liberty. A little guy climbed the rope hand over hand to the ceiling. "I'm Bakunin!" he shouted.

At Socialist headquarters Antonio Casal managed to work up the members, too. Linotypist of *El Demócrata*, thirty-six years old, married and with three children, Casal had been a Socialist ever since he began to shave. Kautsky's *Road to Power* had converted him to the doctrine, but he had never accepted any party post. But Ovid Lodge had ordered him to take over the leadership and, despite the opposition of his wife, he had accepted.

His unruly shock of hair contrasted with the premature baldness of Cosme Vila and Future's glistening waves. He was fascinated by the class struggle; but the idea of the dictatorship of the proletariat enraged him, as well as the doctrine that converted terrorism into a religion. With a prominent nose and a small, tight-lipped mouth, his peculiarity lay in always carrying some cotton stuck in one of his ears, "to make myself deaf when it suits me."

His triumph was also a noisy one because he used a direct, energetic language to which the people of Gerona, and particularly those of the UGT, were little accustomed. He started out by stating that the first thing the members had to do, before asking for a raise in salaries, was to pay up their dues. Then he added that no one had to stay in the union if he did not like it; that if after a union meeting someone went out and read St. Teresa, he was wasting his time, the union's, and even St. Teresa's. That as long as Major Martínez de Soria went riding through the Dehesa, and the Diocesan Museum received enormous appropriations from City Hall, there was little hope of bettering the living conditions of those employed in the different trades affiliated with the UGT; that what mattered, therefore, was to force elections before the end of the year—and win!

Nothing else.

Léon Blum smiled down from the wall. Canela wanted to unionize herself, and Tower of Babel applauded wildly. Casal made his way through the clusters of people and left because his wife and children were waiting for him.

FORTY-EIGHT

THE Costa brothers reopened Izquierda Republicana with full honors, and everybody was back in place. Mateo and Ignacio, on the way home from Professor Civil's, saw the leaders of the different parties come down the stairs, stand in knots arguing, and then break up and go their separate ways.

The two boys got along very well now, and, by tacit agreement, they very rarely discussed politics. They—especially Mateo—were up on everything that took place in the city and on all the forces mobilizing their strength. But their studies took up most of their time—above all, that of Ignacio, who kept hard at it in accordance with the pattern of life he had set himself. He buried himself in his books every night until he could not keep his eyes open. From the bedside table, it seemed that St. Ignatius wanted to study too, for he looked down at the open pages over Ignacio's shoulder.

The first thing Ignacio had done, once he felt completely cured, was to forget his promise to climb to the Hermitage of the Angels. On the other hand, he did not forget to accompany Matías Alvear to the Neutral now and then, or to go with Carmen Elgazu on occasional visits to the Church of the Sacred Heart. Neither did he forget to send Canela a message which said: "Thanks a lot."

He knew from *El Demócrata* that, despite the recommendation to join forces, the anarchists refused to play ball with the Communists, and Cosme Vila and Casal refused to cooperate with the Costas. All of them, apparently, could have benefited by a talk with Mosén Francisco: perhaps they could discover the formula of harmony. Ignacio knew from the blond ex-anarchist that performances of musical comedies were to follow the wrestling and boxing matches: comedies in which the tenor would be the Good One and the baritone the Evil One or vice versa, to maintain the tradition. He had read the speech of the notary Noguer, but—he did not give it much thought. For the moment he devoted himself to Pilar, in return for the company she had kept him during his sickness. He joked with her about the dressmaking establishment, or her "dear diary," and he egged her on to telling stories about the nuns, roaring with laughter at them, which delighted his sister. Sometimes he treated her to a movie, or some chestnuts, or crullers; always some little treat. Then, he had also written to César, thanking him for the book on Teresa Neumann. It was a long letter that left the seminarian flabbergasted. "What has come over Ignacio?" he asked himself. The letter was that of a fine, sensible, believing boy. César showed it to his Latin professor, who answered with a smile that he had read it before César. The seminarian was filled with a great happiness. "Ignacio converted! Ignacio converted!" His prayers had been answered. It made up to him in part for the closing down of the Bernat workshop.

But, above all, Ignacio had written with emotion he had not anticipated to Ana María. He started the letter out of politeness and found himself reliving the moments at San Felíu: the naturalness of the girl, her green eyes, the blue ball, the unforgettable expression of distaste on her face when he was rude on the beach. He wrote: "No, I am not mayor yet—a notary is mayor—nor a lawyer; but I will be: And then—yes, Muntaner 180, I remember perfectly—I will appoint you councilman, or perhaps my head clerk. Who knows, we may win, you and I, a lot of hopeless cases. At any rate, I have just won one: thanks to a sickness for one thing, and then to a priest with a preposterous hat." Ana María answered him by special delivery. That day she put on her best earrings.

MATEO, who was of draft age, got Major Martínez de Soria, thanks to Marta, to endorse his appeal for temporary deferment as a student. So he was safe, for a while anyway, and could breathe freely again; Pilar could breathe again too. It wasn't that he was looking out for his own convenience; serving his country seemed a great honor to him; but like J. Campistol, chief of the squads in Barcelona, whom he visited, he felt that his place for the time being was in Gerona, wearing the blue shirt, and not in any old barracks of the peninsula in a khaki uniform.

Don Emilio Santos was happy at having his son at his side awhile longer; Carmen Elgazu would have been sorry to see him go; Professor Civil, who was proud as Punch of his two students, would have suffered a real disappointment; not to mention Raimundo, Mateo being one of his few clients who took a mustache trim and massage.

"When you need deferment," Mateo said to Ignacio, "we will have a talk with Marta, and the major will fix you up."

One thing troubled Mateo: his heart. He could not account for what was happening to him, but the fact was that when he went up to Ignacio's house, with his head filled with "eternal values, the blue ocean, yokes and arrows," not to mention Roman law and economics, Pilar's dazzling youth, her firm, rosy cheeks, her bright dresses hemmed and stitched by her own hand, her tilted nose and saucy eyes, filled him with a great sense of well-being. Before going into Ignacio's room to study some difficult lesson with him, he would sit in the dining room beside the stove a few minutes, next to Carmen Elgazu and facing Pilar. On these occasions he found the girl's high spirits contagious. Everything about her was becoming familiar to him, and it seemed logical to him that he should know at what hour she went to the dress shop, when she left, what she did after work, whether she came right home. Matías Alvear with the head-set on, or reading the paper, thought: "I wonder if one of those arrows Don Emilio Santos talks about flies through this dining room and unites these two kids." Carmen Elgazu, as she sat knitting, had an air of preparing the way of a new being into the world.

All that worried Mateo because at first he had thought it was Marta who would interest him. Castilian profile, horsewoman, a student at the School of Fine Arts. The introduction of a ringing word into the conversation aroused her. But, in spite of all this, the most he felt for her was admiration and esteem, considering her a magnificent comrade. She could establish the feminine division of Falange in the city. It never occurred to him, looking at Pilar, to ask her what she thought about José Antonio.

"And what do you talk about at the shop?"

"Well—nothing. About boys."

"And movies?"

"Naturally."

"And what boys do you talk about?"

"Really! About you, maybe."

"I didn't say that—"

Ignacio would open the door to his room for the third time and say: "Mateo, Roman law awaits us."

THE speeches of Cosme Vila, Future, and Casal had been published in their entirety in *El Demócrata*. Everybody read them. The general impression was that they had a tone of great violence; but in spite of that, Professor Civil remarked that this violence was only a pallid reflection of the violence that was really in the heads of those men. He was sure that Cosme Vila's objectives went far beyond those which he had outlined, and only the fact that this was Future's maiden appearance had restrained him from speaking of bombs, which was what he had in mind. As for Casal, the professor insisted that his was the most incendiary mind in the city. "You will see. He is a box of explosives."

Ignacio was not sure what to think. He tried to be fair. He followed the advice of Mosén Francisco. Instead of trying to calibrate the dangers all this might hold for the city, he reflected on the three men who had come forward as leaders, and tried to find the possible causes for their explosiveness.

To his old theories about the decisive importance of childhood—what could have been the childhood of Cosme Vila, of Casal?—he had already heard the story of Future's—he now added many others. Physical make-up, temperature of the flat in which they lived, and, above all, the greater or lesser degree of intensity in their family relations. The fewer family ties—members of the FAI, Warning Voice—the greater the violence. The greater the family ties—his parents, Professor Civil—the more the moderation. There were exceptions like El Responsable, living with his daughters, but the examples to back his theory could be counted in the hundreds. The whole middle class. The teller, who since he had adopted Paco had turned into a sentimentalist. Ignacio thought of his own case. When he had found himself spiritually distant from his family, he had jumped up on a bandstand and destroyed a trombone, and had wound up swimming in seas of pus. Now, when he sometimes sat down beside the stove like Mateo, with his parents and Pilar, he had moments of great unrest, but he knew how to control it.

And Cosme Vila? Was he, too, an exception? Would his tone moderate when his companion delivered to him the child she now carried in her womb? Perhaps. Perhaps in the face of the child's helplessness he would have less desire for absolute powers for the State.

Ignacio realized that in thinking about those things he was examining them either in a mildly ironic light or with an air of self-sufficiency. This upset him. He was afraid of being guilty of vanity, of self-sufficiency, of being too subtle and smug. Perspective was all right for Professor Civil, bowed with years, and a scholar of Latin and Greek! But he was a green kid, who made twenty-five duros a month and studied first-year law. There lay the pitfalls of virtue. He could not figure out how César managed to avoid the sin of vanity. It was necessary not only to keep silent, but to silence certain voices that arose from the silence. Mosén Francisco spoke of showers...perhaps he was making a mistake not to follow this piece of advice before all others....

But he did not have to go overboard in that direction either. No, he was not as unfair as he was making himself out to be. The fact was that he loved his neighbor, with exceptions like Canela and Mosén Alberto. But it was beyond his power to fight that. The important thing was for him to maintain his serenity. He had a foreboding that all of them, together, were approaching a great catastrophe, and for that reason he loved his neighbor more than ever. Now instead of the Russians, Rousseau and Voltaire, and the rotogravures of *Crónica*, he read his textbooks and the book on Teresa Neumann. And the Bible! Great heavens! "Those eighteen upon whom the tower in Siloam fell."

How many things he saw clearly! In Gerona it was enough for one man to come forward—a Cosme Vila, a Future, a Casal—for a political party to acquire prominence. Where then lay the permanent value of the doctrine? That very thing, of course, was what had always happened to him. Perhaps that was the new, the dangerous tower in Siloam. In any case, the constants in the city were the rebellion of the lonely, the instinct of conservation of the families, the struggle between the haves and the have-nots, and the walls.

One fact stood out even clearer than the others: he continued classifying Mateo among the fanatics.

It also seemed evident to him that Marta, mounted on her mare or afoot, dressed all in black, was the most beautiful woman in the city.

FORTY-NINE

THE double wedding of the Costas was, as expected, an event, and it took place despite the fact that the house under construction was not yet completed; for the time being, they would live in two rented flats.

They were not married by the Bishop, as Raimundo had predicted; nevertheless, the religious ceremony was spectacular. It took place in the parish church of the Carmen, which was decked out in such splendor that it looked like the headquarters of the CEDA.

The fact that the Costas had chosen such wealthy brides was widely commented upon. Some considered it undemocratic, others said that it had no bearing. In any case, the Costas shot the works. They did not limit the guests to their sister Laura, Commissioner Julián Cervera, the committee of Izquierda Republicana, the manager and assistant manager of the bank, the many friends they had made in jail—Julio, David, Olga, and others. They invited all their workers: those from the quarry and the foundry, from the lime kiln, the marble cutters. It rubbed some of these the wrong way to have to enter the church, but down deep they felt flattered.

The brides had been more restrained. They had brought their parents—solid-looking property owners—and half a dozen relatives in starched collars. As their witnesses they had a notary from Figueras and a rice broker from Pals.

After the religious ceremony there was a banquet at the Hotel Peninsular, with music by El Rubio and his orchestra. The one hundred and forty-four workers of the Costas were accommodated in the dining hall opening out from the room where the wedding party sat. The in-laws of the two industrialists glanced uneasily at those men who did not know how to hold a fork and who drank like Carlist soldiers. When the dancing began, they trembled at the thought that their sons-in-law, for the sake of their democratic principles, would expect their daughters to dance with that rabble. The mother said: "This is too much." They were reassured by the smiles of their daughters, which told them that it would be over in no time and that afterward nobody could take away from them the name whose mere echo mobilized every bank in the city. Nevertheless, they foresaw unpleasant conflicts over questions of politics.

The Costas were prudent. A new and opportune handout of cigars was the signal for a democratic withdrawal. "Holiday until Monday," they went about telling the workers; and the workers, in their Sunday best, flushed with champagne, and with an air of excited expectancy, made their way out of the hotel, slapping one another on the back and carefully avoiding tripping over the pots of flowers installed beside the entrance.

The Commissioner—Don Julian Cervera—was one of those who remained. He danced with the two brides. Julio García also remained, and he was among those who spoke after the banquet. The managers of the banks stayed till the end, glasses on high, with the director of the Arús Bank, footing dance after dance with Doña Amparo Campo, who was blissfully happy. Major Campos tried to soothe the nerves of his wife, who had to sit out every dance. David and Olga had left. Casal and Cosme Vila, as had been foreseen, had declined the Costas' personal invitation.

A little before six o'clock the two couples disappeared. They left, nobody knew for where. Laura had scarcely had time to exchange two words with her new sisters. They seemed easier to get along with than she would have supposed. On finding herself alone with the parents, she looked over the guests one by one until her eyes came to rest on Julio.

Laura had a very low opinion of Julio because of what she had heard of him. But despite that, the policeman won her over. He struck her as very intelligent. He told her about the life of turtles—not everything, because there was not time—and most curious bits of information about African music. He recited some verses of Hafiz. "I never would have guessed you were like what you are. I really thought you were a roughneck."

Julio, who was in his cups, replied: "The roughneck is my wife."

Laura could not restrain a guffaw. "I am very happy," said the girl. Perhaps this stemmed in part from the fact that all of her brothers' workers, one by one, had come past to greet her and to say goodbye. "Poor dears, poor dears," she said to them, easing their embarrassment.

Don Julián Cervera, the Commissioner, had reflected a long time on the invitation before accepting. Julio had told him: "Don't worry about it. Warning Voice will be marrying in no time and we will make sure that you are invited. Then everybody will see that the Commissioner is impartial."

Many girls pressed their noses against the windows of the hotel to look in on the banquet; one of them was Pilar. If Mateo saw her, he would be furious, she thought, but the whole shop had decided to go; it was impossible to refuse. All of them, including Pilar, were disappointed to find that the newlyweds had left already. Two automobiles? Each couple separate? What do you think of that! All of them admitted that Laura looked very nice and that the wife of Major Campos was a real fright. Pilar, on catching sight of Julio dancing, thought back to a couple of years before when the policeman asked her: "So—you like the springtime?" She blushed on recalling the question.

FIFTY

EXCEPT for Cosme Vila, Casal, Julio, Major Martínez de Soria, and a couple more, nobody in the city had taken the local Falange seriously. The national Falange—Castile, Madrid, and the rest—was something else. The extremists of the Left never stopped talking about assassinations, and the extremists of the Right looked on the FAI as their target. The fact that some people here and there attended the Falangists' meetings out of curiosity did not eliminate the real feeling that they were only a handful and would not constitute a national threat unless those in power opened the doors to them. Gerona had known from the first that the son of the manager of the *Tabacalera*—with his shock of hair and blue shirt—had arrived with the intention of opening a breach. Noguer the notary, Don Santiago Estrada, Mosén Alberto, and others among the city's first citizens considered Mateo a bright adolescent with a spectacular idea or two in tow, but completely ignorant of the psychological realities of the region. El Responsable and many of the workers—both employed and unemployed—predicted that he was in for some rough handling; on the other hand, David and Olga felt that the virus was more contagious than it might appear. "People act by mimicry, especially in periods of transition like this."

Some ladies felt attracted to the new movement without knowing exactly why. There was something secret, mysterious, knightly about Falange. Mateo was not aware of it, but he aroused certain sighs of admiration as he passed by.

Mateo's goal was to bring together six members as soon as possible. He did not consider this impossible, for he was convinced that the same thing was true in all communities: there were a number of young men who were Falangists without knowing it. And there were others who were openly in sympathy, who read the speeches of José Antonio carefully, but who, lacking a local leader, did nothing. What was needed was fervor, example. "In the barbershops, in the cafés..." At the first sign of sympathy, take the novice aside and then put him to the test. Tell him that Falange offers him no advantages, nor a fatter pay envelope, nor a way of passing examinations without studying; at most, what it offered was the possibility of serious trouble. Hand out the circulars, very clear on this point. If, notwithstanding, the fellow came to attention and answered: "*¡Arriba España!*" he would receive his membership card.

Mateo's right-hand man was Octavio Sánchez, a local employee of the Treasury Department, membership card number two. Mateo, who classified intelligence as heavyweight, featherweight, and flyweight, placed Octavio in this last division. By flyweight he meant the faculty of sparring and awaiting an opening to land the first blow. He said this because Octavio never allowed himself to be beaten to the punch. When at the office they asked him captious questions about Falange, he answered straight from the shoulder. He did the same thing at the boarding house where he lived.

An odd thing had happened at this boarding house, near the Plaza Municipal. Octavio, who called himself a "humanist" because he much preferred having a drink in the company of friends to scaling a peak of the Pyrenees or exploring a cave, had for some time been prolonging the after-dinner conversation with the keeper of the house and his daughter Rosario, until one day he told the girl he loved her. She ran up to her room crimson and then came down a little later to confess that she had been waiting for him to speak for days. The boarding house keeper was pleased with the development, for he felt that having a relative in the Treasury Department could do nobody any harm.

The simplicity with which all this had come about was frightening. Now Octavio wore a blue shirt and his sweetheart, Rosario, ironed it for him. Things could not have been more perfect. Octavio liked Ignacio a lot, and hoped for the day when Ignacio would occupy one of the seats in Mateo's study. "Don't kid yourself," Mateo told him. "Ignacio has a gene in his blood that pulls in another direction."

Octavio did not insist. He had great respect for Mateo, looked on him as the leader, and was prepared to obey him blindly. Octavio was well aware that he had been Mateo's first comrade in the city; so the more smoke, the greater the tension, and the more circulars scattered about the study in which they held their meetings, the happier he was at not being just a pen-pusher at the Treasury office, at being able to contribute, even with his lisping "s's," to the "awakening of Spain." He would have seen eye to eye with the Martínez de Soria brothers, even though they would have struck him as a little presumptuous. Something comical was taking place now. He was managing to win some respect for Falange at the office, at the Neutral, everywhere except at the boardinghouse. The boarding house keeper, a tall man with a great midriff, always said to him, flourishing the bread knife: "Listen to me, Tavy. You get my daughter mixed up in any monkey business and I'll send you back to Andalusia in little slices."

Mateo and Octavio had put their shoulders to the wheel. The preparations being made by all the other forces in the city acted as a spur to them. Mateo told Octavio: "We have got to get up to six. Six men doesn't seem like much, but the way we work that will be enough to get our foot in the door. There are surely six potential Falangists in Gerona. You wait and see—within a month they all will have presented themselves of their own accord."

Mateo's calculation of probabilities turned out to be just about right. Twenty-five thousand inhabitants: there had to be at least six. The first turned out a dud, but the rest were all the real article.

The dud was Lieutenant Martín. He presented himself, declaring that he had already been a member of Falange in Corunna. Mateo turned a deaf ear. He wanted to have as little as possible to do with the military, especially of the fancy-pants stripe of Lieutenant Martín.

On the other hand, they accepted the younger son of Professor Civil. This was curious in view of the fact that the professor had told Mateo and Ignacio: "None of my sons will ever belong to Falange: I have educated them in the classics." His younger son, Benito Civil, a draftsman, had been unemployed after the events of October, but was now working for the architects Ribas and Massana. When he found out that Mateo was studying law with his father, he turned up one day at Mateo's house and said: "Comrade, I should like to know exactly what the movement is all about, but I think that in principle I am already with you."

Mateo looked at him steadily. At that time Benito was still out of work. Mateo replied: "Falange doesn't promise to find you work; on the contrary, you will probably have to help us pay off a few debts."

Benito Civil blinked.

"Are you married?" Mateo asked.

"Yes."

"Do you have children?"

"Yes. Two."

"Then, think it over carefully. This is dangerous."

"Why is it so dangerous?"

"Because Falange loves Spain above everything, including one's own children."

Benito Civil felt a cold shiver run through him. His wife had told him: "Keep away from them. That business can bring us nothing but heartaches." But something drew him and kept him standing there in Mateo's study in the shadow of the stuffed bird.

He took the circulars home with him. He read them feverishly. Benito Civil had known from the time he was a boy that he would not be satisfied to live in Gerona, hating technology and the Jews, which were the ideas his father had hammered into him. All this struck him as fanaticism. But on reading in the circulars: "The idea of Country is the exact point of balance between the local or regional concept—the rachitic concept—and the concept of the wiping out of frontiers and the establishment of the universal society—the vague and illusory concept," and "For us, Spain is our Country, not because it gave us birth and sustains us, but because it has fulfilled the three or four great transcendental destinies that have characterized the history of mankind: defense of Catholicism, discovery of America, etc.," Benito Civil put on his green-checked sports jacket—the draftsman liked colors—and walking, like his father, the professor, with a certain stoop, presented himself to Mateo and, raising his arm, exclaimed: "*¡Arriba España!*"

Now they were three. Half their quota had been reached. The fourth was the son of Dr. Rosselló. Miguel Rosselló began feeling himself a Falangist the day he had first heard his father talk against the Falange. "When my father knocks something, it must be good," he said to himself.

The gulf that had always existed between Dr. Rosselló and his son was one of the basic dramas of the city. Miguel Rosselló kept track of his father's doings and considered him an undesirable being, possessed of strange personal ambitions. When Miguel Rosselló left his house he would look up at the blue sky and draw a deep breath, filling his lungs. Having virtually broken his family ties, he sought something into which he could pour his student energies. One day he read a speech by José Antonio and was carried away. He came to know Octavio at the Neutral. Octavio told him: "Falange would condemn people like your father—who use the sick as a means to an end—to life imprisonment, or worse." Miguel Rosselló asked to be introduced to Mateo. Mateo looked at the buttonhole in the lapel of the candidate's jacket, which displayed a button with the trademark of a make of automobile.

"Are you an automobile fan?"

"Yes."

"Why?"

"I like speed."

Then Mateo asked him about his other interests. Miguel Rosselló wanted to study medicine "to save the people my father destroys."

"I can't understand your talking that way. Your father has the reputation of being a very competent doctor."

"He is, but he is not a good man."

"Do you think that before being a doctor one must be a man?"

"No doubt about it."

Mateo nodded in approval. He yanked the Studebaker button from Miguel's lapel. He gave him the circulars. "Come back in three days." Miguel Rosselló, tall, almost beardless, with a face that conveyed absolute frankness, and with great energy concentrated in the corners of his mouth, came back and shouted, shoulders squared: "*¡Arriba España!*" Afterwards, returning home, he told his father what he had done.

Dr. Rosselló answered: "If you don't have your name removed from the rolls immediately, you can find a new roof for your head."

The boy replied: "I will find a new roof."

The fifth comrade was Juan Roca, a student of languages. He was the son of the doorman of the Labor Office—the rival of the assistant manager in knowledge of Masonic affairs. He made his living by giving German lessons and filling out identification cards for the local government. He liked everything German, beginning with the language and ending with the cameras. His father told him that German was awful, and that all it was good for was to recite poems and to sing hymns. But Juan Roca kept on studying and teaching German with absolute conviction.

He presented himself to Mateo because he was convinced that Falange had its origins in modern German theories. When Mateo told him that he was mistaken, that the negligible non-Spanish part of the Falangist doctrine had come from Mussolini, the boy tried to withdraw. But Mateo kept him from leaving. He had liked his looks. He gave him the circulars. Juan Roca read them and thought: "What the hell, this is all taken from the German no matter what he says. Or at any rate a German could have thought it up." He went back to Mateo's study and, extending his arm, said with a smile: "*¡Arriba España!*"

Mateo told him: "Before I give you the membership card, you will have to have a couple of lessons. You have to rid yourself of all ideas of foreign influence."

The last to join was Conrado Haro, a good-natured, remarkably well-meaning kid from a very modest family. His father was a city policeman. Conrado wanted to be a sailor. Everything that had the slightest connection with the sea went straight to his heart. He was disconsolate because the Republic did absolutely nothing in that sense and had utterly neglected the merchant marine. When he read on a scrap of newspaper that Falange proclaimed that Spain would once again be a naval power, he did not hesitate for a minute. He presented himself to Mateo.

Mateo told him: "It is true. As you see, even the color of our shirts is blue."

Conrado Haro shouted: "*¡Arriba España!*" He did not make much out of the circulars. He skipped the paragraphs that did not make any reference to the "sea," murmuring: "O.K., O.K., very good." Mateo accepted him because he saw in him a pure heart with a concrete ideal for which he was prepared to make sacrifices. He promised himself that he would not be content until he saw Conrado Haro in white uniform on the deck of a ship.

Now that they were six, Mateo decided it was time to hold a meeting. They barely knew each other as a group. Octavio knew Rosselló; Roca and Haro had said hello to each other on the Rambla at some time or other; and Benito Civil was a good deal older than any of the others—twenty-nine, the oldster of the group. They had to be brought together and worked into a compact body. The idea of unity was essential.

Mateo was delighted with their diversity of backgrounds and even the diversity of motives that had inspired them. He told himself that the six formed, in miniature, a complete world. Octavio was the subtle, instinctive Andalusian intelligence. Rosselló was the rebel. Benito Civil was very primitive intellectually, but with a moving emotional capacity. Juan Roca had great tenacity. Conrado Haro was the uncorrupted spirit. When all these spiritual forces became welded in a common desire for the greatness of Spain, Gerona would begin to assert herself, and the bravadoes of *El Tradicionalista* would collapse of old age and Casal's panaceas based on production and transportation would ring hollow. The Costas were ingenuous, Estat Català was shortsighted, El Responsable and Future were a couple of dangerous romantics. The most dangerous was Cosme Vila, because his theory also represented a total conception of life. Unfortunately, it was based on materialism, wishing to replace the four arms of the cross—the four points of the compass, the four elements of nature—with the five-pointed star, which, according to Professor Civil, as early as Babylonian times, had represented perfect science, perfect power—that is to say, God.

Mateo told himself that he had to unite the comrades and some other people, too. A romantic idea—probably a dangerous one, too—suggested itself to him.

And he put it into practice. He organized a dance at his home to celebrate his birthday, St. Joseph's Day. He told Orencia, the maid: "We'll be thirteen. Prepare thirteen cups of chocolate."

Don Emilio Santos readily agreed. Don Emilio was keeping a careful watch on his son's every action without Mateo's realizing it. Sometimes he stooped to acts unworthy of his graying temples: he listened at keyholes. When

Mateo and Octavio shut themselves up in the study, Don Emilio Santos would slip down the hall and eavesdrop. Thanks to this, he discovered the meaning of that little party, and that the first public manifestations of Falange in Gerona would occur in June.

Saints in heaven! The thing was moving fast. The hubbub of the other parties was swelling like a tide. The Communist Party had headquarters of its own in the Plaza de la Independencia, magnificent headquarters displaying on the balcony a huge sign in red letters reading: "Communist Party of Gerona."

All the guests began receiving invitations to the dance. The first were Ignacio and Pilar. Carmen Elgazu was delighted. It seemed very natural to her that her children should enjoy themselves. "Dances at private homes don't bother me at all," she said. Matías Alvear replied that if he had ever gone off the rails it had been at just such private parties.

Mateo told Ignacio and Pilar: "There will be surprise guests." Ignacio replied: "Sure, I know! Octavio, Rosselló, et cetera." Mateo smiled and added: "And someone else."

The person who took the party most to heart was the maid, Orencia. Orencia would have been hard put to it to justify before any judge why she had become a spy. She had always been a quiet girl, even devout, a bit of a dreamer, but very dutiful. For that reason Carmen Elgazu had warmly recommended her to Don Emilio Santos. But—she had begun going with Salvio because she wanted to marry and Salvio was a good-looking, reliable man. That was where the business got its start. As soon as she found out that her sweetheart was a Communist, she felt it her duty to keep him posted from A to Z on Mateo's activities. "You'd better tell Cosme Vila that they now have six members, and that besides—"

"Don't mention Cosme Vila to me," Salvio interrupted. "I am a Trotskyite."

Orencia was perplexed and thought that the day she had a chance to enter Mateo's study she would look that word up in the dictionary.

The day of the dance she decided not to miss one detail of what took place. Mateo had begged her, in spite of its being St. Joseph's Day, to stay and serve the guests. To make up for it, he promised her two afternoons off.

As the guests arrived, she looked them over one by one, making to herself silent comments of an inexplicable violence.

There was the young gentleman of the house, Mateo, wearing new shoes to make an impression. There was the son of Professor Civil and his wife, with a face like a nincompoop. There was that one from Treasury and his sweetheart, looking as though butter wouldn't melt in her mouth, who probably spread Falangist propaganda at the boarding house. There was the Alvear boy, really a refined type, who would be a lawyer some day and refused to join Falange. There was Pilar, plump and baby-faced, who couldn't keep her eyes off of Mateo. There was Rosselló, not dry behind the ears yet, and his sisters, who didn't know what it was to wash dishes...or spend a holiday afternoon preparing thirteen cups of chocolate. Also there was one Juan Roca, as ugly as sin, and one Conrado Haro, who looked as though he hadn't been weaned yet.

That's it, sip chocolate and nibble cakes next to that dried-up old bird, and with that photo of José Antonio presiding!

While the tinkle and clatter of teaspoons and plates drifted into the kitchen, the maid fed her bad humor. But she could not keep it up. As soon as she heard the chairs being pushed back and saw all the lights in the house turned on, she cocked her head. The phonograph started up! It was a tango. The first few bars went down with a little bitterness. But as she heard the moving feet of the dancers, she pushed the kitchen door shut, took off her apron, and gave herself up to languid solitary turns embracing an imaginary Salvio.

Nobody cared about her. What a dog's life while one was single! The guests each lived his own tango. What a house, what furniture! They danced in the study, in the hall, in the dining room. A magnificent dizziness had taken possession of the house.

"Full house." Ignacio had said to Pilar: "You see who was right: there you have the surprise guests." And the sweep of his hand took in Rosselló and his sisters, Octavio, and the rest in their blue shirts. Pilar had to accept the fact. But what did she care? Mateo was enough for her. A magnificent dizziness, indeed! Above all when the others danced in the study and the dining room and she and Mateo remained alone in the hall. In those moments Mateo would stop and draw her closer to him. Pilar could feel his cheek against her temples, their hair intermingling, and their feet moving on a single tile of the mosaic floor.

Mateo also felt a wild happiness. At last he had managed to be with Pilar without Carmen Elgazu darning socks alongside them. There was not a fire on in the whole house, yet he was constantly pulling out his blue handkerchief to mop his brow! Pilar arrived wrapped in a heavy coat, but when she took it off she was wearing an incredibly airy, delicate dress. Mateo's hand trembled against it. It even trembled as he tried to light his pipe with his flint lighter, a gadget that drew shrieks of enthusiasm from the sisters Rosselló.

Professor Civil's daughter-in-law relived the parties of her salad days. Octavio did flamenco singing in a style that made the records seem pale and aroused the party to a frenzy of enthusiasm. Ignacio, completely given over to the natural gaiety of the house, recalled as belonging to another existence other Sunday afternoons when he had spent the best of himself in a rose-colored room with Canela. What an acrid taste it left in one's mouth, and afterwards what a sensation of death in one's soul! Having the kind of friends he had now was to live, to have a soul!

It seemed very odd to him to be dancing with his sister. He found her much lighter on her feet than he had imagined. "Having a good time?" he asked her.

"Don't tell a soul, but I am completely happy," she replied. Ignacio kissed her on the forehead.

Suddenly, when everyone least expected it, the doorbell rang. Mateo went to the door; it was Marta. "I knew there was one cup to go," the maid thought to herself.

Marta was dressed in black, as always, and wearing high heels. Her hair, as never before, swooned on either side of her face. Pale, with bangs almost to the eyebrows over her serene, steady eyes, she extended her expressive hand to each of the guests, one by one. She smiled almost shyly, but at the same time with a certain inner assurance.

Ignacio received one of the strongest impressions of his young life. He managed to isolate Marta from everything connected with the Military Tribunal, with the orderly assigned to accompany her on her gallops through the Dehesa, with the distance she and her mother established between themselves and other women. He accepted her as a vision, as something beautiful and grave rising up from the depths of an ancient city and coming to him that afternoon of St. Joseph's Day, crossing that threshold and shaking his hand. When she reached Benito she asked: "You are the Professor's son, aren't you?" When she came to Ignacio she said: "And you are Ignacio." Pilar waited in vain for her to say: "And you are Pilar." She thought for a moment that perhaps the flower she was wearing in her hair might have displeased Marta.

But that was not the case. When Mateo introduced them, saying somewhat solemnly: "Marta, here is the friend you deserve," Marta smiled at Pilar in a way that made it evident that she wanted to please her. When Marta found out that Octavio had been born in Seville and Ignacio in Málaga, she lifted her cup of chocolate toward each of the boys, saying: "A toast to Seville and Málaga." Pilar was amazed at such daring, but she recognized that the girl did it without any affectation. Octavio, however, objected to toasting Andalusia with chocolate. "The next party will be at my house and things will be done *comme il faut.*"

The get-together was perfect. In other places—crowded movies, the Ateneo Popular—the festive afternoon advanced more sluggishly. Many people at UGT, in Estat Català, at the Communist Party—spoke of a united front:

thirteen people at Mateo's house achieved it. Not to mention the Costas, who had also achieved it in the honeymoon setting of Mallorca.

When Ignacio put his arm around Marta's waist, he observed that the girl kept her distance when she danced, but held his hand firmly. A worthy daughter of Major Martínez de Soria, he thought to himself. Yet nothing in him rebelled against that thought. Apparently his prejudices of the past were dead.

Except that he recalled with absurd insistence her two brothers in Valladolid. They looked so much alike, with their blue shirts, and their small revolvers hidden on their hip. But Marta was less ironic. She listened attentively. When she followed the argument, she assented vigorously; when she did not, she raised her hand to her forehead and pushed her bangs off to the sides of her forehead. Mateo, who never stopped observing her, decided that she was finding Ignacio a little disconcerting, for she kept moving her bangs with disturbing regularity.

They danced until eight o'clock, when the phonograph lost its voice. Then they all went into the study, the chairs were returned to their places, and cognac was substituted for the chocolate. The object was to gossip a little, and it was fulfilled. Pilar's opinion was that it was worse than the dress shop! Octavio told fabulous stories about Seville, about women who would sell their mattresses to buy a ticket to the bullfight.

Mateo wanted to avoid at all costs the subject of politics. But he could not prevent Benito Civil's wife from alluding to St. Joseph as "my favorite saint," which drew from Octavio, who was by way of being an atheist, a couple of wisecracks about the flowering of certain rods, which scandalized the group. Professor Civil's daughter-in-law told herself she would never again attend one of those parties; along with the maid, she was the dissenter at the party.

Pilar was brilliant in explaining the error men fell into by thinking that women dress to please them. "What really interests us is to make other women envious." The Rosselló sisters agreed wholeheartedly.

"So, then, Marta put a white choker over a black sweater to make you all foam at the mouth!" Ignacio said. Everybody laughed. Marta finally confessed openly, to everyone's delight, that that was precisely the case.

Octavio's sweetheart, Rosario, laughed, but somewhat timidly. At the boarding house most of the guests were like her father: they would have preferred red wine to chocolate and would have talked about fishing or how to cook a good stew instead of St. Joseph. For that reason she was grateful to Octavio for introducing her to a higher level of society. Looking at the picture of José Antonio now and then, she decided that he was beyond doubt much more distinguished than El Responsable.

Rosario took it for granted that everybody there was a Falangist, and she supposed that not only Marta, but also the wife of the draftsman, and certainly Pilar, knew by heart the definition of "vertical union or corporative system" as opposed to the "political syndicates," which Octavio always was quoting. She was very fearful of beginning the study of all that, but she was more afraid not to. "I must be different from the others, for the fact is that I dress to please Octavio and not other women," she thought to herself.

Rosselló and Juan Roca, Haro and Civil looked each other over with great curiosity. They burned with a desire to talk to one another, to communicate their respective enthusiasms, to ask: "Have you read the latest speech?" or "Do you know what it means to stand guard above the stars?" But they had to limit themselves to exchanging looks of understanding.

Two of them—Rosselló and Roca—knew that there was one dissident at the party: Ignacio, who was pretending not to know what was going on. "If the discussion gets hot, there will be quite a dust-up here," Mateo thought to himself.

Fortunately, Marta opened and closed the subject in the same breath. On realizing that Ignacio had Socialist leanings, she exclaimed: "There's nothing to that. Why, in Valladolid all the Socialists come over to Falange."

Ignacio bit his lips. To get even, he decided to take the soapbox, forgetting Mosén Francisco's advice, and dazzle Marta, Octavio, all the faithful, and even Don Emilio Santos, who had just come in from the Neutral. He talked uninterruptedly for a long stretch to the delight of Pilar, who said to herself: "My brother's got real class." He spoke of many things, none of which had anything to do with Socialism or Valladolid. He spoke of the bank, where he said there were employees who had worked side by side for years eight hours a day without having found a thing in common, and who would witness the disappearance of one another without the least comment. He spoke of the law, which he was studying with the greatest interest because it taught one that there were ways of reconciling differences without coming to blows. And he spoke of Teresa Neumann. "She is even more significant than that French soldier of the war of 1914 who was wounded simultaneously in five places: both hands, both feet, and the left side—in other words, exactly the five wounds of Christ." In conclusion he spoke of the modern dance, conceding that its rhythm was certainly obsessive, but that, in his opinion, the honors would ultimately go to purely melodic jazz and the South American rhythms.

Ignacio had his say, and Rosselló and Roca, holding no grudge, smiled cordially. The reconciliation of these differences brought an added good cheer to the members of the group, who had completely forgotten that it was time to go home to supper.

The party had been a complete success. Mateo was happier than anyone else. Now they were "six," perfectly united, and Pilar was enchanting. The idea of inviting Marta had been an inspiration—now Marta was incorporated into the group, and, above all, she and Pilar were on a footing of friendship. Ignacio had seen his men at close quarters, and some of their ideas would stick. What better return could he have hoped for from thirteen cups of chocolate?

Marta was happy too. During the whole of Ignacio's speech she pushed aside her bangs only once: when she heard that several men could work side by side eight hours a day for years and remain perfect strangers, without establishing one square inch of heart contact.

The part about Teresa Neumann interested her immensely, despite Octavio's snickers. "The first to show the stigmata was St. Paul." What did it all mean? She would have to learn more about it. Further information was indispensable. It was a beautiful subject, and Ignacio seemed very well informed. Don Emilio Santos, who had arrived after the remark about the Socialists in Valladolid and Falange, considered the money for the party well spent, and took satisfaction in the good sense displayed by all. "So far, Mateo hasn't given me much cause for worry, in spite of the arrows." Also, he liked Pilar a lot. If, instead of studying to be a seamstress, she had studied typing, he would have gladly given her a job at the *Tabacalera*. The only person who left with a bad taste in her mouth was the wife of the draftsman. She had the feeling that her husband, without any need to be, particularly now that he had work, was mixed up with people who were "too smart." If she had known what Don Emilio Santos was thinking, she would have said to him: "Don't fool yourself. You'll have plenty of worries."

FIFTY-ONE

LIFE was rolling on at a dizzying pace. On the 14th of April, the fourth anniversary of the advent of the Republic, Izquierda Republicana staged a noisy celebration. Mosén Alberto began his excavations in Rosas in search of the Greek city that so interested the scholar Relken, Julio's friend. The Costas' sister, Laura, went to the office of Warning Voice to have a tooth pulled, and the editor-in-chief of *El Tradicionalista* asked her in a tone that strangely disquieted her: "And you, Laura, aren't you going to marry?" Every fortnight David and Olga received a visit from the new inspector of schools, appointed after October, who told them: "I'd advise you to keep politics out of your teaching...." The elder son of Professor Civil, the architect, got the contract to build a group of summer houses at S'Agaró, the fashionable beach, and he signed up all the Murcians from the Calle de la Barca as laborers. They packed up and left with their wives and children, while the rest of the laid-off workers continued getting up late and washing in the kitchen after giving their wives a shove. And before they knew it, it was Holy Week in Gerona again! Silence came once again to the Alvear home, and the images were draped in black. Carmen Elgazu cried out again during the ascent to Calvary: "Forgive us, O Looord!" The olive trees began to rustle again, the stones to take on meaning. Ignacio once again wigwagged twenty times with his torch during the procession, and Pilar again failed to spot him from the balcony. This time it was not Ernesto who went along behind the horse of Major Martínez de Soria gathering up the droppings, for Ernesto was in the insane asylum. Haro's father, the city policeman, took the job to earn the extra pay.

Holy Saturday came and went, with the bells tolling all day; nobody threw any bombs into the episcopal palace. Spring came, and the painters returned to the San Daniel Valley, drinking water from the wonder-working fountain, and Jaime, from the Telegraph office, once more twisted his hands together during the *Juegos Florales*, awaiting in vain the announcement of his name as a prizewinner for his latest poem, *Woman*. And while Raimundo held forth in the barbershop, proposing as the only remedy for the evils that plagued Spain the establishment of a choral society and theater group in every village, Don Pedro Oriol assured one and all that there could be no progress until the men in government, whoever they might be, devoted their efforts to carrying out a thoroughgoing reforestation program.

Meanwhile, Doña Amparo Campo said to Julio: "Julio, time passes by and you still haven't taken me to La Molina, so I suppose this summer you don't plan to take me anywhere either...."

It was for Cosme Vila, however, that the tempo of life was at its giddiest, though with his squared shoulders and slow walk he managed to keep his footing.

The opening of the new headquarters had been his moment of emancipation. He quit the bank. His wife set about weaving baskets at home. Her parents, at the rail crossing, prepared her work for her between trains. With the money that came in from the baskets and a remittance that Barcelona promised, the leader had at his disposal an office, and the city its first Communist Party headquarters.

By Corpus Christi, Cosme Vila was already able to watch the procession from the balcony of the headquarters. On seeing the immense carpets of flowers covering the plaza, he thought to himself that spring was beautiful, and as his offering to spring he decided to name the local committee.

He did not have much regard for Victor, whom he considered so much dead weight; but he was a one-time glory and had to be respected. As treasurer, he could be put in charge of the photo morgue and the illustrations for the little weekly—some day to become a daily—they planned to publish.

Gorki would be his right-hand man, as Octavio was for Mateo. Gorki was from Aragón, short and stocky, with eyes like a lynx and a small round belly; he had a store of information. He was strangely fanatical. Nobody could understand why he manufactured perfumes. "Going about the province with a sample case, one learns a lot of things," he would say. He would be the managing editor of the weekly, which they decided to call *El Proletario*.

The fourth member of the committee was Murillo. He was a unanimous choice. Cosme Vila was well aware that a man without scruples would come in handy some day. Naturally, they would have to keep an eye on him. But if he ever washed that raincoat, he'd lose half his value.

The fifth member, and perhaps the most fanatical, was Teo. Teo Arias, the giant drayman, the best in the city. He worked for himself, and owned a dray with an immense platform, from the center of which, straddle-legged and reins in hand, he drove two superb chestnut horses, also his property, with their manes flying. He made twenty trips a day to the station. Every time he passed at a trot in front of Gorki's laboratory, every beaker and bottle on the shelves began to dance. When he passed the Communist Party headquarters, the panes in the windows rattled. "There goes Teo," Victor would say, lifting his head.

Teo's importance rested on his own attributes—and the fact that he suddenly announced that the taxi driver killed at police headquarters on October 6 had been his brother. None but his most intimate friends had known this. The day of the funeral, standing in front of the grave, Teo had sworn that he would avenge his brother, Jaime Arias. He felt that now that he was a member of the committee of the Communist Party, the opportunity had arrived.

Cosme Vila was confident that these four collaborators were all he needed for the time being. Another general assembly would have to be called, and the introductory course in Marxism would continue. But the most important thing, before anything else, was to assign to each member of the committee his exact function, and with regard to the work to be carried out, to dot the "i's" and cross the "t's."

Seated at the desk in his office at headquarters, Cosme Vila thought about the bank and his typewriter. As the hours ticked by he would say to himself: "Now the manager is coughing, lighting his pipe, and asking for the endorsement. Now the assistant manager is pulling out his box of snuff and unfolding *El Debate*. Now Padrosa is eating a ham sandwich. Now Ignacio is rolling a cigarette, with a sly smile."

How wonderful to be able to devote the whole day to one's ideal! Cosme Vila recalled the letter, addressed to a brother of his, which his father left on the dining room table before hanging himself: "I can't bear to see my wife and children go hungry. Help them as much as you can, and may God reward you."

How bitter that was, how distant, and yet how near!

Seated beneath the hammer and the sickle, the pictures of Marx, Lenin, and Stalin, the map of the province of Gerona glued to the wall, Cosme Vila, in shirtsleeves and wearing a wide leather belt given him by his father-in-law, met with the committee, prepared to get down to brass tacks. The two adjoining rooms were bustling with the members washing windows, sweeping the floors, putting bulbs in the light sockets, and moving everything from the barbershop but the mirrors and cuspidors.

His first task was to curb the enthusiasm that gripped the members of the committee and their desire to set about doing things with an eye to immediate results. He pulled a penknife out of his pocket, and as he pared his nails he told them that if anything would imperil the progress of the party and the revolution, it was speed and sentimentality. He quoted from the texts, particularly Lenin: "First decide, then vote.... The directors of a revolution should be professionals."

"So let's be practical. There are five of us on the committee, as against three hundred members and a whole mass of sympathizers. Whenever it is possible we will do what we can to satisfy these members and improve their lot; but if circumstances require that they be used for determined ends, we will do that too.... In Russia in 1920, millions of Russians were sacrificed....

"You already know the ultimate goal: the total destruction of the bourgeois setup in the city and the province. The means we will use are those which best fit each case, so nobody is to get upset if we shout *viva* for something one day and *muera* the next. We believe that what counts is the future. Why are you looking like that? It is strange that it should be so difficult to convince people that what died is dead, and that tears are only water. You, Gorki, did you see any tears in Zaragoza that were anything but water? I didn't here.

"Here's something else for you to think about. Stick to politics rather than economics when you talk to the people: it is a lot more effective to put an idea in someone's mind than a dollar in his pocket. We need a couple of factory workers on the committee without a doubt, because they have the class instinct; but they must be tied short. If they aren't, they will soon be asking for the same things as the bourgeoisie. A good revolutionist turns hunger to better account than prosperity.

"So, then, the most important thing is to create a climate of revolution. Keep in mind that everything must be repeated endlessly. That's the advantage of a simple program—the nine points I outlined in the barbershop—and posters and the press. The walls must be covered with posters that always say the same thing, and the same things must appear in the newspaper every day. Therefore the weekly *El Proletario* will be made up of three sections, always the same: one for the peasants—written in simple language, for they are suspicious; another for the industrial workers—lots of statistics: and a third for the fishermen—written in poetic language, for they are superstitious. I'll handle the simple language and the poetry; Gorki can do the statistics.

"Within the party the basic thing is the organization. There must be a hookup with every factory and every workshop, and an agrarian cell in every village. We won't really start rolling until the map of the province is covered with little flags. And keep this firmly in mind: we on the committee are responsible for the whole operation. We will begin by meeting every night without fail. Then goodbye to all luxuries. Chairs and tables are all the furnishings our homes require. No more movies, no more dances, and no more wasting time chewing the fat with the boys. And, above all, forget about dressing up like the Mayor or the Costas. Either go bareheaded like me or stick to a railroadman's cap. I don't want to see any felt hats, any handkerchiefs sticking out of breast pockets, or neckties. And no cologne, no matter how hard it will be on Gorki's business. We have to watch the details, even those that seem trifling. We must keep in constant contact with Barcelona and visit Vasiliev periodically. Iron discipline and no explanations. Every now and then we will have to make an example of somebody. It goes without saying that we must study every minute. Anybody here who is not willing to die for the cause, to go to jail or to sacrifice his family if necessary, had better go and join Izquierda Republicana."

The committee gave its approval to the line of conduct laid down by Cosme Vila. Gorki told himself there was a great day coming. Cosme Vila reached into a drawer of his desk and pulled out a sandwich, which he began to eat.

Cosme Vila felt equal hatred for the landowners, the military, and the clergy. He felt the same way about the dissident elements within the party, particularly Pedro, a kid who lived on the Calle de la Barca with his father, who spent all day in the kitchen with a bee in his bonnet. Perhaps Cosme Vila's favorite target was the clergy, not out of any conviction, but by temperament. He belonged to the organization called "the Godless Militants," which had just been founded in Barcelona, formerly known as "the Godless." It was his contention that antireligious activities should go even farther in Spain than in Russia.

Nevertheless, he was intelligent and he did not harbor too many illusions. He had a very precise understanding of those who surrounded him. He knew very well that his in-laws would admire him, no matter what he did; but that, on the other hand, the members would give him the heave-ho unless he constantly demonstrated his authority. He also realized that Gorki, a man of integrity, would not forgive him one slip nor tolerate the least deviation; and he knew that when Murillo slowly stroked his mustache, it was a sign that he was chewing the cud of some grievance.

But none of this was important. He would give them proof of his indomitable will. For the time being, he did not leave his desk even to step out on the balcony, not even when Teo rumbled past on his wagon, making sparks fly from the paving stones.

This was the great virtue of the leader, as the party was aware. He was immutable. The members admired his firmness. They realized in the barbershop that they were now playing for keeps. Cosme Vila always said that the prime defect of the bourgeoisie was frivolity, which would be its undoing.

After analyzing every one of the decisions taken by his adversaries, Cosme Vila came to the conclusion that they were all frivolous. The notary Noguer was frivolous when he thought that a city could be cleansed by an efficient garbage-collection system; Casal was frivolous when he thought that a plug of cotton in one's ear kept one from hearing; the Costas were frivolous when they became ecstatic because no sooner had they reopened their headquarters than there were more members than before the events of October 6, and when they solemnly named the martyr Joaquin Santaló Perpetual President of the party and Most Exemplary Republican.

THIS was the life of the city. If Mateo dreamed of Marta heading the feminine wing of Falange in the city; if Izquierda Republicana made propaganda with the bones of Joaquín Santaló, and the Communist Party was ready to sacrifice its members; if the Socialist Party and its syndicate won back lost ground with remarkable impetus; if Future had turned the head of El Responsable's older daughter to the point where she proposed that they put into practice the theories of Bakunin and run off together to France or wherever it might be; if Mateo worked day and night to consolidate the initial enthusiasm of the recruits, and orthodox old Don Jorge proved a bulwark at Liga Catalana against those who wanted to turn it into a cooperative bank, all these things formed part of the ebb and flow of the city—and of its history, like the river or the handsome head of the Commissioner. To be sure, it filled the present—the daily life, the streets—with inescapable harshness. The diversity of the groups affected the entire existence of the city, from its institutions to its commercial life. The fact that every man had his political headquarters—and each headquarters its own janitor—meant that every woman had her chosen bakery or fishmonger. To live each day in accordance with one's ideas: this was the iron rule. Nothing in this world would have persuaded a member of the UGT to put one peseta over the counter of a Radical. Moreover, every citizen read a single newspaper, which chiseled his mind into given form as though it was stone. Each newspaper's advertising space was bought by certain individuals, and the readers knew that those who advertised in other papers were their enemies. This practice gave rise to a remark by Matías Alvear in the Neutral one day which was repeated for months and particularly delighted Julio García: "If things go on as they are, we will be able to tell from the trademark in a man's socks where he stands on the mystery of the Incarnation."

Matías Alvear talked like this half in fun and half in sadness. It depressed him that there was such a lack of tolerance and that the newspapers did not advertise all brands of socks. At the same time, he found cause for happiness in that freedom to organize and express one's opinions which was proof that things were back to normal and that the specter of a military dictatorship, which had been feared at one time, had disappeared. Matías Alvear, almost without being aware of it, was little by little regaining his confidence in the Republic. He would repeat for Don Emilio Santos, who was less optimistic, the lines from the song: "With a little gray matter and some honest republicans, everything will go rolling along." Sometimes he was even willing to accept the idea of one man at the top, a leader. Not Gil Robles, "a hypocrite," not Azaña, "full of resentments," but somebody new, sensible, with honest intentions. Matías Alvear believed that such a leader would come forward some day, that there was no reason to despair. "Meanwhile, why get all stirred up about it?" he would say.

What was happening was that Matías Alvear, a realist, was happy because the Catalanist business at the Telegraph office had become a dead issue and, above all, because among the things that had gone back to normal was his family: Santiago, tranquil in Madrid, with José working in a used-car business, and his brother in Burgos out of jail for some time now, with his daughter about to get married. Both of them—as well as the boy—were back in UGT. Considering what had happened, the balance was favorable. Including his wife's relatives, there were thirty members of the family, and, all told, the total loss came to four fingers, those lost by the brother-in-law from Trubia, who nevertheless was back as factory foreman. Everyone accounted for in Bilbao and in San Sebastián. Carmen Elgazu also gave thanks for that. Her prayers now were that Ignacio would continue as he was, studying and not getting mixed up in the secret strife of the city; that César should come home soon—she missed him so much!—and that the interest Pilar felt for Mateo should lead to a happy ending.

FIFTY-TWO

JUNE. A great torpor had come over the city. Movements grew languid, bodies loathed changing posture. One glance at the sun drove home the conviction that it would soon be pouring down rays of fire. At certain hours the streets seemed those of a deserted city. Everybody was saying: "I don't know what's the matter with me; I could sleep all day."

Ignacio and Mateo passed their first-year law examinations at the University of Barcelona. Ignacio telephoned Ana María. At the sound of his voice she felt as though her heart would jump out of her breast. They went for a boat ride around the harbor. Ignacio made another speech....

Mateo's and Ignacio's families were waiting for them at the station. Professor Civil was there, too. Hugs, kisses, presents all around. The first year past! A chant went up at the Arús Bank: "Ignacio Alvear, office hours from three to seven."

Pedro, the dissident and solitary Communist, wanted to buy a radio on the installment plan to get the party line straight from Moscow. His father, the old man in the kitchen, said to him: "Go and see what you can do." Pedro inquired about the terms and was told: "We can arrange it, but you'll have to sign these notes." Pedro refused. His father had warned him, even as a child: "Don't sign a paper, Pedro. I signed one once, and that's why I'm here in this kitchen all these years."

The series of major festivals started. The orchestras were swamped with contracts. Thanks to this, the former anarchist El Rubio, "the Goat," was finally hired as saxophone player by the most important orchestra in the city, Pizarro Jazz. And Mateo had given him a job in the warehouse of the *Tabacalera*. When Mateo said to him: "But don't you musicians feel the crisis?" El Rubio answered: "Don't be foolish! The worse things get, the more people dance." El Rubio was turning out to be a useful person.

Another useful person was Mosén Francisco. The priest of San Félix got a contract, too. He was invited to take his student choral group to Perpignan to sing *sardanas* and folk music. Mosén Francisco wanted his boys to learn a song in French to sing in Perpignan, but his efforts were fruitless. He had selected *Frére Jacques*, but the chorus made a mess of the pronunciation. "We're not going to Perpignan until you can sing *Frére Jacques*!" The boys made all sorts of excuses. "Mosén, it's so hard to enter on the right beat." Finally they managed to enter the round at the right moment, and Mosén Francisco took them to Perpignan, greeting the sleepy station masters en route with his immense hat.

ALARM in the Alvear home. César arrived unexpectedly. He came from Collell carrying a letter from his Latin teacher which read: "Make him sleep. He has spent whole nights here praying without feeling fatigue."

Matías took him by the chin and asked him: "Is this true?"

César nodded his head. "But I feel just fine."

Matías Alvear did not know what to say. It was a fact that the boy looked well. Carmen Elgazu untied her apron and, quickly pinning her hair in place, went to see Mosén Alberto. César had spent whole nights in prayer without feeling tired. "What is your opinion of that?" Mosén Alberto, to whom the director of Collell had already written in this connection, was of the simple opinion that César was a saint and that this was evidence of grace. Carmen Elgazu raised her hands to her cheeks and cried: "Jesus!" Her joy was so great that her eyes filled with tears that perhaps were water, perhaps not. "A saint! A miracle! My son performs miracles!"

Mosén Alberto endeavored to calm her. "These are supernatural cases, without doubt. The absence of sleep is one of the typical manifestations of the state of contemplation, especially of ecstasy. Just like the lack of a need for food. St. Catherine of Siena—incidentally, that is a magnificent image of her that you have—slept for half an hour every three days, and St. Lydwina slept three hours in thirty years. Nevertheless, you must be calm. Forget about the miracles. And, above all, don't say anything about it to César. Make him go to bed."

All of a sudden the sun unleashed its offensive. No sooner had it appeared behind the crest of Montjuich than a sultry heat gripped the city. The big electric fans of Izquierda Republicana were turned on; the little ones of the Arús Bank took a perverse delight in blowing the papers about; but there were people for whom there was no escape. The city policemen, the father of Haro on Piedra Bridge, the street venders, the bricklayers, the farm workers. The sun's rays fell on them like hammer blows. It was like a kind of drunkenness. First the body was soaked, and soon after the skin began to boil. And then the brain.

Especially the brains of the unemployed. There was the rub. The theorizers on the subject of hunger had said to them: "Don't worry; living is no problem in the summer." The unemployed found that it was worse then. The heat, the sweat, the interminable hours. Suddenly they would leap up from the curb where they were sitting, caps pulled down over their eyes, sick of the sun and themselves. They sought a little shade, something cool for their parched lips, a little conversation. Even their tobacco had a bitter taste. The carts rolled by: "Ice cream, delicious ice creeeam!"

Besides, the weeks of want had been piling up since October. Their reserves had been exhausted long since, and the help of friends. The women could no longer find washing to do in the river, and the river itself was nearly dry. "So-and-so will get you work; they say So-and-so is going to be hiring men." Lies. The So-and-sos were packing their suitcases and going on vacation.

Noguer the notary, from his Mayor's desk, carried out his promise to the best of his ability. He managed to get the City Council to approve unanimously the construction of a covered market over the Oñar. It was a bold undertaking. A first allotment of eighty thousand pesetas was voted for it. The women were delighted. A covered marketplace! But the number of workers hired was less than forty. Forty workers in rubber boots began to lay the foundations, while the neighboring bridges filled up with sidewalk superintendents.

That was the best Noguer could do. That and the fifty Murcians who had left several weeks before for S'Agaró, under the orders of Professor Civil's older son, the architect. There was nothing for the others. Two hundred and fifty men without hope until at least September.

And as if this was not enough, disturbing news began to come in from the Murcians. It seemed that they had established themselves and their families on the beach of S'Agaró in shacks they had thrown up, whereupon the summer visitors had driven them out, on the grounds that they were turning it into a pigsty.

El Demócrata published the news. "They have had to set themselves up alongside the road in some ramshackle sheds. And they have ordered them out of those, too, because they want to use them as a gas station."

The CNT came out in defense of the Murcians, because it was the syndicate to which they belonged. "Working in the killing sun, and they haven't the right to live near the water!" The two hundred and fifty jobless supported the cause of their comrades.

But they accomplished nothing. The rights of the tourists won the day.

The jobless were outraged. They threw themselves on their beds at night naked because of the heat, and this added to the sense of abandonment they felt.

The exodus of vacationists to the beaches began. Cars sped by with canoes fastened on top, or with top down, carrying men dressed in white, beautiful women bareheaded or wearing scarves over their hair. *El Tradicionalista* ran advertisements of reasonably priced bathing suits and maps outlining "itineraries of breathless beauty."

Some among the unemployed looked upon all this as the natural order of things. It was life, rolling along like the tires over the road. Others felt it to be an insult, a bad joke the world was playing on them.

Among the latter was Salvio—though he himself was working—who had founded the Trotskyite cell. But nobody paid any attention to him. The Communist Party, the UGT, and Salvio were powerless to find a solution. The only ones who seemed to understand the Murcians and the unemployed were El Responsable and Future.

Future was everywhere, and he was the only pleasant human contact the jobless had. "Nothing in my right hand, nothing in my left hand," and he suddenly pulled a peseta out of the nose of those beings who had not a penny.

Future directed the offensive, a nocturnal campaign against the whiteness of the walls, the house-fronts. Heading a group of men filled to overflowing with anger—for among those leaving for Mallorca and Puigcerdá were Warning Voice, Don Santiago Estrada, Don Jorge, and the Costa brothers with their wives—they spent their time filling the city with signs. "Down with this one. Down with that one." Streets and squares bristled with threats. On the door of the assistant manager they wrote: "Long live the FAI," with a skull underneath.

Noguer the notary had no choice but to appoint a brigade of night watchmen. César's miracle—going without sleep—was repeated among the unemployed, though in their case Mosén Alberto was unable to come up with an explanation. Now they could not even sleep, so not only were the days interminable, but the nights too. And as the vigilance squad made it impossible for them to spend the night under the stars, the men gathered in any tavern that was open, drinking and playing cards till six in the morning, while Future, at the other end of the city, heading a squad of his own, broke shop windows or made the metal shutters rattle with deafening noise.

Noguer the notary suffered. And he called on the Civil Guard for help. At this the unemployed wrote more than ever on the walls. But Future said to them: "Comrades, they'll catch us here, and besides this isn't getting us anywhere. I've got another plan."

"What is it?"

Future ran his hand over the glossy waves of his hair. "Tomorrow," he said, "everybody's to be at the Dehesa at twelve o'clock sharp. In front of the swimming pool."

The sun rose earlier that day and sank more deeply into people's brains.

Everyone was at the swimming pool at the appointed hour. The young anarchist was waiting for them, accompanied by El Responsable's older daughter.

When they were all gathered around, Future picked up a rock and laid it in the middle of the huge open esplanade unsheltered by the trees, known as the Field of Mars. He placed a match on the stone, and beside it a piece of glass. The sun's rays fell so plumb that in a few moments the match quivered and burst into flame. "This—in the woods," said Future.

Everyone understood. The woods, the woods! Sow the woods with matches and pieces of glass. This was the great sleight-of-hand trick Future had devised for the province. While Cosme Vila's companion was giving birth to a son, the youngest Communist in Spain and the world; while Casal at UGT headquarters, comparing his committee with that of Cosme Vila, and realizing its frightening inferiority, sought and obtained the collaboration of David and Olga—Olga, treasurer, David in charge of propaganda; while Major Martínez de Soria crossed foils in the infantry armory with Colonel Muñoz, the number-two fencer of the garrison, a group of men was making its way to the nearby and the distant hills carrying matches and pieces of glass.

It was the grandiose moment. It was vengeance, swift of effect. Fires began to spring up, first near the city, than farther, ever farther away. Nature is an arbitrary thing. Some of the fires began haltingly, some were stillborn. A few impotent flickers shrank in fear from the scabs on El Cojo's lips and disappeared. Others tried to advance, but the earth refused to transmit their red words. Others achieved strength enough to turn a family of pines, some scattered olive trees, to ashes, but nothing more. Only the snakes fled with violent contortions. And Don Jorge's tenants returned to their houses with shovels and other implements, ready to fight the fire.

But at other spots, especially in the direction of the Hermitage of the Angels, Rocacorba, and Arbucias, the fires took spectacular hold. The flames, aided by invisible elements, clasped hands. This was the miracle conceived by Future. The villages and farms along the hillsides saw a fantastic glow light up the summits. The sight was repeated simultaneously here and there, real tricks of legerdemain. By the light of this glow, pines and cork oaks sank mortally wounded. The whole province became alert. The fires of the Hermitage of the Angels were visible from Gerona, from the rooftops, from David's and Olga's school. The mountains and the forest were ablaze, and Future, El Cojo, Ideal, and others returned, some indifferent, some excited, others a little frightened at what they were doing.

The first impression was one of utter stupefaction. Professor Civil went up to the roof to view the scene. Colonel Muñoz stood at the armory windows. Julio García went outside the city walls. Some of the canons climbed up to the

Cathedral bell tower. The whole city sought the high places. Ignacio went to the Postal Building and climbed to the cupola with his father; there they gazed in silence upon the horizon in flames, their suffering twofold: for the men who had set the fires, and for the destruction they spelled.

Don Pedro Oriol's car raced about the province. His woodlands seemed to have been the special target. His wife said to him: "The important thing is for everybody to be saved."

Everybody was saved, but not many cabins in the hills, nor many snakes, nor equipment, nor whole families of pines, oaks, and cork trees. The earth lay blackened, smoking. From the ravines came the laughter, the crackling of living tongues. Don Pedro Oriol wept, Professor Civil recalled Nero, Paco made sketches, Noguer the notary issued warnings to careless smokers.

Mateo and Octavio, Benito Civil and Rosselló, Roca and Haro felt that the moment had come. On their return from firefighting, for which the troops had been called out, but in which many volunteers took part, they laid their hands one upon another on Mateo's desk before the photograph of José Antonio.

The next day letters of enormous size—like Teo standing in his wagon—in black paint, one on each tree, appeared on the trunks of the trees in the Dehesa. Read together they spelled out: VIVA FALANGE ESPAÑOLA. All Gerona turned its gaze upon those ancient sycamores, which, in a sense, seemed charred, too. That VIVA—and similar ones in other places—standing out in black, produced a new and disturbing impression, particularly as it alternated with the MUERAS written on neighboring trees and walls by the unemployed. The Falangists, too, worked under cover of darkness, for the night patrols had been transferred to the mountains. They, too, went about the streets with their faith, with similar cans of paint, similar crayons. For the time being there were no meetings beneath the stars. Nevertheless, many people felt that the physical presence of Falange in Gerona was an even greater calamity than the fires. "So that boy at the *Tabacalera* was in earnest," they said. The newsboys selling *El Demócrata* and *El Proletario* were on the lookout at street corners, expecting any minute to receive a brickbat in the head.

Then the pamphlets began to appear. Saturday, market day, the six Falangists chose strategic spots and handed out the first Falange pamphlets, with the arrows at the top. Some read: "What has happened is not the work of careless smokers, as the Mayor believes. The forests are burning because the people are suffering, are full of hatred, and hatred ignites matches with its mere glance." Others explained that the people who were suffering were the unemployed or others who had work but who thirsted for justice and a Country. Others stated that the forests of Spain were dying—and with them the birds—because for many years the governments had not fired the soul of the Spaniards with a living, dominant ideal. At the Rightist headquarters flyers were being handed out, saying: "Every Spaniard should be half monk, half soldier."

The pamphlets caused amazement. The workers said: "They're following the priests' line: they say they love us so much."

Cosme Vila spread a copy of each pamphlet out on his desk and remarked: "These fellows are nobody's fools."

Benito Civil's post was at the exit of the railroad station, so his audience was made up almost entirely of people from the country, peasants wearing caps and cummerbunds, who asked, as they looked at the arrows: "What's this?" and who, when they read about igniting matches with a mere glance, thought it an advertisement for a new brand of matches. An occasional young boy whispered: "They're Fascists." And those words made Benito Civil the object of looks whose meaning he failed to fathom. Mateo took charge of the slums and workingmen's quarter; Octavio visited the offices and banks; Dr. Rosselló's son, Roca, and Conrado Haro were assigned to the center of the city, especially the Rambla.

It was an eventful month. The damage caused by the fires was incalculable, and many people refused to believe it was the work of sabotage. "No one could do such a thing." Mosén Francisco and the boys in his catechism class saw one of the fires from France, on their way back from singing *Frére Jacques* in Perpignan. "Our country is ablaze," was the young priest's thought. The boys had never seen such a magic mountain. Mosén Alberto, for his part, firmly believed that the Falangists had had a hand in the matter. "You'll have to keep an eye on them," he warned notary Noguer.

Yet the automobiles went rolling along. Life followed its pattern, vacations began with mathematical punctuality, and every day the traffic toward the resort centers increased. The fires in the mountains had made more people select the beaches. As a result, the fashionable spots along the coast, from Blanes to the frontier, including San Felíu and S'Agaró, were jammed. The members of the Murcian colony were pushed farther and farther back. They were in the way everywhere. They resented these shifts because "it was wonderful beside the sea," and, to make matters worse, they had to go a long way for their drinking water. Only the sight of the statuesque bathing beauties reconciled the nomadic heads of households to the summer visitors who were driving them out. But this calm was only momentary. Suddenly a great rage would come over them as they sat smoking and watching the sailboats and the blue balls.

The invasion of the coast had led certain property holders to post their lands, to put up walls and wire fences to make themselves private beaches. It was said that some of the places belonged to North American movie stars who had discovered that corner of heaven in Spain. Madeleine Carroll's name was mentioned. Others belonged to eccentric painters, who, with foreign visitors, formed a nudist colony.

The fences aroused a storm of indignation. "They're taking even the landscape for themselves. Apparently they own the sea, too." Everyone tore down the fences or climbed over them and dumped all kinds of filth into the walled-off places. Future, tired of bathing in fresh water, took a little trip there, and small fires soon broke out in the pines. He respected the property of the supposed North American artists, for Blasco had sternly warned him: "Be careful! We could start an international incident."

If popular opinion was bewildered by the fires, the political leaders of the Right and Left were not. They knew what the score was. And they assumed that punishment for El Responsable and Future would be harsh. Warning Voice came back from Puigcerdá breathing fire and brimstone and, accompanied by Don Pedro Oriol, went to police headquarters with witnesses who had seen the anarchists in the mountains.

But the matter proved difficult. Not only were the necessary proofs lacking, but the fires had burned themselves out. Moreover, the Commissioner flatly refused to admit that the two anarchist leaders had had anything to do with the setting of the fires. "How can you think that? El Responsable spends his day at the gymnasium, and Future at the swimming pool. Dozens of people have seen them there morning and afternoon."

So El Responsable and Future were not at all worried. They could count on the personal friendship of the Commissioner, Don Julián Cervera. The Commissioner had liked them both from the start. He said to El Responsable: "I like people who stick to their beliefs." He asked Future, laughing: "Is it true, Future, that in Barcelona you once lifted up an astronomer on your left arm and a second-hand bookseller on your right?"

It was a profitable friendship. The Commissioner not only turned down the complaints of the landowners who had suffered losses, of the Institute of San Isidro, and of left-wing and rightwing party affiliates, but even argued so hotly with the Costa brothers, who had come by taxi from the town where their wives had been born, that the two industrialists finally shrugged their shoulders. "In the last analysis," they said to the Commissioner, "it's you people who represent the government who've got the most to lose."

Casal's reaction was more violent. He could not accept the idea that an attempt of this nature against the forest wealth of the region should go unpunished. He was enraged; however, he was not going to take reprisals against El

Responsable and Future on his own. "If the powers that be think this is going to help anybody..."

No, apparently that was not the explanation. The powers that be did not think that was going to help anybody, for the incident, which had given rise to different reactions, revealed even more clearly the differences that divided the parties of the Left, and this seemed to them a bad omen, for the summer was passing and elections probably would be called for the end of the year. And wasn't their chief concern to come to these elections united, all forming a common front, from FAI to Izquierda Republicana?

It was at this time that Dr. Relken made his appearance in the city. Julio received him in his home with full honors and introduced him to his friends. Doña Amparo was flushed with pride. "At last, guests of distinction."

When the doctor learned of the havoc the province had suffered, he remarked as he polished his thick glasses: "Alas, there's no way to make you Spaniards reach an agreement. May I have a glass of water, Doña Amparo?"

FIFTY-THREE

WITH César at her side Carmen Elgazu was the happiest woman in the world. His nine months of absence had seemed so long to her that she realized once more that to give a son to God was to lose him from the human standpoint. Home three months a year; and when his studies were finished, God knew where he would be sent.

She feasted her eyes on him, and it seemed impossible to her that he should have grown still more and know so many things. She had always believed that César knew much more than Ignacio. In her scale of values the whole body of the law was worth less than a new detail of the liturgy or a scrap of theology.

César once more took possession of his bed, his chair in the dining room, the window looking out on the river, the balcony. He took possession of his dog-eared Bible, observed that the statue of St. Ignatius was taking on a proper patina. Pilar's eyes, and the happiness his sister revealed in every gesture, made him realize that her love affair with Mateo was much farther along than he had gathered from letters. As he listened to Ignacio at the table, calm and master of himself, discussing dispassionately what had happened, he saw that his brother had made great strides since he last saw him in October, when Ignacio had been all wrought up about the revolution. He did not know that Ignacio had been sick. He attributed the change to prayer, and perhaps to the influence of Professor Civil, of whom he had heard the highest praise.

The thing that impressed him most in the home were the images of St. Francis of Assisi and St. Clara, which Murillo had sent in accordance with his promise.

Carmen Elgazu had put them in Pilar's room, which the seminarian rarely entered. They had told César nothing about them, so they were a joyful surprise for the boy. He gazed rapt at them where they stood, each on a little pedestal, beside his sister's dainty bed. "This is the best thing that has come from the Bernat workrooms," he remarked. Then he said that he would have to go and thank Murillo. Matías Alvear scratched his nose, but said nothing to discourage him for the time being.

The thing that most impressed César in the city was, on the one hand, the fires, and, on the other, the emergence of Falange—and, consequently, of Mateo—on the scene.

His reaction to both these happenings was astonishment. With regard to Falange, his immediate feeling was one of uneasiness, perhaps because Mosén Alberto had said to him, pointing to the mountains: "If your mother knew the kind of person Pilar has got mixed up with, she would not let her go out with him." But that was not all. From the first moment, the word "Falange" was identified in César's mind with the word "Fascism," and this awakened a special fear in him. A fear that increased when his Latin teacher in Collell told him of the persecution the Catholics suffered in Germany, adding that Mussolini, at the start of his career, during his Syndicalist days, had published a pamphlet entitled: *God Does Not Exist*, as well as horrible blasphemies against Jesus.

Nevertheless, he refrained from condemnation. In the first place, one of the boarding pupils at Collell, who had a picture of José Antonio hidden in his night table, always said that José Antonio was, above everything else, a Catholic; and as for Mateo, he seemed to be not only a Catholic, but a devout one, not to mention his knowledge of the Bible, which according to Ignacio was amazing.

Moreover, Mosén Francisco, whom he had visited shortly after his arrival, had said to César: "Mateo dangerous? Pshaw! You know Mosén Alberto and I rarely see eye to eye."

César could not understand what had happened in the mountains. He could not grasp the idea that anyone could set mountains on fire. At Collell he reveled in the sight of them, and would never forget how they looked at Christmas, all covered with snow. As for the trees—there were times when he even thought they had souls. During the nights he had spent in prayer, every now and then he had gone to the window, and if the moon was shining, or a light in the patio was burning, had watched the poplar leaves trembling as though greeting him, or at times as though weeping slow tears. No one was capable of setting fire to them deliberately! Not to mention the cypresses, which seemed to him the trees that had the most reason to believe in God.

Yet there were the facts: the embers on the mountainside. And there were the VIVAS of Falange in the Dehesa. And the pamphlets. Could the fires be the work of Falange? He did not know what to think.

It was more of an effort than before for César to integrate himself with the lives of other people. He felt himself absent. Nevertheless, he observed Mateo carefully, and every time he talked with him he had a good impression. He could not raise any serious objection to the things Mateo said. Just one phrase in the flyers displeased him, where it said: "The people who suffer, hate." César admitted that, unfortunately, this was true in many instances, but said that, put that way, it might give the impression that such hatred was legitimate.

Mateo answered him: "My dear César, don't lose sight of one thing. We are not addressing ourselves to persons like you, who wear a penitent's belt, but to workers who are rejected, pushed back everywhere they go by the resort visitors, and who, as your brother says—your brother talks very well—'see how their wives age, that the water they need is a long way off, and that they have no place to hang their caps.'"

César nodded thoughtfully. It was all so complicated.

From the practical point of view, his plans were less concrete than the preceding summer. Calle de la Barca? The other workshop? All that seemed so far off, he could not say why. Should he make up during the day the hours of sleep he lost at night? He was living on the other shore. Coming from Collell, he was bewildered a little by Gerona, as when one arrives in a big city. But it even seemed to him that he lived on the opposite shore from his own parents! Even Carmen Elgazu. He even reached the conclusion that the burning of the trees pained him more than the fact that Murillo—he finally heard of it—was a member of the committee of the Communist Party. César suffered deeply, and he realized, at the same time, that Ignacio was aware of it. He did not know what to do. When he took communion he prayed for serenity. In the street he stopped when he heard the bells. He would have liked to go into Pilar's room often to implore St. Francis of Assisi to guide him with the light that shone from his stigmata; but if Pilar was not there, he lacked the courage; and if she was there, he did not want to distract her from the lyrical entries in her diary.

FIFTY-FOUR

IGNACIO and Mateo had arranged with Professor Civil not to resume classes until the first of October. So as not to lose touch completely with their work, however, they would meet with him one day a week for an hour. Matías had suggested this plan because, among other things, the saving of three months' tuition would be a real blessing. Mateo had steady work now; Ignacio spent his spare time strolling around the Dehesa, swimming in the Ter, or going to the UGT to audit the classes in economics which Casal went on giving to the members.

David and Olga were overjoyed to see him there, and it was like reliving the days when they had been so closely linked to him. They loved him sincerely. There were times when they said that Ignacio's affection was the only thing they really considered necessary. "You wander off to other pastures," David reproached him with a smile. "And there they talk to you about very pretty things, such as St. Paul and historic missions. St. Paul—that's not my province. He was a tent maker, and I have always had great respect for tent makers. But when it comes to historic missions—there's the case of Italy. Mussolini is already talking about a historic mission in Abyssinia."

To hammer the point home Olga added: "When Mussolini or one of the others shouts 'Long live our historic mission!' you ask yourself how many coffins are going to be needed."

Only the religious problem kept Ignacio from believing wholeheartedly that Socialism was the solution for Spain's problems, for to his discovery that the circumstances of isolation, climate, physiological make-up, and so on, had a direct influence on the individual, he now added, with even more conviction than when he had argued with Mateo under the arcade of the Rambla, the economic factor. The fires, the colony of Murcians in S'Agaró, the hundreds of workers milling about UGT headquarters with their immediate problem of existence, made those ideas of sea routes and all the rest of that nonsense seem chimerical. Casal in his classes proved clearly that in the historical process whole races had succumbed because of lack of the means of production. "To be sure, one can be poor and sing flamenco," said Casal, "but the voice soon goes. One can also be rich and have no twinges of conscience: just draw the shades. Spain is a poor country, and, in addition, inept. A factory of photographer's supplies went broke in Madrid because the workers refused to use special gloves, saying that they bothered them. It is tragicomic, therefore, to talk of autarchy. We have a lot to learn. The first thing to drive home to people is a little civic spirit. In France there are mountains of butter in the stores—and in the homes. At closing time the markets give away fruit and potatoes. But the people there obey the laws, and besides they manufacture lots of automobiles. Civic sense and industrialization, that's the answer. In my opinion, the French Revolution had something to do with all this. In a word, the pattern for Spain is clear."

As Ignacio listened to Casal he felt that there was great truth in his words. All that he was saying seemed closer to a sense of reality than any other doctrine. Matías Alvear spoke a similar language, and that offered Ignacio the best of guarantees. He had come to admit that his father was a man of great common sense, and now he constituted him the arbiter of all his problems, big or little. There was nothing dramatic about believing in paternal wisdom; Rosselló paid no attention to his father, Mateo did not even listen to Don Emilio Santos; nevertheless that did not alter Ignacio's judgment. Matías Alvear might be wrong in the remedies he suggested, but his diagnoses were infallible. The telegrams he handled continued to reveal to him the connection between events and taught him to synthesize; and there were his years in Madrid, his married life, and his children to back him up. Without mentioning the fact that he was not a one-newspaper man.

On the other hand, it distressed Ignacio beyond words that his mother, Carmen Elgazu, could not find words harsh enough for the UGT. Because his mother, too, was level-headed and had practical sense. She did not believe that the objective of the UGT was to give away fruit and potatoes. "Wherever David and Olga are," she said, "I don't expect them to give away anything but bad advice."

Ignacio laughed to himself and wondered: "How can I convince my mother?" At the same time, she might be right. The boy took good care not to discount Carmen Elgazu's arguments as childish, even when it came to politics. Ever since he had kissed her neck that day in the dining room after his illness, and then had gone with her to church several times, and even to buy an umbrella one day, he had listened to her attentively, admitting the existence of a knowledge that did not come from books, but was direct and efficacious.

And as though this was not enough, how could one hold out against her strength of character? Ignacio now regarded his mother with admiration. And how she repaid him, a thousand to one! A loving son, God keep him! He would come crawling into the kitchen on his hands and knees and scare her by tickling her legs. At times, when she was sitting sewing, he would stand behind her and let down her hair—its black mixed with white—amazed at its length, for it came almost to the floor—and comb it as he had done when he was a child in Málaga. At other times he organized little plots among the family so that Carmen Elgazu would not have to get up even once at mealtime. Ignacio, Pilar, César, and Matías Alvear himself took charge of bringing in everything and serving. Carmen Elgazu was forbidden to move. She was just to preside at the table and eat—nothing else. The four of them admitted that all together they could not do what she did alone, but their thoughtfulness made her happy. Listening to Casal, Ignacio asked himself uneasily if the industrialization program might not carry with it the disappearance of human beings like his mother. David answered that, on the contrary, there would be many more. "Many women today would like to be Carmen Elgazus and can't, because they have no stove in the kitchen or table to preside over."

At other times Ignacio thought about Marta. In spite of the fact that in Valladolid the Socialists had gone over to Falange, the word "Socialist" seemed to fill her with horror. She did not talk much about it, but it was evident. She said of Casal: "The very sight of him frightens me."

When Ignacio asked her why, Marta answered: "That's the worst of it, I don't know why. But he frightens me."

Ignacio had noticed that this system of passing judgment without following it up with an explanation was habitual with Marta. Perhaps she wanted to give the impression that she was a woman of intuition; perhaps she really was.

Nevertheless, her frequenting of the family circle was making him nervous. Ignacio continued to feel a strong sensation every time he saw the girl, for she emanated a magnetic quality, but it was a disturbing impression such as a star out of its proper place might produce. He was at a loss to explain what bond there could possibly be between Marta and his sister. They were so completely different, and, above all, the vital differences of intelligence and even upbringing between them were so great. Evidently Pilar's high spirits, her unexpected sallies, and the health she radiated made a conquest of everybody. There was Mateo as a living testimony.

Pilar would say to him, for example, nudging Mateo with her elbow: "Ignacio, what would happen if I went to the UGT and while Casal was talking about transportation I took the cotton out of his ear?"

That was the explanation: Pilar's gaiety was contagious. It was a waste of time to try to talk seriously when she was around. A number of people had tried it—César, Julio—but they never got anywhere. Perhaps the only one who at times was successful was Mosén Alberto.

César failed completely. Pilar would tweak his nose, or roll his head back and forth with her hand, saying to him: "Come now, my lad, you are living in this world."

At times she would run her hand over his shoulders and say with an expression of comical astonishment: "What's this I feel here? Don't you realize that you are sprouting wings?"

She teased Julio openly. Ever since she had Mateo's picture on her bedside table, Pilar had been afraid of nobody, not even the policeman. And that annoyed Julio. With nothing to do since he had been dismissed from the force in spite of all Colonel Muñoz's efforts, he visited the Alvears more frequently now, even though he noticed that Ignacio was cool toward him. This did not bother him. With regard to Ignacio he told himself: "He'll come back. He's already gone back to UGT." As for Matías, Julio knew that he could always count on him. So the only member of the family he could not get around was Pilar.

And the truth of the matter was that he had always liked her very much, even as a child. In the policeman's mind Pilar had always stood for the eternal feminine; she was the imperious, the unattainable desire of his maturity. He was attracted to Doña Amparo by vice; Olga might have attracted him by her strength; but those rosy cheeks of Pilar meant more to him than the triangle of the Lodge.

The only person who brought seriousness to the girl and to the house was Mosén Alberto. Perhaps because the priest always discussed matters of deepest import which disturbed Pilar and made her bite her nails—leprosy, for example, or the fires.

If Mateo was not present, Mosén Alberto talked about Falange, "inspired in the pagan doctrines of central Europe," leaving Carmen Elgazu deeply perplexed. There were times when he even talked about death.

Indeed, this had been the priest's favorite theme ever since he had begun the excavations in Rosas, for which Noguer the notary had put up part of the money. Because, apparently, something strange had been discovered there: the Greek city did not emerge, but they had discovered hundreds of skulls. A necropolis. So many skulls, in fact, that not only was the Alvear dining room full of them in abstract, but they threatened to become a reality, for Mosén Alberto was confronted with the problem of where to put them.

It was useless for Pilar to interrupt, saying: "But, Mosén Alberto, couldn't you talk about something more amusing? Why don't you tell about Jonah and the whale?" A waste of time. Mosén Alberto was loaded down with skulls.

He found an ally where he least expected it: Mateo. The subject interested Mateo from the start, and all of a sudden he said to the priest: "Mosén, I'd appreciate it very much if you would bring me one of them."

Good heavens! Matías Alvear raised his eyebrows, and it would have given him great pleasure to break his fishing rod over the head of his future son-in-law. Carmen Elgazu thought what the priest had said about the doctrines of central Europe must be true. But Mosén Alberto, on the contrary, was greatly pleased. At last he was beginning to find a place for the skulls. "You shall have one, Mateo, you shall have one."

Then, suddenly, running his hand over his cheek, he asked him: "But what kind do you want, a man's or a woman's?"

Everyone caught his breath, most of all Mateo. It had never occurred to them to establish such a distinction. They had always supposed that death made all human beings absolutely the same. Finally Mateo asked for a man's skull, and, in a measure, this restored Pilar's peace of mind.

THE matter of skulls to be had for the asking overflowed the limits of the Alvear dining room and entered the public domain, thanks to the information on the excavations in Rosas published periodically in *El Tradicionalista*. And that excellent observer Dr. Relken suffered his first surprise when he learned that nobody was interested in acquiring one. "How horrible!" was the general reaction.

"I don't understand it," the doctor remarked at Julio's house. "I had believed that the Spaniards were not affected by the idea of death." Dr. Rosselló assured him that this was not true, that it was religious propaganda.

Mateo had only two imitators: David and Future. David asked for one specimen—male—to place on a pedestal in the classroom, near the aquarium. Future asked for another—female.

And, as always, the young anarchist used it for his tricks. He took the skull to the gymnasium and put it in the middle of the floor. The anarchists seemed the only people in the city on whom the object made no impression, a fact that would have given Dr. Rosselló food for thought. They gathered around it with a matter-of-fact air, asked it questions, and stuck their fingers in the cavities. Blasco took out his brush and brushed its utter baldness. Everybody asked what that line of holes around the brainpan was. Ideal suggested: "Maybe the dame had an operation." And El Cojo bore him out: "Those are sutures." Then they speculated on whether the woman had been married or single, which gave rise to obscene jokes. From that day the skull became the mascot of the FAI, just as Joaquín Santaló—the whole skeleton of Joaquín Santaló—was the mascot of Izquierda Republicana.

FIFTY-FIVE

THEN the fortnight of love set in. Its first beneficiaries were Laura and Warning Voice. Ever since the day the dentist had asked the sister of the Costas: "What about you, Laura, aren't you going to marry?" she had been all aflutter. He had asked the question in a special tone of voice. And inasmuch as several of her teeth needed attention, she had been at his office a number of times. At the last of these visits his intentions had been so unmistakable that Laura finally said to her brothers: "You know, I think I made a mistake in not accepting the first floor of your new building."

Next Octavio and Rosario. Octavio and the daughter of the boarding house keeper were living a kind of honeymoon. In her presence the Treasury employee forgot his concept of Country and devoted himself to doing away with, in so far as he could, the distance between their bodies. Fortunately the owner of the boarding house kept a watchful eye on them, knife in hand: "Tavy, don't you get my daughter into monkey business—of any kind."

Then Mateo and Pilar. And Cosme Vila and his companion and their baby, who was a darling. And Outstanding Drafts and his sweetheart, who were talking about getting married. And the assistant manager and his files. And Noguer the notary and his covered market, which was making progress. And David and Olga and the UGT.

Gerona, it would seem, was granting itself another truce, similar to the one at Christmas, before mustering its forces for the elections being talked about.

Dr. Relken, too, was one of the beneficiaries. He was becoming fond of Gerona, he said. He was interested in the excavations, and for this reason he visited Mosén Alberto. He was interested in the Cathedral, in the old images. He found the Spaniards very hospitable. In Barcelona he had been the guest of a Socialist deputy who showered attentions on him. In Gerona he hardly knew how to repay the cordiality of so many people: Julio, the Commissioner, Dr. Rosselló, the architects Massana and Ribas. Fortunately for him, the doctor drank only water. He drank water in such quantities that Doña Amparo Campo considered him a saint.

Fortnight of love. At the Neutral, Ramón, thanks to Dr. Relken, traveled on a magic carpet. The doctor, with his blond hair cut *en brosse*, his German collar and thick glasses, told him of incredible adventures. Cairo, Prague—he had been everywhere. Even Vladivostok. Ramón, licking his lips and occasionally raising his eyes to the ceiling, lived the most exciting fortnight of his life.

"And Tangier? Have you ever been in Tangier, doctor?"

"Indeed! I spent the winter of 1928 there."

"Tell me about it. Lots of smugglers, aren't there?"

The doctor drank a glass of water and replied, lowering his voice: "More than you think."

The Costas' workers had their fortnight, too. Buses at their disposal, taking them as far as Valencia. The sweet oranges attracted them. On the other hand, Paco, the teller's adopted son, still pursued tragic themes. To the extent that he went to the hospital to ask the attendant to let him go into the morgue to sketch. The attendant granted him permission on condition that he draw a picture of him in his blue cap.

Matías Alvear, on the contrary, became more and more calm, and drew Don Emilio Santos into the orbit of his ways. Matías's love of fishing induced Don Emilio to follow him up the Ter every afternoon, where the fish might or might not bite, but where they could roll themselves a couple of cigarettes, breathe deeply of the fresh air, and make satisfied allusions to the "pair of turtledoves," Mateo and Pilar. The manager of the *Tabacalera* sought in vain for a suitable proverb to describe this unexpected development.

Touching examples of the state of affairs manifested themselves on all sides, and Mosén Alberto felt sure that the area of Rosas itself would prove generous, that the Greek colony would emerge beneath the skulls. Colonel Muñoz, tall and elegant, granted a company of the garrison a furlough, and the soldiers rose up to call him blessed once again. He organized open-air entertainments for the people of the city: swimming and aquatic contests at the pool, in one of which Teo the giant wont first prize. On St. John's Eve the traditional bonfires were kindled, bonfires whose innocence filled the anarchist eyes with nostalgia.

Raimundo, the barber, picked up interesting news flashes. The barber had a passion for those of his customers who had a mustache trim and massage, and he gave them preferential treatment. During that fortnight he said to Mateo: "Mateo, I have some information for you."

"What is it?"

"I know how you can—make a friend."

"A friend?"

"Yes. Pedro."

Mateo said nothing. The barber added, clicking his scissors: "Give him a radio."

Mateo pretended to take no notice, but the idea remained fixed in his mind. And at the meeting the following Saturday he laid the matter before his comrades.

All of them were amazed. Benito Civil settled his green-checked sports jacket and asked: "A radio to a Communist?"

"Why not?" Mateo answered.

Octavio said thoughtfully: "It would be an honor for Falange to win Pedro over." But then he added that there was not a cent in the treasury, that it had all gone into the flyers.

Rosselló suggested asking for contributions from the people who were on their side, like Marta and Lieutenant Martín. He himself would give so much. Said and done. Nobody quite knew how they managed it, but in a few hours of youthful enthusiasm they had collected the amount they needed. El Rubio, the saxophonist, gave twenty-five pesetas. Don Emilio Santos was generous; Matías Alvear, though he did not understand just what was going on, had to dig into his wallet. By seven o'clock Monday evening the gleaming radio was in the barbershop of Raimundo, who was astonished to see that his suggestion had been taken seriously. A committee was organized, made up of Mateo, Ignacio—who knew Pedro—Octavio, and El Rubio, and, accompanied by Pilar and Marta, they set off, elated, at a brisk stride to the home of Pedro, who lived in the Calle de la Barca.

When the boy opened the door of his dingy flat and saw Mateo with a radio under his arm, and the others on the stairs, he put his hand to his forehead, gaped with eyes as wide as saucers, and finally, not knowing what to do, bent down to touch the case.

Then they all pushed into the dark dining room and helped him to look for an outlet, which they finally found at floor-level in a corner. Octavio stood up on a chair and connected the aerial. When the tubes lighted up and the radio began to hum, a shout of satisfaction went up. Pedro was so overcome by emotion that he stood benumbed. Then suddenly he went over to the radio and began to turn the knobs. But he could not get Moscow! It was not the time for its broadcast.

All that was on was waltz music. It was so tempting that Pilar took Mateo's hand and they began to dance. Ignacio held out his hand to Marta.

Until all of a sudden a cadaverous face, with two tufts of eyebrow, appeared in the door of the kitchen. Everyone grew quiet, and the radio was turned off.

"What's the matter, what's the matter?" the face asked in a frightened voice.

In the fifty years Pedro's father had lived in the flat, it was the first time he had heard music there.

THE fortnight was propitious for Ignacio, too: vacation. With San Felíu out of the question, for David and Olga had given themselves over heart and soul to UGT, Ignacio determined to get out of Gerona for a change of atmosphere. He thought of the country. But where to go? Jaime, the telegraph operator, had said to Matías: "If any one of you would like to spend a few days at my folks' house in Cerdaña, just let me know."

The trip was arranged in the twinkling of an eye. Ignacio would pay what it would have cost him in a boarding house, and he would be treated like a member of the family.

Ignacio left, prepared to assure Jaime's father and mother that their son was the best poet in Catalonia. The town where they lived was near Puigcerdá, where Warning Voice spent his summers organizing golf clubs that invariably petered out in the winter.

From the moment he arrived, Ignacio blessed Jaime's offer as the soldiers on furlough blessed Colonel Muñoz. What beautiful country, set around with mountains whose forests had not been burned, and peaceful flocks and fruit trees! The house had a garden and a threshing floor. Many rabbits that hid in the grass and peered out stupidly. Ignacio could not understand why Jaime had left all that, why he preferred to sit hour after hour in front of a machine that went: "Ta-ta-ta."

Jaime's parents said to Ignacio: "That's the way it is, boy. The city attracts the young people. Jaime would like to make his way in Gerona with his poetry. But he says he doesn't know the right people."

Then they went on to tell him that the priest of the village was an excellent man and that the watchmaker was crazy. When a stranger arrived, he would call him in and show him a clock that had stopped, saying: "I'll start it the day the revolution breaks out."

The expression on Ignacio's face when he heard talk even in Cerdaña of revolution resembled that of the rabbits. But he paid little attention. The country and the valley and that house filled his heart at once. There were the roads that the sun fatigued during the day, but which, toward evening, stretched, awoke, fetching and carrying across the plain wagons, alfalfa, mystery. At that hour Ignacio saw the grass of the fields quiet and yet moving, the mountains of Nuria darken and yet grow in stature, tree trunks and solitary walls which, even though it was night, still received impacts of light. And then he slept completely, as he could never manage to sleep in Gerona, and, at times, at dawn he looked out the window, seeing that everything was in its place, that all the clocks of Cerdaña—except that of the crazy watchmaker—were keeping perfect time. Threshing fields, strawstacks, dogs and cats, elms and poplars, the frontier of France a scant mile and a quarter off, the road to Seo de Urgel, the byways of the smugglers, the water of the Pyrenees, which Dr. Relken would have enjoyed, the old Carlists sitting on the stone benches of the village square, all had their norm and their law.

If it had not been for the crazy watchmaker, Ignacio would have said to César on his return to Gerona: "Now I understand why in Collell it seems to you at times that everything in nature has its own soul, that in unison or separately everything greets you, that some things weep, that many of them make an effort to learn your name and that of your Latin teacher." But the watchmaker, who called Ignacio over the first time he saw him cross the street—screwing into his left eye the horrible monocle of his trade—told him that all that was very fine—the flocks, the water—but that the people of the village were much less healthy than Ignacio might think. Cousin married cousin; there was more poverty than the authorities would admit; many families emigrated to France; life in the winter was hard because they were cut off, and because the tunnel of Nuria, which Primo de Rivera and then the Republic had promised them, was still on paper.

"The happy country. Oh, yes. See this clock? You wind it and it runs backwards. Yes, bank employee, life is unbearable here in Cerdaña in the winter. My father said he did not want to let himself be baptized because the church was ice cold. He was right. It is very pleasant to come to Puigcerdá in the month of July and go about the way you do, in sandals and a silk shirt embroidered with your initials. But in the winter... Why do *I* talk about the revolution? Because my trade has taught me that the little wheels are as important as the big wheels. Which are the big wheels? Those who come to play golf. Which are the little wheels? Those who go into the forest to gather firewood. But there's a day coming. Look at the clocks: tick, tock, tick, tock. There's a poison that will kill the whole world. A clock that covers the whole wall—that's what they ask me for. They think that because they have money I'm going to give them a thirteen-hour or twenty-four-hour clock. Not on your life! Tick, tock, tick, tock. The last poison is Abyssinia. Have you read *El Diluvio*? Now we're trying to imitate them here. They tell me that you're handing out circulars already in Gerona."

Ignacio returned to Gerona somewhat obsessed by that man. Gerona brought him back to reality. There was less quiet grass—though the walls there, too, received impacts of light in the night—and there were more initialed silk shirts.

Carmen Elgazu thought that he had put on weight. César said to him, unexpectedly: "Today I went to the San Daniel Valley. I saw the walls of the cloistered convent."

As for Gerona, the festivals there were at their height. The fortnight of love had reached its apex. Every district had its summer festival, just as in Cerdaña every road had its wagon. Colored paper streamers swung from balcony to balcony, traditional wooden puppets danced in the air, there were platforms for the musicians, ice cream stands.

It was the festival of the Rambla, and Matías Alvear was on the organizing committee. The family felt that they had a personal stake in the festivity. And, besides, such a strategically located balcony.

Really, from their balcony the Alvear family had a box seat from which they could see everything, the comings and goings, the laughter, the bald spots of the musicians, the microphone through which El Rubio greeted the "dear public," then puffed on his saxophone. Teo walked by with a strange woman who came to his navel; Gorki with one who was a head taller than he; Lieutenant Martín with a bargain-basement siren who left a wake of perfume as she passed. Under the arcade, Murillo and Canela were dancing cheek-to-cheek, and she was wearing new earrings. The children deliberately stepped on their elders' toes, there were two chess players in the Neutral, the soldiers tossed their caps in the air, and a group of taxi drivers passed by, clowning and pinching the girls, shooting off firecrackers and knocking the water bottles over.

The residents of the neighborhood, however, were unwilling to let the celebration get out of hand. They decided to take part in it themselves. Respectable businessmen, more or less "bay windowed," came out of their shops with their wives and danced. The memory of their young days brought a flush to their cheeks. Everyone took part; there were no class distinctions. Liga Catalana and CEDA, Radicals and Izquierda Republicana mingled fraternally. A half-dozen gaffers brought their chairs out to the edge of the sidewalk so they would not miss a thing. The servant girls were blissfully happy.

Pilar and Mateo, from where they were dancing in the street without moving too far off, kept calling to Matías and Carmen Elgazu, who were on the balcony, to come down and do a waltz for them. Carmen Elgazu, though she laughed, refused in spite of Don Emilio Santos's efforts to persuade her.

The last day Matías said: "Now you're going to see something!" He drank a glass of mineral water, and offered Doña Amparo Campo his arm.

Thanks to this concession, Julio managed to get a dance with Pilar. The policeman's hand was damp against her hand. Mateo never took his eyes off them.

Then, the whole length of the Rambla, the final *traca*, the chain of fireworks, was set off.

FIFTY-SIX

THEN came the fortnight of disasters.

The heat set in again, and it was like a curse from Africa. The Oñar practically dried up; what water remained stood stagnant. The workers struggling with the foundations of the market complained that the smell it gave off made them sick. It was a dead river in the middle of the city.

The festivals of the outlying quarters were but feeble imitations of those of the Rambla and the Plaza de la Independencia. Matías laid the blame on the committees in charge, saying that they lacked initiative; but it was really the heat. By night everyone was exhausted, and with the first light of dawn the sun climbed the heavens in unchallenged majesty, drinking the blood of the inhabitants.

Perhaps it was because of this red mist that a crazy idea occurred to one of David's and Olga's pupils, the eldest of them, Santi, who now followed Future around wherever he went and acted as a kind of office boy or doorman at the CNT. He went around to the Calle de Rutila to look up two of his friends who thought themselves tough *hombres*, and said to them: "Let's go to the school. I've a plan."

The boys could not resist their curiosity. They were more intelligent than Santi, but he dominated them because of his brutality. When they reached the school, the budding anarchist pulled a glass cutter out of his pocket and cut a hole in one of the panes, as though it was a shop window. He put his hand through the opening and released the catch. The three of them climbed in through the open window. "What are you going to do?" Santi, floating along on his big feet, walked over to the aquarium and, in spite of the thickness of the glass, cut a hole in it. The water began to trickle out through the hole. The twenty bright-hued fish swam madly around their enclosure. The water was nearly gone, and the gasping mouths of the fish denoted their cosmic terror. The two boys Santi had brought with him reacted instantly. In the face of this gratuitous act of cruelty, one of them grabbed Santi's wrists, holding them crossed behind his back as David had taught them, while the other hit him a jolting blow in the face. The blood from Santi's nose dripped into the aquarium as though to prolong the life of the fish a few seconds. They might have drunk it avidly had they not suddenly found themselves in the fountain of the garden, where they at once began to inspect their new home, circling it without pause. When David and Olga returned, they were at a loss to know what had happened, for the rescuers of the fish did not inform on Santi. Informing was forbidden by their code.

No one ever learned one word of how the idea of killing twenty goldfish had suddenly sprouted in the mind of the office boy—or doorman—of the CNT. But the two other boys, who adored Olga and David, passed judgment on Santi: "He'll wind up in the electric chair."

Another disaster, another drying-up, took place in the barbershop that had once been Communist. When the party moved to its new headquarters, the customers disappeared. The barber thought of attracting new trade, even of turning his place into a deluxe establishment. He bought two new American-type chairs, framed his mirrors in gilt. He put on a spotless white coat. But all for nothing. He had lost his few old customers and was unable to attract new ones. It was a sad sight to see him standing in the doorway, his hands in his pockets. "Maybe the CEDA will bite," he thought to himself, and pasted a small picture of Gil Robles on the window, but, for the time being, that did not work either. The assistant manager of the bank asked: "What has come over that fool?"

Next on the list of victims was Don Jorge. Don Jorge was informed by the manager of the Arús Bank after one of the meetings of Liga Catalana that his son and heir had just joined Falange.

It was as though Don Jorge had received a blow in the chest. How could such a thing have happened? He jammed on his derby and started for the door. The years were drying up Don Jorge's face. This fact and the somber clothes he wore imposed respect. And life in his home kept its silent, disciplined rhythm. As Noguer the notary used to say, "it was a house as upright as Teo's could ever be, and equally necessary to perpetuate the multiplicity of man's destiny."

What had happened had happened very simply. As Don Jorge's oldest son was coming out of the station on the Saturday when the handbills were being distributed, Benito Civil handed him one of the leaflets about the forests, the birds, those who suffered and hated, and the one illusion. The heir had just witnessed the setting afire of a wood of live oaks on one of the family properties in the Pyrenees, and the caretaker had said to him: "I hate to say this to you, sir, but this was bound to happen." The boy, who for a long time had been flouting his father's orders in his dealings with the tenants, said nothing. In the caretaker's house he observed the pile of sacks of potatoes labeled: "For Don Jorge." He noticed two of the man's children, with nobody to look after them, leaning over the garden cistern to see the disk of the sun in the water below. The caretaker kept repeating: "If you only knew—"

When Jorge got to Gerona, he went to the Arús Bank and asked for his father's bank balance, but they told him they could not give him the information without written authorization. The same thing happened at the other banks where he called. He looked at himself in the mirror, and his face showed no sign of his inner conflict. Even his name disturbed him—Jorge, like his father. His mother loved them all, but when her husband was around she hardly ventured to speak. Young Jorge, after reading the handbill Benito Civil gave him, locked himself up in his room, wept, prayed, and then went to Mateo's house. Mateo said to him: "It depends on your capacity for sacrifice."

Don Jorge's decision was identical with that of Dr. Rossclló a few weeks before. He said to his heir: "Either you take your name off Falange's list, or you can find yourself another place to live."

Strange month of August, when it might have been said that the sun's rays were opening up human hearts. Ana María, in San Felíu, fixed her hair in expectation of seeing Ignacio. He, in turn, daydreamed: tic, tac, tic, tac. And the sound became confused with the *trap-trap* of the horse that Marta rode.

Dr. Rosselló had his troubles, too. The Sisters of the hospital suspected that the doctor was giving the incurable patients lethal injections. The case of a countrywoman who had suffered an accident made them absolutely sure of this. With the starched wings of their caps bristling, they surrounded the doctor and questioned him. He denied their charges. The Sisters went to see the Bishop. The Bishop said to them: "But what proof have you?" The Sisters replied that their only proof was the woman's corpse.

Don Pedro Oriol cast up the accounts of his losses from the fires. The figure was overwhelming. Half of all he owned! Warning Voice said to him: "And they say patience, have patience! How long?"

It was an ill-starred fortnight. The assistant manager suffered a frightful humiliation. The father of Roca, a doorman at the Labor Office, got hold of certain information on Freemasonry in Italy which the manager did not have. Was King Victor Emmanuel a Mason or wasn't he? Roca's father went to the Arús Bank and, pressing his small head against the window, waved the precious paper before the assistant manager's eyes.

People planned something and it turned out just the opposite. César, for instance. It happened the last day of the festival on the Rambla. While his parents were out on the balcony listening to the music of Pizarro Jazz, César stayed in the dining room, contemplating the parched river and praying. The dance numbers reached his ears as though muted. Suddenly his prayers transformed that profane music into angelic music. He heard violins. The boy almost smiled as the thought came to him that in Pilar's room St. Francis of Assisi and St. Clara were serenading St. Ignatius in the next room. Like a sleepwalker he opened the door to see! His sister's room was dark, but it seemed to him that he saw a light, a light at the feet of St. Francis on his little pedestal. Fascinated, he approached it, and then discovered that it was a reflection, from the windowpane overlooking the river, of the electric lights in the houses across the street. But in any case it was a moving light that rose from the feet of the saint, ascending his habit and coming to rest on his face. The face took on a spectral, supernatural quality. Beyond doubt, St. Francis of Assisi was getting ready to speak to him. He looked at César as though he saw him small, very small, and shrinking ever more, as the seminarian's knees began to bend and he sank to the floor. And undoubtedly the saint would have spoken if he had not been interrupted by a sudden catastrophe: Pilar, who had been dancing with Mateo, burst into her room, laughing and still whirling about. Not seeing César in the dark, she bumped into him and gave a terrified scream. The light descended once more to the saint's feet, the whole family rushed in to see what had happened, and Matías said to César: "Son, I should think you could do your praying in your own room."

Mosén Francisco had remarked to Ignacio one day that living with a saint was no easy matter. Ignacio had answered him: "Dear Mosén, living with anyone, even a normal person, is no easy matter."

THE two final catastrophes to befall the city affected a limited number of persons, but they were irreparable. They had only one thing in common: their outcome, death. One of the protagonists lived far from the city; the other near at hand. The family of one of them lived in the city; the other's, far off. Neither one affected Ignacio directly; yet in both cases his sad reflection was: "The worms never lack for food."

Someone—Ignacio could not recall who—attributed these gusts, these sudden charges of suffering, to the planets. According to this theory, the planets suddenly pointed to a city on the earth and said: "There." And a typhoon of their invisible armies swept down, sowing ruin. "It's not always Mars," the person had said. "Those who think it is Mars or Jupiter are mistaken. All the planets collaborate, all of them. All the planets are always looking at the earth, waiting for the moment. And the worst of all is the moon. The moon sinks ships, gives pregnant women nausea, causes drought, and, above all, inflames the mind. Whenever you see minds on flame, look at the moon; it's laughing. In these days it's laughing fit to kill. Until the time comes when they make a rocket or a shell and blow it to bits."

It seemed to Ignacio that this time Gerona was the target. Apparently the moon was not yet satisfied; it selected Pedro's flat. It sent an army to Pedro's flat and set a mind on fire, that of the old man in the kitchen, the father of the young Communist.

From what Pedro told Mateo and those who went to see him, it was something unheard-of, incredible. Since they had had the radio, the old man had seemed rejuvenated and had spent the fortnight glued to the speaker except at such times as his son tuned in to Moscow. Suddenly one afternoon he came out of the kitchen with a suitcase in his hand. Pedro asked him in amazement where he was going. The old man replied with great seriousness: "I've got nothing to do here. I'm going to America."

Pedro thought his father was joking, though he was astonished nonetheless, for his father never joked. "You go put that suitcase away and come and listen to the music," he said to him.

But the old man walked on through the dining room, saying: "What for? There's nothing for me to do here. It's better for me to go to America."

And he walked on, on until he had crossed the sill of the balcony, which stood open, on until he hit the balcony, fell across it, and disappeared on the other side, his body shattering against the stones of the Calle de la Barca.

Pedro could do nothing but stand there on the balcony with an expression of terror on his face, his brain paralyzed by the dull thud his father's body had given as it hit the ground. Afterwards he was inconsolable. Because it was clear that he could have prevented it, that he could have got up and blocked his father's way when he saw him making for the balcony. But, despite his surprise, he had been convinced that his father was playing a joke with the suitcase.

It was a humble drama that left everyone deeply perplexed. They all did everything they could to comfort Pedro, but it was useless. Moreover, he told what had happened only once, in a low voice and with very few words. An ambulance took away the old man's body; a policeman listed the contents of the suitcase: a pair of long underdrawers and a pencil. A pencil! What was that for? Julio decided to wait a week before calling on Pedro to ask him for a photograph of his father; but on card 371 of his file he made this entry: "Jaime Bosch, aged 67, prominent eyes."

Ignacio and El Rubio, Mateo and his comrades, and Teo—representing Cosme Vila—accompanied Pedro to the cemetery. Benito Civil suggested:

"We ought to order a headstone." Everyone stared at him. Then he remembered that it was Pedro himself who carved headstones.

The second death notice was picked up by Matías Alvear. The telegram from Valladolid was addressed to Major Martínez de Soria: his older son had been riddled by bullets in front of Free Youth headquarters as he was pasting a Falange poster on the wall.

As the major read the telegram he stiffened to attention, while his wife burst into wild sobbing; Marta went to her room and knelt there. When her eyes had become as dry as the Oñar, her father said to her: "Pack your bag. They are waiting for us for the funeral."

In Valladolid the family, including José Luis, and a guard of blue shirts, accompanied Fernando to the cemetery. After their return to Gerona, when Marta appeared in the doorway of the Alvear dining room, the whole family got up, and Pilar went over and took her by the hand.

Marta said nothing. She sat down in a corner beside the little table covered with Pilar's thread-lace. César asked if Fernando had had time to confess.

"Death was instantaneous."

Marta's grief was silent; but the major reacted in a manner that was disconcerting. He had aged five years in Marta's opinion, and at the cemetery in Valladolid he had lost his last dark hairs. Now, back in Gerona, he was trying to get himself in hand. When he was at home he could not fail to be affected by the state of mind of his wife and daughter, and he frequently accompanied them to church; but when he was at headquarters he gave no sign of what he was feeling, joking with the officers as though nothing had happened.

Letters of condolence were constantly being left at his door: Major Campos, Noguer the notary, Warning Voice, Colonel Muñoz. The last one he opened was that of Mateo, in which the young man said to him that in the struggle for the daybreak in Spain, it was inevitable that the best should fall.

The major stood with the letter in his hand, trembling with rage. "What does this imbecile mean by that twaddle about daybreak?"

His wife tried to quiet him; then Marta explained to him that this word formed a part of Falange's lexicon. "It's a figure of speech. It means that Falange will bring the light, or something like that."

The major tore up the letter and stood by the window, thoughtfully watching the shadows descend upon the city's rooftops.

FIFTY-SEVEN

AFTER the lapse of a few hours the outer dimension of the disasters was limited to comments. The people of Gerona had a great capacity for absorbing punishment. At the Neutral, Dr. Relken said they were stoics.

Major Martínez de Soria's state of mind, however, elicited more than the usual comment. The red blotches on his face had turned so dark that many of those who had been arrested in October remarked feelingly: "If he were trying us now—!"

Julio said; "Don't be so sure you're out of the woods. There are plenty of the military with red blotches, and it may be that any day now they will call for a mass trial of us."

This was the rumor that was circulating about the city. Julio said that there was unrelenting pressure on Gil Robles to bring off a *coup d'état*, and the fact that many of the active and even the retired generals were republicans was no guarantee. Many of these generals had gone over to the enemy when Azaña's law was passed, and it was said that Martínez Barrios himself, referring to Franco, had said: "I don't like those little generals one bit...."

Among those who refused to give any credence to these rumors was the assistant manager. He said to Ignacio: "Why, half the army are Masons, and they're talking about *coups d'état*! Who would pull it off in Gerona? The commanding general is a Mason; Colonel Muñoz is a Mason, and Major Campos, the Commissioner. People would do better not to waste their breath."

Matías Alvear took the position that the military were much more intelligent than the miners of Asturias. "They're not going off their rocker because the son of a major has been assassinated or Estat Català is beginning to lash its tail again."

Nevertheless, Major Martínez de Soria's grief weighed on the city. And the more erectly he carried himself, and the more glasses of rum he ordered at the officers' café, the more Teo cracked his whip as he drove his dray back from the station, the more Casal reminded the UGT that a united people constitutes an irresistible social force, and the more pictures of Joaquín Santaló were distributed in the streets, the more El Responsable jammed his cap down as he said to the Commissioner: "Winter's coming and there's no work. Do you think the unemployed can't set fire to anything but pines?"

The most serene among them all was Don Santiago Estrada. He had returned from his vacation, and he dreamed of giving great impetus to the Christmas campaign. "This Christmas the CEDA must distribute overcoats and mufflers to all the poor of the province." Possibly, when it came to serenity, Cosme Vila was not far behind. Seated in the presiding officer's armchair at Communist headquarters, he went on steadily stamping papers of every sort. Each stamped paper was a little flag on the map; each little flag a link with a factory or a cell in a village. Santiago Estrada thought of filling the province with mufflers; the executive committee of the Communist Party thought of filling it with fanatics.

The ground-swell that arose everywhere when it became known that elections had really been scheduled for February 1936, five months off, changed the whole tenor of the city. The streets took on a strange activity having nothing to do with that of the festivals. Each mind deployed its batteries; the women walked faster; shops, fish markets, and cafés crackled with allusions. Many light bulbs were broken, nobody knew why. All political parties instructed their doormen to double their vigilance in checking all who came into headquarters.

And then the rains came, as though to wash away all traces of the past, of the depression of bodies and spirits. It rained so much that the Oñar recovered from its sterility and began to rise, dragging off garbage, weeds, stenches. It swelled so that in its incontinent fury it dragged away the foundations of the new market. Scoffing laughter from the enemies of Noguer the notary, the aldermen who had voted against the project, the members of other parties, echoed through the City Hall. Noguer was crushed. "Drawing a will is not the same thing as city-planning."

Don Santiago Estrada called him up to say: "Don't worry. We'll start it over again."

The appearance of the Dehesa changed too. The rains cleared everyone except the anarchists from the swimming pool, and lent the trees a yellow tinge. The words *Viva Falange* grew blurred on the trunks. And suddenly the first leaf fluttered down. It said farewell to its branch, hung in the air for a moment as though hesitating in its choice of a new home and grave. Finally it came to rest in a footprint beside a puddle, which to the leaf seemed the sea. The other leaves assumed that it was free, that it was coming to know other worlds, and they, too, left their branches. From time to time a gust from the Pyrenees set them all dancing, and the Dehesa was turned into an Orphic grove, a huge vegetal chorus.

The humans, Casal and David and Olga in UGT, El Responsable and Future in the gymnasium, Gorki and Victor at Communist headquarters, all the Leftists of the city felt a great quickening of hope. Elections! The three hundred prisoners of October recalled their turns around the prison courtyard, the gypsy crying: "A penny an amen, a penny an amen." "Remember the baskets, with our names written on the tag?" People snatched copies of *El Demócrata* from each other's hands, and *El Diluvio*, *Claridad*, *Mundo Obrero*.

Santi, bare-chested and red-haired, looked at his big feet as he sat at CNT headquarters, thinking: "I'll soon have a new pair of shoes."

The forces were perfectly aligned. And to each leader clung his shadow, the inferior soul, fawning, subservient: Teo to Cosme Vila, David to Casal, El Cojo to El Responsable, Octavio to Mateo, the Commissioner to Julio, and Julio to Dr. Relken, the tourist with a German accent.

Santi was the slave of the CNT. He was the slave of the CNT in abstract. Any of its members could order him to steal a bicycle or kill goldfish. The shadow who best knew what he was doing was Teo. Teo was Cosme Vila's slave because of a sense of discipline. "If Cosme Vila orders me to throw myself under the dray, I do it." And he would. For the party he might even have consented to disinter his brother; at least that was what he said to Gorki one day when the Aragonese asked him.

The least excusable was Julio. His hat tilted over one ear took on a ridiculous air in Dr. Relken's presence. When the latter talked about Spain—beggars, illiteracy, excessive gesticulation, fanaticism—Julio nodded abjectly. And when the doctor, after photographs of Prague, Vienna, St. Petersburg, brought out pictures of primitive tribes—Bushmen, Kaffirs—and stated that the difference between these savages and a Nordic or central European was greater than the difference between the former and a trained dog, Julio, in spite of the fact that he knew much more about racial psychology than the doctor, had the feeling that somehow he, and all the other Spaniards with him, were only halfway up the ladder leading from the trained dogs to the Nordics or central Europeans.

Matías Alvear was slave to no one. For that reason, when he met the doctor at the Neutral, he was far less impressed than Julio, and said: "I can beat him at dominoes and many other things, and so can Don Emilio Santos."

Nevertheless, the fact that there were slaves meant that there were masters.

Now, the two most enslaved slaves were the Costas. They were the slaves of their wives. The executive committee of Izquierda Republicana was in despair. Ever since the Costas had married, they divided their time between their homes—finding a place to put the things their wives bought—and their business enterprises. They had hardly any time left for the party.

Fortunately, the executive committee was made up of married men who grasped the situation perfectly. "We are pregnant, we want you with us," the Costa wives said. How could the brothers refuse? Not to mention the fact that their parents-in-law came in from Pals at the least excuse—in a 1900-model car—and went looking for them wherever they might be, at the foundry, the lime kilns, the quarries, to inquire: "Are you being good to our little doves?"

The Costas solemnly promised the committee that they would get around these difficulties. "We'll do everything that has to be done."

"You understand," the committee told them, "at election time it's the example that counts."

There was one last pawn: Warning Voice. Warning Voice had voluntarily declared himself Laura's slave. The wedding announcements had been sent out. The Costas were overcome. "Imagine us having Warning Voice for a brother-in-law! The man who goes around saying that if the military don't prepare a *coup d'état* they must be blind! Imagine us...."

That was life for you, and Laura, blissfully happy, going about saying: "The workers dangerous? Why, they are lambs. If I were in my brothers' place, you'd see how they would all be reading *El Tradicionalista*."

So the sign of that summer and beginning of fall was slavery. Professor Civil affirmed this. At the classes, which Ignacio and Mateo had resumed, he intimated to them that he was deeply worried. He saw the future black, and was almost glad to be as old as he was. The fluctuations in the weather had wearied him very much; in his opinion, the enormous machines the Costas had imported from England were germs that would destroy whatever was still healthy left in Gerona. "People will leave the land and come to work alongside these monsters. The moment will come when we'll all be proletariat. In a few years, if you go to Puigcerdá," he said to Ignacio, "you'll find no one there but the mad watchmaker. He will never cross the frontier, I can assure you. No real poet ever deserts his country."

As a matter of fact, Professor Civil was dissembling a little the cause of his concern. Mechanization was an old story, and there was no reason for him to get more upset now than on other occasions. It was a different microbe that worried him, a different import: Dr. Relken. Professor Civil was convinced that Dr. Relken was a Jew, and he was beside himself. "Poor Gerona. You can see for yourself. The first thing that man did was to call us illiterate; the second, to buy up antiques for three reales apiece."

FIFTY-EIGHT

IT gave Ignacio great pleasure to talk of Teresa Neumann, the stigmatic, for he saw that by so doing he made Carmen Elgazu happy, brought a glow to César's eyes, frightened Pilar, and held Marta's attention. He always chose interesting details, having such an air of verisimilitude that Matías himself often found that the cigarette he was holding between his lips had burned to ash.

Ignacio had a presentiment that one day César would receive some special mark of grace from heaven. For that reason he emphasized the supernatural character of the manifestations of the Austrian stigmatic, for he felt that any day César might give them a similar surprise.

With regard to the stigmata, Ignacio assured his audience that Teresa Neumann was the most complete stigmatic there had ever been, for she not only had the signs on her hands, feet, and side, but the imprint of the thorns on her forehead, the lashes of the flagellation on her back, and on her shoulder even the mark of the cross. And as for her visions, which was the aspect that interested them all most, he told his listeners that the invalid followed the liturgical calendar: at Christmastide she saw the cave of Nazareth, on Good Friday she was present at the death of Jesus on Calvary, and so on.

Marta was particularly interested in the visions. "But does she see everything in detail?" she inquired.

"Of course. She is present at the events. She sees Christ as I see all of you. And she hears Him talk."

"How is that possible?"

"And the apostles. Just as they were. She could draw them."

"But how can it be known that she hears them talk?"

"Because often, during the vision, she repeats aloud the words she hears, so those who are present can put them down."

"Does she talk in Latin?" asked Pilar, fidgeting in her chair.

Ignacio shook his head. "Not Latin. There was a Munich professor who questioned her when she awoke after a vision of the Nativity. The woman had heard songs and could not remember them or repeat them. The doctor tried to stimulate her memory. He recited the 'Glory to God in the highest' in several ancient tongues, but she kept shaking her head. As soon as he began to recite it in Aramaic, Teresa instantly exclaimed: 'That's what I heard. But it was much longer.' Then she repeated words which, she said, she had heard from the lips of St. Peter before the Sanhedrin; the professor recognized them as the dialect of Galilee. During the vision of Christ stumbling under the weight of the Cross, Teresa sat up in bed and shouted *'Kum, kum,'* which means 'Arise!' It was the soldiers who were shouting this to Christ, and it seems that Teresa heard the same word, *'Kum,'* on Christ's own lips when He revived the son of the widow of Nain. And when she saw Christ appear among His disciples after the Resurrection she heard: *'Shelam, lachen!'* which means 'Peace be with you. It is I.' And you must remember that Teresa Neumann never had a teacher of Aramaic—not to mention the fact that she described the streets of Jerusalem, the houses, the faces."

Carmen Elgazu was radiant. "What you're telling is wonderful, son."

Ignacio, looking at his father, and convinced that Carmen Elgazu would burst with happiness, added: "To be sure, there are many people who laugh at this, while they put complete faith in a horoscope that costs them twenty dollars. Me, I'd rather believe in Teresa Neumann, who, at least, has clear eyes."

"Really?"

"Yes, blue, except when they weep blood. Besides, on the days when she can lead a normal existence, she cares for the sick, and her mother raises birds. Oh, I left out one detail," Ignacio added. "While she is in an ecstasy she cannot say the number three, but says one and one and one. That is to say, she is in an infantile state."

"All that scares me," Pilar repeated.

"Not me," Marta said firmly. "And I only wish that all this were happening near here."

Matías Alvear laughed. "Don't complain. We have a similar case here in Gerona."

"Who?"

"El Responsable."

"That's right," Ignacio went on with the joke. "El Responsable can hypnotize you and make you believe that you are listening to the Sermon on the Mount."

"And if he wanted to he could bring out wounds on more than one."

"He nearly brought one out on me here," and the boy touched his jaw reminiscently.

Yes, Carmen Elgazu was happy. Neither Julio García, nor David and Olga, nor the tumult of youth, nor the elections of the UGT had been able to uproot the faith of her son. A warning from heaven—the New Year, that terrible sickness—had been enough to turn his eyes back to what she had taught him. Carmen Elgazu smiled in the kitchen as she polished the faucets and murmured jokingly: "*Kum, kum.*"

She felt proud. Let the letters in violet ink keep coming from Bilbao; she would keep writing back: "Don't worry, Mother. Everything is going well. César is a saint. Pilar is very lovable. Ignacio has become his old self again." The letters from Madrid were answered by Ignacio, who poked fun at the anarchists in his own inimitable way.

As for César, he had realized that everyone was expecting something similar to the phenomenon of Teresa Neumann from him: his Latin teacher, Ignacio, Mosén Francisco.... He said to Ignacio: "Don't be foolish. The stigmata are received only by those who earnestly desire to share the sufferings of the Passion with Christ. And I am only a sinner like everyone else."

Mosén Francisco said to him: "Yes, but at Collell you did not sleep."

The seminarian shook his head: "Oh, that lasted only a little while."

The fact was that César had a feeling of guilt. The summer was drawing to an end, and he had not accomplished anything of what he had set out to do. He felt guilty of a grave lack of charity. Other people did not exist for him. The thirst for an apostolate, for action, which he had felt the previous summers had now been replaced by an irrepressible desire to be alone and to pray. To pray in the silence of his room, or in the church. Only that. Without even thinking of his family or the city. He and God. He comforted himself in part, thinking that he would not have been able to do anything anyway, for in the Calle de la Barca the children were all scattered. Some of them had grown too big, most of them were in S'Agaró.

Mosén Francisco tried to cheer him up, by showing him that there was no sin in that. "Don't be silly. One goes through periods of withdrawal. The action of grace is as evident in you now, in your desire to pray, as it was last summer when you could not be still for a moment. And if you don't believe me, let's examine it. What happens to you when you pray? What do you feel?"

César shrugged his shoulders, somewhat confused. "Why—nothing happens to me. I try—to bring the image of Jesus before me, that is all."

Mosén Francisco nodded his head. "And do you achieve it?"

"Sometimes it seems to me I do."

"How do you see Jesus? Under what circumstances?"

César thought for a moment. "It's nearly always at the moment of the Transfiguration."

"Robed in white?"

"Always."

Mosén Francisco looked hard at César, struck by the concentration the seminarian's countenance revealed. "Tell me one thing. Does the body of Jesus emit rays of gold?"

"No, no," answered César with assurance, "rays of white."

"Is Jesus carrying anything in His hand?"

"No, nothing at all."

Mosén Francisco marked a pause. "Do you see Him on the mountain's peak?"

"Yes. On the peak of a mountain."

"And where do the rays come from?"

"From his heart."

Mosén Francisco nodded his head again. "Don't you realize? All this is very great, César." The seminarian said nothing. Mosén Francisco added: "But, tell me in more detail what it is you do. What do you feel, or what do you say?"

"Feel—I don't know," César answered. "At times a great peace. At times it seems to me I don't feel anything."

"And what do you say?"

"I say: 'O Lord, my God.' Or at times I sing the *Magnificat*."

Mosén Francisco rose to his feet, overcome by emotion. And he repeated that it would be silly of César to worry. All that was as valuable as charity. What did it matter if he did not think directly of others? "Those white rays, César, traverse your soul, never doubt it. And through you they reach the others. Your family—you have seen the results—your superiors, everyone."

César bit his lips. "I would wish them to reach other persons, too."

"Who, for instance?"

"Many—I can't say. The whole world."

"Well, give me a few names. At Mass we two will pray for them."

César smiled and rubbed his ear. "Well, I'd like to be able to help—my cousin José in Madrid."

"We'll pray for him."

"And Murillo. A fellow by the name of Murillo, and Bernat." And then he added: "And all those involved in the forest fires."

SOMETHING else made Carmen Elgazu happy: that Marta should have fallen in love with Ignacio. She no longer had the slightest doubt. She had been young herself, and there were unmistakable details. Why did Marta choose to visit Pilar at the very hours when Ignacio was at home? Could the boy be so blind that he hadn't noticed this?

Carmen Elgazu was pleased by this development "because Marta is well-bred and had a Christian upbringing." Carmen Elgazu said to herself: "Her mother must be a fine woman, I don't care what they say in the shops." As for the major, she hardly knew what to think. She felt him so removed from what they, the Alvears, were. Such an aristocrat, with his left shoulder hunched forward in that typical gesture of his. Nevertheless, it was said that since the death of his son he caroused less, and that even though he drank a lot, he made up for it by going to church more often with his womenfolk.

As for Ignacio—Carmen Elgazu had come to the conclusion that any day now he would find himself trying to tell Marta he loved her, and unable to get the words out. It could hardly be any other way. Marta was the girl with the strongest personality her son had ever met, and Ignacio was not going to fall in love with just anybody.

Carmen Elgazu avoided talking of the matter with her son. But she said to Matías: "Matías, you see the way things are going. Any day now I can see you taking fencing lessons from Ignacio's father-in-law at the armory."

FIFTY-NINE

SEPTEMBER put people in their place. César went off to Collell, heartened by his talks with Mosén Francisco. Warning Voice and Laura were married and left on a short wedding trip, for Warning Voice said he could not stay away with elections pending.

This was the city's obsession, the elections. All other problems had been relegated to the background, with perhaps one exception: Dr. Relken. This topic came up all the time, for in addition to the fact that the doctor's appearance aroused much comment—his planed-off blond hair, his Germanic occiput—nobody knew just what he was doing in Gerona. He was the subject of inexhaustible discussion: he was a scientist; he had told Mosén Alberto he had made a mistake in his choice of site for the excavations; he belonged to a foreign company that was prospecting in the Pyrenees; he drank water enough to float a battleship; he could not get used to Spanish cooking with olive oil....

But aside from the political leaders, who never took their eye off him, most people thought he was just a scientist. At the Arús Bank, Padrosa said he had seen him around Montjuich wearing a pith helmet and chasing butterflies.

What really mattered, however, was the elections. The parties of the Right were certain of victory. Especially the CEDA. Huge posters of Gil Robles were going up on all the billboards and walls in the province, as throughout the rest of Spain. Meetings, trucks equipped with loudspeakers, balloons painted in the likeness of Gil Robles, and mufflers waiting to be handed out at the opportune moment. "Our goal is three hundred. Three cheers for the honest workman!"

It quickly became evident that there were to be three major tactics in the campaign: first, the build-up of the leader, Gil Robles; second, the glorification of the honest workman; third, the systematic insulting of the opposition.

At the meetings the revolution of October was savagely attacked. The memory of the citizenry was refreshed with regard to the atrocities of Asturias, and figures and facts were adduced of the mismanagement and ineptness of the first government of the Republic.

The assistant manager said to Ignacio: "No one can fail to be swayed by a campaign of this sort. People are not fools. Those with money want to keep it. The middle class wants to see the peseta stabilized. And as for the workers, except those who are blind, they are fed up with promises."

Ignacio smiled. "So it's in the bag?"

The assistant manager frowned. "Under normal circumstances, yes. But everybody knows what victory means this time. So they'll do everything they can think of. First they'll try to form a united front. And if even so they lose, they'll resort to force."

"What do you mean?"

"They'll destroy the ballot boxes."

THERE was an optimistic climate at Liga Catalana, too. Their faith rested on the same principle as the CEDA's: that people were tired of radical experiments.

Those who believed in an overwhelming victory of the Right expressed the opinion of the majority. Many people felt that the candidates supported by the parties of the Right offered greater guarantees than the Mongoloid head of Cosme Vila and the brilliantined waves of Future.

Warning Voice and Mateo were the only ones who did not share the general optimism. Warning Voice, while still on his honeymoon, had said to Laura: "Nobody realizes the numerical mass the workers represent. You find them everywhere. It is ridiculous to be sure of winning. Take Andalusia, for example...."

Mateo's misgivings were based on less statistical reasons. Mateo was of the opinion that the Rightists would lose, first, because they deserved to—they had spent two years asleep at the switch—and second, because they would not unite, "whereas their adversaries, no matter what the assistant manager believes, will in the end close ranks. They are less vain, more realistic. They will all unite. Here in Gerona the Costas will join up even with those who would like to see their enterprises in the receiver's hands."

This was not so clear to Ignacio. He was rather of the belief that the ones who would unite were the Rightists, who were divided only by minutias, whereas the divisions among the others seemed to him unbridgeable. "How can Cosme Vila, who does not believe in private property, unite with David and Olga, who want to own their own home? Just mention Future's name to Teo and see how he reacts."

For the moment Ignacio seemed to be right. The differences among the Leftists had been growing steadily.

It was a situation of the sort that Professor Civil loved to discourse on. It was risky to make predictions on this occasion, he said, for often at the last moment events having no bearing on the basic principles could make public opinion veer unpredictably.

"That's the worst of elections," Mateo said to his comrades. "The future of the country is at stake, and public opinion depends on the outcome of a football game or an attempt on a minister's life."

Professor Civil could not have been more right in the matter of veering opinion. Autumn brought events that decisively influenced the political climate. These were "facts," facts that people were asking for to clear up their ideological perplexities.

The first of these took place in higher governmental circles. It was splashed in headlines across all the newspapers. Certain members of the government were involved in a shady deal, had covered up a huge swindle: a type of roulette called *straperlo*. It was said that Lerroux's adopted son had been paid millions to allow this fraudulent game to be introduced into Spain. There were many who claimed that Gil Robles was in on the deal, in cahoots with the Minister of the Interior.

At the bank, the assistant manager talked himself hoarse, insisting that Gil Robles had had nothing to do with the affair, that the Radical Party was exclusively responsible for the business; Tower of Babel commented ironically: "So when the chief says our goal is three hundred, what he means is three hundred million pesetas...."

Don Emilio Santos said to Matías Alvear: "That roulette has cost them fifty percent of their chances to win."

Matías Alvear doubted that the matter was that serious. At the Telegraph office many of the employees, once their first indignation had died down, remarked: "You might as well make the most of your chances."

And one of the mailmen said to the others: "If I'd been minister, I wouldn't have passed up the opportunity."

Meanwhile, the second hammer blow, whose impact was to be far more serious, was about to fall. When Matías Alvear picked up the news on the radio, he removed his earphones and muttered: "This is the last straw."

The news was of an international nature, and it set off a buzz of comments. Nobody would have imagined it would have such repercussions in a little city like Gerona. Repercussions even in the fanatical way many women kept on buying at only one certain butcher shop and no other. On October 4 Mussolini had ordered his troops to march into Abyssinia in spite of the warnings of the League of Nations, which was presided over by a Spaniard, a liberal.

The news stirred the whole city. People went about the streets waving *El Demócrata* and muttering insults. "Something should be done! You can't let him get away with this!"

The first to turn this spontaneous popular indignation to his advantage was Cosme Vila. He lowered the flag in the window of Communist headquarters to half-mast and called a general meeting. He first explained to the members what kind of person Mussolini was—"and there is one here who would like to copy him." Then he went on to describe the simple, peaceable life of the Ethiopians, "whom Fascism is hunting down in their homes just as Lerroux did the miners of Asturias here in Spain at the time of the October uprising." He said this was the first of a series of crimes that Germany and Italy were planning, and that unless the proletariat of the world reacted immediately, it would be too late. And he assured his hearers that Russia had been the first nation to protest the aggression against Abyssinia.

When, shortly after Vila had delivered his speech, Victor was on the point of taking the full text to the press where *El Proletario* was printed, Teo pulled up his dray in front of the building, and the giant rushed panting up the stairs. He had just heard over the radio, in the Gran Vía Café, that His Holiness had blessed the tanks leaving for Africa.

Cosme Vila did not move a muscle. "All right," he said, "now go"

Teo put on his cap, said "*Salud*," and left. Cosme Vila called Victor back and had him draw a cartoon of Pius XI and Mussolini in profile, driving a tank over an Abyssinian who lay in a pool of blood, his horrified eyes raised heavenward.

Casal was less lurid. He preferred statistics, and to reason his position. In his economics class he explained that patriotism carried to a frenzy, as in Italy, led to an increase in the birth rate, with the consequent need for expansion—that is to say, war.

As for El Responsable, he was planning a reprisal of some sort, but Future beat him to it. He took the skull Mosén Alberto had given him, painted it black, fitted a wig of short, kinky hair over it so the resemblance to an Ethiopian was unmistakable, and with some fifty followers made his way to the house of an Italian businessman who acted as Consul. All the windows were broken, and the front of the house was covered with menacing scrawls.

In the final analysis, however, what mattered most was the climate that was created, and the effect on the undecided and the members of the middle class. Julio said at the Neutral: "Mussolini has done us a big favor." *El Demócrata*, in a special section, described the flight of the Ethiopians under a hail of bombs. The figure of the Negus, with his umbrella, took on a legendary quality. People who had never thought of themselves as extremists were deeply stirred and employed language of great severity. Matías Alvear looked at Marta with a different expression on his face when the girl came to visit Pilar; and very especially at Mateo, something that was not lost on the latter.

In the absence of Warning Voice, Don Pedro Oriol in *El Tradicionalista* supported Mussolini in his venture. This started a chain reaction and gave the Costas their chance to regain lost ground. They saw their opportunity and seized it; besides, they felt the cause keenly. They came out strongly in favor of the Negus, and started a subscription, heading it with a huge sum, which won them many admirers. It was Izquierda Republicana that launched the most systematic, reasonable, and intelligent campaign against the Italian action.

Izquierda Republicana, which was managing things so skillfully, decided to take a delicate step: to invite Dr. Relken to give a lecture at headquarters. "Abyssinia, Its Life and Customs"—so ran the title on the posters. Wonderful! The doctor knew the country backwards and forwards. *El Demócrata* carried a photograph of the doctor in Addis Ababa, standing beside a camel.

Mosén Alberto, who by reason of his Catalanism was at heart on the side of the Negroes, and to whom the subject of the lecture was of absorbing interest, lamented the fact that it was to be given at Izquierda Republicana, where he could not go. His absence, however, was not noticed. The place was jammed. One of the Costas introduced the speaker, and Dr. Relken achieved an absolute triumph. He made no allusion whatever to the war; he merely said that those who thought the Ethiopian a primitive civilization showed complete ignorance. The Ethiopian civilization, of ancient origin, was rich and flourishing, and it was thanks to the influence of Ethiopia that many of the peoples of Africa had risen above their savage state. For example, in the musical aspect, certain tribes, such as the Bongos, had achieved rare perfection. Dr. Relken showed his audience slides of harps, small guitars, mandolins, and, in the easternmost region, flutes, all of which had been introduced in the interior of Africa by the Ethiopians. Also sculpture, wood carving, and so forth. Not to mention the tom-tom. The tom-tom was not exclusively of Ethiopian origin, but characteristic of all the Negroes of the continent; however, according to Dr. Relken it had a special resonance in Abyssinia. The emotion of the audience as the doctor, employing only his hands and a table, imitated multiple varieties of tom-toms, all having an obsessive rhythm and unquestionably the basis of the musical revolution in the world and in jazz, was indescribable. Everyone felt his skin turning into a drum, and saw fires, deserts, and Negroes dancing, Negroes dancing the dance of death around the Italian tanks. Dr. Relken received an ovation. It was the best lecture the city remembered.

The success of the act organized by the Costas was so great that others wanted to do the same. David and Olga said to Casal: "We ought to invite the doctor to give a lecture here." Casal replied: "All right, but not right away. Later on." Dr. Relken also received invitations from various villages.

Cosme Vila thought this was all very clever, but he shrugged his shoulders. "I'd rather invite Vasiliev." It was evident that Dr. Relken was not a Communist, and Cosme Vila did not allow heretics at his center.

The speaker of the evening said to Julio with a smile: "I never had such a success." And in spite of the repeated requests, he seemed in no hurry to give the lecture again. He told people that he did not like to speak in public. It was plain that he preferred small gatherings. "I am a man of—what is that pretty word you use—?"

"For what?"

"A group of people that meets regularly."

"*Tertulia*?"

"That's it—*tertulia*. I'm a man of *tertulia*."

That was true. Dr. Relken preferred, rather than speeches before a large audience, to improvise a gathering at the Neutral, for instance. Improvise, that was the word. For he always arrived there alone or, at most, accompanied by Julio. But it was not long before the group began to gather. The doctor's figure always attracted attention, as well as his great seriousness, in spite of his constant smile. Soon a small group had collected about him, especially if Julio raised his voice or asked one of those present a question. In this event the doctor willingly acceded to a general conversation. And the same thing always happened: he was soon describing faraway places, distant things he had seen, which filled Ramón with delight. And as he talked, his audience grew. At the end there came, of its own accord, what Julio called the "questions and answers" period. Strange, unexpected questions, which never went unanswered unless their intent was humorous. When this happened, Dr. Relken stared and gave the impression that he had not understood. It was because of his lack of a sense of humor that Matías Alvear had said of him: "I can beat him at dominoes and other things; and so can Don Emilio Santos."

"Is it true, doctor, that in Russia the workers live like rajas?"

The doctor replied that Russia was very big. Certainly, other things being equal, they lived better than in Spain. Possibly they worked longer hours—but this was voluntary. They wanted to see their country progress.

"And what about Germany?"

The doctor took off his glasses. "Well, Hitler is trying to do the same in Germany, but Hitler is not concerned with the workers. He flatters them for his own ends; but what he wants is power, power. He trusts in his star...."

The theme of National Socialism, Fascism, and, indirectly, the Falange came up frequently. Because of the war on Abyssinia the first serious offensive had been launched against Mateo and his comrades, even though there were many who laughed at them, calling them a handful of muddle-headed fools, who were beginning to get what was coming to them, "as happened in Valladolid."

The doctor stretched his neck as he heard this. He did not share the opinion of the scoffers. "You are wrong to think the Falangists are a joke, just because they are only a few. The Nazis began as a few in a beer hall, and the same thing happened when Mussolini was starting. Here, from what I have seen, Fascism bases its doctrine on very old theories, which date back to the expulsion of the Jews and the Inquisition. In that aspect, naturally, it will founder against the knowledge all of you possess of these facts. But they are very shrewd in other aspects, such as, for example, glorifying the conquest of America without telling people about the mass murders—forgive the severity of my words—carried out by the conquerors. And, above all, they are very astute in injecting their followers with a very dangerous political idea, the idea of Unity. This is, in fact, more serious than would appear. This was the arm that Hitler used, the same as Mussolini. You wait and see how their ranks grow, and how the members come to look alike. Unity, all united to create strength. It is an idea which, repeated again and again, becomes a steamroller."

Someone interposed: "I don't see what they can steamroller here."

"Don't you?" The doctor smiled. "No democrat ever sees it, and for that reason, when he does, it's too late. You put too much faith in individualism. The Italians were individualists, too, and Mussolini seized power. What they can steamroller here is nothing more or less than the Republic."

A silence followed. "By winning the elections?" asked another listener.

"Well, Spanish Fascism will not win them," replied the doctor. "But the Rights can win them if the republicans do not unite first. And if the Rights win this time—allow me to make a little prophecy in my role as foreign observer: before a year the Fascists will have imposed their will. All they need is to be sure of the collaboration of a few generals, which will be much easier than it seems, for, from what I have seen, in many places the Falangists are sons of the military."

Julio indicated that he was in agreement with the doctor. "You know what I think. But it is hard to get these ideas across to most people. Here, unless the bull is big, we don't take it seriously."

"There's only one defense," the doctor concluded. "Unite before they do. Form a bloc."

Someone objected that it was difficult to harmonize all the different tendencies, and that there were conflicting interests.

The doctor shrugged his shoulders. "Afterwards all that can be discussed. A foreigner sometimes sees things more clearly than those on the inside."

Someone asked: "It's easy to unite people in Germany, isn't it?"

"Easier than here," the doctor replied.

Julio added, smiling: "And those who do not want to unite are expelled, isn't that so, doctor?"

"How well I know!" said the archaeologist, getting to his feet.

SIXTY

MAJOR Martínez de Soria was nervous. His wife, who always seemed to be walking on carpet, went over to the window and as she drew the curtains said to him: "Go for a little ride. It will make you feel better."

The major was nervous because he believed that the army was the backbone of the country, and it so happened that he did not like either the present structure of the army or the hands guiding the country. At the time of the *straperlo* scandal he had said, with an oath: "It is absolutely grotesque to have to serve a government of thieves!" As for the army, everything led him to believe that the debacles of Cuba and Africa would be repeated, if the occasion arose, for many of the army leaders seemed bent on turning Spain into a colony of some other country.

His wife tried to soothe him. "Be calm. Don't precipitate matters." Her words had a double sense. What she meant to say was: "Do what you have to do. But make sure of success." The major looked at his wife, took her hand, and gave her a kiss. It heartened him to know that she understood him. The he tweaked Marta's bangs and shut himself up in his office or went to the barracks library, where he followed operations in Abyssinia step by step—it was his opinion that the Spanish infantry, with half the materiel, would have advanced much more rapidly—and read everything having to do with the electoral campaign, which was at its height.

Marta admired her father for his patriotism. Every third word on the major's lips was Spain. As he looked at the map of Abyssinia, he regretted the absence of a government that would organize a similar enterprise in Africa or somewhere. Marta said to him with a smile: "From that to the idea of daybreak is only a step."

The major roared: "Don't use those idiotic words!" Although his grief over the martyr of the family was unassuaged, he still fulminated against the Falangists.

He shuddered when he thought of the elections. He was one of those who were convinced that the Leftists would unite, and that if they won, great disasters lay in store. All those whom he had sentenced for their share in the events of October would be converted into heroes; he would be coming face to face with Joaquín Santaló's coffin every time he turned around, and probably with his own before too long.

All these reflections had renewed the bond between him and Warning Voice in their conversations in the café. The same thing happened again and again. He would come to the conclusion that the dentist was a sycophant and unfair toward the lower classes; but after avoiding him for a time, he would have to resume the association.

The major's wife was a supremely tactful person. She possessed the art of advising her husband without his being aware of it. She did not say the name of Spain at every other word, but it was the object of one out of three of her thoughts, the other two being her husband and her children.

She never spoke of Fernando. He had died, his course was run. He was a lamp that burned in her heart. José Luis went on studying in Valladolid, and pasting up posters. When he returned from his brother's burial, he went to the very spot where Fernando had fallen and wrote: "VIVA." As for Marta, she was her mother's immediate comfort, her consolation, but also her immediate problem; even more immediate than the one arising from the major's plans.

Marta's mother was worried about her daughter's association with the Alvears. On the whole, she liked the family. The Alvears had one essential virtue: they were not Catalans. The major's wife would never be able to understand the Catalans. To her they seemed unpatriotic, materialistic, and blasphemous. Whereas she had heard that Matías was a foursquare man, Spanish through and through, very witty, and a consummate angler; she could bestow no higher praise on Carmen Elgazu than to say she was Basque; and she found Pilar enchanting. She loved her naturalness, her gaiety of spirit. She was always saying to Marta: "You couldn't have found a nicer friend." The member of the Alvear family who worried her was Ignacio.

The major's lady felt that it would be no great effort for her to give up the idea of a count or duke for a son-in-law, which had filled her dreams when Marta was born. A lawyer—preferably a first-class lawyer—would suit her very well, but not one who belonged to the UGT. A lawyer of the UGT would be as out of place in her home as the red star in Don Jorge's office. She knew that Marta was not easily influenced, and she often said of her that her bangs were a curtain she put between what she was thinking and what others were thinking; nevertheless, once love entered the dance, everything changed. "In religious matters, it is the man who gives in; in politics and social ideas, it's the woman." And if Marta refused to yield, the marriage would be a failure.

Marta's mother's misgivings stemmed from several sources. First, her personal opinion. She had seen Ignacio in the street, and he had seemed to her a well-bred boy, intelligent-looking, bubbling over with youth—but not wearing a uniform. As she looked at him, she realized what this meant to her: at Ignacio's age Major Martínez de Soria already had his first bars. Then there was the uneasiness she felt over some of the things Marta told about him. For example, his criticism of her love of riding. He had said that when he saw her return on horseback from the Dehesa, her head at the level of the balconies, and followed by an orderly, she seemed to him as remote as a Moorish princess. "How is it possible for him to say such a thing, when in those countries he considers models it is the normal thing for women to ride horseback?" And, finally, Mosén Alberto's report on the lad had frightened her. When she asked Mosén Alberto his opinion, he had tossed his cape over his arm, and replied: "To be frank with you, Ignacio is the sour note in the family."

The priest's opinion put Marta's mother on guard. To her, family unity was of vital importance. She knew that the man who married Marta would form a part of the heart and the life of Major Martínez de Soria, and to a certain extent would have to share his fate or there would be grave trouble. The present circumstances of the country would not permit of two men of conflicting ideologies sharing the same roof. Moreover, in her opinion what Spain needed was very clear: an iron hand to extinguish the volcano and point each Spaniard to his place. God protect us from the democrats, those who felt they had a right to threaten Italian consuls!

Fortunately for Ignacio, he had a friend in court—and a good one—at the major's house: Pilar. She adored her brother, and she said everything good there was to say about him, embellished with certain inventions of her own. She provided a kind of counterbalance, especially where the major was concerned. The major loved the girl dearly. No matter what she said, he found it amusing. When Marta's mother heard Pilar talking about Ignacio, she smiled indulgently; on the other hand, the major hunched his shoulder and conceded with a smile: "All right, all right. I am convinced that Ignacio is wonderful." At times he added: "Much better than that crackpot you have taken up with."

Deep down, the major was jealous of that crackpot, Mateo. The man found Pilar delightful. He liked to look at her, make her blush, take her chin in his hand. As a rule he paid her compliments, teased her; but at times he liked to hear her opinion about serious problems he had on his mind. He always said that Pilar was much smarter than she seemed. "That's enough of your brother. Now you listen to me. What is your opinion of Dr. Relken?"

One day when the war communiques had been especially exciting, he asked her what she thought about the Italo-Abyssinian conflict.

"Me?"

"Yes, you. What do you think?"

Pilar looked thoughtful. "Well—if it had been the English who attacked them, everyone would think it was fine."

The major let out a roar of laughter. It leaped to the eye that Pilar had not thought that one up herself. He became even more convinced that she was an exceptional person.

"That's the pity of it," he remarked to his wife that night. "I think Ignacio is a fine match for Marta, but Mateo will make a doormat of Pilar. That imbecile will talk to her about nothing but Gibraltar, and he won't remember to tell her how becoming her new coat is."

And Pilar returned the major's affection. She often talked about him at home, saying that he was much more modest and unassuming than people thought. Among other reasons, she liked him because he would mix her a cocktail, on the sly, just like those the Hollywood stars drank. The one thing she could not forgive him was that he was always sniping at Mateo. "Thank Heaven he likes Ignacio."

One day she added, as she was talking to Matías Alvear: "At least, he hasn't declared war on both the boys, like Mosén Alberto."

"Both the boys?"

"Yes, sir, both of them."

"Let's see if we can get this straight."

"It's very simple. Here all Mosén talks about is German paganism, and this, that, and the other. At Marta's he advises them to throw Ignacio down the stairs."

"For God's sake!" Matías Alvear saw red. He had his own opinion of Mateo, but he did not want anyone else meddling in the matter. The first chance he had, he tilted his chair back and said to Mosén Alberto, half-joking, half in earnest: "Mosén, do you dislike the idea of Carmen Elgazu and me becoming grandparents some day?"

SUDDENLY cracks began to seam the Alvears' happiness. And it was Mateo who was to blame. Someone had told them: "The Falangists are volunteering for Abyssinia."

The family was astounded. They did not really believe it, but the meal was a silent one, and everyone was waiting for Mateo to arrive to question him, face to face and without any beating about the bush.

When Mateo arrived that evening he noticed something in the air. And when Matías formulated the question, he answered, without hedging: "It's true, there has been talk of it. In Madrid, León, and Seville they wanted to form a phalanx to be assigned to a company of Black Shirts; but it was finally decided that Spain needs us now. So the idea was given up."

Pilar asked: "But—would you have enlisted?"

"Of course," the boy answered.

Pilar was speechless. She got up from her chair, went into her room, and threw herself on the bed in utter despair. As for Matías Alvear, he felt a wave of indignation flooding his breast. He, too, got up and crossed the dining room. When he reached the door he turned back and said, rolling a cigarette: "We'll talk this matter over further."

The second crack in the happiness was caused by Ignacio. Ignacio was in a bad humor again.

It was Pilar's opinion that it was because of the Abyssinian war. At Marta's house she told them: "In my family, Papa is on the side of the Negroes. You can tell because he listens to the radio. Mamma feels terribly sorry for them, but the Pope's blessing has left her all confused. But the most fanatical is Ignacio, naturally. He calls the Italians aggressors, and says that after Abyssinia they'll want more and then more, and something about Somaliland. And that it's all because of too high a birth rate. And he's all hot and bothered again about politics."

That day, when, after Mateo's blunt declaration, Carmen Elgazu had followed Pilar to her room, Ignacio tilted his chair against the wall and said to the Falangist: "So the reason you're not going off to Abyssinia is because Spain needs you."

Mateo looked him steadily in the eye and answered: "That's it."

Ignacio nodded his head. "Firing a few shots wouldn't bother you at all?"

"Well, it might bother me. Sure it would!" Mateo went on. "But I'd do it."

Ignacio did not pursue the subject further, following the example of Matías Alvear. He picked up his law books from the table; Mateo got up and did the same. He did not know whether to knock at Pilar's door or not. He finally decided not to, and the two boys set out for their class with Professor Civil.

Once they were in the street, Mateo strode along firmly; his steps seemed to keep time to a military rhythm. Ignacio, on the contrary, walked thoughtfully and hesitantly, with uneven motion.

Two petitioners passed: "For the widow of Joaquín Santaló." In the balconies many flags, including that of Cosme Vila, were at half-mast. Santi brushed past them, on his big feet. He was carrying an envelope.

The fact was that for the last few weeks the excitement of the city had aroused a strange unrest in Ignacio; now Mateo's rhythmic steps seemed to be pounding in his brain.

Mateo was holding forth as he walked beside him: "Oh, I can see that this has made a bad effect. We are nothing but a gang of assassins. Volunteers for the war to kill Negroes! Horrible! As though anything great in this world had ever been accomplished without the use of force."

"For the widow of Joaquín Santaló, for the widow of Joaquin Santaló!" Santi ran by again, this time without the envelope, past the unemployed sitting on the curb in front of the Café Cataluña.

"Other nations have occupied half the world, but Italy can starve. A Latin nation—what difference does it make? Lo, the peaceful and civilized Ethiopians! Did you know that many of them are still cannibals? It would be fun if Léon Blum and Azaña and a few more of their champions were to land over there, in the interior. They would roast them with special care to show their gratitude for their speeches. To be sure, to be sure, peaceful nations must be protected. The BBC says so and we believe it. What is at stake is the lifeline of the English Empire, and we'd be capable of defending it with the gold reserves of the Bank of Spain."

Ignacio did not answer him. He had turned up the lapels of his overcoat and held his law books pressed to his side.

They reached Professor Civil's house. Ignacio was deeply troubled. Where had Santi been going with that envelope? Perhaps to some other aquarium. He was not alone in his cruelty, which had finally come to light. Other boys his age were growing up with similar tendencies. Something deep was giving way in people. On Professor Civil's desk lay a copy of *El Tradicionalista.*

Ignacio had acquired more experience, and he no longer saw only one face of the coin as before. He tried to be fair. His distress arose from the fact that he saw the lack of balance not only in Mateo, but wherever he turned his eyes. He was just as troubled by the fact that Mateo did not for a moment take Pilar into consideration in his decision to go off to Abyssinia as by the fact that David's and Olga's rationalistic pedagogy was responsible for Santi. On the other hand, the pedagogy of the Marist Fathers was responsible for Mateo! And that of the Jesuits for Warning Voice.

It seemed to Ignacio that he himself partook of this duality, that he was in part Santi and in part Warning Voice. Otherwise, how was it possible to explain that the argument that the Ethiopians were still cannibals left him cold, whereas it made him see red to hear Dr. Relken in the Neutral poking fun at the religious fanaticism of the Spanish women?

It was clear that the dividing line was being laid down in him. On one side the Alvear inheritance, on the other the Elgazu. The Seminary, perhaps, and the UGT.

Kum, kum. In the matter of faith, he had arisen. Ever since the beginning of the year. He did not doubt God, but it disconcerted him to know that the Pope had blessed the tanks. He did not doubt in social matters, either: maternity clinics, education, work, and burial had to be guaranteed to everyone. And, above all, freedom; but it aroused his indignation that in the name of these principles Future should display a skull, and Teo should crack his carter's whip as he pleased.

Perhaps his least clearly defined attitude was that of Country. It seemed to him that he had already thought of a number of the things Dr. Relken laid at Spain's door, and had even thrown them in Mateo's teeth in the course of their arguments; but it enraged him to hear a foreigner say them. To such a degree that at moments he even justified Mateo. How humiliating that a group of Spaniards should gather at the Neutral to listen complacently to the man vivisecting bullfighting, the wearing of mantillas, the state of the highways, and the opposition to the Reformation! Bullfighting was cruel, but brave and more artistic than cockfighting. A mantilla was far more attractive than the pith helmet Dr. Relken wore at Montjuich. If the highways were poor, at least they led somewhere, and the Counter-Reformation had halted spiritual fragmentation. To hell with those speeches of his! It was all right for someone to come from Prague to explain what a democracy should be; but that same someone should mind his own business with regard to what Spanish mothers wore on their heads.

And yet it was clear that the Alvear inheritance, and David and Olga, and even Dr. Relken himself were right on many counts. That was Ignacio's drama, and for that reason the phrase Carmen Elgazu used when she wrote to Bilbao was too simple: "Ignacio has become himself once more." To be content to be silent, to pay attention and all the rest, seeking individual peace of soul when the city where one lived was girding itself for a struggle to the death, were acts of incalculable selfishness. Spain was poor, the land grudging, the standard of living low. Spain had contributed nothing to pure science, to systems of philosophy, to mechanics. Not even Professor Civil would deny that. If there had been a time when it had produced geniuses in other fields, that day had long since passed. Spain did not even produce inventors. Anything new and revolutionary, whether in medicine, astronomy, or any other field, came from other countries, not Spain. What had gone wrong? The contention of David and Olga, Casal, and so many others, that the Spanish genius had been locked in the sepulcher of the Cid seemed inescapable, and for that reason all the panaceas put forward by Gil Robles or José Antonio would perish in that same sepulcher.

But, on the other hand, when he thought of Marta, for instance, of her Castilian profile, her nobility, and her austerity, the land of the Cid seemed so vital, so lovable!

Moreover, might it not be that each nation had its mission to fulfill, and that Spain might carry out its own, not constructing philosophical systems in books, but guarding in the collective consciousness, as in a ciborium, something of perhaps greater worth, and certainly more enduring: religious faith and unity? Besides, would it be possible, or even desirable, for a Goya to appear every five years? Wasn't it enough that Spain should have produced him once? And the music, and the songs, and dances, and the majesty of the landscape, and that sky? The only thing that interested Carmen Elgazu was the salvation of her soul and those souls which had been entrusted to her care. Possibly this basic thought lay at the bottom of the indifference of the race toward science and thoughts that perished. Possibly Spain did not want to "specialize" because she thirsted for things eternal, for something all-embracing. Otherwise how was it possible to understand why David and Olga, instead of confining themselves to teaching their thirty pupils, should endeavor to penetrate to the very fiber of their being, to exercise an all-pervading influence over their potential as persons?

It was an obsession with the transcendent. Ignacio recalled that a simple doorman at the Labor Office was exercised over whether the King of Italy was a Mason or not. For that reason he, Ignacio, in the Seminary not only had wanted to study Latin, ethics, rhetoric, and theology, but had wanted to hear about human poverty and receive infallible prescriptions for saving the world. For that reason Miguel Rosselló had complained that college textbooks were superficial. He wanted to know not only the prehistory of every country, but its future. Perhaps because of this aspiration to totality, the *Espasa Encyclopedia* had over eighty volumes, *Don Quixote* was a compendium of human sentiments and aspirations, and St. Francis Xavier had reached Japan, on the other side of the world, before anyone else.

But what calamities this type of mentality engendered for the business of daily living! Things lost all proportion and restraint. Men like Mateo, who believed in the eternal values of Spain, came to dream of hunting down Ethiopians; while others, who clamored that Spain should retrace her steps and "Europeanize" herself, managed only to demoralize the country and create an inferiority complex.

In this connection Ignacio recalled the unanimity of opinion on the part of the Spanish intellectuals of the preceding epoch—Giner de los Ríos, Ganivet, Joaquín Costa, and others—and those of the present, Ramón y Cajal, and so on—with regard to Spain. They were all in agreement with David and Olga, and, virtually, with Dr. Relken. "The backwardness exists, and it is due to the closing of the Pyrenees. The air has not circulated between Spain and Europe." Unamuno alone, the one who had spoken of the human snails, represented the opposition, assuring his listeners that people on the other side of the Pyrenees were even less happy.

The destructive work of the first group distressed Ignacio, but Unamuno's defiance—"Let them do the inventing"—seemed to him ridiculous. Was it really impossible to harmonize the preservation of religious faith with the importation of the tractors that were needed? "Let them do the inventing!" But in Spain there were 700,000 people without work, and unrest, and a bitter, fratricidal social conflict.

Ignacio talked in this vein at Professor Civil's house that day, and the professor thought to himself: "The two Spains face to face. The Spain of Unamuno, Carmen Elgazu, Major Martínez de Soria, the secret emotion of this boy as he looks at the map of Iberia and hears pure Castilian; and the Spain of Julio García, David and Olga, Giner de los Ríos, Ramón y Cajal, and El Responsable, the secret rebellion of Ignacio as he listens to Mosén Alberto or sees Warning Voice." The family of Bilbao and that of Madrid and Burgos. It was evident that such contrasts were as harsh and varied as the contrasts in the country's geology. Those who hung pictures of Philip II and the Escorial in their office, like Major Martínez de Soria, were supporters of Mussolini and gave fencing lessons; those who sympathized with the Negus—Tower of Babel—had a picture of Gandhi in their room, and a view of Versailles. But if Tower of Babel, a peaceful person, donated blood at the hospital, he also went to the Calle de la Barca to find out from exactly which floor Pedro's father had fallen to the street, and he listened to Dr. Relken as though he was an oracle. And if Major Martínez de Soria, a bellicose man, sentenced Joaquín Santaló to death and kept Olga standing during a four-hour questioning, he would lay down his life for Spain without hesitation, and he raised the tone of a street by simply walking through it.

For his part, Ignacio was thinking that there must be a trace of opportunism in Mosén Francisco's advice. For there was nothing harmonious about all this, and yet it was by paying careful attention that he had discovered this fact. A complicated life, a complicated war with Abyssinia, complicated elections.

SIXTY-ONE

WHEN the assistant manager read in *El Tradicionalista* that the new commander of the garrison, General Carlos Zurita Belaustegui, had arrived to assume his duties, he remarked: "The battle is on."

Clean barracks, better rations, passes. The general was so short that without his uniform and the force of his watery eyes, continually darting back and forth, nobody would have noticed him. But the uniform gave him solidity, and his eyes brought his staff to instant attention. He arrived with his wife and three daughters, and their quarters were a huge old house near the infantry barracks. The terrace looked out on the patio of the Seminary.

Colonel Muñoz and Major Campos were waiting to receive the general. Three days later, in the Calle del Pavo, he was also received by the Commissioner, Dr. Rosselló, the architects Massana and Ribas, Julio, Casal the linotypist, and the others. The notice that had been sent out to all the brothers read: "Very important meeting."

After signing the roster in the atrium, each brother took his place in the workroom. Colonel Muñoz presided, for in the Lodge the general's rank was lower than his. The general greeted the new brothers. He expressed himself in brusque language, interspersed with startling interjections. He was welcomed, and the work began.

It was a long, tiresome work, all facts and data. The general had to be brought up to date. One by one the topics were dully ticked off except for the last: the union of all the forces of the Left, from Izquierda Republicana to the FAI. A united front had to be drawn up, the Popular Front.

Julio was deeply disappointed. He had always imagined that the general would be carrying in his sash the order for his reinstatement as Chief of Police. Julio felt an urgent need to get back to his office once more. He had been suspended for more than a year. Doña Amparo Campo could not understand it: "They've probably dropped you to the bottom of the list." At times Julio felt contempt for his wife because, ambitious though she was, she pinned her hopes on the regular channels of promotion.

"Are you short of money? Do you want for anything? No? Well, then don't annoy me."

Colonel Muñoz said to Julio: "For the moment this doesn't strike me as being important. The thing that matters is to win the elections."

All during the Work session one man kept moving his fingers nervously in his white gloves: Casal the linotypist. In the first place, he never felt at home in the Lodge, even though he knew that one of the knots in the black frieze stood for him, even though the eye of the triangle regarded him, too, and even though he knew as well as anyone else that JAKIN meant fecundating principle, BOAZ, fecundated principle. But doctors, architects, bank directors, colonels, and now a general! Besides, at times he had doubts of its utility. The Commissioner had never paid any attention to him, and yet he protected El Responsable. And above all, the lodge rooms seemed to him too severe and chill. There were times when he felt that they were bound to come out on the losing side in a city where the Cathedral towered so majestically, where the walls stood like eternal witnesses. He found it hard to persuade himself that people with posts of such authority could possibly be democrats. Once a general, always a general! He suddenly heard the latter's voice addressing him: "With regard to the Socialist Party, there'll be no obstacle in the way of union. At least, I hope not."

Casal the linotypist felt as though the cotton in his ear was working its way into his brain. He had known for a long time that the order the general's words implied was bound to come, but he still felt as though the cotton was getting into his brain. His wife had always said to him: "I think you will have to obey them. They are your superiors, and they know what is needed." He had held out, for he knew his party members and he had his own ideas; but perhaps his wife was right. Possibly his point of view was too local, too circumscribed, failing to take into account the fact that Socialism is international. Probably they were right, and the union of all the parties of the Left was absolutely indispensable.

Yet how could he defend a cause he did not feel? And how could he convince the members? The linotypist considered feasible a coalition with Cosme Vila, for as the latter's program was utopian, it would collapse of its own accord at its first contact with reality; but a coalition with Izquierda Republicana would be suicidal. Izquierda Republicana was a bourgeois party made up of people no different from Noguer the notary, and the worst of it was that they did not realize it. Socialism's worst enemy was Izquierda Republicana. Casal expounded his point of view and ended by saying: "At any rate, terms would have to be agreed upon once we have won."

Colonel Muñoz declared the meeting adjourned. "I have no doubt Brother Casal will act along the lines indicated," he said.

On the way home Julio García remarked to the linotypist that the shrewd thing would be to pretend that Izquierda Republicana was laying down the terms. "There is beyond doubt a good share of the middle class that is frightened by the disorders. I think the Popular Front should play up a platform of moderation. Otherwise the elections would go against us. In fact, I think we really must be moderate. I have given it much thought, and I firmly believe it."

The linotypist's hair was damp with perspiration when he got to his house. He looked around his bookshelves and said to himself: "I don't know whether I've read too much or too little." Antonio Casal loved his wife and children passionately. The day when, as a child, he had seen his father sprinkle bread crumbs on the windowsill to lure pigeons from the square and then grab one of them, and a few minutes later had heard the sputtering of fat in the frying-pan, he had realized that poverty had to be done away with or there would be no more pigeons. From then on he was a Socialist. He wanted to make sure of maternity homes and decent burial even for the pigeons. The enemies, in his opinion, were superstition, ignorance, backwardness, and the concentration of capital in private hands. For that reason he had joined the Masons, because Freemasonry was fighting those very things, because it believed in Culture, Progress, Brotherhood. That night, after tiptoeing into the room where his three children were sleeping, and looking at them for a moment in silence, he went into the dining room, where his wife sat sewing close beside the brazier, and said to her: "Well, everything's set. Before long you'll see me arm in arm with the Costas."

"You must do as they say. They outnumber you, and they know better than you what has to be done." Fine—agreed. But how to go about convincing David and Olga, Tower of Babel, and, above all, the dozens of rank-and-file members who were just waiting for their hour to come?

The linotypist was so worried that he could think of only one thing: to talk the matter over with Cosme Vila. It happened to be the day of San Narciso, the patron of the city, and all Gerona was ablaze with lights. Casal walked past the Blouse of Fear, the snake charmer's, the doughnut stands, thinking: "In this country reasons to grant a truce can always be found." A huge crowd was pouring out of the bullfight, another from the football stadium, another was coming down the steps of San Félix after visiting the sepulcher of the saint whose body was preserved uncorrupted, according to that morning's issue of *El Tradicionalista.* The first group had seen fresh blood on the sand, on the sword blade; this latter had seen the coagulated blood of San Narciso.

Casal found Cosme Vila contemplating his son, who as yet neither walked nor said Papa or Mamma or Stalin. The dining room was small, and in the middle of it Cosme Vila's mongoloid head looked like a huge light bulb. The flat overhung the river, like the Alvears', but no fishing rod had ever come through its dining room window. The place was damp and depressing. One of the chairs was occupied by Cosme Vila's wife, who looked upon him as a god, a god whom all the world would soon acclaim—perhaps after the elections—who would divide land and money among all those in the province who had never had any. The other two chairs were occupied by Cosme Vila's parents-in-law, the grade-crossing watchman and his wife. The father-in-law was a tall, timid man, who without the signal flag did not know what to do with his hands. The mother-in-law did not take her eyes off the baby.

"Hello, Casal. You don't look well."

"I'm all right. That doesn't matter."

"We have nothing to offer you."

"I don't need anything."

Cosme Vila sensed at once what had brought Casal. But he behaved with complete indifference. The only thing that interested him was to talk about his party, about Teo, Victor, Gorki, and Murillo, who was selling images to Dr. Relken. "I'm interested in my own people, you understand. I have to build from scratch. I have to convince all that crew that you can't be a Communist and make perfume. I've finally brought Teo around. He will go on driving his dray and cracking his whip at the horses, but the equipment all belongs to the party, as well as the profits. He will have enough to live on, and to buy himself a cap once in a while; but Gorki is playing dumb. I see you are getting impatient; I don't know why the devil you're always in such a hurry. Of course, you've come about something that interests you; but you already know my opinion. Communism is not in the least sentimental. You might as well understand that. What I'm interested in is Teo, Gorki, Victor, and Murillo. You people spend your time consulting one another, and meanwhile the fanatics keep forging ahead. What do you hope to accomplish without fanaticism? When I was at the Arús Bank I saw that those who made money were the fanatics, the ones who counted their dollars as though they were pearls. And from their point of view they were right. I have to fill the province with fanatics. I am already finding some, along the coast and in the hills. The day will come when we'll organize the march on Gerona. You'll get nowhere teaching arithmetic. The first thing to do is to convince them that it is a sacred subject, and then shoot the person who makes a mistake in addition. Now, personally, friend Casal, I have all the respect in the world for you. We have always got along well together, and my wife likes yours very much. But this matter of the elections, to be sincere with you, gives me a pain. It strikes me as being as ridiculous as to think my kid could pass an opinion on the purposes of the executive committee. So all your arguments are superfluous. We are tacticians, and that settles it. We will join up with anyone, everyone. We have to open a breach. We'll join up with the Costas, with you, and we'll accept the votes even of the anarchist bootblacks. But listen to me carefully: we're out for our own ends. I repeat, I have all respect for you personally."

Casal realized that he had annoyed Cosme Vila by coming to see him at his home. He had wanted to make it clear that there, or at headquarters, he was always the leader. It seemed to the linotypist that Vila was overdoing it, and this certainly did not make his task any easier. He knew with whom he was dealing. "All right, all right..." he stammered, and looked down at the child. And suddenly he felt pity for it. The child was trying to put its foot in its mouth. Casal had a feeling that history was going to be pitiless toward that handful of human flesh. Cosme Vila had enrolled him in the party without asking the child's opinion. It was evident that no one was ever going to ask his opinion. He would hold out his hand, first to one and then to another, to have his fingerprints taken; and if one day he refused to have this done, or made a mistake, a bullet would write finis to him.

Cosme Vila's wife's eyes were red. She was sewing, and her smile was like her father's. She asked Casal: "How's your wife?"

"Fine. Fine."

A silence followed. The linotypist was having a hard time. This was as bad as dealing with generals. "Have you people had dinner?"

"We don't eat dinner. We have just one meal a day."

Casal felt utterly disconcerted. He would talk with David and Olga. The teachers were really friends. Olga was the perfect treasurer. David and Olga would give him heart.

Cosme Vila asked him: "How did you like the cartoon we published in *El Proletario*? The one of Mussolini and the Pope."

"I didn't see it."

"You didn't see it? Don't you read *El Proletario*?"

"Well, to tell you the truth, no."

This seemed perfectly natural to Cosme Vila. "I don't blame you. Those are commonplaces."

Another silence. Then Cosme Vila said: "Did you know we have a woman on the executive committee?"

"No, I didn't."

"Gorki brought her. She's from Valencia. You would hardly believe the perspicacity a woman can show."

He paused. Casal leaned back against the wall. "I have Olga."

"That's different. Olga is a man. That is, she and David have created a neuter sex. A woman, to be a woman, has to have had children, like your wife or mine, or this one from Valencia, who has had five. I'm very pleased with her, though Teo can't take his eyes off her and I don't know what may happen."

"In what way do you think you are going to find her useful?"

"Well—there are moments when one shrinks, feels pity, or something. Then you look at this woman and you get over it."

"And are you moved by love or by hate?"

"By discipline."

Casal made an ironic gesture. "Do you believe man comes from the monkey?" he asked unexpectedly.

"Ah, that's a good question. I believe in evolution, in the blind evolution of nature."

"In evolution toward what?"

"I've already told you—blind evolution."

Casal added, after a pause: "And what conclusions do you deduce from the fact that your son wants to eat his foot?"

"That he has no awareness of the fact that his members belong to him, and that we are a bundle of instincts."

"The day he acquires this awareness, what will have happened?"

"You're just wasting your breath. You know my opinion: tears are water."

The tall, timid father-in-law was listening open-mouthed. He had a huge wart under his left ear. Cosme Vila had prophesied to him that a day would come when there would be electric watchmen at the grade crossings which would never make a mistake; then, by a further evolution, the grade crossings would be done away with. The trains would all run underground.

"But don't worry," Cosme Vila had said to his father-in-law, "you won't be left without a job."

Casal looked at Cosme Vila's wife, his child, and the watchman and his wife. In their way they constituted a model family. They were joined in an ideal. To the parents-in-law Communism was a romantic dream, starry, perfect. To Cosme Vila it was both an art and a science. To his wife it was a simple way of settling all the problems of the province, and for her to become the wife of an emperor; for the baby it would be an uninterrupted series of fingerprintings.

Cosme Vila took him to the door. Casal looked tired. As he helped him with his overcoat, Cosme Vila said to him: “Remember me to your wife.”

SIXTY-TWO

THE propaganda activities of both sides had turned the city into a battlefield. Political animosities and personal animosities joined hands. Anything went that would win a handful of votes, from the white lie to out-and-out calumny. And the timing made the whole situation especially painful, for Christmas was at hand.

All those who had been imprisoned because of the events of October of the previous year remembered that this was the first anniversary of their liberation. How much ground had been covered in a year! From having their political headquarters closed down, they had swung to a militant alignment of all available forces. Everybody recalled the great snow the year before, when Gerona had become one immense communion wafer. Now all the footprints would be stamped clearly in the snow, as though everyone were wearing army shoes. Dr. Relken's print would stand out among all the others, for he alone wore hobnail shoes.

It seemed to Don Santiago Estrada that the moment had come to distribute the mufflers and other winter garments that had been collected by the CEDA. A committee of ladies was appointed, one of whom was Laura, who ever since her return from her honeymoon had been the moving spirit in all the beneficent activities of the city. But the undertaking proved a dismal failure.

The people refused to accept anything. "What are you trying to do? Buy our votes? On your way. We don't need anything here."

"We don't need anything." This was the usual response. This and curses. Laura was aghast. The ladies could not understand how it was that the poor needed nothing, or why they, being rich, could not give anything. "If they were as cold as they say they are, they wouldn't be so touchy and would take what we offer them."

Nevertheless, the ladies decided to keep up their efforts until the New Year, for the winds from the Pyrenees were blowing colder and colder. They even decided to spend New Year's Eve visiting the homes of the poor, especially in the San Félix quarter, the only one to which they had not gone. This was the end of their pilgrimage. On one of their visits they had such a distressing experience that they completely gave up their apostolate.

The owner of the Crocodile Bar had said to them: "Over toward the Baños Arabes, Number 5, lives a woman so ragged and awful that it's a pity. She comes in here every day and I give her a glass of anisette to warm her up."

By the light of the street lamp they found Number 5 and knocked at the door. La Valenciana, Gorki's paramour, whom Cosme Vila had mentioned to Casal, opened the door. This feminine member of the executive committee of the Communist Party received the ladies with a smile and invited them in. But she no sooner had them in the room than she turned on them in a fierce rage. "So, the last day of the year—" Reaching over to Don Santiago Estrada's wife, she jerked off her glove. "You don't feel the cold with these on, do you?" And she threw the glove on the floor, rubbing her fingers against her skirt.

It was all so incredible that it made Laura cry when she recalled it. The woman, of an indeterminate age, with stout, heavy legs, ripped open her dress. "Five children, five children," she said, "by five men." Then she showed them newspaper clippings and photographs of herself in Valencia with clenched fist raised. She did not talk politics. Nothing but obscenity flowed from her mouth. It was New Year's Eve, and she had probably had a glass of anisette at every tavern. Gorki's name came vaguely into her ramblings, and she spat as she mentioned Teo.

The return of the Ladies' Auxiliary of the CEDA was painful. The streets were full of drunks singing: "Jesus was born in a manger." Don Santiago Estrada had prepared a collation for the ladies at headquarters, but none of them felt like eating. Warning Voice was waiting in his car for Laura, and they drove home in silence.

MOSÉN Francisco refused to be dismayed over the fact that all the news that reached his ears reeked of violence. He assembled the children of his catechism class and began his campaign. He drew a huge poster for the vestibule of the church: "Say the Blessed Rosary." He printed leaflets and pictures bearing the inscription: "Say the Blessed Rosary." He distributed the leaflets in the streets. He slipped them under the doors. "We face difficult times. We must appeal to love, not hate. Let all Christians say the Blessed Rosary." At the conclusion of Mass, he turned toward the faithful, folded his arms, and said to them: "In the name of God, we have had enough of fratricidal struggle. Let us say the Blessed Rosary. And every family add a Pater Noster for the peace of Spain."

Mosén Francisco was so carried away by his Christmas campaign that he proposed to the faithful that they should all say the rosary at the same hour. "At half past nine at night, when you hear the bells, gather about the stove and say the Blessed Rosary."

The first person to do as he said was a woman who had never had any confidence in the organized distribution of winter clothing. This was Carmen Elgazu—Carmen Elgazu, who adored Mosén Francisco. At the first chime of the bells she would say "Sh-sh-sh," and then, with the last stroke: "Now let's begin." She would cross herself, and Ignacio would begin the "Hail Mary, full of grace, the Lord is with thee." At this point Matías would get up. Neither before nor after Mosén Francisco's advice had Matías Alvear been able to say the rosary sitting down. He had to do it walking about. He would go from the dining room to the front door and back again. Ignacio as a rule imitated him, taking the opposite direction, and the two of them would pass each other in the middle of the hall. Carmen Elgazu complained that she could not hear them from the dining room. If Pilar dozed off, her mother would tap her on the knees with the scissors or the lid-lifter.

Another home in which the priest's injunction was carried out was that of Major Martínez de Soria. "It's time for the rosary." Marta led, and the major, too, walked up and down. At times his wanderings led him much farther than those of Matías Alvear and Ignacio, sometimes to the far end of the apartment, to his office, for example, where he occasionally became so engrossed in the map of Abyssinia that he did not return to the dining room until the set of mysteries they were saying was over. His wife prayed with eyes downcast, the silver beads slipping over her immaculate black skirt. Marta from time to time pushed aside her bangs and sighed. When she began the Pater Noster for the peace of Spain, the major would stop for a moment, looking up at the ceiling. Then he would raise his left shoulder, feeling a struggle going on in his heart.

Dozens of families followed Mosén Francisco's advice as the lights of Christmas fell livid in the river. The figure of the young priest seemed to hover about the stoves like a beneficent shade calming the spirits that were waiting for February 16. They said the rosary in Don Pedro Oriol's silent home and at Noguer the notary's, the litanies translated into Catalan. At Don Jorge's house the two maids took part in the family prayers, seated on stools beside the kitchen door.

The rosary was said at the assistant manager's flat, in that of the doorman of the Labor Office, in that of the Alvears' cleaning woman.

The priest had particularly recommended this prayer because it seemed to him that it comprehended better than any other all the elements of human existence. Especially the Mysteries. First the Joyful Mysteries, symbolizing the pleasure man receives from the birth of another man. The priest had baptized dozens of children, and had always noted the same smile on the parents' faces. Then the Sorrowful Mysteries, symbolizing the earthly struggle crowned by death. Mosén Francisco had been present at dozens of burials, and had always heard the same weeping. Finally the Glorious Mysteries, symbol of the resurrection and heaven.

In the priest's opinion, everything was contained in it. "The day that all Spain says the rosary, the Pater Noster for peace will be unnecessary."

But when would this be? Of the two hundred and fifty jobless, only ten or twelve had followed Mosén Francisco's advice. The others were putting up posters, some of them designed by the architects Massana and Ribas at the table next to that used by their first draftsman, Benito Civil.

SIXTY-THREE

ON January 15, when Matías read the proclamation officially announcing the constitution of the Popular Front, and saw that there was nothing in the program that did not sound fair and reasonable, he remarked: "It begins to look as though common sense has finally won out. Let's see if Azaña can save the Republic this time."

His satisfaction would have been complete except that Mateo's behavior still troubled him. The boy not only had made no apologies for his stand on Abyssinia, but had persisted in his attitude, especially when he saw that Pilar had come around. There was the weak link. After she had had her cry out and had talked things over with Marta, she made an about-face and announced that Mateo would have been a hero if he had gone off to the war.

Because Matías Alvear believed that young people would always return to the fold if they had had a good upbringing, he could not make up his mind to break things off between Pilar and Mateo. And he felt sure that this would be the case with Mateo, for it was impossible to forget that he was the son of Don Emilio Santos, a gentleman if there ever was one, and the first to deplore his son's violence. So he let Pilar continue to go out with him, trusting also that the victory of the Popular Front at the polls would settle Falange once and for all.

As for Mateo, he was living uneasy days. His prophecy had come true. The Leftists had united. The Popular Front was a reality. And meanwhile the Rightists were sending up balloons and boasting in the Casino of their coming triumph.

He had still another worry. He was not completely satisfied with his fellow Falangists. He regretted having admitted Don Jorge's son. The boy went around whey-faced over his father's threat that if he did not tear up his membership card within two months at the outside, he would disinherit him. On the other hand, Miguel Rosselló was likely to pull off some crazy stunt at any moment. He was in such a state of frenzy and indignation over what he considered the country's lack of awareness that he was always wanting to do something about it. He was living in a boarding house, and loneliness was playing hob with his nerves.

Mateo would have liked to enlarge his group, organize it more quickly, and not find himself all the time in the position of having to explain everything, justify everything.

"Why is it that in some provinces we are putting up a candidate, if Falange does not believe in parties, either of the Right or the Left?"

"Because until better days we have to have a forum where we can make ourselves heard. And there's no better place for that than Parliament."

But in spite of everything, Ignacio was absolutely convinced that Mateo knew where he was going and that nothing could make him turn back. "He's waiting for orders from Madrid. As soon as he gets them he is capable of putting Rosselló's plans in practice, all at once."

Not for one minute did Ignacio stop thinking about the elections. And he felt, like the rest of the employees of the bank, that the outcome could not be predicted. Nearly everyone felt the same way. And what made the doubt so serious a matter was the fact that everybody knew that this was not just an ordinary election. "This election will decide Spain's next hundred years."

"Spain's, and maybe Europe's." This was Professor Civil's dictum. Professor Civil believed that in the two Spains which Ignacio bore within himself, and which would meet at the polls on February 16, lay the seeds of the coming struggle in the whole world. He still believed that the structure of democracy was tottering everywhere, in part as a result of natural wear and tear, and in part because it had fallen into the hands of Jewish leaders; but unfortunately the forces opposed to it might be even worse.

"And why do you think that in Spain we are anticipating the struggle?" Ignacio asked.

"Because there is greater fanaticism here than anywhere else. Ideas instantly acquire body and soul here."

Dr. Relken seemed to share the professor's views. He spent his days at the Neutral extolling the epic quality of that struggle. The day the proclamation of the Popular Front was published he remarked: "You people are magnificent. On Twelfth Night I saw you out with your children. They were asking for dolls, erector sets, bicycles. Later on they will ask for the head of their adversary. No, I'm not saying this as a reproach. Quite the contrary. You act at the bidding of racial instinct, and there are contradictory emotions in your race. For that reason the struggle here is always on a grand scale. Each one of you defends tooth and claw the things he believes in." After a moment he added: "It's a pity that sometimes you get too obfuscated."

"What have you in mind?"

The doctor set his glass on the table. "You have a proverb that I think fits the situation neatly. You say: the one who doesn't run, flies."

"So—?"

Julio explained that Dr. Relken must be referring to Major Martínez de Soria, who had just left for Rome.

Everyone looked perplexed. The doctor took off his glasses and nodded his head: "That's it."

"He's showing the white feather."

"What's he so scared about?"

"It's strange that he should have left his family here."

At this point Julio shook his head: "Oh, no, he's coming back. This is a round trip. He went with several generals and Goicoechea."

A number wondered if he had gone to see the Pope. The doctor shook his head. "No indeed. They asked Mussolini for an audience, and he granted it."

There was a general stir. One of those most affected by the news was Matías Alvear. On his way home he kept thinking what a boil on the neck Mateo and his sort were turning out to be.

Ignacio was particularly indignant because Marta had not told him a word about the matter. "Why didn't you tell me anything about it?" he asked her that night.

"So you wouldn't put your own interpretation on it."

"It seems to me there is only one way to interpret it."

"You are mistaken."

Mateo, at any rate, interpreted it joyfully. So joyfully that he took Pilar to the movies. He needed to let himself go. At last a light in the distance! He did not have much confidence in the men who could bring off the coup; they were acting in self-defense rather than out of any deep-seated desire to renew their country. Nevertheless, perhaps Falange could demand an outstanding post and channel events.

"That would be the worst thing that could happen to you," said Professor Civil. "There is nothing more dangerous for a political party than to come to power while its inner structure is still incomplete."

The comments at the Neutral continued. Meanwhile Major Martínez de Soria, unaware of the conjectures to which his trip had given rise, returned. Several persons observed that on the return trip he was wearing civilian clothes.

He returned three days before elections and was as silent as the tomb, to the despair of many. Not a word did he say at the officers' café, or even to Marta; he spoke only to his wife and Lieutenant Martín. His wife asked him: "What's the matter?" and he answered: "Things are going badly. On the 16th they will destroy the ballot boxes like a charge of Cossack cavalry."

PART IV

February 16, 1936 to July 18, 1936

SIXTY-FOUR

AROUND midmorning the assistant manager called at Don Santiago Estrada's house and said to him: "Everything seems to be going all right in the province, but there's a real tussle here."

The head of the CEDA got to his feet and said: "How do you mean a real tussle?"

The assistant manager explained to him that, as they had planned, the young men of the CEDA had gone out to protect their voters, standing guard at the polling booths, but that suddenly squads of Communists and anarchists had appeared and were lined up along the sidewalks with an expression that boded no good. Teo, in particular, was leading a group of about a dozen men his size, and when they had dispersed one line, they went to another.

Don Santiago Estrada had trouble understanding. "But are they beating anybody up?"

"The dispensaries are full."

"Of our people?"

"Nuns and such. You ought to go and see for yourself."

Don Santiago's wife was terrified. "For heaven's sake, be careful!" she said to her husband as he put on his overcoat. When he got to the street, Don Santiago realized that nothing was going to be easy, and that the calm of the past days had been completely misleading, perhaps planned that way. And the inroads of Teo on the one hand and Future on the other were not the worst that was happening. The worst was the sudden frenzy that seemed to have seized the militant Socialists. David and Olga and dozens of their fellow members were posted along the streets leading to the voting booths, and at the drop of a hat they considered that they had been insulted and hurled vituperation and threats at the voters.

"There by the Cathedral, Olga grabbed by the hair a woman who had her ballot in one hand and her mantilla in the other and made her go back."

Don Santiago thought this must be exaggerated. It could not be. The Popular Front had been stuck together so artificially, and there had been nothing to forecast this joint action.

When he reached the polls in the Rambla he received a disheartening impression. His young men, wearing a CEDA armband, were pacing back and forth under the arcade like caged animals, without venturing to approach the line of voters. Many railroad workers were sitting on the ground with newspapers in their hands. He saw Roselló—with five arrows on his shirt—taking away a wounded person with the help of a policeman. Julio García was arguing with some stranger wearing a hat and carrying a cane. Against the wall above the policeman's head was a huge poster with the picture of Joaquín Santaló.

The Rambla was swamped with portraits of the dead man. The posters carried around were signed "Paco."

Farther off, toward the barracks, many of the balconies were draped with Catalan flags, as was Raimundo's whole barbershop. Many members of Izquierda Republicana were wearing buttons in their lapel reading: "Long live Free Catalonia!" "For the freedom of Catalonia!" "The Catalan people will avenge their October martyrs!"

Some of the polling places were orderly; at others there were shouts of. "Long live Russia!" Don Emilio Santos had managed to get to the polls without interference. Matías Alvear had been among the first to vote, at eight that morning, while the Rambla was practically deserted.

Don Santiago Estrada set out for the polls of his district, cast his ballot, and then went to party headquarters. "How are things going in the villages?" he asked.

The reports from the villages were more encouraging. Someone spoke up: "The one who is winning the fight here is that kid from the CNT, Santi."

The assistant manager nodded his head. He had seen Santi in action, wearing his customary pointed shoes. The minute he saw a priest—Mosén Alberto knew something of this—he sneaked up from behind and gave him a kick in the shin.

The morning wore on. From time to time a truck came by carrying a load of unknowns shouting: "Long live the Popular Front!" The members of Izquierda Republicana had set out in a bloc, taking up a strategic position. They did not insult anyone. They smoked and scraped the soles of their shoes on the edge of the sidewalk as they watched their allies put into practice the theory of direct action. Whole families were moving quickly, holding hands. The rooftops were black with watchers. From that height the street encounters resembled skirmishes among insects. Occasionally a little blood was shed on the stones, giving rise to great agitation.

The person most astonished at what was happening was Don Santiago Estrada. The person most cognizant of what was happening, Cosme Vila. The most curious, Dr. Relken.

Olga, without knowing why, had lost control of herself. She was patrolling the city, up and down, followed by several of her students. Near the station she saw a taxi pull up to let out a group of infirm people protected by two boys from the CEDA. She recognized them as nuns of the Pauline Congregation, the most implacable enemies of her school. They had carried on a vigorous campaign against Olga and David. When she saw that they had even hired a taxi so that the paralyzed nuns could vote, Olga did something that she was unable to account for when she thought about it afterwards. She went over to them and shouted: "Pigs!" The two CEDA boys stepped forward menacingly. Just then David appeared, accompanied by half a dozen of the UGT. Meanwhile the nuns were standing on the sidewalk, looking from one group to the other in bewilderment. David said to one of the CEDA boys: "Go on, get them away from here; that's the best thing to do." The boys were preparing to obey when one of the nuns, taking a firm decision, made her way forward and handed her ballot to the architect Massana, who was in charge of the table. At this point David himself stepped aside to let the others by.

Perhaps those who best kept faith with themselves were the Costas. They had ordered pictures of Joaquín Santaló handed out, and around noon, when things took a favorable turn, they began distributing pictures of the Negus, which were received with loud enthusiasm. Otherwise they were good liberals. Their wives, who had just had babies a few days apart, wanted to vote, and the Costas let them have a car, even though they knew they would vote for the Right. That was their privilege. "Each one is each one," their husbands said.

The most provocative of the Rightists was Lieutenant Martín. Impeccably uniformed, he made his way to the voting place in the square where the moving-picture theaters were, and there he came face to face with El Responsable and his nephew, El Cojo, who was wearing a red handkerchief and had borrowed Future's skull for the morning. The lieutenant said as he came abreast of them: "Long live Spain!" The remark was uncalled for. El Responsable gave him a long look and, after a moment, spat. At this the lieutenant put his hands on his genitals. El Responsable spat once more and, making a half-turn, walked away. But they had made an appointment in time. From a distance El Cojo kept twirling the skull and pointing his finger at the lieutenant.

Major Martínez de Soria and his wife voted without difficulties. Mosén Francisco refused to vote until the priest of San Felix ordered him to do so.

Don Jorge wanted his son the Falangist to go with him. The boy said: "All right, I'll go with you, but I won't vote."

"What?"

"Falange doesn't believe in parties," the boy replied.

Don Jorge slapped him as hard as he could, and said to his wife: "Jorge is not to leave his room."

Tension rose as the rumor got about that the military were going to seize the ballot boxes to prevent the counting of the votes. Tight cordons of men stood on guard around the voting places. Some of them were asking for arms; others already carried them. The early returns began to come in with news that the Popular Front was winning in the country, and shouts of enthusiasm were heard. "That's hogwash. There hasn't been time to count yet."

Late in the afternoon, Future, who had had half a bottle of brandy at the Crocodile, saw Gorki and La Valenciana pasting up pictures of Stalin. He went over where they were and shouted: "Russians! Renegade Spaniards! Sons-of-bitches!"

"We'll see who's who, tough guy," La Valenciana answered. And with a swipe of her brush she affixed the leader of the Union of Soviet Socialist Republics to the door of Liga Catalana.

Professor Civil watched the movements of the crowd from his balcony. "Our youth was not so hectic," he said to his wife.

WHEN it became known that the victory had gone to the Popular Front, a howl went up from the earth. The victors demanded their place in the sun. They began elbowing their way toward the positions of honor and power. They had a majority in Parliament. The people had expressed their will. The time had come to settle accounts. A river of champagne, provided by the Costas, flowed through the streets, wetting the triumphant voters' whistles. The victory was said to be sensational, a landslide. The newspapers ran big headlines. A new era had begun for Spain.

The less excitable denied that the victory had been a landslide. "The Rights polled almost as many votes as the Lefts on a country-wide basis. But the Popular Front carried the big cities, and under the present electoral laws that gives them a majority." The bank cashier broke down the figures and stated that, bearing in mind the fact that the Basque nationalists had joined up with the Left for separatist reasons, the total number of votes of the Center and the Right was actually greater than that of the Left: 5,051,954 as against 4,356,559.

But nobody paid any attention to him. A majority in Parliament. The assistant manager of the bank charged that what had happened was a scandal without precedent anywhere in the world. He claimed that certain railworkers had voted four times; and no one would ever know how many of the Rights had been kept from voting. "The same thing happened all over Spain. When the votes were being counted they falsified the returns, adding those they needed to win. It's an out-and-out steal, but this is not the end of it, by a long shot." Tower of Babel conceded a certain amount of probable fraud, but said that aside from the fact that the Popular Front would have won anyway, the Rightists had done the same thing in certain regions of Navarre and Castile which they had carried. What gave people most food for thought was the difference of opinion between the large cities and the small towns. Dr. Relken remarked: "That is further proof of the fact that when the workers unite in large numbers, their revolutionary spirit is multiplied."

Cosme Vila said to his baby: "You see, little man. We must build big factories. We must found huge colonies of workers."

Matías Alvear was amazed. He had voted at eight o'clock in the morning. For the Popular Front. He did not like those audiences with Mussolini. But he had never dreamed all this would happen. What had become of the police? Vacationing? He was glad the Popular Front had won, but he would have liked cleaner elections. Fortunately Azaña seemed on the side of law and order.

Carmen Elgazu had crossed herself a thousand times that election day. She had watched everything from the balcony. A few days before, she had received a letter from San Sebastián in which her brother said: "Remember that you are first and foremost a Basque." And both Matías and Ignacio had filled her ears with accounts of what the military were up to.

Nevertheless, the evening before, she had gone to ask Mosén Alberto's advice, and he had said to her: "My dear Doña Carmen, you know that I am a Catalan and I could say the same as the Basques; but this time vote for the Rights."

Carmen Elgazu obeyed. And then she said to Matías: "There you are, now. This is the liberty you were preaching. Now we'll see what's going to happen."

Ignacio suffered intensely. Not a single detail had escaped him. And the expression on Marta's face was eloquent, especially when she saw the pictures of Stalin and the Catalan flags on the street. He had gone to UGT and had found David and Olga in an incredible state of excitement; Casal, on the other hand, let it be seen that he was not too pleased by the methods employed. Casal knew Ignacio, and said to him: "But don't worry too much about it. These things are inevitable, and, besides, for centuries they have done the same thing. What matters is that now being a bank worker or a stevedore or a slaughterhouse worker will not mean getting starvation wages. Besides, things won't take us by surprise or without experience as happened in 1931. I think now we know where we're going. Go on, be your age, and learn to see things as they are."

What Ignacio saw, however, was Olga with her hair disheveled, something he had never seen in the teacher before, and his uneasiness grew. As he came out of the UGT he ran into a crowd rushing down the steps of the Seminary. Someone told him these were the common prisoners, who had received a general amnesty. There were many gypsies among them, and various bearded characters, some tall, some short, some better dressed, some worse dressed, but all with a special glitter in their eyes. Evidently the amnesty had been conceded throughout most of the country, especially in Asturias, where there were still prisoners of the October Revolution.

Ignacio asked Tower of Babel: "But who gave the order to unlock the jail here?"

"I don't know, but it was probably your friend Julio García," Tower of Babel answered.

Ignacio was perplexed. Of course, Julio had probably been reinstated in his job. And he was making up for lost time. Matías Alvear was of the opinion that it was a great mistake to release the common prisoners. And the proof was that in Bilbao a number of them, in company with those who had been held after the 1934 business, had attacked the prison, setting fire to it. The fires! There is nothing more dangerous. They spread swiftly, and then nobody can check them.

The family in Burgos was more than happy. And in Madrid, Santiago, José, and the Parliament stenographer were bursting with satisfaction to judge by the postcard received from them. In it José advised César to forget about Latin and study something useful.

It seemed to Ignacio that he could see a wonderful side to that general happiness. It could not all be compounded of deception and gullibility. Something deep and significant evidently had been shut up in the bottle. He had a kind of fantastic dream as he lay in his bed beside the little image of St. Ignatius. It seemed to him that an unending line of the poor of Gerona, pick on shoulder, was making for the walls that encircled the city and undermining their foundations to the rhythm of the Pizarro Jazz orchestra, and that all of a sudden the cyclopean stones fell down, burying Warning Voice and poor Don Pedro Oriol, and that in place of the walls fertile fields opened out, with fruit trees like a paradise. Santi was leaping among the melons and the vegetables, followed by El Cojo and Future. All the city seemed overjoyed. And at the very moment when Dr. Relken bent over one of the flumes that watered this paradise, took a drink of water, and then straightened up, pointing to the headless angel of the Cathedral, saying: "Now, there!" Ignacio awoke. He awoke and found himself covered with sweat. He did not know whether he had formed a part of that pick-carrying caravan or not. He did not know whether he was one of those who had been buried.

At that moment his mother came into the room. Ignacio asked her: "Mother, what do you think about all this?"

Carmen Elgazu answered: "Son, all I ask of you is to be very careful."

Warning Voice had disappeared from the city. He and Laura had left by car, saying to Dolores: "We'll be away for a couple of weeks, or a month." Laura followed him like a lamb. Ever since the failure of the attempt to distribute winter clothing, Laura had lost confidence in herself. Now anything the dentist said was article of faith to her.

Many people meeting in the street felt that their feelings toward one another had changed. The children said terrible things picked up from their elders. In the Barca section a number of people were utterly outraged, among them La Andaluza. La Andaluza, who was something of a snob, preferred to have her girls consort with the military rather than with *hoi polloi*. She even let the impression get around that her daughter had been sired by someone important. Someone asked: "Don Santiago Estrada?" to which La Andaluza always replied: "Much more important."

Among those who looked searchingly into one another's eyes in the street were Major Martínez de Soria and Colonel Muñoz. For the time being, no words passed between them. They smiled. The major hunched his left shoulder and saluted. The well-groomed colonel raised his hand to his cap. "See you on Saturday." "On Saturday." On Saturday, in the armory, they put on their helmets as though nothing had happened and crossed foils in their customary fashion. It was a strange bout. Lieutenant Martín enjoyed it. When Colonel Muñoz achieved a coup, Major Campos smiled too. The three daughters of the general had asked to be allowed to watch the fencing matches, but their father had said: "Get along with you. Go out on the terrace and watch the seminarians play football."

One of those who suffered most was the draftsman Benito Civil. His wife had said to him: "There, what did I tell you! They've got you docketed now, and Heaven knows what's going to happen to us."

Fortunately, Mateo braced his spirits a little. As soon as the official election results were announced, Mateo called a meeting of his six comrades and said to them:

"Comrades, what had to happen has happened. They have won because they deserved to. The Right's two years in power have been the crassest display of impotence the country can recall. Don't swallow the argument that the Popular Front stole the elections. That is of little importance. They used force; more power to them. You know that doesn't matter—if you are in the right. If the new government goes about creating a great Spain, it will have been all for the best. But I am afraid that that is not what is going to happen, in which case we, in our own fashion, will brand them as doubly responsible. I know that you are impatient and somewhat discouraged. At least that's what I read on the faces of some of you. Now, I shall tell you my opinion: this is the beginning of our triumph. This opinion of mine coincides with that contained in a circular I have just received from Madrid: 'Now you will see how people from all sectors will soon be coming to Falange.' Today there are seven of us here; before two months are over we will find that we cannot accept any more applicants. The first to come will be those youngsters who have been wearing green armbands for two years. They have learned their lesson: all the slogans in the world don't mean a thing unless they are backed by a doctrine having true spiritual content. Then there'll be many monarchists, lukewarm army officers, middle-grounders. All except the members of Liga Catalana, who would rather dance *sardanas* to the crack of Teo's whip than join José Antonio and those of us who believe in a whole, united Spain. And then the ones that interest us most will come: the workers, for the Popular Front will defraud them. It will not bring Spain anything but senseless acts of violence, strikes, disasters. No one will be better off, except perhaps Julio García and a few shrewd operators. Then the workers will come to us if we make our position clear. And when that happens, I want you to know that the door of this house will be opened to them with all honors. It will be a joyful day for Falange. We are more interested in one worker who joins up than in a hundred members from the middle class. And if he happens to be a Communist or an anarchist, so much the better; we will get along better with him. Now, I feel it my duty to warn you that we are in danger. I know for a fact that we are among the first whom an effort will be made to silence. We are considered the 'most aggressive wedge.' This, too, is an honor. In other words, possibly one of us here is going to have an unpleasant experience. If that should happen—the rest of us will continue to stand guard, sword in hand. We are neither for nor against the Popular Front. We are against everything that threatens Spain or the integrity of Spain. And we shall defend ourselves. Today each of you will leave this room with a revolver. Octavio will give them to you. That is all, for the time being. *¡Arriba España!*"

Octavio underscored Mateo's words by carrying out his order. At the Treasury Department he had expounded the same theory as his leader: "This is the beginning of our triumph." The bewildered old employees decided once more that he was crazy.

At that meeting Haro and Roca proved that they were brave.

Roca said: "You watch and see how the number of my English students increases. Every time things swing Left, the number of students of English increases." Conrado Haro saw his possibilities of entering the navy fade away. Don Jorge's son kept easing his stiff collar by running his finger around it.

Forty-eight hours after the elections, Don Emilio Santos said to Mateo: "Son, your brother's in jail in Cartagena." He showed him a letter. Then he added: "I am feeling my years. I know that my gray hairs matter less to you than other things, but the fact is I feel old. I have a feeling that neither you nor I are ever going to see your brother again. You, here—should do what you can so I won't be left alone."

THIS series of events exhausted Ignacio because he was unable to grasp their inner meaning. Something told him that it was not worthwhile to nail one's individual destiny to these mutations. "Maybe those who watched the crowds from the housetops are right." It seemed to him that men handed over the scepter of authority to one after another, spelling each other in vengeance. The moment one group reached the summit, the roar of those who hoped to pull them down came from below. Two attitudes were possible: drift with the river or turn the brain into an island, the breast into a barricade. Go to the Dehesa and shout: "Go ahead and kill yourselves, I will live on my own among the green leaves!" Perhaps there was a third position: to have a share in history with the others, but without giving oneself over to it completely, reserving something independent and individual within oneself: the faculty for judging—or one's heartbeats.

The truth was that Ignacio was feeling his heart trying to assert itself amid the ballot boxes and the ideological conflicts. It was useless to try to fight it by putting forward prejudices, class struggles, politics. In the midst of the crowd, there would come a moment when he would feel himself lonely; when he had achieved solitude, he would want company. And he realized that all this did not happen to him by chance, but was induced by an external agent who stood guard over him as the Socialists stood guard over the polling places. A being who winked an eye at him from the other end of any street that he took. An agent who covered the horizon and then suddenly turned into the slight figure of Marta.

The time had come for him to admit it to himself. He was in love with Marta to the marrow of his bones. With Marta of the tiny feet, who always did and said the right thing; with Marta, a little taller than Pilar, a little shorter than he. With her solemn eyes, her hair parted in the middle, and her bangs. In spite of her riding horseback and being the daughter of Major Martínez de Soria.

Worn out with the arguments at the bank, struggling with the subject matter of second-year law, which Professor Civil's teaching art made endurable, he told himself that to get ahead on life's hard road he needed the spur of a soul that by some miracle was linked to his, and that this soul was Marta's.

All this was very satisfying, for he was convinced that Marta felt the same way about him. Otherwise, why did she come to the flat on the Rambla so often, why her sudden silences when he pretended indifference, the melancholy look he had several times surprised in her eyes as he turned to her? And, above all, how explain otherwise that on the last day of the old year, his twenty-first birthday, Marta had come over to him and said: "I lost eighteen years before knowing you; I won't be satisfied until I have spent as many knowing you."

Thinking about all this, Ignacio went off in a daydream. When he came to, he said to himself: "I love her." On his way to the bank he repeated: "I love her." When he heard the bells pealing he thought: "I lost twenty years before I knew her. I won't be satisfied either until twenty more have gone by."

One morning he rang her up. He had never heard Marta's voice over the telephone. The eagerness with which she talked made him think that she must always have been waiting for him, for her first words revealed surprise but not confusion. Marta talked as though the most important thing in the world for her was to talk with him, even though it was in the middle of the morning and to do it she had to let her room go without tidying. Ignacio asked her to go out with him, as it was Saturday and he had no class. Just the two of them, as they had done on Twelfth Night, when they went to see the Japanese lanterns and the cavalcade and found that his friend El Rubio was taking the part of the Black King, riding a magnificent gray horse from whose back he greeted them and even blessed them, promising them all sorts of toys—erector sets, dolls, bicycles—and perhaps the toy of a future spent together in perfect communion.

Marta accepted, and they went out, filling the day with intimate, mutual enthusiasm. And then they spent all Sunday afternoon together, besides having seen each other, along with Mateo and Pilar, at Mass. And they kept going out together, and the two of them were convinced that they really needed very little to make them happy: just to be together. When they were together, time took on a fullness of meaning; walls gave the impression that they could walk right through them; their feet danced over the ground with a gnomic tintinnabulation, as though they had a life of their own; and, above all, they felt such good humor, interspersed with moments of emotion and tenderness. The least thing amused them and made it necessary for them to link their little fingers together: a cab that went by with many suitcases piled on top, one of them about to slide off; a bobtailed dog; the birds sitting like philosophers on the telegraph wires. They found the telegraph poles lots of fun. Ignacio would go over and put his ear against one of them, telling Marta to do the same. When they heard the buzzing, he would say: "You hear? That's my father at the Telegraph office." One day Marta took a little round mirror out of her purse, and when Ignacio saw it he let out a shout of delight. He put his head up against hers to see if they would both fit in the little round circle. They laughed like fools because they could not manage it. Marta said: "Shall I throw it in the river?" Ignacio replied: "That's what it deserves." Marta tossed it away, and they both stood watching while the water swallowed the disk in which perhaps their two half-faces lived on.

Marta had a blind faith that Ignacio would become a man in the full sense of the word. "All he needs is to channel his energies in one direction." The thing she liked doing best of all was to go with him to the Cathedral and the walls. Much more than sitting on a stool at a bar. It seemed to her that in those places their love took on solemnity, that it wasn't something that had just happened.

Ignacio yielded to her wishes. And when they found themselves surrounded by the old stones and ivy, he gave silent thanks that the picks he had seen tearing down the wall had been only a dream. On the road to Calvary he was deeply moved, for he recalled Carmen Elgazu walking along it with the rosary between her fingers. And when they reached the hermitage keeping its age-long vigil, Ignacio took Marta's hand in his, their fingers intertwined, and the two of them gazed out over the valley. All the history of the city, and their own history, the limpid Mediterranean sky, and those tones of green which even in winter did not completely wither, united them in one being, capable of surmounting all obstacles.

It was a love that set Ignacio at an infinite spiritual distance from Canela and sin, filling him with a great sense of responsibility, just because it was not easy, because, in a way, it was superior to him, or set on another shore. Marta was glad that Ignacio was considerably taller than she. And at times as she caressed his face she said things that Ana María had already said to him: "I like your eyes, too, and those high cheekbones you've got."

It was a love that worried Matías Alvear greatly every time he thought about Major Martínez de Soria's trip to Rome.

Pilar realized that the affair was really serious, and she was beside herself with delight. "Do you realize," she asked Mateo, "I'm going to have Marta for a sister-in-law?" For Pilar loved Marta almost as much as Ignacio, even though her brother was still unable to understand it, the two girls being so different.

Talking to the two of them, Carmen Elgazu said: "You girls are now women. Remember that a man is, in a great measure, what a woman wants him to be. Above all, do not forget that religion is the cornerstone of a home." And then she added, looking at Pilar: "And—great purity."

Carmen Elgazu could not say why, but in this respect she was less easy in her mind about Pilar than about Marta.

SIXTY-FIVE

JULIO García in fact had given the order to open the jail. From the moment the Popular Front victory was officially conceded, Julio turned into a giant, a kind of viceroy of the city.

The Commissioner of the Generalidad had his office on the mezzanine; police headquarters was on the floor below. The Commissioner had been invested with far-reaching powers by Barcelona; the first thing he did was to telephone Julio. The latter put on a heavy overcoat with a black fur collar, settled his hat on his head, and descended the steps of his house. A few minutes' walk brought him to the huge building. Several plainclothes men stood up when they saw him. He walked in and took possession of headquarters.

It was a satisfying moment, for which he had waited a long time. He called in all the members of his staff and, pointing to a motionless object in the corner, said: "Before we go to work, I want to introduce my secretary to you. Her name is Berta." The policemen looked where he was pointing, and saw the turtle.

Julio García would have liked to be alone for several hours in his office, taking its measurements as he walked back and forth and filling it with the smoke of his cigarette to savor his triumph. But there was no time. It was as though the news of his reinstatement had been broadcast. So many people came to see him that for the moment he did not notice that there had been a change in the office, in which he had not set foot since 1934. The old paperweight was gone and in its place was a glass one with a snow-covered village inside. When one moved it, snow began to fall upon the belfry and the tiny houses.

The Commissioner gave Julio a free hand, and he used it. The task awaiting him was an arduous one. He needed only a few days to convince his wife that the moment was at hand when, like Sancho Panza, he would be master of an "island" and the whole province. The Popular Front was not going to dilly-dally.

One of the measures that seemed to him most urgent was the appointment of new mayors throughout the province, as the Commissioner had ordered. It was an easy task. Many mayors had automatically handed in their resignations; in other cases the parties of the Left had telephoned saying: "Everything has been taken care of."

Another matter had to do with the illegal possession of arms. Julio ordered a search, with the result that more than one hundred and fifty persons of Rightist affiliation were brought in for questioning. Names were mentioned, among them that of Mosén Alberto.

Julio was anxious to settle the problem of unemployment. The sight of men out of work for months and months was a disgrace. He talked with the Commissioner, with the Costas, with the city architect. He received a delegation of workers, who came away from the interview well pleased. As a first step they were to receive relief payments. And within two weeks they would be hired for public works the provincial government was starting. It was about time.

Something strange was happening to Julio. He had cherished plans of revenge, but now that he was back in power his guiding thought was really to accomplish something worthwhile and even to take a hand in matters that did not, properly speaking, come under his jurisdiction, but which he considered indispensable to the smooth functioning of the province.

Among these worthwhile measures was the overhauling of the administrative systems of the Provincial Hospital, the orphan asylum, the insane asylum, and other charitable institutions. Their state was a flagrant indictment of the authorities responsible for them. Julio sent for Dr. Rosselló, who quickly outlined a plan of what, in his opinion, was needed: "At the orphan asylum, fewer striped smocks, better food, and more exercise. At the insane asylum, less squash and turnips, and more psychiatric treatment. At the hospital, more beds, more medicine, fewer nuns, and more graduate nurses."

Another problem was education. During his enforced vacation Julio had visited the outlying districts of Gerona and had seen for himself that the number of children who did not go to school was very high. And he received disheartening reports with regard to the situation in the villages. He got in touch with Barcelona and persuaded the Generalidad to appoint David and Olga Supervisors of Education, with authority over all the teaching institutions in the province, including the religious.

He found the necessary person for every task. Julio was satisfied, and his happiness was shared by everyone from his faithful lieutenant, Officer Antonio Sánchez, a shrewd Extremaduran, to the Commissioner and, very especially, the Costas.

The Costas were so highflown with their election as deputies that they called a meeting of all their workers and delivered a speech that was all brotherhood and love. The workers listened with unwavering attention. At the end, one of the quarrymen spoke up: "We are very pleased to know that you have such good intentions, for in that way we suppose there will be no difficulty."

"Difficulty? Difficulty about what?"

"Haven't you received a communication from the union?"

"We haven't received anything."

"It doesn't matter. You will."

The Costas shrugged their shoulders, a little perplexed. But the atmosphere of good feeling and the recollection of the fact that Izquierda Republicana headquarters was crowded from morning till night soon restored their optimism.

The dismissals and the new appointments changed the fortunes of certain persons and, indirectly, that of the city. Noguer the notary had to resign as Mayor, and Massana the architect was appointed Mayor pro tem to fill out his term. The architect was well liked in many sectors. He had been the moving spirit behind the modern part of Gerona, and it was said that he had vast plans for city development. When he took office, he ordered an extra month's pay for all the municipal employees, which won him their unanimous support.

David and Olga were among those most aglow with well-being. Olga's hair was once more combed with its usual neatness, and she was wearing her turtleneck sweater. They were entranced with their job as Supervisors of Education, to which they now devoted most of their time. They received reports from teachers all over the province, and the conclusions they arrived at were disheartening. For one teacher who fulfilled his duties, twenty were smoldering with resentment because their salary was too low or because the villagers preferred to have their children work in the fields rather than go to school. Many of the teachers felt themselves practically forgotten: they received no money for supplies, and their school buildings were ramshackle affairs. The teachers of the border zone complained the loudest, for "in France, villages of four houses have a teacher who is well paid, with a decent school and everything they need."

David and Olga said to them: "Set your minds at rest. All this will be attended to."

Then came the turn of the religious schools. "It's incredible," David told Julio after his visit of inspection. "The nuns devote an hour and a half to prayers, religion, and so on. The textbooks are full of exaggerations; the punishments they impose are absurd. And then those habits they wear, with crucifixes around their neck, and those starched wings that distract the pupils' attention. You should see what happens among the Pauline Sisters. At church they separate the charity pupils from those who pay. The paying students are first in the line, and if they only study a little they can be sure of good grades. The Dominicans are, more than anything, just incompetent. Hardly one of them has a normal-school certificate. They put on plays representing angels and devils, and the devils' tails always fall off. The Sisters of the Heart of Mary are intelligent, but terribly fanatical. Only the Carmelites carry on useful work, caring for foundling girls. But you only have to look at their pupils' handwriting to realize the kind of education they're getting. It's an anemic handwriting, without any character to it. At the Brothers of the Christian Doctrine we have discovered, incidentally, a case of homosexuality: the sexton. The Marists resemble the Pauline Sisters. Now, if the Generalidad gives us permission, we'll go about setting things right."

"What is your solution?" Julio asked.

"First of all, a qualifying examination for all nuns and friars who do not hold a degree; and then forbidding the use of the habit."

This latter measure was the most painful aspect of the reform that was inaugurated. Those affected by it felt themselves outraged. There were nuns who did not know how to dress in lay clothes, how to put on stockings and garters. Those who wore their hair cropped looked as though they were getting over an attack of typhus, while others removed their coifs to discover that they had a beautiful head of hair. The Marist Brothers each got a black suit, but they refused to wear stiff collars because they made them look like Protestant ministers. There were ejaculatory prayers, tears, shame. Lord, what humiliation! When Pilar went to visit the Sisters of the Heart of Mary and saw Sister Beethoven, who did not know how to walk without her habit, she couldn't keep back a laugh.

Few passed the qualifying examination. Two thirds of the teachers who took it were declared incompetent.

Some people considered all this an act of provocation. Carmen Elgazu said: "It's the old story. The first thing they do is persecute religion."

Don Emilio Santos was afraid that when you came right down to cases, that was all the Popular Front was going to do: harass priests and the Civil Guard. "Maybe a pot shot at some capitalist, but nothing serious."

Don Santiago Estrada found a thousand and one things to criticize, as did the assistant manager. Ignacio said to the latter: "All right, but you people held all the trumps for two years and didn't do a thing."

What most frightened those who wanted to keep to the middle of the road were the activities of Cosme Vila on the one hand, and El Responsable on the other. A kind of steady hum came from Communist headquarters, and dour-faced people were continually running up and down the stairs. They seemed very sure of themselves and paid not the slightest attention to the other parties or the authorities. They stopped wherever they felt like it, pushed people out of their way, and put up a poster. They entered people's flats and nailed flags on the balconies. They organized small street meetings, and when they shouted a "Down with" they looked aggressively at the passersby as though demanding endorsement of what they were saying. Jaime assured Matías Alvear that in certain of the outlying districts Communists went into the bakeries and other stores and paid for what they bought with IOU's they left on the counter. "Any day now," Jaime added, "they're going to decide the time has come for a showdown, and all hell will break loose."

The anarchists seemed to have adopted different tactics. El Responsable gave out that what the CNT was interested in was the social problem. "Less chest-thumping and more results." As El Rubio told it to Mateo, El Responsable was planning a steady series of strikes until a complete change had been effected in the situation of the workers. "Casal," said El Rubio, "is also planning something along those lines, but apparently he is waiting for the new Commissioner of Labor, who is to be sent out from Madrid, to arrive; El Responsable, on the contrary, doesn't give a damn about that."

At the same time, the anarchists had registered their disapproval of architect Massana's appointment as Mayor. "With him everything is going to be the same as before. City taxes and all that crap. And having to pay to ride a bicycle or keep a dog."

Nevertheless, Gerona was much quieter than most cities, according to reports Julio García received. In Madrid the churches of Santa María and of Our Lady of Mercy and a monastery had been set on fire. It seemed that in Valencia there had been a pitched battle, with a number of casualties. In Alicante, following the flight of the Governor, one Botella y Pérez had taken control of the city and had addressed the crowd from a balcony, saying: "Comrades, I leave you in complete freedom to do as you please; you are the masters of everything." Along with Botella y Pérez, Comrade Milán, the local head of the Communist Party, had instantly organized the looting of all shops, churches, and even the homes of persons of the Right, sparing only their lives, and the same thing had happened in Yecla and other places. As Julio filed away these reports, he said to his faithful lieutenant, Officer Antonio Sánchez: "These are the inevitable outbursts of the first days. Later on, everything will settle down." The Costas hoped the situation in Gerona could be brought under control at once.

The only person who ventured to make a public protest against the measures adopted in regard to the institutions of religious instruction—especially that forbidding the wearing of habits—was Mosén Alberto. He published an article in *El Tradicionalista* charging the Minister of Public Education in theory, and David and Olga concretely, with being "enemies of freedom" and not observing the promises of tolerance made before the elections. And then he said from the pulpit: "To be sure, it is the Christian's duty to respect authority. But when the obvious intent of the authority in question is to persecute the representatives of the Church and prevent the normal fulfillment of their activities, then disobedience is justified."

As soon as these words had been spoken, everyone felt that they were a lamentable mistake. They soon became public knowledge, and more than one person stated that this was practically inciting to riot. At the same time it was said once more that in the Museum directed by Mosén Alberto two double-barreled shotguns had been found near the case containing old chasubles.

Julio felt that there was no reason to take official action. When Cosme Vila heard that the policeman had passed opinion to this effect, he said: "You'd think we were playing hide-and-seek."

Cosme Vila had a special grudge against Mosén Alberto. Years before, when he had worked in the bank, he had had to send him a letter with his statement, and he had addressed it: "Mosén Aborto." On the present occasion he seemed to have lost his customary calm, and kept repeating: "Yes, you'd think we were playing hide-and-seek."

Abruptly he opened a drawer and took a card out of it. It was a square yellow card, and in the center of it was a photograph of the priest at the very moment when he was saying to the prisoners in the prison courtyard that man can derive great spiritual good from his misfortunes.

He got up and went over to see Casal, who received him at once. Cosme Vila showed him the photograph and then said: "But that's not what I am interested in. It's this." He pulled a carefully folded paper out of his pocket and laid it on the table.

It was an article. The photograph was only to illustrate it, but the important thing was the article itself. What Cosme Vila wanted was for Casal to publish it in *El Demócrata*. "You understand why I am asking you to do this. *El Proletario* has a much smaller circulation than your paper."

Casal finished reading the article and wiped his forehead with his handkerchief. He looked at Cosme Vila, who had got to his feet, saying: "You sign it if you want to; if not, use my name."

Casal seemed very nervous, as though he was mentally gauging the importance of this move. When the head of the Communist Party had left, he called in David and Olga and showed them the article. The teachers read it and thought it over for a moment. Finally David remarked: "When all is said and done, what it states is true."

Casal pushed the cotton farther into his ear. The next day all the readers of *El Demócrata*, and soon all Gerona, learned of the case of homosexuality discovered by the Supervisors of Education in the school of the Christian Brothers.

The scandal to which this information gave rise was indescribable. Santi put on his pointed shoes. Future picked up his skull, Teo his whip. La Valenciana tore open her dress, shouting: "Five children, five children!" Dr. Relken said at the Neutral that a thing of that sort had little importance in Nordic countries, but that in Spain it was unpardonable.

Almost immediately some thirty members emerged from the headquarters of the Communist Party carrying a poster which read: "Monks and the Vow of Chastity!"

Leaflets were circulated giving details and the name of the accused: "Brother Alfredo, sexton." Then followed his physical description: "Short and sickly-looking, with soft, blue eyes; he offers the pupils candy and licorice sticks."

El Tradicionalista published an indignant denial, signed by the director of the school, defending Brother Alfredo as a "man of irreproachable conduct." The calumny was doubly shameful because "Brother Alfredo has been a sick man for many years."

Nevertheless, a cloud of gloom seemed to envelop the building of the Christian Brothers. The maids who called for the small boys when school was out rushed them off in great haste. Some families took their children out of school "until the matter is cleared up." Those who remained faithful won the director's undying gratitude. Brother Alfredo, unaware of what was going on, asked on noticing the many gaps on the chapel benches: "What's the matter with the boys?"

"Nothing," the director answered. "Grippe. The usual thing."

SIXTY-SIX

THAT the pace of events should speed up was only natural. The protagonists had been kept throttled down for a year and a half.

It became apparent from the first moment that the four main focuses of popular indignation were Mosén Alberto, Major Martínez de Soria, Warning Voice, and Mateo.

The first thing the dentist learned on returning from his trip with Laura was that his clinic was first on the list of residences that had been searched. His maid, Dolores, handed him a summons from police headquarters ordering him to appear "at the earliest possible moment to answer charges of possessing a pistol, a rifle, and six hand grenades hidden in an old chest on top of the water tank." His status as army officer saved Major Martínez de Soria from being searched for arms, but he knew that the three hundred who had been arrested in October had addressed a petition to the general asking that the, major be tried by "a court of the people's confidence" and worded in a manner that had his wife and Marta thoroughly frightened.

As for Mateo, he had been obliged for the first time to open the door of his study to non-Falangists. Three detectives whom he recognized as three regular attendants of the UGT called at his house. Don Emilio Santos was shocked and amazed to see them, and the maid went back to the kitchen quivering with satisfaction and curiosity. Mateo took out his blue handkerchief and his flint lighter. The detectives refused the cigarette he offered them and smiled at the stuffed bird. They stopped before José Antonio's picture and asked: "Someone in the family?" Suddenly, with restrained violence, they began to open drawers and bookcases. They discovered no weapons. "Where do you keep the pistols?"

Mateo shrugged his shoulders and answered: "I don't have any."

The detectives searched his bedroom, the dining room, the kitchen, the pantry, and finally Don Emilio Santos's bedroom. They went over the mattress carefully, and the manager of the *Tabacalera* said to them: "You can spare yourselves that trouble." They went back to Mateo's study and picked up Pilar's picture. They asked for the membership file.

Mateo paused and said to them: "What do you need it for? You know better than I do who we are." There was no card, no document referring to Falange. "Besides," added the Falangist, "the party is legal. Its statutes are registered at police headquarters."

One of the detectives answered him: "You're way behind in your information." They finally left, but with a peculiar smile. Mateo, who was disturbed by the last remark of the detective, knew that this was no more than a truce. He supposed that they were on their way to the homes of Octavio, the draftsman, Roca, and Haro, each and every one of the comrades. God, Don Jorge would be fit to be tied when the detectives began searching his nuptial couch!

Mateo went into the dining room, where Don Emilio Santos sat utterly crushed. He was going to speak, but his father interrupted him: "I was afraid they were going to take you away handcuffed."

Mateo remained standing in front of him. He regretted what was happening, but was more determined than ever. "What do you think the detective meant when he said I was behind in my information?"

Don Emilio Santos, who had heard nothing, shrugged his shoulders. Mateo could not stand his doubts. He combed his hair quickly, ran down the stairs, and made his way to the Alvears. Between the Telegraph office and the bank they were posted on everything. He found Ignacio studying in his room and Pilar cleaning the wardrobe mirror.

In answer to his question Ignacio said: "It's true, there has been an important piece of news—important for you, anyway. You should know it."

"What's happened?"

"Your leader has been arrested."

"Which leader?"

"José Antonio Primo de Rivera."

Mateo stood rooted to the spot. "How do you know?"

"It was on the radio. In Madrid, for illegal possession of arms."

Mateo's face had turned so red that even Pilar was frightened, afraid to go near him or say anything to him. "José Antonio, held incommunicado in the basement of police headquarters." The news was stark and harsh. "That's what is known as aiming straight at the head." Ignacio had gone back to his book, and Pilar did not know what to do.

Mateo took his leave abruptly and left the house. He went to the Treasury Department and informed Octavio. The two of them called a meeting of all the comrades. They even notified Marta. All attended except the draftsman, whose house was being searched.

After the initial shock of the news had passed, the first thing they decided to do was to send a telegram of support to Madrid: "At your orders, always. *¡Arriba España!*" A telegram that Matías Alvear transmitted slowly, with a thoughtful air. Then all the comrades turned toward José Antonio's picture, regarding him with the greatest respect and at the same time the greatest helplessness. They all felt the same fear, though none of them put it into words. The wave of violence was rising so high throughout the country that the worst could happen: José Antonio might be assassinated at any moment. Mateo was thinking: "He is the age of the predestinates: thirty-three." J. Campistol of Barcelona had called him at the *Tabacalera* to express the same anxiety.

Mateo turned his back to the picture, and in a firm voice told the comrades that not even this setback could postpone the day of victory. "The more they hound us, the sooner will come the day when we shall have to close the membership roll."

Two days later came a circular written by José Antonio himself from the basement where he was held. The national leader gave a résumé of the activities of the Popular Front during its scant month in office, warned once more that the regional statutes would bring about the disintegration of the country, foretold the inexorable advance of the Communist Party, informed them that most of the Falangist centers had been closed, and summoned all the comrades to the perilous task of the reconquest of Spain. They were all deeply moved by the circular, for it had a tone of great confidence and, at the same time, great bitterness. It set things straight for Mateo: "the inexorable advance of the Communist Party" reminded him of the key position held by Cosme Vila, and "the disintegration of the country" recalled the aspect of the Rambla now, with dozens of fanatics kneeling at the sound of the ritual *sardanas*.

The boy recalled his long talks with Ignacio, and Matías Alvear's re-aroused fear that he might be transferred to some other city, Cuenca or Guadalajara. Companys was President of the Generalidad again, and all the separatists who had been in exile were back, demanding compensation. This seemed to him the source of infection. And the return of another wave of exiles—Margarita Nelken, La Pasionaria, and others—added to it. Mateo had heard that a number of agitators had reached Barcelona from Russia—Losovsky, Neumann, Bazine—and had been placed under the orders of Béla Kun.

Mateo pondered the importance of these events. And he seemed to note a difference. Whereas the separatists had begun their operations immediately, Cosme Vila, in spite of his haste in the matter of Brother Alfredo and Mosén

Alberto, seemed to be holding off for a few weeks, though not many, before unleashing a general offensive. On his way to meet Pilar, Mateo said to himself: "To be sure, Gerona has powers of resistance. What Cosme Vila is going to start is a war of nerves. Wear people down, create unrest. And then all of a sudden some spectacular move. Some unexpected decision, like all fanatics."

Pilar was happy beyond words to see Mateo that day. She always feared the worst when they were separated. Fortunately she kept on reading her rose-colored novels, but everybody frightened her.

People were so nervous; that book of prophecies by Mother Rafols, which the nuns had given her to take to Carmen Elgazu; the rushing about of Mosén Francisco; and, above all, Marta's worried face.

"Are you afraid for your father?" Pilar asked her friend.

Marta answered that she was, in spite of the fact that Major Martínez de Soria said at home: "Don't be silly. There is a surprise in store for them. A surprise even for the general. They won't be able to take any steps against me, not even get me transferred."

This encouraged Mateo. This and the decision of his comrades, including even Don Jorge's son. Through Marta, Mateo was coming to have confidence in Major Martínez de Soria. "Perhaps he's not as superficial as I thought," he told himself. "And besides, he gave a son, a son who's standing guard on the other shore."

Ignacio lived under the same tension as his friends, to which the temperament of the assistant manager of the bank contributed, now more pessimistic than ever. He informed Ignacio that the person mainly responsible for whatever might happen in Gerona was Dr. Relken. "He's a Mason. He will lead the city to disaster. There is nothing worse than foreign agents. What does the country mean to them? He's already asked for the best room in the hotel. Everyone is carrying out his orders without knowing it. Before a year is up, he'll have accomplished all he set out to do. He'll go away with a bulging wallet and an album of photographs of all the ruins and fires. And those of you who think all this is a long way off are very much mistaken," he concluded.

Ignacio's only consolation was when he could manage to make Marta smile. Then all the storm clouds disappeared, and he felt himself a man once more, a man with a life of his own. For Marta, too, love was a source of strength. They still went up on the walls. The days were growing longer, and the San Daniel Valley stretched before their eyes more resplendent than ever. Often from the railroad trestle they looked at the very spot where the little round mirror had fallen into the river.

SIXTY-SEVEN

EL Responsable and Future were convinced that the Popular Front owed its victory to the anarchists. If their million and a half members had refrained from voting, as in 1933, it would have been a rout.

This made them fully aware of their rights, and their violent nature prevented their accepting an orderly evolution in social conditions. As though this was not enough, the Gerona anarchists had received a visitor from Barcelona who said to them: "Comrades, you have to help us. We must try out an experiment in Gerona." To this end, they presented to the Labor Board, on a take-it-or-leave-it basis, a work code demanding workers' control of the factories, profit-sharing, salaries for the owners, and so forth. Unless this was accepted, a general, unlimited strike would be called.

These demands were made known, and the whole city was outraged. The Murcians working at S'Agaró left their shacks and came into Gerona, where they paraded the streets carrying signs reading: "We hail the CNT-FAI demands and the emancipation of the worker."

Casal, Cosme Vila, the Costas, and the authorities took the matter as a joke. "They are a pack of fools," said Casal. The Labor Commissioner—a brand-new Commissioner who had just come to Gerona, a personal friend of Largo Caballero—sent for El Responsable and asked him indignantly: "What do you think you are doing? Do you suppose people are going to hand over the keys to the safe just like that, and that you can run a factory the way you run a car? Two months after you took over, all there'd be left would be a few broken-down machines and people starving. Profit-sharing! Why not share the women too? The thing for you to do is—you'll have to find the way—to run a note in *El Demócrata*. Find some way to postpone the matter. You are an intelligent man and will hit upon an out of some kind."

El Responsable, who was rolling a cigarette, sat poker-faced. "Is that all you've got to say?" he asked.

"That's all."

El Responsable left, and called a general meeting. "Comrades, since 1933 a retrograde government has been doing this to us"—and he made the motion of turning a screw. "Now that the people have won the election, the CNT has presented its code, and we are told that management will not accept it, and that we would ruin everything. Comrades, in Gerona there are three thousand families working for a dozen owners. The CNT is ready to fight and hereby calls a general strike."

Strike, strike.... The word instantly reached the ears of the whole city.

When Julio read the notice, he called the gymnasium by telephone. "You are a bunch of jackasses," he said without any preamble. "You are going to force me to call out the Assault Guards."

Santi, the only anarchist who had remained on guard, answered him. He put the receiver down and went: "Ugh, ugh!"

The anarchists of the city were joined at once by those of the outlying districts, and by certain workers who were dissatisfied with the slow procedures of the UGT.

It was hoped that the movement would be chaotic, purposeless, but this hope soon vanished. The strike was organized along the most orthodox lines. El Responsable was much more competent than the Labor Commissioner had supposed.

Cosme Vila and Casal published a note addressed to their respective groups. "Report for work unless the strikers use violence."

El Responsable pondered this for a long minute. His daughters were at his side. "If you back down now, you'll be a laughingstock."

El Responsable said: "At twelve o'clock on the dot, everybody on the Piedra Bridge."

The order was carried out to the letter. As the hour approached, the group grew. From her balcony Laura calculated at one thousand the number gathered there.

The workers not backing the strike made a joke of the affair. "When are you going to bring out the tanks?"

But they soon would have to change their tune. At quarter past twelve, on an order from Future, each group set out in the direction to which it had been previously assigned. Trucks had arrived before them and were unloading sacks of sand, stones, and bricks on the sidewalk. At the sight of these materials, the enthusiasm of the strikers mounted. El Responsable rolled his eyes from side to side.

In the twinkling of an eye barricades had sprung up in front of the entrances to factories and workshops. The stones and bricks were on the ground, within easy reach.

Among the buildings thus occupied were the Central Electric, the most important power plant in the city, the gas plant, and the waterworks, though El Responsable had ordered that for the moment there was to be no interruption in these services.

The whole city was taken by surprise at this sudden display of strength. Cosme Vila and Casal received evidence of the fact that not one single industrial plant had been overlooked. "At least their file is as complete as ours," they had to admit.

Most astounded of all were the Costas. They realized that no exception or differentiation was being made between them and monarchist owners like Don Pedro Oriol. Their foundry, quarries, and lime kilns were blockaded. Then they understood what the quarryman had been alluding to at the feast of brotherly love. However, they were not going to take it lying down. "We'll dot the i's and cross the t's."

The Costas went to see Julio, who received them stroking Berta, which left them somewhat disconcerted. The two industrialists briefed him on the losses they and the city would suffer because of this stupid strike. Julio answered them: "There's only one thing I can say to you. I'll talk with the Commissioner, the Mayor, and everyone. We'll do what we can to make the strikers see reason. But I have to remind you that strikes are legal, and that the Popular Front was formed to win certain liberties. I am sorry to have to talk to you like this. I wouldn't say this to everyone, but I feel that two republican deputies have enough political savvy to understand that, one month after winning the elections thanks to the votes of the workers, we can't call out the police because they go a little too far."

"A little?"

"Or a lot, it doesn't matter. Besides, to talk to these Murcians about losses would make very little impression on them. They would answer that they have never had anything to lose."

The Costas left Julio's office more than disturbed, and only their sanguine temperament kept them from making some rash decision. Their wives said to them: "If we were in your place we'd shut down everything. When all's said and done, with what you've got in the bank and what our folks have, we've got enough to live on. Think it over. We could go and live in Pals. Papa and Mamma would be tickled to death to have the babies there."

The Costas had a heavy load of responsibility to carry. Izquierda Republicana was in a bad humor over the strike and the news the papers carried.

Revolutionary demonstrations were on the increase in Toledo, Madrid, Cádiz, Granada; and in many other places the fires leaped from one church tower to another. The Costas said that Azaña was doing all he could to bring the situation under control, and so was Indalecio Prieto. "It seems that Azaña is counting on Catalonia, the Basque Provinces, and Galicia to help him hold the reins firm. For that reason he granted the Statutes and is giving facilities of every kind. Yet, in spite of all this, you see what is happening. Even here, where moderate opinion prevails, men like El Cojo are allowed to run loose with brickbats in their hand."

Seventy-two hours after the strike started, the Commissioner telephoned Julio: "El Responsable has just sent me an ultimatum."

"And what did you do?"

"Nothing. Refused to accept it."

Julio congratulated him. The answer of the strikers' committee, however, followed swiftly: the wrenches went into action, and electricity, gas, and water were cut off.

This triple suspension gave rise to the worst confusion the city could recall. Everything was left dark. The Commissioner tried to call Julio again. The shops closed immediately, the faucets dripped their last tear, the wildest curses filled the kitchens.

The Commissioner, Cosme Vila, and Casal felt that the insolence had gone beyond all tolerable bounds.

The cutting of the power caught Casal just as he was preparing to run *El Demócrata* through the press. The machines stopped dead and the lights went off. The printer's devil lighted a candle. What had gone wrong? Candles were being lighted everywhere. Casal realized at once what was up, and he set out for UGT headquarters. As he came into the building he had the strangest feeling, as though he had gone into a church, for David and Olga had lighted four candles. The same thing was happening at police and Communist Party headquarters. Cosme Vila's office looked like an altar, with Stalin as patron saint, for his picture was surrounded by candles.

Casal and Cosme Vila began discussing the situation at once, urged on by Julio, whom Doña Amparo Campo had gone to see, informing him that he would have to eat in the restaurant because it was impossible to cook without water.

Cosme Vila grasped the fact that El Responsable, despite the housewives' complaints, was on the point of winning a solid victory, for the reaction by and large was favorable. It almost seemed that the anarchist plan of carrying things to the bitter end was winning the support of people who would be the losers by it. Symptomatic phrases could be overheard: "Of course they're right. The Soler factory earned six million pesetas in 1935.... If the authorities are not doing anything about this, it's because they know they've not got a leg to stand on.... It's worthwhile going without water a few days if at the end of the year we get a check...."

Cosme Vila said to Casal: "You know how I feel about it. The anarchists are a bunch of gangsters. I told you we were handling them too gently. Now that's over. You will have to decide whether you want to follow my lead. What I am going to do is to ask for armed help, and go out and get it."

Casal drew his eyebrows together. "I don't understand," he said. "What are you planning?"

"On Monday morning, at eight o'clock sharp, your members and mine are going to work, come what may."

Casal scratched his head. "Julio won't want to help you."

"Julio will help. He's got more to lose by this than we have."

Casal realized that the mistake had been not to resist at the start. "We should have gone in in spite of the barricades."

Cosme Vila did not share his opinion. "You always see only half of the picture. If we had done that, they would have been martyrs; they would not have been allowed to express their opinion. What could be better than for them to discredit themselves? Don't forget this law: always try to make the enemy cut his own throat."

THE agreement reached by Cosme Vila and Casal got to El Responsable's ears quickly. El Responsable, who prided himself that he knew whom he was dealing with, said, after analyzing the situation, that not only would the Communists come out en masse at the summons of their leader, but that, as always happened, they would drag Casal's followers with them.

The only possibility of resistance, if the forces of order took a hand, would be, in his opinion, the intervention of all the anarchists of the province. That, however, could not be depended upon. El Responsable knew that Cosme Vila controlled the rural population. "The Andalusian peasants," he explained, "are anarchists; but in this province they are conservatives. They trust in the handouts from Moscow."

He spent all day Sunday visiting the different barricades. And he sensed at once that it was not going to be easy to control his men. The strike had given them a taste for fighting. Moreover, they gave little thought to the other syndicates. Their principal enemies, in their opinion, were the capitalists, the presidents with their coaches, the priests, the military, who strolled past smiling ironically at those crude breastworks. The enemy was still Warning Voice, the Costas, Mosén Alberto, Major Martínez de Soria, and the Falange of Gerona, which at any moment might start sniping from the rooftops.

By late afternoon El Responsable felt that he had convinced his comrades. "We must avoid bloodshed."

"Why?" asked Blasco, who was standing guard at the power plant.

"Because they'd kill us like flies," El Responsable answered him. Then he added: "We'll give them their medicine some other way."

But when night came, the darkened city excited the strikers all over again. Bonfires were built along the barricades, to wait for the dawn. The anarchists' wives kept them company. In many places they were drinking and even singing and playing guitars. Future was the ideal companion for improvising a celebration under the stars. Santi was jumping around everywhere.

At half past seven Monday morning the first squads of Assault Guards made their appearance. This gave the Socialist and Communist workers who had been ordered back to work the confidence they needed.

At ten of eight the first workers began to show up, keeping close to the wall, when an unexpected, spectacular element entered upon the scene: the cavalry. Julio sent mounted policemen to the most heavily guarded spots, and the horsemen rode up to the barricades clearly prepared to go into action. That decided the contest. There was a moment of confusion among the anarchists, which proved decisive. The lines of workers opened the factory doors, taking care not to jostle any of the strikers or tear down the barricades, and started to walk in amidst a dead silence. At the gas works El Cojo threw a brick at a sickly-looking worker, setting off a noisy protest, but it did not go beyond that. At the Costa foundry El Responsable's daughters scratched the face of a woman cleaning the office, but that was all. The anarchists felt foolish, and from their horses the mounted policemen said to them: "The best thing you can do is to go back to work too, and that way you'll have a paycheck on Saturday."

They felt foolish because each group was made up of a small number of men. But as other groups that had also been dislodged began to appear, the increase in their number multiplied their indignation. The horses made it impossible to organize the real concentration of strikers to which that might have given rise. Suddenly the machines began to turn over. What was happening? The street lights went on in broad daylight. The electric plant had yielded, too. In the kitchens and in the washtubs the faucets began to gush. The women congratulated one another from balcony to balcony.

At this point El Responsable ordered in a low voice: "Break it up, but go get the bombs...."

The word had a magic effect on the strikers. To most of them the decision seemed to carry such a weight of responsibility that not a single one took it upon himself to act independently, as might have been feared. The leaders of the groups instantly recovered their authority. All this took place between the Piedra Bridge and the Rambla. Both Laura and Professor Civil from their balconies saw Future set out toward the Plaza de la Independencia at the head of a dozen comrades, while El Responsable and a similar number, following the river, seemed to be heading for the football field or the Costa quarries.

The police, who had not heard El Responsable's remark, decided that the strikers were finally dispersing and that the whole thing was over. They went on patrolling, but with a bored air.

They showed no signs of animation until the first explosion was heard about ten in the morning. It came from the Dehesa. The first bomb had gone off in the Dehesa. Future had set it. He had selected that spot because it seemed fitting to him to begin in that setting of ancient sycamores. Nobody was going by at the time; only a solitary water-colorist was sitting on a camp stool near the swimming pool, and over by the bridge there was a camp of gypsies. All the rest was deserted. It was a wintry Dehesa in tones of gray and violet with a misty vapor.

Future selected an intersection of two walks where Bernat and his friends bowled on Sundays. The bomb raised a great cloud of dust, a comet of sand and dead leaves, and then died away. The trunks of some of the trees were hit by shrapnel, cutting splinters in them, one of which Bernat later found useful to hang his cap and watch on.

Although the explosion was heard only by the people living in that part of the city, the news of it spread quickly, sowing panic. Casal left the print shop of *El Demócrata* for UGT headquarters. David and Olga did the same. Work was halted at the bank. The Commissioner, beside himself, issued an order: "Put a guard over the Telephone Building."

A quarter of an hour later came the second explosion, a much louder one, this time from the direction of Montjuich. Someone said they were blasting at the quarries, but it soon came to light that it was something much more serious: the powder magazine.

"That's impossible," shouted the Commissioner.

Julio shook his head with an expression that left no room for doubt.

Colonel Muñoz was never able to understand how it was possible that the bomb caused no casualties. Apparently the squad on duty happened to be some distance away cutting wood, and the sentinel was sitting behind a rock some three hundred yards off. This was held to be neglect of duty, but the sentinel preferred that to being blown to bits.

Fortunately the powder magazine was nearly empty. A week after elections the stores had been withdrawn. Nevertheless, sufficient powder was left so that the explosion was loud enough to terrify the women washing in the brooks of the San Daniel Valley; and on this side of the mountain the entire personnel of the cemetery was frightened: the gravedigger and the dead. Soldiers of the African war opened their eyes as though they were back in 1921, caught in ambush by the Moors.

The living, on the other hand, seemed indifferent. Only the women and children shut themselves up in the house, and some shops quickly rolled down their metal blinds. The rest of the population—taxi drivers, bank messengers, waiters—stood in groups on the street corners, in spite of the fact that the Assault Guards were energetically trying to disperse the gatherings.

Julio said to his faithful lieutenant, Antonio Sánchez: "That's the worst thing about these people: they're poets. Where will the third one go off? No one knows. Impossible to predict in time or space. The police squads searched the streets in vain for anarchists. They had all disappeared. Did they use time bombs? Did they drop from the sky? Perhaps there won't be any more."

At exactly eleven o'clock the people who happened to be in the Plaza de la Independencia heard the third explosion. This was nothing but a hand grenade. It scared everyone, but that was all. It went off right in the Labor Office. The new Inspector, Largo Caballero's friend, threw himself to the floor and crawled under the desk. When he saw that no damage had been done, he clenched his fist and shouted: "You're soon going to find out who I am!"

At that moment the whole city felt itself helpless, at the mercy of El Responsable. Even Colonel Muñoz. He had reached the point where he was suspicious even of a scrap of string on the barracks floor.

Everyone felt himself at the mercy of El Responsable—except Cosme Vila. Cosme Vila, whom Teo kept informed of everything that was happening, realized, on the contrary, that El Responsable had completely lost the battle the minute he set off the first bomb.

"Just analyze the situation," he said to his people, who were uneasily watching the unfolding of the anarchists' plan. "Don't let yourselves be swept away by the fireworks. Consider the facts. What was the CNT's objective? To shut down the factories by means of the barricades. What is the result? The factories and workshops are humming away like mad; the barricades are gone. Then they cut off the light, the gas, and the water. There, too, they capitulated stupidly. Like fools, for that's a one hundred percent revolutionary weapon. The noise you hear now is nothing but the funeral march. The one thing they should not have done was to let themselves be scattered and then set off bombs.

They should have done exactly the opposite: refuse to move and let them make martyrs of them. But there you are. People don't like to hear shrapnel go whining past their heads. So they've missed the boat. The powder magazine! What did that amount to? Gave the general a chance to strut. The Dehesa, the Labor Office—it's stupid, it's absolutely crazy to pick a fight with the Labor Inspector and throw a grenade at him in his office."

Cosme Vila's listeners scratched their heads. They could not help feeling that to have a city at one's mercy was a display of strength, whatever came of it.

"Don't be fools. The thing that matters is what comes afterwards. They've got public opinion against them."

Teo spoke up: "But they have sowed."

"Sowed? That's right—for us." His hearers looked bewildered. "The Inspector will be eating out of my hand now," Cosme Vila elucidated.

Nobody seemed to think this of much importance.

"It is absolutely essential, bearing in mind the fact that Saturday, at the latest, our turn is coming. Isn't that true?"

"What turn?"

"The presentation of our program," Cosme Vila explained, "a serious program, a scientifically revolutionary program."

The leader looked at his audience one by one. It seemed to him that his words were taking effect. La Valenciana was nervous and seemed to be asking what they were waiting for.

Cosme Vila addressed himself to her. "Well," he said in that tone all recognized as the prelude to a sudden decision, "you'd like to get your two cents in, wouldn't you? I can see I haven't convinced you."

She sat down, with a bored expression.

"Well, if you want it, there's a job waiting for you," Cosme Vila went on, walking over to his desk. "You can help him." And he pointed to Murillo.

"Help me with what?" asked Murillo.

Cosme Vila, whose expression had grown serious, opened a drawer, took out a package, and handed it to him. "Help you to put the finishing touches to El Responsable's reputation."

Everyone stood around in utter amazement. The package contained a small, oval object, incredibly heavy. Cosme Vila had seated himself.

It had all happened so unexpectedly. "Where are we to take it?" they asked.

"If no one has any objections," answered Cosme Vila, "I would choose the Diocesan Museum."

It was an order. An order that was received with a strange mixture of fear and delight. Teo sat huddled in a chair, utterly dejected because the choice had not fallen on him. Victor ran his hand over his hair. Murillo, with his dirty raincoat and his walrus mustache, balanced the object in his hand as though hefting some precious metal.

Things could not have gone more perfectly. The order was carried out without loss of time, with incredible celerity. To the point where the police and the taxi drivers who were in the Plaza Municipal, where the Diocesan Museum stood, were completely at a loss to explain how the thing had happened right under their noses while they were watching. When they heard the jarring explosion, close at hand, terribly close at hand, for the wood and the windowpanes of the balcony just over their heads went flying through the air, they threw themselves to the ground, holding their breath.

Murillo had calmly strolled into the Museum, for it was a visiting-day. He had walked through it from one end to the other, without this causing any surprise, for he often went there to look at the old images. Before leaving, he left a souvenir of himself behind a door. It was this souvenir that exploded a few minutes later.

Cosme Vila would have preferred One of the rear rooms where Father Claret had slept; but Murillo, for reasons of his own, preferred the rectangular room with a high ceiling where the collection of polychrome virgins stood on little pedestals.

La Valenciana, who was waiting with him in the street, approved of his plan. She approved of it because suddenly, as the policemen and taxi drivers threw themselves to the ground, she saw come pouring out of the balcony a flood of detached members of those virgins. The sight filled her with enthusiasm, especially when a head of the infant Jesus went bouncing over the cobblestones and came to rest at her feet. She was on the point of picking it up and shouting: "Another child! Another child! Six children!" But the movements of the police caught her attention. Something was happening. Several of them had got up and were hurrying into the building. It was then that Murillo heard a taxi driver say that one of Mosén Alberto's maids had been found behind a door with her head crushed by the explosion.

The Plaza Municipal quickly began to fill up with angry-faced people, the account of what had happened spread, and while El Responsable and Future at the gymnasium received the visit of several detectives who asked them to come along, the crowd in the Plaza Municipal saw an ambulance drive up to the Museum, come out with a stretcher, and drive off toward the hospital.

Someone said that the woman's heart was still beating and that Dr. Rosselló would do what he could to save her.

Mosén Alberto was at the episcopal palace when he received the news.

He turned pale, leaned his hand against the wall, and then, taking his cape and hat, descended the stairs. On the way to the hospital he felt as though something in his breast was bursting. He did not even know which of the two maids it was. The only thing he was sure of was that they had told him she was dead.

He reached the hospital, and a nun took him up to the operating room. Dr. Rosselló, who was just coming out, confirmed the fact that there was nothing he could do. Mosén Alberto went over to the operating table, where the outlines of a body could be seen under the sheet. He turned back the sheet. He had expected to find a gentle, calm countenance, and what he found was a horrible mangled face. He was still ignorant of which of the two maids it was. He did not find out until he saw the younger of them kneeling beside the corpse with her face buried in her hands.

He did not know what to do; he felt like laying his hand on the head of the survivor to comfort her, for it was plain that she felt utterly alone, empty, as though the death of her sister had drawn off her vital substance too.

Mosén Alberto suggested saying the rosary, but the nuns told him that the director of the hospital had forbidden this. And, besides, they had to vacate the operating room.

The priest walked slowly away. In one of the corridors he came face to face with Carmen Elgazu, dressed in black and accompanied by Pilar, who, when she recognized him, came toward him with an expression of great grief.

Mosén Alberto said to them: "It would be better for you not to go in." Pilar looked around the white corridors in utter panic. If someone went by, she felt better; but if the corridor was empty, a kind of vertigo seized her and she clung to her mother's arm.

Carmen Elgazu insisted on seeing her dead friend. She said goodbye to the priest. Once in the operating room, she displayed her admirable fortitude. She laid a print of the Virgin of Begoña on the maid's breast. She said to Pilar: "This, my child, is death." Pilar had stood as though hypnotized before the dead body. It was the first she had ever seen. Carmen Elgazu helped the younger sister to her feet and led her away in the direction of the Museum, offering to stay in the house with her and look after everything.

The Plaza Municipal was empty except for two Assault Guards standing watch at the door of the Museum. The street cleaners had piled up in a corner of the patio the members of the virgins which had fallen to the street. Dr. Relken was there, with a Romanesque arm in his hands, and had asked permission to examine it. Pilar said to her mother: "That's Dr. Relken." The only thing the city was talking about was bomb number four.

The two guards had said to Dr. Relken that the anarchists were going to have a tough time. "That poor woman had done nothing to anyone."

Dr. Relken asked them if there was proof that the anarchists were responsible. One of the guards looked at him with surprise. "It doesn't matter whether there's proof or not. Everyone knows they did it." The doctor shook his head.

SIXTY-EIGHT

IGNACIO had followed the course of the disturbances with a deeply troubled mind. It seemed incredible to him that the authorities had not settled the matter at one stroke. He said to David and Olga that it was shameful to allow such a state of affairs to continue beyond all reason. David and Olga, who were themselves greatly upset, answered: "Now they're paying the consequences."

The teachers were convinced that Casal's efforts would finally bring the situation under control. "There have been no more bombs. And Julio has been questioning El Responsable and Future for twenty-four hours straight. What more can be done?"

As Ignacio listened to them he became still more furious. The death of the maid had affected him more than if it had been a minister. David and Olga told him not to exaggerate. "Oh, sure, don't exaggerate," answered Ignacio. "It's easy enough to talk when you're on the safe side of the fence." And the same thing happened to him in the bank. At the bank the death of Mosén Alberto's maid was a matter of utter indifference. The only thing the employees—with the exception of the assistant manager and the teller—were worried about was that not a vestige had remained of the proposed labor code, and the only thing that encouraged them was the rumor that Cosme Vila and Casal were going to present demands that would be the answer to those put forward by El Responsable.

Ignacio's only source of satisfaction was in his family. In his mother, washing dishes at the Museum; in Pilar, offering to sit up at the hospital with the dead maid; in César, writing from Collell: "I have finally learned to give injections. I have given eighteen this month without breaking a single needle."

And in Matías Alvear. Matías Alvear reconciled Ignacio to mankind, for he saw that his father was suffering as much as he was, even though at the Telegraph office, as he said, life went on. The telegrams kept coming in as though nothing was happening in the city. "Arriving tomorrow afternoon."

"It's a boy. Love." The day the maid died more than twenty boys were born in the province.

What a man his father was! He suffered, but he did not lose his serenity. Along with Don Emilio Santos, he followed every detail of what was happening. There was something comforting about seeing the two of them walking along the street, so neat, so courteous, greeting the humblest acquaintance with cordiality. When they separated they did not shake hands, but tipped their hats. In Ignacio's eyes they were irrefutable proof that the bombs were not destroying everything.

And he needed this proof, for many people were disillusioning him—David and Olga, Julio García—and also because he was disillusioned with himself. How was it possible that the spectacle of Gerona, instead of benumbing his flesh, aroused it? He was thinking of Canela again! What a complex thing the human body was! Fortunately there was Marta, the thought of whom was always with him. Marta, a true source of satisfaction. Praise God for the day when she had crossed his path, when she had touched his face and said to him: "I like your eyes, and those high cheekbones of yours." The girl was wonderful, and had a strength of character that even the general strikes could not bend. Confronted with the chaotic state of the city, she had said: "We can reach no collective solution because of the authority being in the hands of those who hold it; but each one of us, personally, should be at his post."

That afternoon she felt, and Major Martínez de Soria agreed with her, that her place was in the Diocesan Museum, alongside Carmen Elgazu, bringing order into the rooms that had been wrecked. Without fear of the groups roaming the streets, captained by the bootblacks, she left her home and made her way to the Museum. Under her arm she carried a blue smock that had been her father's. When she reached the building she greeted the two Assault Guards and went up. Carmen Elgazu was deeply moved to see her. Carmen Elgazu was wearing a huge black kerchief tied over her hair to protect it from the dust. "Just look at this, my child."

Ignacio learned about all this from Matías Alvear. The boy went out on the balcony, thinking about the two women in his life. Trucks carrying sacks from the barricades passed by. The Neutral was closed. The lights trembled nervously on the fronts of the buildings.

Suddenly he felt that his place, too, was in the Museum, beside his mother and Marta. Vague fears seized him. He hurried out of the house, passing by the Cataluña, where a loudspeaker was belching slogans. He went up the stairs of the Museum and walked in. He found Marta in the room where the bomb had exploded, surrounded by mutilated virgins. The girl looked at him. Carmen

Elgazu came in and she stood looking at him, too. He asked what he could do to help. When he saw Marta in her blue smock, he asked for something to put over him. Carmen Elgazu brought him an old cassock she had turned up somewhere, and he slipped it on. Without a word he set to work, while the two women looked at the cassock with contradictory emotions. They swept the debris and broken glass into piles. Ignacio was afraid that Mosén Alberto might suddenly appear, but he need not have worried. Mosén Alberto was receiving a steady stream of visitors, of people who were volunteering to attend the maid's funeral, which apparently was going to constitute a real manifestation.

It made Ignacio suffer that little by little his emotion, which should have been sorrowful, was being transformed into a pleasant sensation as he watched Marta put the arms and legs of polychrome wood into a box with the greatest respect.

THE funeral, spectacular in itself, promised to be even more so because a recent order had forbidden all religious manifestations, including funerals, outside the churches. Therefore no priest or altar boy bearing the cross would accompany the servant girl.

That night Carmen Elgazu returned home exhausted with the work at the Museum. And she could not get out of her mind the implications of that order. As she ate, with Pilar serving dinner, her eyes filled with tears.

Suddenly there was the sound of a key in the door, and Matías and Julio came in. They had been at the Neutral. Julio did not give up his habits; on solemn occasions he still came to see the Alvears.

Julio had aged in the preceding months. They all thought the same thing when they saw him come into the dining room. His tilted hat seemed out of place on him now. His mustache was set in a framework of wrinkles.

Both Matías and Julio realized that Carmen Elgazu had been crying. Julio felt embarrassed. He almost regretted having come up.

Carmen Elgazu got up and prepared them coffee as usual. Ignacio came out of his room, tired of studying. And it was Pilar who asked, blurting it out:

"Tell me, why can't they carry a cross at a funeral?"

The policeman was disconcerted. He had not expected such a direct approach. "Don't ask me, child," he answered. "I didn't issue the order." And he sat down.

"They want to eliminate it everywhere, daughter. That's the whole thing."

Julio stroked his mustache. It was strange that they should ask him those questions. But what could he answer? The truth of the matter was that he was too fond of those people. He told them it was best to look on the bright side of things. "What can I say to you? Changes take place!" The look in Carmen Elgazu's eyes forced him to go on. "But I don't suppose anyone is going to demand an accounting of your inner feelings." And then he added: "What they are trying to do is to separate State and Church completely. Not to mix religion in public life."

Ignacio spoke up, unexpectedly: "Listen, Julio. It's better to drop the subject, don't you think?"

At that moment Julio made up his mind to get up and go. But he did not have time. Carmen Elgazu, feeling that Ignacio was on her side, sat down in front of the policeman and said to him:

"You have no call to be offended, Julio. Ignacio is right. You know better than we do what is going on. They are doing everything they can to banish the name of God. That's all they concern themselves about, and to accomplish it they seek the support of anybody, even people like El Responsable. There's something that blinds them, and that is hatred of religion. To them a cassock or a crucifix is as deadly as poison. Mother of God! They could not be more mistaken. Without religion there is only hatred. Religion is the only brake, even though you don't think so. If I had not made the sign of the cross over Ignacio so many times, who knows what might have become of him? And the same is true of Pilar. You are not going to pretend that everything is going as it should, are you? You heard what they are yelling in the streets. A family gathered together, as we are here, is old-fashioned, out of date. One should do like David and Olga, or what they do abroad. It's all so distressing. Because it is so useless, you know. They won't accomplish a thing. Do they think they've hurt the maid? She's where she wanted to be. Listen carefully to what I'm saying to you, Julio. They can fight God, but they'll lose. There are still many people like the maid; don't let them forget that. They have their work cut out for them. Nor should they think they've won because they see us weeping. They can burn down as many churches as they like. They can forbid crosses at funerals, and altar boys; but they'll never be able to stop us from praying here"—and she pointed to her breast—"and that's what counts."

SIXTY-NINE

IT wounded Warning Voice's pride that the Leftists should be warring among themselves. "They think we're so harmless they don't even worry about us."

The funeral was being discussed everywhere. The Alvears decided to let Ignacio represent the family. Major Martínez de Soria decided to go in person, as did Lieutenant Martín and several other officers close to the major. Don Jorge dressed himself as befitted the occasion, and ordered all his children to do the same, except Jorge, the disinherited, to whom he said: "You do as you like."

Mateo had to make a difficult choice. On the one hand he wanted to attend, but on the other he was afraid that his presence might be interpreted as support of the line followed by Warning Voice. In the end he decided not to go, but to send two of the comrades. He chose Octavio and Conrado Haro. "Wear your blue shirts," he said to them.

The funeral notice published in *El Tradicionalista* announced that the ceremony would take place at three o'clock in the afternoon. By two thirty the plaza was jammed. When the hearse appeared and stopped in front of the hospital, there was a moment of tense expectation. The presiding committee lined up—Mosén Alberto in the middle, Don Jorge on his right, Major Martínez de Soria on his left. Then the coffin was carried out and the hearse was filled with wreaths.

The mourners followed on foot. The only reminder of past funerals was the Miserere. Mosén Alberto murmured it in a low voice, and Don Jorge and the major said the responses. "*Dies irae, dies illa...*"

When the hearse reached the river, instead of going toward the cemetery it turned off toward the center of the city. Knots of curious spectators formed along the way.

The police stopped the driver. "What route are you taking?"

The driver answered: "Past the funeral parlor."

The policemen stepped aside, keeping at a prudent distance, with their night-sticks in their hand.

As the funeral procession moved farther into the city, the curiosity of the people grew. Fortunately the Plaza Municipal, where the Museum stood, was not far off, and the procession quickly reached it.

The driver drove slowly around the square past the building where the tragedy had occurred, and everyone felt a shiver run down his spine as he looked up at the shattered balcony. The bystanders took off their caps. Only a couple of taxi drivers gave the impression that they were taking an ironical attitude toward the affair.

Octavio and Conrado Haro followed the procession in silence, shuffling their feet like the rest. But suddenly, as they passed by the City Hall, where a huge Catalan flag was draped across the front, Octavio felt something tighten in his throat. He looked at Major Martínez de Soria and shouted: "*¡Arriba España!*" And then: "*¡Viva España!*"

Everyone was disconcerted. Only Conrado Haro answered him, in a reedy voice, and Lieutenant Martín. Nobody else, not even Major Martínez de Soria.

The policemen came over immediately. "On your way to the cemetery," they barked. Protests could be heard among the spectators, and the taxi drivers were struggling with their desire to reply to the provocation. "Throw them out! Down with them!"

Haltingly the procession reached the riverbank and finally started toward the cemetery. Nobody turned back. All who formed a part of it knew the route was a long one, but nobody wanted to desert. Those walking beside Octavio looked at the Falangist out of the corner of their eyes, without saying anything.

The gravedigger had been notified that the whole procession was arriving, and he threw the gates wide open. It was only by an effort that Don Jorge could keep the pace set by Mosén Alberto and Major Martínez de Soria. His left leg was failing him.

The driver put on his brakes in front of the gate and got down. There was a stretcher on the ground, and the coffin was lifted onto it. The gravedigger pointed the way: "Over there, over there," pointing to the middle path between the cypresses.

The niche in which the maid was to be laid away belonged to Mosén Alberto. It was in the east wing. The stretcher, carried by the employees of the funeral parlor, led the way. Then came the presiding committee, and then the huge crowd, beneath whose feet the sand squeaked with a metallic sound.

Everybody wanted to witness the ceremony, but this was not going to be possible. The cypresses and the funeral vaults obstructed the view of those in the rear.

The arrival at the niche was dramatic, for it coincided with the appearance of the implacable police guard at the head of the stairs leading to the northern part of the cemetery.

The stretcher was laid on the ground. All eyes converged on the coffin. Mosén Alberto moved his hand, feeling the physical absence of the hyssop. He would have wished to say a requiem, but the presence of the police made this impossible. In the end, he made a sign to the gravedigger to wait and began the Lord's Prayer.

In a flash the policemen had leaped across the three steps that separated them from the spot. Mosén Alberto stopped. And instantly a concert of shrill whistles broke out on the other side of the wall.

Mosén Alberto understood and ordered the gravedigger and the assistants to lay the coffin in the niche. They obeyed, and the box was slipped into the opening with rare precision. Then the gravedigger picked up mortar and trowel and, with six bricks exactly like those the anarchists had used for their barricades, began to seal the opening. The laying of the last brick, which fitted perfectly, coincided with another concert of whistles, this one more remote.

When the ceremony was over, Don Jorge went up to Mosén Alberto, took his hand, and kissed it. Major Martínez de Soria did the same, then Don Pedro Oriol, then Don Santiago Estrada. As it was impossible for all to reach him, Mosén Alberto raised his right hand and traced a benediction in the air.

Those in the rear had already left the cemetery. Professor Civil said to Ignacio: "Come, let's go."

The wife of the gravedigger, who was leaning against the gate with a child in her arms, seemed to be waiting for something to happen. The calm, however, was complete. The people were leaving without incident. The whistling had ceased. Only Lieutenant Martín seemed reluctant to leave.

Octavio and Haro asked him: "Are you coming?"

"Not just yet."

Nobody else noticed that the lieutenant was staying behind in the cemetery—not even the police.

Octavio and Haro asked each other what Lieutenant Martín was up to. They saw him hide behind a vault bearing the inscription: "Cobera Family" and light up a cigarette.

A few yards from the vault stood a handsome tombstone with the name carved on it: "Joaquín Santaló." Some twenty yards to the right, on a mound of earth, on a pile of earth curved like the belly of a woman, was a marker, one of those used in the potter's field, which read: "Jaime Arias, Taxi driver."

Jaime Arias, the brother of Teo, who had died on October 7 of a bullet through the temple. Lieutenant Martín compared the tombstone of Joaquín Santaló and the marker of Teo's brother. The difference between the two seemed to him to obey an inexorable law: for a deputy, a handsome tombstone; for a poor taxi driver, the potter's field. And, farther to the left, the niche of the staff major who fell from his white horse, killed by the bullet fired by the Izquierda Republicana deputy.

Lieutenant Martín, tall, dark, with close-clipped mustache, tossed away his cigarette, crushed it out, and, taking hold of the cross on Joaquín Santaló's grave, moved it back and forth until he had pulled it loose. Then he took a handful of damp earth and smeared the tombstone with it, obliterating the name.

This done, he went to the mound where he read: "Jaime Arias, Taxi driver." He tried to efface the name by rubbing it with his shoe. But the paint would not come off, so he stamped the marker into the mud. All that was visible was the word "Taxi driver." It gave the impression that Jaime Arias was still offering his services to the inhabitants of the place.

Lieutenant Martín then crossed the main avenue and walked to the cypress-encircled niche of the staff major. He stopped, stood at attention, and saluted.

At that moment the wife of the gravedigger saw him. His presence surprised her very much, and she called to her husband. Her husband was talking with a group of strangers near the gate. The lieutenant walked through and past them without speaking and set out for the city.

He had not gone more than twenty yards when the gravedigger went into the cemetery for a round of inspection, like a dog on a scent. He was certain the officer had committed some outrage.

When the Costas received word of the desecration of Joaquin Santaló's tomb, their indignation knew no bounds. "We are going to swear out a warrant against those responsible for this."

When Cosme Vila heard what had happened at Jaime Arias's grave, he said to Victor: "Go to the cemetery right away and take photographs."

Everybody tried not to let the news of what had happened get to Teo. Nobody knew what might happen when the giant found out that his brother's grave had been profaned.

SEVENTY

THE strike, the bombs, even the corpse of the maid, were pushed into the background. For the moment Lieutenant Martín's exploit, fully described in *El Demócrata*, based on an official police communication, monopolized attention.

Everybody realized that the cancer had not been cut out by the mere fact of winning the election. Finis had to be written to the Rightist chapter. To effect this a meeting of the Security Committee was called.

This committee was made up of the Commissioner, Don Julián Cervera, presiding; Julio, Chief of Police; the Costas; the architect Massana, Mayor; the architect Ribas, representing Estat Català; Cosme Vila; and Casal. Special agent Antonio Sánchez acted as secretary.

Julio had attended the meeting at the urging of his wife. Doña Amparo Campo said to him: "You follow Dr. Relken's advice and be practical. Don't forget that they have their eyes on you in Madrid, to see if you've got what it takes." The architects Massana and Ribas were a little frightened; the Costas were sputtering with rage. As a matter of fact, the only really serene person aware of what was happening and what needed to be done was Cosme Vila. His mongoloid head and his broad leather belt were to dominate the meeting.

After a brief discussion it was agreed that Lieutenant Martín should be handed over to the military authority, whose duty it was to take action in the matter. "The general will know what steps he should take."

As for the Falange, in view of the fact that one of its members, Miguel Rosselló, had been found carrying arms, and that two of them, Octavio and Conrado Haro, had uttered subversive shouts in the Plaza Municipal, it was decided that the party should be dissolved, its headquarters closed, the three members in question put under arrest, and a statement secured from the leader, Mateo Santos.

Following this, Julio read out the findings in the one hundred and fifty arrests for illegal possession of arms. Most of the accused would be punished with a fine. Don Jorge de Batlle, Warning Voice, and other landowners of the province, however, would be taken into custody because the arms found in their possession were high-caliber weapons and because they had not turned them in of their own accord.

The Costas frowned when they heard the name of their brother-in-law. But it was not the moment to make a family matter of it.

Cosme Vila inquired how it was possible that Mosén Alberto's name was not on the list in view of the fact that "two double-barreled shotguns" had been found in the Museum.

Julio replied that this was not true, that it had been made up out of whole cloth. "The truth of the matter is that we found absolutely nothing there."

The meeting proceeded at a leisurely pace. One after another the topics Antonio Sánchez had listed on the agenda were taken up, without any change in the tone of voices. It was as though they could make the gravest decisions without this tone altering.

The architect Ribas brought up the problem of Major Martínez de Soria. "It would seem that we had forgotten that most of us here were in jail and were tried by him. I can't understand why the general has not reached a decision on this matter."

Julio answered: "The fact is that Major Martínez de Soria has backing in high places. Not only has the Captaincy General ordered the affair halted, but even the ministry of War."

Julio's words caused blank amazement. What they implied was that there was a chain of reactionary-minded officers, at strategic points, who protected one another.

There was a moment of silence, of which Cosme Vila took advantage to raise his hand and ask for the floor. "I should like," he said, "to bring two important matters to the committee's knowledge."

"What are they?"

"First, Jaime Arias. The Communist Party demands that the outrage against the brother of our comrade Teo be avenged, and that Lieutenant Martín be sentenced within thirty days."

In the midst of the silence his words had caused, Cosme Vila went on: "Second, I wish to inform you that the Communist Party will shortly present its program. It covers three aspects: industry, commerce, agriculture. And along with these a plan of reforms having to do with the political structure of the municipalities and the province." As he said this he looked at the Mayor of Gerona, the architect Massana.

The latter shook his head. "I don't know what you are referring to," he replied. "I hate vague allusions."

Cosme Vila raised his eyebrows. "If you will permit me," he said, "I will make these allusions concrete." He pulled a piece of paper out of his pocket and began to read. "Certain irregularities noted at first glance: first-, second-, and third-class funerals are still being held. In Gerona, infant mortality has not declined since 1920. Dozens of workers live in the Calle de la Barca, in the Pedret quarter, and in the caves of Montjuich as though they were living in the time of the cave dwellers. There is not a single instance of the son or daughter of a working-class family in Gerona studying at the university. No space is available to organize workers' free schools, and yet the Seminary takes up two blocks. The city subsidizes a football team, which has its own playing field; if the workers ask permission to play on it they are told that they will spoil the turf. At the moment there are as many police in the city as under the dictatorship of Primo de Rivera. If we were to search the homes of our ranking municipal authorities—asking the pardon of some of those here present—we would find that their standard of living and their furnishings are far superior to those of the workers I have mentioned. Churches and convents bursting with gold, and a dozen establishments for religious teaching. Concerts organized by the Musical Association—Dr. Rosselló, president—but admission by ticket only. A magnificent Casino, with a billiard room, a library, a room for this and a room for that, but for members only. I should like to draw for you a comparison between this state of affairs and what goes on in Russia, where any economic, artistic, or scientific activity is designed for the benefit of the proletariat. Here that does not carry any weight. We have been in conference here for two hours and I have not heard the word 'people' mentioned once. In Russia all the meetings are for the people, and every municipal body is at the service of the people. There is much more that I could add to this. I repeat that the Communist Party holds that the way of life of the workers must be improved. We shall not relax this endeavor. Although that does not seem to be the case, the municipality should be the cornerstone. We shall make all this clear in the program that I have notified you we shall present."

Cosme Vila's statement caused a deep impression, especially because of the tone in which it was delivered. The Costas looked at each other in bewilderment.

The person who had to answer him was Julio. Julio had been on the point of giving an unexpected turn to the meeting by informing those present that the anarchists, fools though they were, had brought in overwhelming proof that it was not they who were guilty of the murder of Mosén Alberto's maid, but the Communist Party. He refrained, however, for Cosme Vila was right in many of the things he said, and it would get them nowhere to whip up feeling.

"Very good, you are within your rights," he finally said. "Present this plan for suggested improvements when you have it ready. Bear one thing in mind, however: we live in a democratic republic, not under a Communist regime. We have many things to do, many, even though you may not think so, and nothing is easy, I can assure you. The easiest way out would be to say: 'Fine, let's use force. I don't like that priest. Off with his head! Nor that major. Out with him!' Very good, but everything has its drawbacks. This is a country full of fanatics; don't think they are all in the Communist Party. And fanatics always give one a surprise. I know that you live in a flat that is not as comfortable as mine.

"That's too bad. On the other hand, Gorki eats much better than I do. Now, we did not come here to argue about human nature. The purpose of this meeting is to cast up accounts, determine where blame lies, and pass the necessary sentences. We have done that, and that is the important thing. Now the members of the force can proceed to carry out their duties."

Dr. Relken gave full approval to the measures adopted. He said to Julio: "Take my advice and get rid of the Falange at once. By themselves they can do nothing, but banded with the military they represent a constant threat. As for Cosme Vila's demands, you will have no choice but to back Casal and the Costas to combat him. If those two give evidence of a revolutionary spirit, the balance will swing in their favor."

Dr. Relken was living days of absolute happiness. He had taken the best room in the hotel, with a telephone and a bell that in two minutes became a chambermaid. His hair had grown considerably since he had arrived in Gerona. He did not wear it so short any more, but combed straight back, and with tight blond ringlets at the neck. His chin jutted out more prominently than ever, and he went on smiling and drinking quantities of water. He spent the day looking through magazines, visiting his friends, giving lectures under the auspices of the Socialist Party, Izquierda Republicana, and even Estat Català, and taking a keen interest in the most insignificant details of the life of the city. He said that he found the Spanish human type enormously interesting because of its multiplicity of variations and because it was always amputating its own qualities from its living body. "You people do not in the least resemble the Czechs," he remarked. "You, especially the Catalans, are more like the Hungarians, and even more like the Romanians. But with a far more interesting quality of pathos."

It was his opinion that the people of Gerona lacked initiative. He would have suggested sweeping reforms. In the commercial area he would have encouraged the opening of large stores in the city, even if it meant sacrificing the small shops. On the industrial plane he felt that the possibilities were unlimited—if they would take the Pyrenees into account. "Raw materials must be sought in the Pyrenees. There is probably even oil there." He envisaged the plain around Gerona and the Ampurdán dotted with oil refineries. In the cultural sphere he praised the choral society, the Municipal Library, the Diocesan Museum, and Archives. And he maintained that the two most intelligent persons in the city were Julio and Warning Voice.

Many people said that the doctor was writing a book on comparative anthropology. At Ignacio's bank it was rumored that he was a homosexual. The assistant manager also believed him to be a Mason, and Professor Civil thought him a Jew waiting to seize the first lode of ore discovered in the Pyrenees. Mateo believed him to be a political agitator with Machiavellian delusions, but a complete fool, inferior to the most stupid Spaniard, a man who in less abnormal political circumstances would already have had to leave the country for Andorra or France.

Be this as it may, Dr. Relken was the first person who read in *El Demócrata* the news that all the decisions taken by the Security Committee had been carried out. He read it at the press, before the newspaper was on the street. He often went there to talk with Casal, to whom he said as he watched him work: "It's impossible to get out a real newspaper with those machines of yours."

Casal answered him: "Real or not, the news it carries is important."

And he was right. The news was important: the jailing of Don Jorge, of Warning Voice, of Rosselló, for illegal possession of arms. The jailing of Octavio and Haro for subversive expressions offensive to the Republic. The dissolving of the Falange and the questioning of its leader. The handing over of Lieutenant Martín to the military for court martial.

At this news, the Leftists rubbed their hands gleefully. Panic spread among the Rightists. Everyone condemned the action of Lieutenant Martín, and Major Martínez de Soria, when he heard about it, regretted not being a general to be able to rip the stars off his sleeve. Carmen Elgazu had said: "You have to be a poor excuse for a man to do a thing like that in the cemetery." Yet nobody had supposed that this would bring in its wake the arrest of other persons, new searches, and the dissolving of the Falange.

Laura turned numb when she saw the officers taking her husband away. "You can't do that, you can't do that!" The dentist had asked for a few minutes to change clothes. He put on his best shirt, his best tie. He stammered out the most unprintable insults. He delayed the moment of leaving his room. Laura was clinging to his neck and saying: "Don't go, don't go." Warning Voice gave her certain instructions having to do with jewels and bonds they had in the house. He dashed off a note to Don Pedro Oriol. "To be published immediately." The last thing he said to her was: "I forbid you to let your brothers do anything about this matter."

Don Jorge reacted quite differently. He looked at the plainclothes men and said: "Very well. Let me tell my family goodbye." He called in his wife and all his children, and one by one they passed before him, each giving him a kiss. Nobody shed a tear. The two maids pleated their aprons between their fingers. Don Jorge asked for his derby, his gloves, and his cane. Turning to his Falangist son, he said to him: "Go get a taxi." The officers informed him that their instructions were to bring him in on foot. Don Jorge said to his wife: "Notify Noguer the notary and tell him to come and see me with a lawyer."

Octavio was at the Treasury Office when the police came for him. Hardly anyone noticed what was happening. Only the cashier, with whom he was always arguing. Nor were there any regrets when people did find out, for everyone considered him bad-tempered and vain. His sweetheart went to see Pilar and flung herself in her arms, hoping that Matías Alvear could do something for him.

Haro said to his father, the city policeman: "I'm sorry about this. Let Mateo know, and bring me books on sailing when you come to see me." Haro and Octavio were put into a cell with Rosselló, who had already been there forty-eight hours. Warning Voice and Don Jorge shared quarters with a gypsy who was dozing in one corner and a peasant with a scar on his forehead who had tried to kill his brother in the barn with a sickle.

Mateo had just received the news of the arrest of his comrades when the same policemen who had been to see him before knocked at the door. The maid opened and, when she saw who it was, called out: "Come in, come in!" The policemen looked at her in surprise, wondering if there was something behind her words. They asked for Mateo, who came into the hall. They handed him a warrant, which he read carefully. He took out his blue handkerchief and wiped his forehead. Then he asked: "Can I get something from my room?"

The police replied: "Absolutely nothing."

"Not even the picture of my sweetheart?"

"Absolutely nothing," one of them repeated, but the other spoke up: "All right, you can take your sweetheart's picture."

Mateo watched the men's every move. Finally he turned and came back with Pilar's picture, which he put on the dining room table. Then the policeman who seemed to have more authority proceeded to seal the study.

Don Emilio Santos appeared at that juncture and watched the operation in silence. "Are you going with them?" he then asked Mateo, who answered: "I suppose so."

The policeman replied: "No, you're not coming with us. You are to come in by yourself at eight this evening."

Mateo raised his eyebrows. "I have a law class at eight."

The policeman shrugged his shoulders. "That's too bad."

It was an anxious afternoon. The Alvears were convinced that Julio would take Mateo into custody. They knew the boy would defend his ideas without yielding an inch, and that he would protest over the arrest of his comrades. Pilar fluctuated between rage and tears, and suddenly she burst out, referring to Julio: "And to think that man comes to our house, and we serve him coffee." Matías Alvear tried to take a hopeful view of the situation, but even Ignacio was sure that Mateo would not sleep in his house any more, and he could see Pilar visiting the jail, carrying a basket of food to him.

Mateo was not so sure. He said that if Julio had intended to arrest him he would have done it already. "The thing for us to do is to think about other things. You, Ignacio, should go to class as usual, and make my excuses to Professor Civil. You, Marta, to your class at Fine Arts. Why not? See if you get the picture of your father finished. Pilar, you come to meet me at headquarters at nine. You'll see that I will be released. I'll be fighting mad, but I'll be released."

Pilar was the most reluctant to take comfort. She looked upon Julio as a monster, and the mere idea that he might arrest Mateo was more than she could bear. "If you're not out at nine, that beast is going to get a piece of my mind. He won't be so high-handed with a woman."

Nobody had much hope of what Pilar could accomplish. They let her give vent to her feelings, but it was a painful state of affairs.

Marta showed the greatest serenity. And she felt that, at heart, Mateo wanted to be arrested, to share the fate of his three comrades.

They decided to follow Mateo's advice. Each of them would go about his business. Unhappiness gripped them as the moment came to separate. It seemed to them that something beautiful was being broken and it might be a long time before it became joined again. Pilar looked at her father as though imploring him to do something. But he did not know what to say, for he realized that Julio was impervious to any sentimental approach.

SEVENTY-ONE

WHEN Mateo arrived at police headquarters, the officer at the door told him to wait while he called Julio's office. A moment later Antonio Sánchez stuck his head out, looked at Mateo, and said: "Please sit down."

The Cathedral clock was just striking eight. Ten minutes later Julio himself appeared at the door. "Come in, please."

Mateo walked into the chief's office, both of them displaying the most perfect manners.

When he sat down facing Julio, what annoyed him most was the presence of Antonio Sánchez, the Extremaduran, with his thin lips and enigmatic expression, who was standing between the chief and the filing cabinet.

The first thing Julio asked Mateo, without any preamble, was whether Lieutenant Martín belonged to the Falange. The question took Mateo by surprise. He answered: "Why—no."

"Just 'no'?"

The boy thought for a moment. "I can give you more information, if you like. He asked for admittance, but was refused."

"Why was that?"

"It was felt that he was temperamentally unsuitable."

Julio lighted a cigarette. "What you seem to suggest is that you people would never have desecrated the tomb of a—Leftist."

Mateo answered: "That's exactly what I mean."

Antonio Sánchez smiled. Mateo looked at him and said: "At the time of the attempt against those of Galán and García Hernández, José Antonio was the first to protest."

Julio nodded his head. He seemed prepared to carry on a friendly dialogue with Mateo, a mere exchange of ideas. "What do you know about a letter written by José Antonio to the army officers?"

"Absolutely nothing."

"The one in which he quotes a phrase of Spengler's saying: 'In the final analysis it has always been a company of soldiers that has saved civilization.'"

Mateo thought for a moment. "I think Spengler is right, but I know nothing whatever about the letter."

Julio leaned back in his chair. "What is your opinion of Warning Voice?"

Mateo shrugged his shoulders. "Bad."

"Why?"

"Because he represents the spirit of selfishness and rancor we are fighting."

"What is your opinion of Don Jorge?"

"There's more to be said for Don Jorge."

"Is that so?"

"He was brought up like that."

"What other people of the city do you condemn or condone?"

"That would take a long time to state."

Julio looked at a paper lying on his desk. "What are your relations with Major Martínez de Soria?"

"Very slight."

"What is your opinion of him?"

"He gave a son to our cause. I have great respect for him."

"Do you think he has received a copy of the letter addressed to the officers of Spain by José Antonio?"

"I know nothing about such a letter."

Mateo realized that Julio was going to go on harping about that until the end. He smiled.

"Now," said Julio, "let's talk frankly about the Falange. What is it you people are after? To increase your numbers and do what?"

Mateo listened to the question without showing any emotion, and replied: "What we are after is for there to be enough of us to give Spain back her unity and her reason for existing."

"And what is Spain's reason for existing?"

"To be true to herself." When this remark was followed by a silence, Mateo added: "And shed her spiritual light over the world."

Julio looked for a moment at Berta, who was crawling toward him. Then he asked, settling himself in his chair: "What would you do with me, if you had the power?"

Mateo gave a gesture of displeasure. "There are many things that could be done. For instance—" and he thought for a moment—"ask you what you proposed to do with Gerona and with Spain." Seeing that there was no reaction on Julio's part, he went on: "I'd also like to put you in front of an audience of three thousand people and have you debate with—let's think whom—with José Antonio. And see what happened." And as Julio still sat motionless, he added quickly: "And then expel you from the Masons."

Julio flushed. He did not grasp the implications of the phrase. "What do you mean by that?"

"Nothing—nothing special." Seeing that the policeman was furious, he went on: "I would expel you for a reason that has nothing to do with—" He paused. "I would expel you because you are an intelligent person." Mateo felt uncomfortable there in the middle of the office, with nothing to rest his back against. He looked at Julio and went on: "I mean it. You're too intelligent to be a Mason."

Julio banged his fist down on the desk. "That will do."

Mateo said no more for a moment and then pointed out: "It was you who asked me."

A silence followed. Julio had himself in hand again. He reached out his arm and pressed a button. Mateo closed his eyes. When he opened them and found that the light was not shining directly in his face, he raised his lids. Julio was looking once more at the paper in front of him. "What is your opinion of Casal?"

Mateo answered quietly: "A person who's mistaken."

"And Cosme Vila?"

"One of the most dangerous persons in the city."

"When you handed José Antonio's letter to Major Martínez de Soria, what did he say?"

"I don't know anything about such a letter."

"Do you think many of the officers of the garrison would follow him?"

The Falangist shrugged his shoulders.

"How many civilians do you calculate would take up arms?"

Mateo maintained silence.

"We are interested in that. In knowing whether many officers would follow the major's lead. And also the approximate number of civilians who would join him."

"I have no idea what you're talking about."

Julio waited a moment. "Yes you do. I am talking about the uprising that is being planned against the government of the Republic."

Mateo made a gesture of surprise. "The government? I didn't know the Republic had a government."

"Didn't you?"

"No."

Julio rested his elbows on the desk. "You'd prefer the government of Gil Robles?"

Mateo shook his head. "No indeed."

"Oh, that's right. You don't believe in parliamentary regimes."

"No."

"Then in what do you believe?"

Mateo shaded his eyes with his hand. "In a man with a prophetic significance."

"Like Mussolini or Hitler?"

Mateo felt dizzy. His posture and the expression on Antonio Sanchez's face made him dizzy. Julio shifted the light for a moment.

"On what grounds do you think we have arrested your three comrades?"

Mateo wrinkled his forehead. "Well—Rosselló for illegal possession of a pistol; Octavio and Haro for having shouted: '*¡Arriba España!*'"

"How do you suppose we are treating them?"

"Decently."

Julio suddenly opened a drawer of his desk and asked: "Why did you have this in your study?" as he pulled out a slip of paper. It was from Mateo's brother, who was under arrest in Cartagena.

Mateo's expression grew sober as he looked at the scrap of paper. Julio unfolded it and read aloud: "'It's terrible to be shut up inside four walls when there is so much to do on the outside. Your news reached me safely. Keep it up.' What news is he referring to? What is it you should keep up?"

Mateo did not answer. Without questioning him further on the matter, Julio put the slip of paper back in the drawer. "Is your brother older than you?"

"A year older."

"Did he join Falange when you did?"

"At the same time."

"And what is it you have to do on the outside?"

Mateo shaded his eyes again. "I don't know," he said in a bored tone.

Antonio Sánchez moved impatiently. Julio then informed Mateo that at that very moment his study was being searched again.

Mateo asked: "Could I be put in jail and my three comrades released?"

"That's a matter for the Commissioner to decide." Julio looked at his list again. "To what do you attribute the fact that no worker has offered you his services?"

Mateo answered: "Because they don't know us here. In other places we have many worker members."

"And why do they join?"

"Because they are tired of demagoguery."

"What you propose is a single syndicate?"

"A vertical syndicate."

"What does that include?"

"It would take a long time to explain."

Julio thought for a moment. "So your doctrine, in a nutshell, is: man of prophetic vision, single party, vertical syndicate."

Mateo shook his head. "No. Our doctrine in a nutshell is love of Spain."

Julio was getting nervous. The monotonous questions and answers were wearying him. He got up and leaned against the wall.

Then suddenly he felt an unexpected emotion opening a breach in him. He thought of Pilar. He thought that Pilar loved the boy sitting before him. And he thought, too, of Don Emilio Santos, with whom he had played so many games of domino at the Neutral. The fact that those two persons, Pilar and Don Emilio, should be devoted body and soul to the Falangist suddenly touched Julio deeply. He upbraided himself for having yielded to the temptation to use the light-reflector on the boy.

Mateo was silent. He showed signs of weariness. He did not know what to do with his handkerchief, which was soaking wet. He felt ludicrous, sitting there on a stool in the middle of the office without anything to rest his back against and the yellow wick of his lighter hanging out of his pocket.

Julio looked down at Berta, who had reached his feet. Then he went over to the Falangist and submitted him to an examination of mounting intensity. He revealed that he was aware of everything Mateo had done since he reached Gerona, from his first contacts with Octavio to the recent enrollment of Marta Martínez de Soria and the telegram to Madrid. "Always at your orders." He questioned Mateo about what he understood by revolution and why up to that moment he had refrained from any act of violence. Why had he been talking with a captain of the Civil Guard for the past two weeks? Why had he had the blond ex-anarchist made orderly to Major Martínez de Soria? Why had he said to J. Campistol of Barcelona over the telephone: "Don't come"? Why had his three comrades, when questioned on this point, looked at each other in astonishment? Why was Octavio carrying in his wallet a list of people in the city, headed by the Costas? Why had Haro written on a paper: "Dr. Relken's accent is not German, but Czech"? Why did Benito Civil often go through the personal correspondence of the architects Massana and Ribas? Why had the son of Don Jorge said to one of their tenants: "I'm going to need a hundred empty sacks thirty-five inches long"? Where had Mateo seen stuffed birds with a little door in their breast that opened when you touched one of their claws? When had he heard a son say to his father: "Yes, yes, I know. But nothing important in this world has ever been done without the use of force"? Why, talking at the *Tabacalera* about a shipment of Havana cigars supposed to arrive in November, had he said: "Bah! Who knows what may happen by November"?

Julio told Mateo that by November nothing unusual would have happened. With regard to the emblem on his shirt, he would have to choose between having no emblem or no shirt; and as for Dr. Relken, he was neither German nor Czech: he was simply Dr. Relken, a distinguished archaeologist, a student of antiquities.

Julio told Mateo that a blue handkerchief and a flint lighter were not enough to start a Fascist cell in a province like Gerona, a frontier province, of great responsibility. A certain amount of experience was required, a sprinkling of gray hairs, and even some ability to make friends. Nor was it enough to say: "I'm going to Abyssinia." What counted was to go—and return, if possible. Above all, he was not to imagine that police headquarters was a debating society. The charges against him were specific, and it was necessary for him to hear them, for in spite of everything, the Republic did not deny any citizen the right of defending himself. He stood accused of having attempted to found in Gerona a political organization that had been declared illegal in Madrid, and of having utilized minors for that purpose, and of having distributed arms, and of being prepared to obey the leaders of this organization rather than the legal government, of participating in a clandestine movement of revolt that was being launched, and of having conveyed a letter to Major Martínez de Soria urging him to take command of the revolt in question in the garrison of Gerona.

Throughout this harangue, Mateo had kept his hand over his eyes to shade them. If there had been anyone listening, he would have made an effort to answer the charges; as it was, he realized that it was not worth the trouble. He was tired. What he wanted was to know his sentence, the fate that was in store for him.

The glare of the spotlight had finally made him so dizzy that at the end Julio's voice was coming to him as though from the depths of a park thick with fog. When silence came at last, it was even more intense, more painful. He had the feeling that some rejoinder was expected of him, some words, the defense that the government of the Republic denied no citizen; but he could not bring it out. He was suddenly absorbed, watching with a kind of stupid fascination something on the desk, the paperweight, in which Julio had accidentally set off a snowstorm.

Mateo had the feeling that the muscles of his face were giving way, that their form was changing. His forehead seemed to have grown to an enormous size. He was sure he was smiling, and he would not have wanted to do that under the circumstances for anything in the world. Julio's voice had become silent. There was not a sound.

All of a sudden came the noise of doors being opened, of footsteps. And at the same time threatening shadows appeared before him, blotting out Antonio Sanchez's smile. Men were coming toward him, perhaps to handcuff him and take him Heaven knows where, on the grounds that he had a cache of arms concealed in the breast of a stuffed bird.

Mateo could not stifle a cry of horror as he recognized, among those shadows right under his eyes, an object from his study, a perforated yellowish object being held in two red-veined hands that trembled slightly: the skull. The skull from his desk. He would have recognized it among a thousand. What had happened? Why had they brought it there?

Then he heard Julio's voice clearly, asking him: "Do you recognize this?"

Mateo opened his eyes. To his amazement, he could see clearly, recognize objects. A great feeling of relief came over him. He looked at Julio and saw that the policeman had rested a framed portrait against the lamp. He recognized the picture of José Antonio, who looked back at him without blinking. "Yes, I recognize it. He inscribed it to me in 1933, at the Escorial."

To Mateo's great surprise, in spite of all that had happened and the gravity of the charges, he was released. Julio went up to see the Commissioner, and when he came down said:

"Good, now you are going to see that we are not as fierce as we are painted. The Commissioner has said we are to release you. So you are at liberty; on the other hand, your three comrades, for the time being, are to remain in jail. However, you are to consider yourself in provisional liberty. Please do not leave Gerona, and report here every forty-eight hours. The officer on duty at the door will have a register for you to sign. Now you may go, and please forgive any inconvenience you may have suffered."

Mateo got up disconcerted. His legs were trembling, and he felt as though his eyes were boiling. He noticed that his yellow lighter was hanging out of his pocket, and he stuffed it back in. He started for the door. He stumbled over a nonexistent object, then recovered his balance and went out.

He had no idea how much time had elapsed. He saw that the officer on duty was a different one. That made him suppose it must be very late. Mechanically he touched his shirt and felt that the emblem had been torn off. He came back to reality, and a wave of indignation swept over him. He walked the final steps to the exit with his customary energy.

As he stepped outside, he at once saw shadows coming toward him. They were Pilar, Ignacio, and Marta. The two girls caught his arm. He asked: "What time is it?"

"Ten. Five minutes of ten."

Before setting out, he looked around him. Pilar, Ignacio, and Marta were leading him down the street. There was a gleaming sky, a May sky, over the housetops. Pilar asked him: "What did they do to you, what did they do to you?"

Mateo answered her: "Never mind. We'll talk about that later." He could feel the girl's hands trembling against his arm. He looked down at her. He saw her brilliant eyes, the sweetness of her expression. He felt a great concern in all her bearing. Pilar was guiding him as though he was an inestimable treasure she had recovered, as though she was defending him against all the other passersby. Mateo felt how much he loved that simple, straightforward being in spite of the way her hair looked that day—for, according to Pilar, it needed washing.

When they got to the Rambla, Pilar wanted him to come up with them.

"No, I can't. I've got to go. We'll talk tomorrow."

"You go upstairs. I'll go and tell your father myself and then I'll come back."

"No, honestly. I had better go home."

Ignacio agreed that that was the most sensible thing to do.

"I'll go with you."

"We'll all go with you," said Marta.

Mateo asked that just one of them go with him: Pilar.

Pilar was grateful for his choice. Once more her fingers closed around his arm.

Ignacio said: "Tomorrow you tell us."

Mateo answered: "Everything went all right."

Marta shook hands with him. "*¡Arriba España!*" to which he answered "*¡Arriba!*"

Mateo and Pilar walked away. They crossed the Piedra Bridge and set out toward Mateo's house. There was a strange calm in the city. It was a mild, pleasant night. Few people were on the streets. Pilar wanted to say many things to him, but they seemed to stick in her throat. They walked very slowly, her head against Mateo's shoulder. The only thing she said, without shifting her position, was: "What were those packages the two policemen who came in were carrying?"

Mateo answered: "The picture of José Antonio and the skull."

Pilar went on: "Your eyes hurt, don't they?"

"A little."

"Shall I go up and prepare you something to eat?"

"No, I don't want anything." In front of the house Mateo stopped. He had Pilar's hands in his. With his eyes, which hurt him, he looked into hers. "I'm sorry. Now you have to go back by yourself."

"That doesn't matter."

Mateo went on: "Tomorrow I'll come over to your house after lunch."

"Fine. I'll call you in the morning."

"No, don't; it's better for you not to telephone."

Pilar was silent for a moment. "Is there nothing I can do? Have you any instructions you want to give me?"

"Yes, I have. Wait a minute. Let me think." He bent his head forward. "Yes. Go and see Jorge and tell him to come by the *Tabacalera* before twelve."

"Right."

Pilar hoped Mateo would kiss her, but he did not. Then she stood on her tiptoes and kissed him on the forehead. Mateo returned her kiss. "Now hurry home."

"I'll go slowly, so I can think about you."

Mateo was just going in the door when he noticed a shadow on the balcony. It was Don Emilio Santos. Mateo felt a great emotion well up in his breast.

"Are you coming up?" asked his father.

"Yes."

He walked up the stairs, holding on to the banister. He felt like putting his arms around his father when he threw the door open.

He did not need to ring. The door was ajar, and his father's head emerged from behind it. Don Emilio Santos clasped his hand and said: "Sh-sh-sh!" and closed the door soundlessly.

"You've got visitors," he said in a low voice.

"Who?"

"In the dining room. Two Civil Guards."

Mateo gave a start. "What do they want?"

Don Emilio Santos replied: "I don't know. But I don't think you have anything to be afraid of."

Mateo looked at himself in the mirror of the hat rack and settled his necktie over his blue shirt. Several steps brought him to the dining room.

The two Civil Guards got up when they saw him. One of them looked about twenty-five years old; the other was considerably older, fat, and with the expression of a person of great fidelity.

Mateo went over to them. The older of them said: "Captain Roberto has spoken to us."

Mateo looked at them searchingly. It seemed to him he was not mistaken in the sincerity he read in their faces. He answered: "It depends on your capacity for sacrifice."

SEVENTY-TWO

EL Tradicionalista informed the people of Gerona that bomb number four had been ordered exploded by Cosme Vila himself, and that Murillo, who had carried out the order, had in the ensuing confusion made off with one of the images that had fallen into the street, and had sold it to Dr. Relken, "who has it put away, together with other objects, in room number 23 of the Hotel Peninsular."

Don Pedro Oriol had supposed that the accusation would cause a sensation. Someone remarked at the Neutral: "What do you think of the doctor! Talking atheism and buying saints!" The assistant manager of the bank was indignant at the idea of the doctor making off with the province's art treasures. "It's the same as the English Masons who took over the Catholic cathedrals," he said. Cosme Vila was indignant, too. What Murillo had done outraged him. In Cosme Vila's opinion the most serious crime a militant Communist could commit was just that: to turn an act of service to his own profit. But aside from these isolated reactions the city paid no attention whatever to the news item. Everyone was waiting for the trial of Lieutenant Martín, that was the important thing. That and the carrying out of the decisions reached by the Security Committee, whose results were becoming known.

Everybody knew that Don Jorge and Warning Voice prowled the prison corridors like caged tigers. Jocose anecdotes were recounted of how they behaved. According to some of these, Warning Voice had suffered a terrible toothache and, not being able to attend to it at his office, had asked the gypsy to yank out the tooth with a string. Others told how the peasant who was in jail for chasing his brother with a sickle had managed to steal Don Jorge's derby, gloves, and cane under cover of darkness and now, decked out in these objects, chased their rightful owner and the guards. Everybody found this highly amusing. Someone remarked: "They ought to let visitors in on Thursdays and Sundays."

As for Octavio, Haro, and Rosselló, it was said that they spent hours singing subversive hymns, such as that of the Foreign Legion, of Falange, *Giovanezza*, and the Horst Wessel song. The guards had had to threaten them with nightsticks. It was said that Rosselló's father had refused to intercede for him. "He wants to have his own ideas; let him take the consequences." Octavio's sweetheart haunted police headquarters as though trying to find a breach by which to enter.

General opinion was that it would be a long time before those held in custody would be released, for as the proceedings moved ahead, new accusations against them came to light. As for Mateo, it was said that he now planned to hold his meetings at the Crocodile Bar. Some thought it a mistake to have let him go. Others replied: "They did it to see if he incriminates himself further." Various smokers claimed they had found clandestine pamphlets in packages of cut tobacco put out by the *Tabacalera*. According to certain soldiers, they had seen the boy talking with Major Martínez de Soria in the armory. "That was where he handed him the letter." "They're going to get a haircut and shave before this is over." "There are Civil Guards mixed up in the business."

El Tradicionalista's denunciation melted like snow under such a variety of problems. Moreover, the denial in the pages of the local publications was crushing. *El Demócrata*, taking as its point of departure *El Tradicionalista's* valuation of the image acquired by Dr. Relken, published on its front page the next day a statement signed by the architect Massana of the wealth in the hands of the Catholic Church in Spain. According to the architect, the jewels of the Virgin alone amounted to an astronomical figure. Not to mention the solid gold monstrances, chalices, and candelabra. "There are altars whose columns are of gold." The robes of the Virgin of Toledo were listed, and of various Virgins of Andalusia, also figures on Montserrat, and the Cathedral of Gerona.

Mosén Francisco, whom Laura's visit had put in a good humor, commented: "Odd. There are details about San Félix I didn't know myself. I didn't know we were so rich."

Carmen Elgazu said: "Naturally, they'd rather see trollops wearing those jewels."

The readers found studies of this sort extremely interesting. But none of them achieved the success of the special issue of *El Proletario* which Cosme Vila brought out two days after the number of *El Tradicionalista* to announce and pave the way for the general assembly of the party, so anxiously awaited.

It was an issue of sixteen pages, with a supplement, printed on good paper. It had an attractive cover and excellent typography. It was a large issue, which was distributed free of charge in Gerona and the province.

Cosme Vila had had the clever idea of covering both the mythological and the real. Employing both dimensions, he managed to interest everybody. The mythological was the sixteen pages completely devoted to Russia; the real was the supplement devoted to persons and events of the locality.

Several days of backbreaking work had gone into the issue, but it had paid off. The report on Russia had been prepared by Gorki. On the first page was a picture of Stalin seated in the Kremlin. At his feet millions of smiling workers acclaimed him. In the upper corners, framed in two artistic medallions, Marx and Lenin beamed down upon their work from the beyond.

Inside were the stories, with authentic photographs and documents. The Communists of Gerona gazed agape at the spectacle of the gigantic enterprises being carried out in Russia: irrigation projects, railroads, smelters, etc. Great tentacles seemed to reach out over the whole country, multiplying its wealth. But perhaps what most impressed them were the conditions under which the Russian workmen lived. The collective dining halls, the hospitals, the number and size of the swimming pools that formed a part of the factories, the athletic fields. "Just compare the swimming pool of Novgorod with that in the Dehesa," was Gorki's caption on page 3, under a huge engraving. "Compare this football field of Odessa with that of Gerona, which you, workers, are forbidden to use on the grounds that you will spoil the grass." Cosme Vila's followers buried their noses in the pages, eagerly sniffing the Grand Canal, the collective dining halls, the Muscovite, housing projects, the Georgian. Especially Teo, whom the sight of those swimming pools had driven slightly mad, for his mania was still the high dive, and he saw that in Odessa, and especially in Novgorod, he could even break his neck.

The faithful repeated what Dr. Relken had said one day at the Neutral: "Of course, one lives much better in Russia than here." The faithful firmly believed that the great mass of workers was made up of volunteers. On the last page Gorki inserted a woodcut of the all-marble subway planned for Moscow.

As for the supplement devoted to the locality, it was perhaps one of Cosme Vila's master strokes.

A cheaper paper was used than for the bulletin on Russia, the printing was much poorer, the format smaller. But this did not matter. It was an unforgettable line-up of personalities of the locality, each with his description. Someone dubbed it: "Family album."

On the first page was Major Martínez de Soria out riding with Marta. The bearing of both of them was dignified; but by a photographic trick, enlarging the mouths from ear to ear, their faces looked monstrous. Everybody laughed at the double exposure—everybody but Ignacio. When Ignacio saw it, he turned pale and stopped breathing. He had found the supplement in the vestibule when he came in from the bank; someone had slipped it under the door.

He could not recall ever being so angry. His father was afraid he was going to do something rash, for Ignacio, as he crushed the paper in his hand, kept looking in the direction of Communist headquarters. "I agree with you, it is a foul thing to do," said Matías Alvear, standing, as though by chance, with his back against the street door, "but there's nothing you can do about it. All this will collapse of its own weight sooner or later." Ignacio, his teeth clenched, finally turned the page with the tips of his fingers and came upon another picture of the major, parade sword in hand, while in a corner a group of tiny workers, reduced in size, peered at him with fear. That was so ingenuous that Ignacio could not restrain a comment that wounded Carmen Elgazu's ears.

He turned the remaining pages one by one. And as he glanced through them he gradually recognized how diabolically clever Cosme Vila had been. There was Don Jorge getting out of a taxi at the gate of one of his farms, sticking his cane into a basket of potatoes the tenant was holding out to him. There was Warning Voice at the officers' café, offering a colonel a light in a fawning attitude. The caption of the picture read: "In a few days this man will be back in the editorial office of *El Tradicionalista*."

Don Santiago Estrada appeared arm in arm with his wife on the middle of Piedra Bridge, both of them laughing uproariously. Then a photograph of the Bishop followed by two pages carrying purple cushions. The Costas smoking long cigars as their workers came out of the foundry. Professor Civil's son holding up a Falangist leaflet. Noguer the notary, Laura, the hooded cloaks of Holy Week, a first-class funeral, with the plumes on the horses etched against the blue sky.

And on the last page, the *coup de grâce*, the masterpiece of Victor's camera: a cut of Brother Alfredo in the patio of the Christian Brothers', handing out caramels to a group of small boys. Brother Alfredo's eyes, which had been skillfully touched up, had an expression of great beatitude.

When he finished it, Ignacio went over to the dining room window, opened it wide, and threw the supplement into the river. Pilar, who was standing at the window of her room, unaware of what was going on, called out: "What are you doing?" Ignacio stepped back and noisily closed the shutters. The girl looked down into the water, and she still had time to see the current slowly carrying off Don Santiago Estrada's guffaw.

Nevertheless, Cosme Vila had achieved his objective. The cafés buzzed with ironical comments on the photographs. Raimundo, who had become strangely aggressive since the Abyssinian war, pasted Warning Voice's picture on the wall. The consensus at the bank was that Laura and Noguer the notary should have been respected; on the other hand Don Jorge sticking his cane into the potatoes was mirthfully received.

The groundwork had been laid for the general assembly. Murillo was easy in his mind, for Cosme Vila had said nothing to him about the sale of the image. A reference in the supplement to Jaime Arias had filled Teo, his brother, with satisfaction, somewhat calming the rage boiling in him because of Lieutenant Martín's desecration. All the members of the Communist Party were living feverish hours, particularly as it had been announced that several of the leaders of Barcelona, and probably Comrade Vasiliev, would be at the Albéniz Theater. Even bomb number four finally came to be looked upon as a clever move of Cosme Vila's.

Cosme Vila did not budge from his desk, opening first one drawer, then another. His wife loved him more than ever; his parents-in-law never stopped thinking of him except when the crossing gates demanded their attention.

Cosme Vila was satisfied because he saw that he was opening a breach in the city. Before elections nearly all the party members had been factory workers. He knew now that several students of mathematics had stated that they were Communists, and as he passed by he noticed that they looked at him with great curiosity and a certain respect. There was talk of an intern in the hospital who was a Communist. A secondary-school teacher, several intellectuals, and even an occasional person of means.

Don Santiago Estrada asked in the Casino: "How is it possible for a person of means to be a Communist?" Nobody could give him a satisfactory answer.

CASAL was greatly surprised to receive a personal invitation from Cosme Vila. "You have a seat reserved for you on the stage, with the presiding committee." The same thing happened to David and Olga: two reserved seats.

On the other hand. Dr. Relken could not understand why his name had been overlooked. He poured himself a glass of water and said to Julio: "As the Russian is going to be there, they have preferred not to have me appear."

Casal suspected that Cosme Vila's invitation had nothing to do with their personal relationship or with any desire for solidarity. David and Olga, on the other hand, were consumed by curiosity.

On the invitation they received there was a postscript in Cosme Vila's handwriting which said: "It would be of interest if you could be present, for in the educational reform plan we are going to present, we intend to use your *Manual of Pedagogy*."

These words filled the teachers with a satisfaction they were unable to conceal. The truth of the matter was that the Generalidad still gave them nothing but vague hopes about their *Manual*. As Supervisors of Education in the province, they could fill vacancies, make appointments, found new teaching institutions, and forbid the use of religious garb; but in the inner workings of the schools, tradition often proved to be stronger than they. Such proposals as washing the pupils' heads weekly or putting them to work at agriculture had been received with outright hostility by some of the teachers. Others, on their own initiative, had introduced reforms that went too far.

In view of the offer of help held out by Cosme Vila, they were inclined to attend the assembly. Casal said to them: "All right, I'll go with you."

Julio, however, declined the invitation he had received, as did the Commissioner. Ever since the meeting of the Security Committee any move by Cosme Vila had aroused their suspicions. "He had better watch his step," Julio remarked on that occasion. "The cavalry would like nothing better than to be called out again."

Cosme Vila had requested the protection of a squad of Assault Guards. According to him, the Trotskyite cell, on hearing of the arrival of Comrade Vasiliev, was preparing some action against him.

The meeting had been set for nine o'clock. But immediately after factory closing time a great buzz of activity had set in around the theater, and many strange faces, rustic in appearance, from all parts of the province, were to be seen. El Responsable and Future, seated in a café, could not decide whether to do something or to accept silently the failure of their movement, a failure that looked as though it might become permanent.

As a matter of fact, only a few days had elapsed since the presentation of the anarchist demands. The eight hundred strikers, therefore, were still holding out; but their discouragement was plain to see, for the machines were running normally, and the blackest poverty had made its inevitable appearance in many homes. The anarchists grew most dispirited at nightfall, when all the lights of the city came on. It was then they understood how short-lived their dream had been. They talked among themselves of the forty-eight hours when Gerona had been without light, when the people had walked along the streets feeling their way by the walls. Santi, particularly, could not accept the idea that the light had returned.

El Responsable said to Future: "Look what they did to us just because we asked for control. Now these brutes are going to ask for much more, and everyone will give in to them."

Future answered: "We were fools. We should have asked for everything, even doing away with money."

And yet none of the workers gathering in front of the theater even remembered the anarchist strike. But for many enterprises its continuation was proving disastrous. The Costas, especially, were in despair. Their wives said to them: "Now maybe you'll pay some attention to what we say! We should all go and live in Pals!" Laura was complicating things even more with her laments. She didn't give a hoot about the strike or the assembly; the only thing that mattered to her was her husband's being under arrest, especially as Mosén Alberto had said to her: "If you don't do something about this quickly, if the Communists get control, the fifteen days in jail will become fifteen months."

"What do you want us to do?" the Costas asked her. "The arrest is legal. Do you think we can change the statutes?"

Mosén Alberto had advised Laura to leave no stone unturned. The priest claimed to know just what the demands drawn up by Cosme Vila, with the approval of the Communists of Barcelona and the teacher recently converted to Marxism, were aimed at. "They have in mind a real revolution like that of Russia, and they plan to hand the province over to the populace." Noguer the notary thought he was exaggerating.

The wealth of details Mosén Alberto possessed was in marked contrast with the complete ignorance of the mass of the Communist members as to what they were going to hear at the Albéniz Theater that evening. As it grew later, the plaza became more and more crowded, and comments of every sort were to be heard. "We are going to give them an ultimatum such as they've never heard before!" Others affirmed that the death sentence was going to be demanded for Lieutenant Martín—that and that the barracks be converted into people's centers "as has been done in Russia."

In view of the growing agglomeration, the attendants of the theater decided to open the doors, even though the meeting was not to start for another hour. In less than twenty minutes the place was filled up. Future, watching from the café, said as he looked at the lines: "A lot of females." And it was true. There were many women, some of them carrying placards reading: "Long live Russia!" Those which read "Long live Comrade Vasiliev!" were at the station, with the executive committee of the party, waiting for the train to arrive.

When it was announced over the loudspeakers of the theater that Comrade Vasiliev and the Communist leaders of Barcelona had reached Gerona, a ripple of emotion ran through the crowd. The gravedigger's son stood up in his seat. Everyone's eyes were fixed on the main entrance, but the loudspeakers informed the audience that the speakers would make their appearance directly on the stage.

Very few knew Vasiliev. His picture had not appeared even in *El Proletario*. Some recalled a photograph of him published by *El Día Gráfico*, in the port of Barcelona, his fist raised, welcoming the sailors of a Russian tanker.

For that reason his appearance on the stage, surrounded by the local leaders, was doubly spectacular. There was no need to introduce him to the crowd: it divined who he was. He stood out unmistakably against the others. A somewhat disordered white mane, thick glasses, a powerful neck. His pale skin was in contrast with that of the dark southerners. Moving both hands in restrained gestures, he greeted the crowd. And just as the loudspeakers struck up *The Internationale*, his fist went up like a human semaphore, dark and determined, dragging after it the fists of all those in the theater. The measures of the hymn sent a thrill through the audience. Teo's immense head, a broad smile on its lips, touched the lower part of the medallion of Lenin in the rear of the stage. La Valenciana, unbelievably dressed up, was at the front. All that was visible of Gorki was his round little belly and his sharp eyes. Murillo's walrus mustache tickled one of the committee from Barcelona. The illuminated head of Cosme Vila was to Vasiliev's right.

Among the leaders from Barcelona, two or three were very short, authentic representatives of the people. They were wearing their railroad caps, which made an excellent impression on the audience. Casal, David, and Olga were seated to the extreme left. The footlights flattered Olga. She looked beautiful.

With the last note of *The Internationale*, Vasiliev sat down, and everybody imitated him. A silence followed, after which Cosme Vila declared the meeting open.

A comrade from Barcelona was the first speaker. He congratulated Comrade Cosme Vila for his achievement in raising the flag of the revolution in a city as reactionary and ecclesiastical as Gerona. The bourgeois forces of the city and province were no doubt feeling in their wallets—in the place where their hearts should be—and in their shotguns—which they kept in the cloakroom—the implacable advance of the new force, the Communist Party.

The speaker assured the people of Gerona that they were not alone in their struggle. Throughout Spain similar groups of the proletariat were gathered at their centers, in other theaters. All along the Mediterranean, and in Extremadura, Asturias, and Galicia. In Madrid, the center of the country, and in Zaragoza, in many places whose names they hardly knew, Communist cells were linked in one network to put an end to the rule of those wallets and those shotguns.

"You are not alone, comrades of Gerona. The Catalan and national directors of the party are at this very moment demanding the nationalization of the banks, of heavy industry, of the railways. Demanding that the forces of order, which are practically blockading the streets, and which are an unbearable burden on the State, be replaced by a people's militia, an armed proletarian force, which, like the Bolshevik militias of Russia, guarantee..."

An earsplitting burst of applause followed his words. Cosme Vila looked toward the orchestra seats and boxes as though looking for somebody. His father-in-law, sitting in the gallery, stretched his neck, for he was sure he was the person being looked for. Cosme Vila was pleased because he had caught a glimpse in one of the aisles of the mathematics students, and near the door the high-school teacher.

The percentage of women pleased him, too. He knew that they constituted a real force. He did feel, however, that La Valenciana had committed a grave mistake in wearing that showy dress.

All the speakers from Barcelona took the same line, patently leaving to Cosme Vila the honor of presenting the local issues. They ridiculed Gil Robles and Calvo Sotelo. They attacked Mussolini and Hitler, and, with special invective, Oliveira Salazar, "one of the obstacles the proletariat must overcome to achieve Iberian union." They attacked Azaña and Casares Quiroga, "bourgeois in disguise, who pretend to be deaf when they are warned that a military uprising is in the making." They attacked Prieto, but spoke favorably of Largo Caballero rather than otherwise. They praised the party heroes, especially Dolores Ibárruri, "La Pasionaria."

One of the speakers was a strange man with a brooding air. Shortly after he began his speech the audience noticed that he had only one arm. His empty sleeve became an obsession for all of them. The man explained that he had lost his arm in the October Revolution. That lent his words a prophetic tone. When he went on to say that he had been studying Russian for many years, that he hoped to make a trip to Moscow at Comrade Vasiliev's invitation, and that possibly he might, with the hand that remained to him, clasp that of Comrade Stalin himself, flames seemed to shoot up from the rows of seats.

"If I manage to see Comrade Stalin," said the speaker, "I will tell him at first hand of the gratitude of the Spanish people for his help. I will tell him how we have lived up to now, how our grandparents, our parents lived, how our children would live if the Russian people had not risen up. We would go on being exploited and humiliated by political bosses like Calvo Sotelo, who only yesterday stated in Parliament that the army is the backbone of the country. We have only one country, the country of all, the country of the proletariat of the world, Russia!"

Cheers!

"Comrades of Gerona, I take advantage of this occasion to propose to you the sending of a telegram of support to Comrade Stalin. You may be sure it will reach his hands, for to him—"

It was impossible for him to go on. Nobody had thought of the possibility of communicating directly with Stalin. The mere idea so stirred them all that the eyes of many of the women were swimming in tears. As for Teo, he would have been happy to set out immediately in his dray for Moscow. The speaker with the brooding air sat down amid the wildest acclaim.

It was then that Cosme Vila got to his feet. And immediately people felt themselves back on solid ground. From the trip to Moscow and the empyrean, the sight of the local leader brought the audience back to Gerona, to their demands.

Cosme Vila was not a brilliant orator. But he was effective because of his grasp of reality. From his first word he galvanized his hearers because he struck by surprise. Instead of confirming what the earlier speakers had said to the effect that everything was going well, he began by affirming that everything was going badly.

"Our comrade from Barcelona has made the suggestion that we send a telegram to Comrade Stalin. We are all in agreement. However, I must dissent. We cannot do this at this time. Not because we do not want to, but because we are not fit. Why? Because our hands are dirty, because there is a traitor among us."

Everyone held his breath, motionless.

"To send Comrade Stalin a telegram, all those of us who sign it must be clean, must have complied with the rules of the party, with the discipline, the work, and, above all, the code of honor. To exploit the party or benefit by it is to behave like the bourgeois. There is one among us whose hands are not clean, and I feel that as long as this one has not received the lesson he deserves, we cannot in good conscience pay tribute to Comrade Stalin, nor stand with head high before his representative here among us, Comrade Vasiliev."

Cosme Vila continued: "You have all heard about the bomb everyone calls number four. Very good. I ordered that bomb set. I admit this and affirm it, and even say that I would do the same thing a thousand times. I am of the belief that until this has been done in all museums of this kind, we have no real hope of forging ahead. As a consequence of this act of service, however, a party member has benefited economically."

Murillo turned rigid. So rigid that his body refused to obey his intention of making his way past the leaders from Barcelona and fleeing. Morevoer, he would not have had time. Cosme Vila was pointing his finger at him, and, in the midst of an impressive silence, walked slowly over to him, ripped off the insignia of the party, and asked the assembly's authorization to expel him from the party and the meeting place.

Rows of fists raised high revealed to the accused the feelings the formal denunciation by the leader had aroused. Two or three young men made a move as though to jump up on the stage; Cosme Vila halted them with a gesture, never taking his eyes off the former decorator of the Bernat workshop. Pale with rage, Murillo met his look defiantly, and that of the crowd, and then with a swift half turn made his way out, stumbling against La Valenciana, and disappeared.

An earsplitting ovation rewarded Cosme Vila's energetic measure. From that moment his mongoloid head had everyone hypnotized.

He reached into his pocket, brought out some papers, spread them on the table, and without delay proceeded to make known the program drawn up by the executive committee.

"If this is accepted, we can declare that our efforts have been effective. If the answer is in the negative, we shall be obliged to call an unlimited general strike."

The Communist Party program was based on the nine points Cosme Vila had outlined in the barbershop one day. On the social level it called for a six-hour work day, labor's control of industry, and a profit-sharing plan. Practically the program of El Responsable, with slight variations.

On a political level, all the authorities were to be immediately dismissed from their posts—Commissioner, Chief of Police, and the others—and elections called to fill the posts in question, elections in which only those holding workers' cards could vote.

On the economic level, it called for the establishment of three workingmen's cooperatives to distribute potatoes, bread, and oil, and for the municipalization of all public services. Every family holding a card of the Communist Party or of a labor union—Socialist or CNT—would be entitled to these free of charge.

In the matter of education, Cosme Vila stated that the Communist Party had great confidence in Comrades David and Olga, who were among those present, for this work.

Cosme Vila then referred to the religious problem. The mention of this theme aroused the keenest interest. The leader said that for psychological reasons, which could not be ignored, it was impossible to reach the desired goal, which would be the complete extermination, in one move, of that factory of lies which was the Catholic Church. This had not been accomplished even in the Soviet Union. The use of the cassock, however, was to be immediately forbidden, and all convents not devoted to charitable ends were to be closed. Those thus vacated, as well as CEDA, Liga Catalana, and the other fascist party headquarters, would be taken over by the workers' organizations.

Cosme Vila had read all this out in a slow voice. He laid down the paper and went on: "There is still much to be done. You all know that arms have been found in the homes of a hundred and fifty Fascists, only ten of whom are in jail. What does this mean? It means that the search has been superficial, and that there has been only token punishment. All of us know that there is not one Rightist who does not possess arms. Therefore we cannot let ourselves be taken by surprise. Comrade Hernandez of Barcelona has alluded to the People's Militia. Let us demand the creation of such a militia in Gerona, for you all know that the military is planning an uprising."

The reaction was unanimous. Shouts of "Arms! Arms!" reverberated through the theater.

When the noise had died down, Cosme Vila went on: "Comrades, when you get home, think over each of these points we are demanding. You will then see that your confidence in us has not been misplaced. They are the elementary replevin of the rights of the proletariat. They represent the first period. Spain can stand in the vanguard of the revolution along with the Soviet Union. You must be willing to employ every necessary means to make our voices heard. If they refuse to listen to us, then all must be prepared to know our implacable will."

There was a new ovation for Cosme Vila of "Long live the Spanish Communist Party! Long live Russia!" Only one thing had surprised the old members: Cosme Vila had not once attacked the anarchists, as was to have been expected. On the contrary, he had extended a hand to them, as to Casal. Some of them decided that this must be a question of tactics.

Comrade Vasiliev's getting to his feet interrupted these speculations. The Russian leader displayed once more the austerity of his earlier appearance on the stage. He received the applause of the crowd without moving a muscle. He only nodded from time to time or raised his fist.

Everybody asked himself in what language Vasiliev would talk. It was said that it was very hard for Russians to learn Spanish. For that reason, when Comrade Vasiliev gave his first words of greeting in Catalan, the crowd went wild. The Russian talked haltingly, but clearly. He had to feel for every word and its pronunciation. But the effect was overwhelming. Every syllable he brought out took on special significance. So, although his speech was brief, it really lasted a long time.

"Comrades—of Catalonia: in the name of the Soviet Union—I bring you greetings from Russia. I congratulate—Comrade Cosme Vila, your leader—for his intelligence—his loyalty. His action—in expelling—comrade—has moved me—I intend to let the leaders of the Soviet Union know about it. Comrades—I approve your revolutionary program, which you, too, have approved. The moment of the—triumph of the proletariat approaches. Comrade Stalin—has requested me—to greet the Spanish and Catalan people. Fight—liberate your brothers. All countries will be with you. Spain—very backward—because of religion and bourgeois dictatorship. But Soviet Union—and Spain sisters. Comrades of Gerona—discipline and heroism! Long live the—proletariat of the world! Long live—Russia! Long live—the Spanish Communist Party!"

SEVENTY-THREE

THERE were several persons whom the frankly revolutionary nature of those demands did not surprise. Among these was Professor Civil. It was his opinion that Cosme Vila had not assumed for one moment that the authorities would accept them; he knew beforehand that with the possible exception of the stipulations regarding religion, they would reject them one after the other. But, in Professor Civil's judgment, that was exactly what Cosme Vila was after. Once the aspirations of the people had been rejected, he would call a general strike, which would coincide with that of the anarchists. The city would be thrown into utter confusion; the authorities would be unable to maintain order; the revolutionary movement in Gerona would be linked up with that forecast in Barcelona. Cosme Vila, according to Professor Civil, would achieve his maximum objective: his ally, stark poverty, would storm the city.

Major Martínez de Soria, for his part, gave special attention to the call for distributing the weapons of the army among the workers' organizations, and the setting up of an armed People's Militia. He asked for an appointment with the general and Colonel Muñoz. He managed to see them together at military headquarters. Both the officers thought he had come to intercede in favor of Lieutenant Martín, which was not the case. "What Cosme Vila has proposed," he said, "is an insult to the honor of the army. On the other hand, if the creation of this People's Militia is not authorized, the workers' organizations will proceed to demoralize the troops. A large number of soldiers attended the assembly, and some of them, I have been told, threw their military caps on the ground and trampled on them. I would request of the general that he take the necessary measures to guarantee the loyalty of the troops of the garrison."

Major Martínez de Soria saw that his words were having their effect, but that the general and Colonel Muñoz were not at all sure that he was not exaggerating. The general, short and squat, his eyes shooting flames, paced up and down the office mouthing oaths. Colonel Muñoz had more self-control.

Besides, he had spent many Saturdays crossing foils with the major in the armory. He said to him: "The general has received a copy of the demands and is preparing a fitting reply. As far as I am concerned, I do not feel myself in a position to advise the general, especially in view of the fact that he has not asked anyone's opinion. I am sure that he will hit upon a satisfactory solution."

Major Martínez de Soria repeated what he had said, and the general replied in a peremptory tone that he would like to be left alone. The major and the colonel went out of the office together. Major Martínez de Soria then said to his companion: "Colonel, for the good of all I beg you to think my words over." And he left.

Warning Voice received the news of Cosme Vila's demands in prison, and it was as though the gypsy really had yanked out his tooth with a string. He had a feeling that he would never leave those walls, that at any moment Cosme Vila would come in and finish him off along with Don Jorge and the other landowners under arrest. He fell into a state of complete panic. On the one hand, he thought that he had made a mistake in forbidding Laura to ask the Costas to intervene on his behalf. On the other, he reproached himself for never having made a generous gesture toward his fellow men, with the exception of his maid Dolores, who brought him his basket of food with exemplary punctuality. Any strange noise, a movement by the gypsy or Don Jorge's cane, terrified him.

"If I were only out..." he thought. He felt that he would be able to persuade Major Martínez de Soria of the need to make a trip to Madrid and talk with other officers who could be trusted. Because the difficult thing was to know which of them would really be willing to carry out the *coup d'état* they had not been prepared to bring off in October, and which would become turncoats at the last minute. Don Jorge had little faith in this. Besides, his reserves of rage were spent. He was obsessed by the thought of his two tenants who had been jailed in the October uprising, and whom he believed responsible for his imprisonment. In the last paragraph of the demands he had read: "Those having to do with changes in agriculture will be announced shortly." Don Jorge did not believe the mob would break into the jail, but he was sure they would seize his holdings. He felt weak and asked the warden if, in view of his age if not his position, he might be allowed to eat at a table with a cloth and sleep in the infirmary. The warden agreed to the latter request; as for the tablecloth, this was forbidden by prison regulations.

Another not taken by surprise was Mateo. Nevertheless, when he read the demands, he had a bad quarter of an hour. When at the end he read: "Long live Russia!" he slumped in his chair, heartsick. What had happened to the country that hundreds of Spanish throats should hail a leader arrived from the lands of the East, that the walls should be covered with posters asking Spanish mothers to adore Stalin? Who was responsible for that? All of them—all—were responsible. The fanaticized masses were the least to blame. It was the rulers, present and past, the enterprises that made millions, and the men who with pen or spoken word did all in their power to uproot the concept of Country. The proof was that there were the hearts seeking themselves another country, far away, on the frontier of Asia....

Mateo's father hovered around him with a sorrowful air, for he had heard nothing from Cartagena for ten days. "Have you any news of your brother?" he asked.

"He's still in jail," Mateo answered, "but he's all right."

Don Emilio Santos was suffering deeply. He presumed that if they had released Mateo, it was so as not to lose touch with the organization, and because they knew that the boy would be rasher than ever.

"My son," he said to him, "I am warning you that all this strikes me as dangerous. Really, I don't know what to think. Sometimes I think you are right, and that we should all be following your example. Nevertheless, there is something in your eyes I don't like. It seems to me that you are just as bad in your way, and that if you could you'd be doing to the others what they are doing to you and your brother. Don't ever forget my advice! In the last analysis, love is always stronger than hate. Make sure you are moved by love, not by the contrary."

For the first time in a long while Mateo took his father's arm and pressed it hard. And for the first time in a long while Don Emilio Santos saw that his son was getting ready to go out without his blue shirt. Without the blue shirt on the outside; he was wearing it under the other, and this had not escaped the notice of the maid.

With the echo of his father's words in his ears, the boy made his way toward the Alvears', where he found them in a state of utter bewilderment. Ignacio was reading a copy of the demands and said despondently: "They made a good impression at the bank..." Matías, when Mateo came in, took off his earphones. The presence of the lad did nothing to dispel the gloomy nature of his thoughts. He still believed that temperaments like Mateo's had had a part in bringing things to such incredible lengths. He had a certain fondness for the boy; it was hard for him not to like someone his daughter loved so much. But he would have preferred a lawyer given to calmer matters, or a telegraph employee. When he learned that Julio had almost made him faint by keeping a light shining in his eyes, he felt a great contempt for his childhood friend. And behind Julio's ambition, as always, he heard the jangling of Doña Amparo Campo's bracelets. Now he was sure that Don Emilio Santos was right: Mateo would be bolder than ever; he would find another meeting place, in the catacombs if necessary. There he would forgather with those who were left, with the new members, with Marta.

Matías Alvear, too, was looking over Cosme Vila's demands, and said to Mateo: "You see what we have come to. They tried to get me to send a telegram to Stalin at twelve o'clock at night."

Carmen Elgazu was nervous because she had arranged with Marta for them to take flowers to the grave of Mosén Alberto's maid. She opened the window to let the May sky in. And seeing that nobody said anything, she asked, turning to Mateo: "Are you sure it was a wise thing to have made El Rubio the major's orderly?"

"Why not?" Mateo asked her.

"I don't know."

Mateo replied: "El Rubio is a more loyal friend than someone more in keeping with our ideas might be."

Ignacio shared his opinion. He was sure they could depend on El Rubio in a pinch.

Marta spoke up: "Of course he can be depended on. My father is devoted to him. He learned to ride at once. Besides, he has a sense of humor. We met El Responsable walking alone in the Dehesa one day and El Rubio stopped and called to him from his horse: 'Au revoir.'"

Carmen Elgazu served Mateo coffee and asked him: "So Julio, as usual—"

Mateo answered: "I can't complain. He let me go."

Pilar inquired: "What do you think is going to happen now?"

Mateo drained his cup at one swallow. "Now—Julio will reject the demands. There will be a strike. Probably shooting. But at least," he added, "Dr. Relken is going to learn that you can't play with Spain."

Everyone looked at him in perplexity. Carmen Elgazu sat down across the table from him and said: "Come, now, no more nonsense! You want to start something else? Dear God," she went on, "soon we won't even be able to go to Mass."

JULIO gave a somber smile as he read the demands. They contained a clause he would never forgive: the proposal that a new chief of police be named. He had barely finished reading them when the Commissioner burst into his office, with another copy in his hand. "This is monstrous, positively monstrous!"

Julio said to him: "Commissioner, this is going to be no picnic. We must get in touch with the general immediately."

Julio spent an hour studying Cosme Vila's proposals carefully. He came to the conclusion that if they were to meet his demands, the setup of the city would be odd indeed: Cosme Vila, commissioner; Gorki, chief of police; Teo, mayor, and so on. The workers would take over everything; the other people would not even have the right to play dominoes at the Neutral. Julio thought: "My wife would love that. She who wanted to see me rubbing elbows with high society." And a picture flashed before his eyes of himself sweeping out Cosme Vila's office or adding his own name to his card index of suicides.

A steady stream of visitors poured into Julio's office. Everyone holding a job of which he was to be relieved under the new order came in person to see him. The Inspector of Labor said to him: "Some favor Largo Caballero did me when he sent me here! First a hand grenade, and now a kick in the ass."

The Judge of First Instance held forth interminably on the illegality all that implied: "For example, the post of judge, you can see for yourself—"

Julio interrupted him: "Of course I can see, my dear friend. Of course I can."

All those persons seemed craven to Julio. All those pleading visitors were grown people, professionals, not born yesterday. But clearly the sight of a thousand railroad workers' caps converging upon them paralyzed their ability to think, their self-confidence, or their shrewdness.

Julio alone did not lose his head. There was no doubt that many people were being swept up by the contagion, by the power that social earthquake exercised, with the result that Cosme Vila's demands were finding supporters even among citizens who had never given a thought to Marxism. But the number of the opponents was large, too. Management, large or small, the bulk of the middle class whose work was definitely outside the "manual workers" classification, and who therefore would have to labor for the collective profits without sharing in them.

It seemed to Julio that it was there that Cosme Vila had made a mistake. After the first shock had passed, bank employees, government employees of every kind, the rank and file of the army, the Assault Guards, foremen, sewing-girls, all those who left their work with clean hands, would unite in protest against this absolute control of the workers. Besides, the splits would come: in the same factory those who ran the machines would consider themselves proletariat, while on the other hand they would deny the name, and the benefits inherent therein, to the bookkeeper and the rest of the office staff.

"Cosme Vila lost a point there," Julio said to Antonio Sánchez, "the smart thing is to gain positions making the fewest possible enemies. Unless," he added, "one has overwhelming superiority of numbers or matériel, in which case it does not matter. But that is not true of Cosme Vila."

And for that reason Julio suspected that Cosme Vila had proposed the creation of the People's Militia because he knew that in every factory occupied, every position taken, there would be a long list of disaffected. In reality, of all the demands the one Julio considered the most dangerous was the People's Militia. The Chief of Police knew that as long as he had the police, the horses, the guns and night-sticks at his command, he could restore normalcy in a minute, as had happened with the barricades of the anarchists.

The general, too, was enraged over the militia. When Julio telephoned him, he barked: "This is absolutely intolerable, and what you people should do is to throw all that trash into jail right away."

Julio did not share the general's opinion. Julio kept a cool head, but when he warned the Commissioner that the situation was serious, he meant it. Things were taking a turn that he would never have imagined, and great tact was going to be needed. There was a moment when Antonio Sánchez stepped out of the office that he felt tired. He played absentmindedly with the key of his desk drawer, pushing it in and taking it out. He thought for a moment of Carmen Elgazu: "The hatred of religion blinds you." Then suddenly, as he caught sight of José Antonio's picture, which, though it was turned to the wall, was still there, he got up, annoyed with himself, saying: "Let's get going." He picked up the telephone book and put through calls to the Costas and Casal.

He had made up his mind to turn down flatly the demands—with perhaps trifling exceptions.

Cosme Vila had set a time limit of one week. During that week measures would have to be taken to counteract the effects of the strike as soon as it was declared.

The Costas gave a shout of joy when they heard Julio's voice. At last! They would never forgive Cosme Vila for having included them in the supplement to *El Proletario*, puffing away at big cigars. Both of them felt that if they were able to smoke cigars, it was because they had worked hard all their lives, and, besides, their ideal was for everybody to smoke them. "Whereas that ape of a Cosme Vila," they said to their wives, "wants us all to smoke cabbage leaves."

Casal, too, was pleased at Julio's call, in spite of the fact that the Socialist leader was not frightened by the program. As soon as he heard it in the theater, he felt positive that it was headed for failure. Subsequent events had only confirmed him in his opinion. The members of the UGT and others who were neutral in the matter felt that the whole thing was madness. Even Casal's wife had said to him: "When I see Cosme Vila's wife, I'm going to tell her what I think of all this."

Only the waiters had said to Casal: "You know, a six-hour day wouldn't be bad...

One thing, however, worried Casal, and this was the struggle he divined going on in David and Olga. He realized that they were being put to the acid test. Casal knew they had too much integrity to sell out their ideas in exchange for the adoption of their *Manual of Pedagogy*; yet they were first and foremost teachers, and their profession was an obsession with them.

Before he set out for police headquarters, he said to them: "I assume that whatever decision I take, you will support me."

David and Olga looked shocked. "Naturally," they answered. And Olga added: "Cosme Vila's attitude is disgraceful."

It was impossible for Ignacio to grasp the fact that his former fellow employee Cosme Vila could go to such lengths. Nor could he forgive the outrage of lampooning Marta in *El Proletario.* There were moments when, looking at his sweetheart, he saw her as in that picture, with her mouth stretching from ear to ear. At such times it took all his will-power to remember his father's advice about being sensible.

The attitude of the employees of the bank did not help any. Without being Communists, they found what was going on an entertaining spectacle. Moreover, he was losing the calm Mosén Francisco had enjoined upon him. He was nervous again; it had been a long time since he had gone to confession.

Ignacio had dismissed as absurd the idea of going up to Communist Party headquarters and punching Cosme Vila in the jaw. But he hoped with all his heart that his revolution would be a failure. He trusted that in that week Julio would prove his efficiency. Matías said to him: "Of course he will; just wait and see."

An eight-day waiting period. Cosme Vila's orders were: "During this week everybody is to go to work and do his job well." It was strange that men should be constantly tolerating one another, conceding days of grace. To be sure, this permitted many things. As, for example, breathing and realizing that spring had once more burst forth, that flowers were blooming and the grass was lush in the San Daniel Valley even though Ribas the architect had not time to go there with his portable easel to paint. It made it possible to admire the serenity Pilar was showing, telling stories of what happened at the dressmaking establishment, where, apparently, good humor was still the order of the day. It made it possible to see Carmen Elgazu observing the month of Mary with a candle burning day and night at the Virgin's feet in Pilar's room.

Blessed truce that made it possible to think things over. What was Mateo planning in connection with Dr. Relken? "He is going to learn that you can't play with Spain." Ignacio had a premonition that made him fear the consequences might be serious for his friend. Moreover, examinations were only two weeks off, and Mateo had lost a lot of time. Not to mention the fact that he was forbidden to leave the city. How would he manage about the examinations in Barcelona? Professor Civil would take this hard; besides, the news that his son Benito was a member of Falange had shortened his life.

A week's wait. On Saturday, Mateo had suggested to Ignacio that they go to the San Daniel Valley. They walked along in silence, looking at the Galligans, turned into a brook, the path bordering it, the walls of the cloistered convent. On the other side of the wall the cypresses raised their heads, and there came the sound of laughter. It was the nuns at the half-hour of recreation allowed them during the day. Mateo paused to listen to this laughter. Did the nuns know what was going on in the city?

Mateo thought about César. He broke a sprig of ivy from the wall, and then threw it away because it had no smell. The frogs were singing in the brook. The boys crossed a small wooden bridge. If they turned their heads they could still see the belfry of the Cathedral. There were wildflowers in the meadows beside the path, daisies, poppies. The dogs watched the two boys walk by. This was the truce that made it possible to think about things, that made possible spring's sweet display.

"There are times when one would like to go off and live on an island," said Mateo.

Ignacio did not answer. Mateo came over to him and clasped his arm for a moment.

SEVENTY-FOUR

JULIO'S meeting with the Costas and Casal—with Dr. Relken present in an advisory capacity—was a failure. Julio's plan was to grant Cosme Vila a part of what he asked—to give the impression of impartiality—and refuse the rest. But when the attempt was made to determine this "part," differences of opinion arose.

When Julio suggested accepting the closing of the Rightist meeting places, the Costas objected on the grounds that this violated the right of assembly the Republic so stoutly defended. When he suggested closing the convents, Casal objected on the grounds of freedom of worship. Worker's cooperatives supported by funds from the bishopric and the banks seemed to the Costas grotesque nonsense. There was no agreement.

Not even Dr. Relken, with his continual harping on "unity," fared any better. So, after wordy discussions, they separated. Yet something had to be done against Cosme Vila! The Costas decided to appeal to the Generalidad. Casal consulted Barcelona, and the Socialist Party answered: "We can't risk spoiling the good relations between ourselves and the Communist Party over some petty local quibble." And in case that were not enough, the Masonic lodge ordered him: "Stick to the general lines laid down by the Syndicate."

None of this, however, altered Julio's decision; the demands were refused. The official communication was signed by Julio and the Labor Inspector. Only number five was granted: the closing of the meeting places of the Rightist parties and the shop where *El Tradicionalista* was printed. All the other demands were considered illegal, and the authorities would take whatever measures were necessary to prevent their imposition by force.

As soon as *El Demócrata* and the radio made this decision known, everybody realized that a critical hour was beginning for the city.

Everybody knew that the executive committee of the Communist Party was meeting in permanent session, along with two delegates from Barcelona who were staying on in Gerona to hear the official answer. It was evident that Cosme Vila's response would be dynamite.

Nevertheless, once more Cosme Vila gave proof of self-control. He received Julio's note. Teo rose to his feet like a tower and asked: "Now what do we do?"

Cosme Vila looked at him and answered: "For the moment, go to headquarters, thank them for accepting point five, and ask when it will be put into effect. Then we'll see."

The two delegates from Barcelona nodded agreement, and Cosme Vila, accompanied by Gorki, set out on the errand.

Julio received them in his office. Cosme Vila was carrying the list of the places affected by the close-down order: the shop where *El Tradicionalista* was printed; the editorial offices of the newspaper, which were also the headquarters of the monarchists; CEDA, Liga Catalana, Acción Católica, Congregación Maríana. Cosme Vila asked: "When does the order take effect?"

Julio answered: "It is already in effect, except for Liga Catalana. Liga Catalana," he added in a firm tone, "is to remain open."

Cosme Vila looked at him but said nothing. After a pause the head of the Communist Party said: "We would like to rent *El Tradicionalista*'s press. We'll pay five pesetas more than the highest bidder."

Julio answered: "We will legally announce that bids are being accepted."

Cosme Vila and Gorki left. It was the middle of the afternoon before Teo came in with the news that the orders had been put into effect as regarded Don Pedro Oriol, Don Santiago Estrada, and the Bishop himself and that the Assault Guards had sealed the places in question. At this point the leader of the Communist Party decided to mobilize his members. He himself broadcast the order for a general strike and ordered everyone to be at the Piedra Bridge at half past three the next afternoon. And he arranged for transportation for the cells in the villages, and especially the peasants, so that they could be present at the demonstration.

Mosén Alberto had seemed a different man since the death of his maid, obsessed by the idea of making himself worthy of the tragic end she had suffered. When he heard Cosme Vila's address, he got up and went to his room, where he knelt and prayed with all his soul that God might have pity on the city.

MATEO realized that the moment had come to take action. He realized that neither the Bishop nor Don Pedro Oriol nor Don Santiago Estrada was in a position to make an effective reply, whereas the Falange's ideological independence left its hands free.

When Don Jorge's son went to see him at the *Tabacalera*, on instructions from Pilar, Mateo brought him up to date on his conversation with Julio and said: "My office has been sealed and the party has been declared illegal. Nevertheless, I have to talk with you. El Rubio has agreed to let us meet at his house. So notify all the comrades to be there at half past seven. All except one: Roca. Tell Roca I'm leaving him out for the simple reason that at least one of us must be safe.... Instead of Roca, there will be two new comrades who have just joined—two Civil Guards, Padilla, who is one of the best, as you'll see, and another by the name of Rodríguez. Let Marta know, too."

Jorge carried out his instructions. Meanwhile Cosme Vila made his statement over the radio. As Mateo set out for El Rubio's house, he was fully aware of the capital importance of the meeting he had called.

The members met in the kitchen while El Rubio went out on the balcony, wearing his Pizarro Jazz cap to distract the neighbors' attention.

Mateo took in at a glance that his comrades were feeling somewhat discouraged. The presence of the Civil Guards raised their spirits a little, but they were all danger-conscious and thinking of the jail where Octavio, Haro, and Rosselló sat impotently biting their knuckles.

"Comrades," Mateo began, "the general strike is on. The situation is going to be chaotic. It is the moment for us to make our voices heard, just as we took advantage of the forest fires to distribute our first pamphlets. This time action is called for. Don't worry for fear our acts will go unnoticed because Cosme Vila at the moment has the limelight; fortunately, Falange has its own trademark, and nothing we do, however insignificant, will be overlooked. I want to lay before you for your approval two things to be done simultaneously. One to prove that we are opposed to all who, in the name of the Left and of social progress, would dismember Spain; the other to prove that we are opposed to all who, in the name of the Right and the defense of Spain, commit atrocities. That is to say, we will proceed on the one hand against Lieutenant Martín;, on the other against Dr. Relken."

There was a stir of curiosity.

"As a lesson to Lieutenant Martín, Falange will go to the cemetery—two of the comrades—and wipe out the offense committed by him against Joaquín Santaló and Jaime Arias. The deputy's tombstone is still covered with mud and the cross is in the dirt. The cross will be set up again, the stone cleaned so the name is visible once more, and five roses will be laid at its foot. The same thing will be done at Jaime Arias's grave. The cheap metal marker is to be removed and a small stone I have ordered from Pedro, from which the word 'taxi driver' has been omitted, will be put up in its place. It reads: 'Jaime Arias, forty-two years of age. Died October 7, 1934. We pray for his eternal rest.' And at its foot, five more roses." Mateo paused. Then he added: "And a Lord's Prayer is to be said at each tomb."

The members were moved, and Mateo went on: "I think Comrades Jorge and Civil are best fitted to carry out this duty. And it would be desirable for them, in spite of the circumstances, to wear blue shirts."

Jorge was the first to react. "Do you think our act will be favorably interpreted?" he asked.

"We are showing that we do not like attacks on those who cannot defend themselves," Mateo answered. "And if the interpretation is not favorable to us, we will have done our duty." And then he added: "If anyone has any objections, will he please state them."

Nobody said anything. The older of the Civil Guards asked: "And the second thing you talked about?"

Mateo pulled his chair a little closer to the group. "As I told you, it has to do with Dr. Relken. I suppose you agree with me that what has happened is disgraceful. He's been here for months talking his head off, calling us cave dwellers, illiterates, beings halfway between savages and civilized man. He doesn't like our olive oil, nor our meal hours, nor the fact that we kill bulls risking our lives. Nobody ever contradicts him, and he is even stealing our Virgins. What he needs is such a beating up that he won't be able to see the strike except from bed."

The response to this was instantaneous. Everyone wanted to volunteer, even Marta. Above all, the Civil Guards seemed to savor beforehand the pleasure of settling outstanding scores with the doctor.

"Take it easy, take it easy," Mateo pleaded. "It seems to me that this should be done while Benito and Jorge are at the cemetery; so there's no question of choice. You two," he turned to the Civil Guards, "in civilian clothes, and I."

"You, too?" Marta asked.

"My dear," Mateo answered, "I wouldn't miss this for anything."

The younger of the Civil Guards spoke up: "You don't think three against one is too many?"

His fellow guard, Padilla, answered: "Why? This is a risky business."

Mateo nodded. "There have to be several of us, for different reasons," he explained. "It's not just a question of beating him up. I think that, besides, we ought to shave that pretty blond head of his."

Marta rubbed her left wrist with enthusiasm. "Wait till Pilar hears about this!"

"Then," Mateo went on, "since he doesn't like regular oil, we'll try him on castor oil."

Jorge wrinkled his nose in disgust.

"And above all," Mateo went on, "we must collect all the images and return them to the Museum."

Padilla, the older of the Civil Guards, seemed experienced, and he spoke of the difficulties in the way of carrying out the plan.

"We'll talk about that later," said Mateo. "But I don't think it's going to be too hard. Tomorrow is Saturday, and they're busy at the hotels."

Jorge and Benito Civil were paying slight attention to the operation planned at the hotel. They were thinking only of their own assignment, of the expression on the gravedigger's face when he saw them come into the cemetery and start looking for the graves of Joaquín Santaló and Jaime Arias. "He's going to think the ten roses are ten charges of TNT."

Padilla kept scratching his head. "There's something else," he said, "we haven't mentioned." He looked around at the lot of them. "What's going to happen afterwards?"

Everyone suddenly recalled that there was such a thing as law and order.

"Nothing is going to happen to you," said the guard, pointing to Benito Civil and Jorge. "Nobody can do anything to you for saying the Lord's Prayer at the cemetery. Nor to us," pointing to himself and his comrade, Rodríguez. "Not a soul in Gerona will recognize us in civilian clothes, and that is all to the good. But when it comes to—"

"Excuse me," Mateo cut in, when he heard him say that nobody would recognize them. "It is absolutely necessary for people to know that it was the Falange."

"They will, my good fellow, they will," exclaimed Padilla. "But it's one thing for them to know it was the Falange, and another for them to know it was Padilla and Rodríguez, don't you see? In a word," the guard went on, "the only one here who runs any danger is you." He turned to Mateo: "What will you do afterwards?"

Mateo gave a gesture of impatience. "Don't worry about me. We'll talk about that later. What interests us now is for people to know why the Falange did these two things. Of course, the doctor will give my name." He thought for a moment. "But besides I think we ought to distribute pamphlets clarifying our attitude." Rodríguez winked his eye in Andalusian fashion. "Throw them off the rooftops, the way they do in Seville."

Padilla approved the plan. Then he asked: "Where will you print it?"

"We still have to write it," Mateo answered.

Marta brushed her bangs aside. "My father has a cyclostyle in his office at headquarters," she said. "He'd lend it to me."

"Are you sure?" Mateo asked.

"Of course I am."

Padilla looked at her. It was evident that in matters of this sort he had little trust in women.

"I often go there to see my father," Marta explained. "The cyclostyle is in his office. Besides, I'll tell him what it is for, and he'll go with me."

"Good enough," Mateo said. "You'll have the copy this afternoon."

"How many shall I run off?"

"As many as you can."

Padilla insisted on knowing what Mateo was going to do afterwards. "I'm afraid that Julio, when it's a question of the doctor..."

Mateo ran his hand over his forehead. "Of course," he agreed. "I don't know." Then he added: "I'm going to have no choice but to go into hiding somewhere."

Marta looked at him, and a sudden emotion gripped her.

"Of course, of course," added Mateo. He reached for a cigarette and his lighter. "Goodbye, sunlight."

There was a moment of silence.

"Now maybe," Padilla suggested, "El Rubio will let you stay here."

Mateo shook his head. Then he gave an impatient gesture.

"Well, let's forget that for now. I'll think about it."

The meeting over, they called El Rubio. The boy appeared in the kitchen door with his saxophone. "What gives?"

Seeing them huddled together so solemnly brought back his anarchist conspirator days. "What an orchestra I've got here!"

Mateo smiled. "We're leaving now."

El Rubio sat down while the others got up. "I hope you're not all leaving together."

"Hardly." Mateo pointed to Benito Civil and Jorge. "For the moment, just those two."

Jorge inquired: "What time for the cemetery?"

"Tomorrow at four in the afternoon."

While the two boys took their leave, Rodríguez said, addressing his leader: "One other thing. All this is going to make it tough for Octavio, Haro, and Rosselló."

Mateo was silent for a moment. Then he said: "We have no choice."

SEVENTY-FIVE

COSME Vila had called the rally of party members and sympathizers for half past three in the afternoon. The morning went by in a kind of ominous calm. No barricades, no violence of any kind. The only strikers in circulation belonged to the previous lot, El Responsable's group. These had their reasons for wanting to go back to work—boredom, hard times—to which was now added the desire to oppose Cosme Vila. Despite all this, El Responsable's orders were: "Hold the line. Everybody knows it was us who opened the breach. Now let's see who the authorities want to deal with, us or them."

El Responsable was living embittered days. He had to stand by, watching the development of the Communist maneuvers. Just as on the day of the assembly when he and Future had sat in the café all afternoon, helpless to do anything but somberly watch the rivers of men wearing railroad workers' caps, and women wearing the insignia of Cosme Vila's party, flowing into the Rambla in the most perfect order.

"Not more than five hundred of them," said El Responsable.

Future was shuffling a deck of cards. "What an optimist! They've got twice as many as we have right now." And the meeting was still an hour off.

On the stroke of half past three not one more person could have squeezed into the Rambla. It was a sultry afternoon. At that very moment Cosme Vila, Victor, Teo, and La Valenciana appeared on the Piedra Bridge. For the first time Cosme Vila was wearing a red necktie, which blazed in the sun.

At the sight of him the crowd became silent. Who was that beside Cosme Vila? Those closest by recognized the mystical speaker from Barcelona, the man with only one arm. His presence stirred them all. A taxi with top down, in which a loudspeaker had been installed, drove up. Gorki was riding in it, standing up, and he was to be in charge of transmitting orders. Many of the city's balconies and many of the shops were closed.

In front of the microphone Gorki read out a list of instructions drawn up by Cosme Vila. They were to parade past the Labor Bureau first, in protest over its failure to accept the six-hour work day. Then to police headquarters and other places. The route was mapped out. Mention was made of CEDA headquarters; its closing down was apparently fictitious inasmuch as the four thousand articles of warm clothing with which it had tried to buy the votes of the poor at Christmas time were being carried down the back stairs.

Everybody was in work clothes, with here and there a pair of clean, new sandals. And the parade got under way at once.

The Labor Inspector, on being notified that the procession was approaching, made a spectacular decision: he closed the balconies and the windows, even the shutters. And he and all the employees remained inside, working as though nothing was happening.

When the crowd had halted in front of the building, Cosme Vila called Teo. He handed him a paper, which was the note of protest, saying "Take this up and wait for the answer." Teo did as he was ordered; the Inspector tore the communication to pieces under the drayman's nose.

Teo clenched his fists and went back. Cosme Vila listened to his report. Then he looked up at the windows and said to Gorki: "Inform the comrades of this." Gorki, standing up in the taxi, described the interview to the crowd over the loudspeaker.

This was the system the Communist leader employed at each stop on the route. At police headquarters Julio received Teo and gave him a written answer: "Police authorities will never allow a dictatorship of the proletariat to be imposed upon the city. And it will proceed ruthlessly against any individual, group, or organization that attempts to disturb public order or occupy the streets."

Each time Gorki communicated to the crowd the answer of the authorities, adding: "Comrades! We have one answer: the general strike."

From police headquarters they set out for the City Hall, by the Calle de Ciudadanos. As they went past the Arús Bank, Cosme Vila looked at the high, opaque windows. A light could be seen inside. He recognized it as that on the assistant manager's desk. The assistant manager would be there, mobilizing invisible armies against Freemasonry.

The Mayor was not at the City Hall, nor the president of the Council, nor a single aiderman. "Has this place been deserted?" bellowed Teo, waving the note of protest back and forth.

An old man came out of a little room marked "Lost and Found Department."

"What's the trouble?" He stared at the crowd outside, at Cosme Vila, with his hands in his pockets. Teo handed him the note.

The old man put on his glasses. "Cooperatives, free public services..." He removed his glasses and looked at Teo. "And His Honor kissing your you-know-what, isn't that the idea?" The faithful porter; fifty years in service.

"You shut up," Teo ordered him. "You hand this to the Mayor and tell him he's to answer in writing."

Gorki shouted over the loudspeaker: "Comrades, you see the wonderful results we're getting from our visits!"

The crowd was growing impatient. Just then patrols of Assault Guards, who apparently had been alerted, showed up. There was a moment of silence. Everyone looked toward Cosme Vila. At the same time, from the direction of the river, came the sound of a bicycle bell. Someone on a bicycle was trying to get through. He wore a red handkerchief around his neck and was shouting: "Let me through, let me through!" There were those who wanted to throw the intruder into the river, but others recognized in him the son of the gravedigger. "I want to talk with Cosme Vila!"

The boy, skirting the edges of the crowd, managed to get to the leader. He dismounted from his bicycle, raised his fist, and informed him that at that very moment two Falangists had gone into the cemetery carrying something red in their hands.

Cosme Vila's face flushed, but he answered: "All right, but we've got no time for Falangists now." And addressing the crowd, he ordered: "Now, on toward the CEDA!"

The mob started moving again. And when it reached CEDA headquarters it discovered that everything really had been removed by a rear entrance. This enraged everyone, particularly La Valenciana. From time to time the one-armed comrade from Barcelona took over the microphone and, addressing himself to the city at large, said: "Citizens, support our strike!" Strike, strike, this was the slogan. The faithful, excited by the sun and their march, were carrying signs and inviting the storekeepers to close their shops. Outstanding among them were the Murcians, who had suddenly deserted El Responsable and joined the ranks of Cosme Vila, as had the waiters.

Cosme Vila realized that the most important moment of the manifestation had come: the demonstration before the barracks. The officers had probably been alerted. What was going to happen? They would have to be on guard.

They crossed the Piedra Bridge. There was a merry moment, for down by the river several fishermen were completely absorbed in their efforts. This, to the Murcians, seemed like treason. "Hey, you!" they yelled at them. "We're on strike!"

Then something unforeseen occurred. Another messenger arrived, this time a fat, elderly man, one of the waiters at the Hotel Peninsular. He elbowed his way toward Cosme Vila and informed him in a loud voice: "Comrade, the leader of the Falange and two unknowns entered Dr. Relken's room in the hotel and brutally assaulted the doctor."

Cosme Vila stood motionless. Falange seemed to have chosen that day for a frontal attack. The cemetery, Dr. Relken...what else were they up to?

But he recovered his calm. He went over to Gorki and gave him instructions. Gorki informed the crowd of the Falangists' attack. "They have broken into the room of a friend of the people, Dr. Relken, three against one, and have injured him seriously!"

A roar went up from the crowd. And then the cry: "Arms! Arms!" Cosme Vila had assumed that the mob would want to go to the house of Mateo Santos; but they did exactly the opposite. Instinct told them that the first thing to do was to demand arms, and the front ranks had already turned the corner toward the artillery barracks. Meanwhile the sky was turning a sultry red. From time to time drifting clouds crossed the horizon, in the direction of the Cathedral, fleeing the sun.

Suddenly the grandeur of the sky was obscured. As though something had come between the crowd and the sun. What had happened? Flocks of birds were taking off from the roof tops. Not birds, but something lighter still. Flyers, which swirled slowly down through space, rising at times in spite of the stillness of the air.

The surprise lasted only for a moment. Propaganda flyers! Everyone, even Gorki, thought this some surprise Cosme Vila had prepared for them, and arms reached up to catch the papers.

From the taxi Gorki finally grabbed one, the first his hand could reach, crumpling it as he caught it. He smoothed it out and prepared to read it over the microphone. But at that very moment Cosme Vila snatched it from his hands.

"Spaniards! Falange Española is speaking to you. Today we have laid five red roses on the grave of Jaime Arias, because it is our belief..."

Cosme Vila clenched his teeth. And at the same time he heard a deep roar, like an angry sea. Everybody who had snatched one of the flyers thinking it was the Communist Party' addressing them, discovering that it was from the Falange, muttered unintelligible words. The Assault Guards, holding flyers in their hand, looked in bewilderment at the roofs.

The barracks were within sight. "Arms! Arms!" Cosme Vila set out, and everyone followed.

The sentinel, seeing the approaching mob, came out of the sentry box. "Corporal!" The corporal appeared and called the officer of the day, a young second lieutenant, who waited to receive the messenger.

As before, the messenger was Teo. The lieutenant opened the note. "Lieutenant Martín...People's Militia...distribution of arms...."

The lieutenant looked at the giant. Then he shouted: "Guard, fall in!"

The soldiers came out and the guard fell in. Some of the soldiers had attended the assembly of the Communist Party, and they smiled beneath their helmets. The lieutenant, on the other hand, was a friend of Lieutenant Martín, and, above all, had great respect for Major Martínez de Soria.

The lieutenant replied to Teo: "Tell your principals that I shall transmit this. That is my answer as officer of the guard." And he added: "As a mere army officer, tell them that I regret not having a cannon at my orders to scatter a ton of lead over the lot of you. About! March!"

Teo pulled his cap down to his eyes. He transmitted the message to Cosme Vila. Gorki communicated it to the mob.

This was going too far. A stone whistled by, smashing a window of the barracks. Cosme Vila realized the gravity of the situation and grabbed the microphone. "Comrades, follow me! Follow your leader! We'll come back here." His idea was to get the mob out of the military area. He had his hands full. Especially with the women, who were insulting the officer, who stood unmoving at the entrance to the barracks.

Only the hope that Cosme Vila would take them to some specific spot from which to launch their attack finally swayed the mob. "Arms! Arms!" They followed Cosme Vila, who seemed to be going nowhere in particular, just thinking. Suddenly, at the other end of the esplanade that stretched beyond the barracks there appeared a swarm of boys, who had evidently just come from school. They were carrying bookbags over their shoulder and playing cup and ball.

The smaller ones, when they saw the crowd, took fright. Some of them ran away; others took refuge in doorways or inside the railing of the military monument on the square, a towering column with a roaring lion on top.

Cosme Vila noticed that some of these children were carrying papers in their hands. Falangist handbills! He went over to them and asked: "Where did you get those?" None of them answered.

"Where did you get those?" he repeated in a furious voice.

One of the boys said: "They fell into the patio of the Brothers." "The Brothers!" Gorki heard the boy say. He looked at Cosme Vila. Cosme Vila nodded his head.

"Comrades, the patio of the Christian Brothers is full of Falangist handbills."

Nothing further was needed. The cordon formed by the executive committee was broken; Gorki's taxi halted, swamped by the mob. Everybody set out on the run for the Christian Brothers'. Dark, tortuous accusations burrowed in people's hearts. Someone went into a garage and came out with cans of gasoline. Teo and La Valenciana were the first to reach the building, which stood quiet and dreaming amid fields of vegetables, gilded by the sun, which had begun to drop behind the mountains of Rocacorba.

The Communists surged into the patio, whose gate stood open. A few flyers were scattered here and there. The crowd went through to the other side, where a door leading into the building was open. They entered, but saw nobody. The corridors were empty. Anyone would have said the school was deserted. Some wandered into the classrooms. Teo and La Valenciana, with surer instinct, started up the broad stairway that rose in front of them. When they reached the first floor they stopped. There was a sound of murmuring voices. "In there!" They moved down a passageway, and suddenly something dark, withdrawn, appeared before their eyes: the entrance to the chapel. Within were lighted candles, an altar, two rows of heads, and a monotonous chant.

The chapel was soon overrun by Communists seeking out the members of the brotherhood. The Brothers turned their heads and, in amazement, got to their feet. The harmonium became silent. Something golden stood out on the altar, with a circle of white in the center. Teo's intentions were vague. "All Over there!" he ordered, pointing to the wall. One by one the Brothers obeyed. Then, unexpectedly, out of the sacristy, carrying a candle in his hand, came a sickly man who, at the sight of all those people, stood paralyzed. Teo recognized him instantly. Brother Alfredo!

In two strides Teo was at his side, and slapping the candle out of his hand and grabbing him between the legs, he raised him up as though he were made of paper.

The sight of Brother Alfredo excited everyone. Downstairs more Communists were coming into the patio. Upstairs the community looked on with incredulous eyes at all that was taking place, and the director never took his eyes off the monstrance. Missals, books of other sorts, chairs, pelted upon the altar. A candle twisted over and little flames shot out.

Teo, carrying Brother Alfredo, went over to the harmonium and made him touch the keys with his feet. There was no answering sound, and that enraged La Valenciana all over again.

Someone approached the altar and poured gasoline around the lighted candles. "What are you doing?" a voice cried out. Two of the Brothers lined up against the wall, tried to move forward, but strong arms held them back.

A sudden flame swept up, hiding the image of St. Jean Baptiste de la Salle behind a curtain of smoke.

Teo was still playing with Brother Alfredo. But when he smelled smoke and saw the fire, he went over to the high windows. He tried to open one of them, but in the twinkling of an eye the Murcians had broken the panes of all of them. Nevertheless, the smoke was making the air in the chapel unbreathable. Everyone was shouting or screaming. The billowing smoke and the sight of Teo carrying Brother Alfredo on his shoulders excited those below.

"Candy, candy!" someone shouted. The phrase caught on. "Candy for little boys." Someone threw a stone. "Crazy fool!" shouted Teo.

La Valenciana could not resist the temptation. She came up behind Teo and gave the frail body of Brother Alfredo a push. Teo held him firm. But those below had seen the move, and, besides, the fire from the chapel was spreading to the benches.

"Throw him down, throw him down!"

Rows of men lined up as though to receive the body of Brother Alfredo, for the window was low. He had lost consciousness, overcome by dizziness from being jounced around by Teo.

Just then Gorki's taxi drove into the patio. Teo never knew what happened to him. He caught the name of Jaime Arias. He raised up Brother Alfredo and hurled him into space, to the right, where he saw an opening and several steps. At the same moment the first tongue of flame burst through the window. A kind of panic seized them all. The Brothers were being asphyxiated by smoke. La Valenciana made her way to the stairs, shouting with enthusiasm. Everyone followed her. Below the stairs many had turned round and come back in from the patio. Several Assault Guards made their appearance.

In a little while part of the convent was on fire. Some of the boys had hid away in the garden. They could not make up their minds which fire to watch: that or the one behind the mountains of Rocacorba.

SEVENTY-SIX

CÉSAR arrived the next day on the Bañolas-Gerona bus. The servants of Collell, who were seminarians, had been obliged to leave in spite of the fact that it was still another month before the end of the course. The peasants of the vicinity had refused to furnish supplies for the boarding students if the seminarians did not leave.

The boy got off at the Plaza de la Independencia, with his suitcase in his hand, and walked slowly toward his house. Nobody was expecting him. People came and went excitedly. He heard someone saying: "The beams are still burning" and "Candy to the little boys."

"Where are the beams burning?"

"At the Christian Brothers' School."

He walked into the flat on the Rambla. "César!" They all rushed to embrace him. The suitcase dropped to the ground. "What's happened? What's happened at Collell?" Carmen Elgazu was holding his face between her hands, covering it with kisses.

César tried to calm them. Nothing had happened to him. He was all right, perfectly all right. He had had to leave because the people in the villages objected. But that did not matter. There was only a month left till the end of the course, and besides they had passed him in everything before he left. What did matter was what was happening in Gerona. What had happened in Gerona that the beams were burning at the Christian Brothers' and the people were running through the streets?

Carmen Elgazu answered him: "Son, whatever you imagine has happened, the truth is still worse."

César looked extremely well. Once more he sat at the head of the table. He read worry on the faces of his family, but at the same time their happiness at having him with them.

Carmen Elgazu had to tell him about the death of Mosén Alberto's maid, the situation in which Mateo found himself—hidden in El Rubio's flat—the situation of Marta, the demands the Communists had presented.

The thing that worried César most of all was to know whether the chapel at the Christian Brothers' had been burned.

Ignacio brought him up to date: "That's where they started the fire."

Carmen Elgazu added: "Yes, the Sacred Form was burned! You see what we've come to."

Matías would have preferred to celebrate the homecoming of César some other way. "Well, well," he interrupted, "I was just saying to myself: when are we going to see César."

César smiled. "Well, here I am."

Later on, Pilar told him how Brother Alfredo had been assassinated. César sat without moving. He touched his glasses. "But why Brother Alfredo?"

Ignacio answered in a natural tone of voice: "They were looking for a victim. It had to be somebody."

The seminarian was visibly moved, but he preserved a strange calm. "And what's going to happen now?" he asked.

"Nothing, son," Carmen Elgazu answered, "absolutely nothing. What can they do? There were over a thousand."

"All right. That's enough about that," said Matías.

César realized that his attitude was intensifying the suffering of the others. Matías had got up and was looking at the river. Turning to Pilar, whose deep tribulation showed on her face, the boy said: "Pilar, when can I say hello to Mateo?"

The girl turned toward him as though moved by a spring. "That's impossible. You'll be followed wherever you go."

César inquired for Mosén Alberto and Mosén Francisco.

"Mosén Alberto is terribly upset over the maid. Mosén Francisco, working as usual."

The doorbell rang sharply.

"Who can it be?"

For a moment the family thought it might be Julio. No, not Julio; perhaps Marta…

"Pilar, you go to the door."

It was Don Emilio Santos. They all got up to welcome him. Mateo's father was greatly surprised to see César, and had a kind of presentiment that he might bring good luck. He ran his hand over the boy's cropped head.

"You'd have been better off staying where you were," he said to him.

César shook his head, smiling. "They sent me away."

Don Emilio Santos sat down. Carmen Elgazu went to make him coffee.

"I felt so lonesome, so I came over," he said.

With one breath they all answered: "That's fine. That was just the thing to do."

"This is all madness, César," he observed, turning once more to the seminarian.

"Have they bothered you?" Matías asked Don Emilio.

The latter shook his head. "But yesterday I had another visit from the police." After a pause he added: "I don't see how Julio can think I am going to inform on my son."

Ignacio said: "I don't know why, but I don't like the idea of your being alone in your house."

"Why? I'm not afraid of anything."

Ignacio went on: "I don't mean that. But a person gets frightened when he's alone."

Don Emilio shook his head. "I'm not afraid, Ignacio," he explained, "but I can't help it. What I most enjoy is family life, you understand?"

Ignacio did not know what to answer. Don Emilio sighed. "It's as though half the world had gone crazy. And what is really frightening," he added, "is to think that the other half will defend itself."

Carmen Elgazu, who had just brought him his coffee, looked at him with curiosity. "Do you believe the other half will defend itself?"

Don Emilio took a sip. "Of course," he said, feeling restored. "Look, I can give you one detail. At the *Tabacalera* the cashier, who is anything but a belligerent person, I can assure you, came in yesterday with one of the Falange flyers and said: 'You've got to admit that this is something.'"

Ignacio gave a skeptical gesture. "You know, what Mateo did was all very fine, but—"

"But what?"

"Well, it's easier to raid a convent."

"Not so easy," said Matías.

"What I mean is that it's easier for Cosme Vila to make converts."

After a pause Ignacio added: "Seriously, I am ashamed of what is happening. I would never have believed that Spain could be like this."

Carmen Elgazu nodded emphatic agreement. "You are absolutely right, son."

"The capacity for hate that exists is terrible," Ignacio went on. "I am really ashamed. There are thousands of Spaniards capable of any atrocity."

Don Emilio Santos put his cup on the table. "Ah, but let's not oversimplify things," he said. "There are also thousands capable of the opposite. And if you don't believe me, just you wait."

Ignacio said nothing more. Don Emilio Santos felt comforted. He was so at home in that house. He looked at César. He wanted to ask him something, and he didn't know what. "What do they say in Collell?" he finally said. "What do they lay all this to?"

César looked at him steadily. "To the fact that society has cut itself off from God."

THE measures police headquarters had taken were, for the time being, two: the questioning of Cosme Vila and the arrest of Teo, and, at the same time, a search for Mateo and the two unknowns involved in the attack on Dr. Relken.

This was the practical reaction of the authorities. Julio had said: "Stern measures will be taken against both groups."

As for the city, the death of Brother Alfredo had aroused general indignation, and many people came forward to state that the accusations against the sexton were completely unfounded. Fortunately, a part of the building was saved, thanks to the speedy action of the fire department. But one whole wall of the convent had collapsed.

Those who reacted most strongly to what had happened were the innumerable former students of the Christian Brothers. In the courtyard of that school many of the citizens of Gerona had played football, and in one of its corners had smoked their first cigarettes. The convent was therefore sacred to them, and they felt that neither the hard life Cosme Vila's followers might have had nor the news of the beating up of Dr. Relken justified setting it on fire.

In a word, "the other half" Don Emilio Santos had alluded to felt for the first time unequivocally that something vital was at stake, that society's very life, the beliefs, history, and traditions by which the country had always lived, were in danger.

His feeling was unmistakable in the heart of everyone, and each revealed it after his own fashion. The old women who, as they came out of the Church of the Carmen, next to police headquarters, crossed themselves as Julio went by. The veterans of the Carlist wars coming together to enjoy the sun in remote spots where they could talk freely. The pupils of the Christian Brothers passing back and forth to look at the rubble of their school, hoping perhaps to find a lost pencil or book. The fright of the ticket sellers in the movies when they saw a blackened hand thrust in at the window. The absence from the Rambla of all but those who carried a worker's card with all the necessary stamps.

This protest, however, was, on the part of the majority, timid. They were legion who answered Noguer the notary's plea for action with: "What do you want us to do? The battle's lost."

In truth, the only place where a will to action, to joint action, was clearly manifest was in certain brains in the city: that of Warning Voice; of certain army officers; of certain conservative youths and members of the CEDA; of the Falangists; and, above all, in that of Major Martínez de Soria.

In the officers' lounge the keynote was silence. The officers looked at one another, read one another's thoughts in their eyes. They played chess, turned the pages of magazines, and read; but the gestures and attitude of each gradually revealed those who were prepared to defend the Popular Front and those who were prepared to put themselves under the orders of Major Martínez de Soria.

Unmistakable proof of this was the way they dealt with the soldiers. Some of the officers saw that their authority was unquestionably weakening and that they were the target of jokes and covert remarks. Others, on the contrary, suddenly adopted an unbending attitude, enforcing the strictest discipline as though defending with each order the threatened prestige of the uniform.

As for the conservative young men and members of the CEDA, theirs was a strange reaction, similar to that of the cashier of the *Tabacalera*; they read avidly and passed around the flyers Mateo had got out. "It is a mistake to suppose that the Communists are doing all this to have a swimming pool like that of Novgorod. Nobody risks his life for a swimming pool. One fights only for a spiritual cause, even though at times the protagonists themselves are not aware of it. The Falange laid red roses on the graves of Jaime Arias and Joaquín Santaló because it respects those who give their life for an idea."

The sons of Don Santiago Estrada could hardly believe what they were reading. They had seen their boarding-school go up in flames in Mataró, and the setting on fire of the Christian Brothers' had revived the scene for them. Mateo's words found their mark in them: "Nobody risks his life for a swimming pool." Nor for warm garments.

These two young men found themselves without a party and with nowhere to go. Their one thought now was how to get in touch with Mateo. What could they do? They did not want to compromise him, but at the same time they wanted to hear concrete explanations from his own lips. Finally, they went to see Marta....

As for Warning Voice, the entrance of Teo into jail brought him to the clear conviction that there were only two choices: kill or be killed. To be obliged to share a cell with the giant was a torture beyond his powers of endurance. Through the bars of the visitors' room he said to Laura: "Go to see Major Martínez de Soria and tell him to give you a pistol. When the time comes we will use it to get out of here and join the forces. Don Jorge's mind is made up, and so are all the others'. The first to disappear will be Teo."

It had horrified Laura to hear her husband talk like that. Major Martínez de Soria, who did not trust her because of the state of nerves she was in, said when she came to see him: "I don't know what forces you are talking about."

As for Mateo, for the first time he ventured to confide to his comrades that it was true, a military movement was being prepared in the event that the government did not take steps to establish order in the nation. After the beating up of Dr. Relken and the return of the image of the Virgin to the Museum under cover of the confusion created by the Communist manifestation, he had gone to El Rubio's house, and there he remained, in the kitchen. El Rubio's mother was under the impression that he was one of the musicians of Pizarro Jazz, and that Padilla and Rodríguez, who, wearing civilian clothes, were the only comrades who came to see him, were musicians, too.

In the absence of Octavio, Haro, and Rosselló, and because the two Civil Guards were the only members not known as Falangists, Mateo had appointed them squad leaders. They would serve in a liaison capacity between Roca, Jorge, and Benito Civil, with whom, in spite of what had occurred at the cemetery, Julio seemed not to be concerned for the time being, and Marta, as well as give instructions to possible new members. Therefore it was to Padilla and Rodríguez that Mateo communicated the news that Major Martínez de Soria was in contact with Barcelona and Madrid "to defend Spain with blood."

"It is clear that there is no other way," he said. "The inertia of Julio and of all the Julios in the rest of our poor land is monstrous. There is a veritable Masonic-Socialist-Soviet plot against Spain. The movements of salvation being launched are many, especially within the army. Falange has given orders to obey only that military leader using the password *Covadonga*, and that was the word pronounced by Major Martínez de Soria when he sent for me through Marta. So now you know. The plan has been scheduled for October or November, perhaps later, when the network has been established with guarantees of success. During the intervening months we will defend ourselves as best we can, winning over all the supporters we can and never losing touch."

Padilla and Rodríguez asked him: "Does Captain Roberto know about this?"

Mateo shrugged his shoulders. "I don't know. The problem of the Civil Guard is a ticklish business. One never knows."

Padilla seemed worried. Then he went on: "Which generals are heading the coup?"

Mateo pulled out his blue handkerchief. "Mola and Sanjurjo, I think. But I'm not sure. There are others."

Rodríguez asked him what was his impression of Gerona, whether they could count on "many guns."

Mateo gave a gesture of uncertainty. "It depends more on them than on us. If they keep on burning and killing, I think we can count on—I don't know, but maybe three hundred men."

Padilla thought the figure too high. He had a very poor opinion of the combative qualities of the Catalans, and thought most of them were "mixed up with the trash."

"You're wrong," said Mateo. "There are greater reserves here than would appear at first glance. People are cautious, that is true, because they've got a lot to lose; but if you hit upon the right word, they will respond the same as in Castile or anywhere else. You see that even Don Jorge asked for a gun."

Rodríguez took his cigarette stub out of his mouth. "Don Jorge has always been a hunter."

Mateo enjoined upon them that under no circumstances was Marta to visit him. "If there's anything urgent, tell her to give the message to El Rubio."

Then he asked them, when they went by the Alvears' balcony, to salute it for him.

As for Major Martínez de Soria, he no longer took the trouble to discuss the "why." All that existed for him now was the word "Covadonga," obedience to the leaders in Madrid, and the number of guns he could count on in Gerona. He felt the wounds of Country as deeply as Mateo. Every "Long live Russia!" on a Spanish woman's lips pierced his uniform, but he wanted the soldier in him to predominate. He was going to be dragging many lives along with his. The fate of a garrison, possibly of the Movement, might depend on him. The province was an important one, a frontier, with outlets to the sea. "Covadonga." He had said nothing to his wife as yet, or to Marta. Marta laughed at his precautions, for from Mateo, and now from Padilla and Rodríguez, she would be finding out everything.

The major counted on the support of several officers of the garrison. He could read their loyalty to him in their eyes. The one who received Teo at the barracks gate had said to him once, as they watched a group of Civil Guards escorting the Christian Brothers to the episcopal palace: "Major, did you know that General Franco had written to the government several times, demanding that it restore order?"

The major twisted his graying mustache. "Demanding is too strong a word. But he did, it seems, warn several of the ministers."

JULIO was furious with the Costas and Casal, who, with their stupid hairsplitting, had refused to back up his plan. "They don't realize," he said to Antonio Sánchez, "that I need more than policemen to handle this mob. I could have ordered my men to fire on the ringleaders, I know that. We could even have brought out the artillery. But that would have made things worse. We have to throw them some kind of sop. God only knows what might have happened if we had not agreed to close the Rightist headquarters. And if we had interfered with the demonstration, instead of setting fire to the convent it would have been the barracks."

Nevertheless, Julio was not discouraged, not in the least. He believed in allowing the revolutionary ferment to wear itself out. As a result he was convinced that, despite the momentary chaos, the ensuing protest that would arise from every quarter would finally engulf the protagonists of the revolution. It was his opinion that the fear, mutterings, glances of hatred, the tragically lonely burial of Brother Alfredo, and, above all, the social and economic disaster the strike entailed and the absurdity and despotism of the demands that had brought it on would be Cosme Vila's worst enemy—worse than the artillery. If the Costas and Casal had backed him, it would all be fizzling out by now. The condemnation of Communist brutality would have been followed up by the offer of a tangible, constructive program. But instead of this Casal had withdrawn the waiters' UGT cards and had ordered his members to be at work on Monday, and the Costas had closed down their factories and had decided—at this late date—to hold a meeting of Izquierda Republicana and send a protest to the Generalidad.

Julio's assurance and his arguments about giving them rope enough convinced Antonio Sanchez, but not Colonel Muñoz or the Commissioner, and even less the general.

"General," Julio had said to the last, "you military men are often guilty of a lack of perspective, and forgive me for talking to you like this. When you see a fire or the city paralyzed, it makes you so nervous that you think such a situation is going to last forever and that the thing to do is to exterminate this one or that one. Allow me to talk to you as Chief of Police. All this is bad—very bad. These people are trying to seize power, I know it. But let me ask you one question. Which do you prefer—to have a little patience, to make use of the forces of order such as Izquierda Republicana, Casal, and those who are loyal to him, to try to work out with the Labor Commissioner some point of agreement, to hit upon a plan to wear Cosme Vila down, or to come out openly against the people, thereby lending support to the military revolt that is in the making? Just a minute," he said as the general gave an angry start. "Which do you prefer, to hear that the people are asking for cooperatives or to see Major Martínez de Soria come into your office with a pistol and a proclamation declaring martial law?"

The general almost insulted Julio. "Just what do you take me for? Do I know, or don't I know, what goes on in the army? Are you going to try to tell me what Major Martínez de Soria can or can't do? Forget it. That's all scuttlebutt. A major is a major—you'll admit that—and a general is a general."

Julio interrupted him to say that it was not only majors who were involved in the matter, but generals too, and not negligible ones. Sanjurjo, Mola...

It was useless. The general was of the opinion that Sanjurjo, after his experience in 1932, was not going to try anything now. "Don't you worry about that, and throw all these savages into jail," he repeated for the hundredth time.

The Commissioner agreed with him, the Mayor too, and many others. As a matter of fact. Julio had only one supporter: Major Campos, an army veteran. Major Campos agreed with him that it would be foolish to fall out with the populace when, possibly before long, they might have to call on it to defend the Republic.

And Colonel Muñoz? Colonel Muñoz was the most unruffled of all. Seated beneath the Masonic triangle at the meeting on the 1st of June, he outlined his views. He did not share the fears of Julio and Major Campos with regard to the military uprising and therefore he did not favor yielding too much to Communist pressure. Neither did he share the fears of the general with regard to the danger Cosme Vila really represented, and consequently he saw no reason to throw the labor leaders and the firebrands into jail. In his opinion, the golden mean was called for once more. What could happen? The strike, to be sure. Everything closed down. It would last a week, maybe two. At the end of that time what would the workers be eating? The anarchists knew something about that.... Would they attempt to loot stores and warehouses before admitting failure? At this point the astuteness Julio had spoken of would come into play. Brother Casal would then step forward, presenting his Socialist program, with its reasonable, concrete, carefully thought-out demands. This would be backed up by the forces of order. The needs of every trade would be considered individually. "And at the same time that these demands are made known, the people will be informed that they have the approval of the Labor Inspector and the authorities. That they are to be put into effect immediately for the benefit of those who pledge their support of them. And what will be the results of all this? That the factory owners and businessmen will see, at last, the possibility of a reasonable understanding. Some factories will be opened at once. As for the workers, aside from a few incurable romantics, most of them will begin to think. Their wives will say to them: 'Do you realize? So-and-so is making good wages, and you're still out on strike.' All this," he repeated, "backed up by the forces of order. Police patrols should be on the move continually.

"My friends, I don't think we should lose our heads. The Popular Front has turned out to be an artificial creation—granted. To try to come to an understanding here in Spain with people like Gorki or that anarchist with the funny shoes is dangerous for those of us who love order and progress, and for that reason the Republic has been concerned about public education ever since it came into being. We must not forget, however, what we feared before the triumph of the Popular Front. With the election we bought the freedom to carry on with social progress, the privilege of not being looked upon by the great nations as a land of slaves and inquisitors. It is only fair that we should pay tribute for this now. But we must not lose our heads because of this. Let everyone stand firmly in his place. They know where they're going in Madrid, and we must not allow the immediate thing before our eyes to blot out the overall picture or obscure the long view. I would ask, on the one hand, that the Chief of Police act firmly, and, on the other, forbearance on the part of those who would employ stern measures. History was not made in a day, and I am of the belief that since 1931 we have taken a great step forward. Let us endure the reverses of the moment for the sake of the ideals that unite us."

Not too many were convinced. Once again the general realized that the colonel was naïve, and recalled that his three unmarried daughters always said of him: "What a wonderful husband he would make!" Julio was in despair over the fact that nobody, not even the military, took the danger of a revolt seriously. Not even after seeing what was happening in the affair of Lieutenant Martín, or the transfer of the major. As for Casal, when he got home he left his white gloves on the table and went to give his three children their customary kiss. At times his jutting nose woke them up. His wife was not advising him, as she used to, to obey those who were his higher-ups. On the contrary, for some time now she had taken a defensive attitude and told him what Cosme Vila's wife had said to her: "Cosme thinks the hour has come." "What does that mean?" she asked. "You be careful. You know my instinct never deceives me."

Just then she caught sight of the linotypist's gloves on the table. She picked them up and remarked: "Heavens, how dirty they are! I must wash them right away."

SEVENTY-SEVEN

COSME Vila had written Julio a note warning of the danger from the military and offering him the support of his members in the province and the city whenever he considered the moment opportune. Julio had struck the table a blow with his fist. It was the first nervous gesture Antonio Sánchez had ever seen his chief make.

Cosme Vila had then called a meeting of the executive committee at which the high-school teacher, Señor or Comrade Morales, depending on who was addressing him, occupied Murillo's place. Cosme Vila felt that not too much heed should be paid to the intellectuals, but on the other hand they brought great prestige to the party.

Teo was absent from the meeting, and La Valenciana was nervous about it. Victor said that he thought what had happened at the Christian Brothers' was going too far and that he was afraid of the effect on public opinion and even among the members when they had had a chance to think it over in the cold light of day.

Cosme Vila cut short the old man's lamentations. "We've come this far; we're not going to quit now, right?"

In Cosme Vila's opinion, the conspiracy of the authorities, the Falangists, and other forces in the city against the Communist Party was so evident that it alone would serve to unite the members in a solid front.

"There is no end to their meetings and discussions about the ways and means of doing away with us. This is all common knowledge, and there is no better argument to justify our conduct. We are acting in self-defense."

Gorki nodded agreement.

"What can happen, anyway?" Cosme Vila proceeded. "Nothing. We have our newspaper and the printing press of *El Tradicionalista* to set forth our case, and, above all, we have the strike to monopolize attention." He looked at Gorki. "Gorki," he said, "you are going to be busy. It is time we turned *El*

Proletario into a daily. Comrade Morales here, being a professor of literature, will help us." Turning to Victor, he added: "The first issue must come out tomorrow."

"Tomorrow?"

"Certainly."

They all thought it was impossible.

"Don't forget that the important thing for us is the strike—that is, our demands. The people applauded them, but the truth is that they don't have any idea of what they signify. They must be explained to them in detail, point by point, pounding away until they have sunk in." After a moment's reflection he said: "There must also be a protest about the attack on Dr. Relken."

"Should we allude to the military coup?" the teacher asked.

Cosme Vila's brows wrinkled. "For the time being we'll lay off that," he finally answered. Cosme Vila's intention was for the newspaper to keep the revolutionary spirit oriented in a positive direction. "That is our mission. What we are after with the strike is something big—in fact, definitive. So not one word that might suggest that it is going to be a picnic. Exactly the opposite. The comrades must be made to understand that it will not be easy; but also that if we stand firm, the authorities will ultimately be forced to give way. There wasn't anything easy about what was accomplished in Russia in 1917."

"It would be advisable to put forward some solid accomplishments for the membership to chew on," Victor said.

Cosme Vila nodded agreement. "Naturally, naturally." He thought for a moment. "Some solid accomplishments—" he went on, concentrating. "We should tell them—this: that, little by little, the authorities will give way. Or, better yet, that the authorities have already begun to give ground. It's the truth, isn't it? So far, we have managed to close up five enemy headquarters. And we have a printing press, rented, to be sure, but ours to do what we want with it. And we haven't even started. What next, you say? Now we'll go after the six-hour day. And for a couple of buildings to be turned over to the people for their use. That is a sure thing. Then we will go after new elections for mayor." He looked around the table. "As long as there are signs of progress, the people will hold firm. The dangerous thing for a strike is to get becalmed."

Gorki mentioned the hunger and the locked stores.

Cosme Vila did not hesitate an instant this time. He felt himself completely in command. "You don't think that we are going to be as stupid as El Responsable, do you?"

"What do you mean by that?" Gorki asked. Morales looked inquisitive too.

"From the very first," Cosme Vila said, "I have been thinking about the hunger problem and our lack of food stocks. I had a long talk about it with the comrades in Barcelona. And, as usual, we came up with a solution."

"Solution?" Gorki echoed.

"Certainly. Why not? I don't know whether you are familiar with the phrase: 'In strikes, the side with the land behind it can hold out the longest.'" In the face of his comrades' expectant attitude, he went on: "We have the countryside of the province behind us."

Cosme Vila then unfolded his master plan. Ever since February he had been receiving visits from tenant farmers and farm hands of the province who had pinned all their hopes of freeing themselves from the yoke of the landowners on him. "At the rally there were more than two hundred farmers, among them five tenants of Don Jorge. Therefore the problem of acquiring foodstuffs is simply a problem of transportation," he said. "Every cell in the province will handle the job of collecting the contribution of the farmers of its area." He paused for a moment and then continued: "We must go all over the province in trucks with signs saying: 'Food for the strikers in Gerona.' Either I am dead wrong, or the result will be surprising. We still have to find a suitable building to store the food when it gets here. Let's see if we can get that place where the Marist Congregation meets, on the ground floor. These foodstuffs will be distributed to the strikers free of charge," he went on. "That will spike the guns of those who thought they could starve us into submission."

Everyone present received the plan enthusiastically. The thought of presiding over a pair of scales and handing out food to the comrades filled La Valenciana with delight.

"Perhaps it could be used to win over new members," Comrade Morales suggested.

"No question about it," Cosme Vila said with a vigorous nod. "If the amount of food we collect is as great as I think it will be, every single worker on strike will get his share, no matter what party he belongs to. We won't exclude even the anarchists."

Gorki patted his stomach. "El Responsable is going to love that," he said.

Comrade Morales looked hard at Cosme Vila. "It would give the people an idea of what the cooperatives would be like," he said.

Cosme Vila shot him a glance. He was enjoying this. "Exactly," he replied.

The collection of the foodstuffs still had to be organized and put into practice. The party would pay only a fraction of the food's value, and this would be all that the farmers would receive. The farmers would be advised to turn over the share of the crop normally set aside for the landowner; if this did not prove to be enough, they would be asked to contribute from their own share.

The question was how to arouse their interest. Cosme Vila felt that the confidence many of the peasants already had in the party would be enough. But it would be a good idea to announce the presentation of the Communist Party program for agriculture at an early date and make it clear that the food collections would be valuable experience for the future.

"We must employ the word 'collectivization,'" he said. "That will encourage generosity, for the peasant knows that when his turn comes he will be treated generously, and that what he has given up is not lost."

Gorki had a question. He wanted to know if barricades would be set up and whether the waterworks and the gas and electric plants would be seized.

"None of that," said Cosme Vila. "We must find ways to help the people, not increase their hardships. If we give them food on the one hand and cut off their gas and light on the other we will only have given them a headache."

"A peaceful strike—" Morales suggested.

"For the moment, as peaceful as possible," Cosme Vila said.

Morales remained thoughtful. He could not believe that things could be so simple. He was sure that there must be some loopholes. "Nonetheless," he finally said, "the people are going to have a lot of time on their hands with nothing to do. Without barricades to defend, without work—we ought to do something to occupy their minds. If we don't, they may get out of hand."

Cosme Vila gave him an approving look. "Occupy their minds of course," he replied. "For the time being, many will be employed in collecting food from the province. Others will work in the cooperative. We must let them think that we're leaving the whole thing in their hands, but never let them forget that the first one who steps out of line will be out on his ear like Murillo."

"I think that Morales is right," Gorki broke in. "That is not enough. The days are long."

Cosme Vila bit his lip. He liked it when they raised reasonable objections.

"*El Proletario* will give them something to read," Victor put in.

"That will take up about an hour," Morales said brusquely.

Cosme Vila realized that he had not given that aspect of the matter much consideration. A solution had to be found and, as always, the best thing was to go to the heart of the matter. He opened the drawer of his desk and pulled out the program. He read slowly and turned the page. At the bottom of the second page he ran his hand over his hair.

"Why don't we put into practice point number nine?" he said abruptly.

"Which one is that?"

"The People's Militia."

La Valenciana made a scornful gesture. "What? With the arms they gave you?"

"Without arms! Without arms!" Cosme Vila interrupted. "Drill without arms in the Dehesa."

"Or we could use something symbolic," Morales suggested. "A shovel or a club."

The idea was well received. "A club, a club," Gorki said.

"We'll see about that later," Cosme Vila said. "The important thing is to start drilling. I've been thinking for days about how it could be done. We must organize sections and squads; and give them leaders. Here we are without any organization, as though we had nothing to do and all day to do it!"

Silence filled the room while he worked out the theory further in his mind.

"Six-man squads. Five clubs to a squad and one militiaman with his rifle. This one rifle can be used to instruct the whole squad in the use of the weapon."

Victor said it would probably be impossible to get permission for possession of even the one rifle.

"That has a simple solution," Cosme Vila replied. "We don't ask for a permit."

No one had an answer to that.

Morales finally spoke up in agreement. The professor liked the whole idea.

"And where are we going to get the *bang-bang*?" La Valenciana asked.

Gorki gave her a scathing look. "We've got some stored away. What do you think we are doing, sleeping?"

La Valenciana shrugged her shoulders. "Excuse it, big boy."

Cosme Vila was enthusiastic. "Occupy their minds..." The countryside would be mobilized, the roads filled with trucks plastered with signs. The food would roll into the city, and everybody would be green with envy. Julio would see that they could hold out for a year. And the drilling in the Dehesa. Neither Julio nor the Commissioner could tolerate this, and much less the general. The cavalry would charge into the Dehesa demanding that the rifles be handed over.... "No problem about keeping the revolutionary spirit alive," he thought.

For the time being, he would play down the militia business within the committee.

"The question of the *bang-bang* will be taken care of," he said. "The important thing now is the depot, the depot to store the food."

Gorki turned to Morales and asked him if part of the building of the Institute might not be used.

The professor smiled. "In the first place, I am not the director," he said, "and in the second, I don't think it would be a very good idea to put the students out and replace them with cabbages."

A suspicious look crossed La Valenciana's face. "Why not?" she asked. "It's food for the people, isn't it?"

Cosme Vila cut her short. "Forget that," he said. "We have to made a bid for the building of the Marist Congregations."

La Valenciana was worried about another matter. "What about the transportation?" she asked. No one, in her opinion, could organize the trucking of the food like Teo.

Cosme Vila looked at her meaningfully. "A few days in jail never hurt anybody."

"Are you sure that the peasants will give us anything?" Morales asked.

Cosme Vila shrugged his shoulders. "I'm counting on it," he said.

Gorki had a lot of confidence too. He had been all over the province with his perfumes, and it looked like a bumper year. "Now is the moment," he said. "If all this had happened in January, it would be a different story."

"It's a good year?" Victor asked.

"I'll say it is. Everything—fruits, grain, vegetables—everything."

Morales nodded. "Of course," he said. "Here it is June already."

Cosme Vila closed the meeting. They all rose, and each received his instructions. Gorki, Victor, and Morales went to the printing plant of *El Tradicionalista*, Cosme Vila to the radio station. He was convinced of the utility of his broadcasts. The day of his talk, in most of the cafés the radios had been tuned in. Cosme Vila was reporting to the members on what had been decided. He would get across that the Communist Party was using more common sense than the CNT. "For the time being, I won't say anything about the militia," he said. "I'll tell them that there will be food for everybody and that the first number of *El Proletario* will be out tomorrow." He also planned to speak of Murillo, who had set himself up as head of the Trotskyite cell and was talking very big.

SEVENTY-EIGHT

IT gave Dr. Relken great satisfaction to hear Cosme Vila talk about him on the radio. He felt even better the next day when he unfolded *El Proletario* and saw his name in headlines over reports on his convalescence.

To tell the truth, he had no grounds for complaint. The sympathy shown him in every quarter was unforgettable—from the owner of the hotel, from Dr. Rosselló, who examined his wounds one by one with extraordinary patience, from the various organizations, such as Izquierda Republicana, Estat Català, and the UGT, which sent delegations to assure him of their support.

There were no words to describe his confusion on seeing Mateo and the two strangers enter his room. When they surrounded him, held a piece of paper in front of his eyes which said "*¡Arriba España!*" forced open his mouth, stuffed the piece of paper in, and compelled him to swallow it, he felt sure they had come to kill him. The first blows confirmed him in this opinion. Nevertheless, the wave of fury that surged up in him after he recovered consciousness was dissipated by the attentions that were showered on him. The Commissioner had come in person to see him the minute he heard the news, and Julio had not been far behind.

The first thing both of them said was: "Doctor, we will not give up until we have our hands on those responsible for this. The honor of the city and of the Spanish people is at stake." Naturally, it would not be an easy matter, for Mateo had disappeared as though the earth had swallowed him, and his two companions had not yet been identified. But Julio had just phoned the doctor two encouraging bits of news. The first was that they had picked up the trail of the culprits after they left the hotel, and the second, that it had been announced that the three Falangists already in jail would be kept behind bars until the culprits gave themselves up.

What annoyed the doctor most was his cropped head. His wounds were more showy than serious; the violent effects of the castor oil were wearing off;

but there was no remedy except a pith helmet for the clipper treatment. As a matter of fact, "the biggest of the three assailants" had left his head practically like a billiard ball, which gleamed outrageously in the sunlight when the doctor went out to take a turn on the terrace of the hospital. He had the feeling that "the other half of the city," which did not read *El Proletario* and had not come to see him, was laughing at him and enjoying his misfortune.

In all Gerona there was only one other clipped head that could compete with Dr. Relken's: César's. Theirs were the two roundest heads in the city, and the barber Raimundo would have contemplated both of them with pride. The first time they met face to face Dr. Relken cursed the authors of his predicament more vigorously than ever. He recognized the seminarian, whom he remembered from the Museum, but he did not say a word and walked back slowly toward the hospital.

César had overcome his bewilderment of other years. They had imagined at home that in the face of the developments in the city he would spread his hands and say: "I don't understand, I don't understand." He did not, however. Now he faced up to the situation, and his reactions were firm. Perhaps this was because he was now getting his sleep at night and because for the moment his feet gripped the ground and the stigmata had not flowered on his hands.

He confessed that he was happy that Dr. Relken had received a few knocks, and when the maid at the Museum asked him: "César, would you like a cup of chocolate?" he replied: "Yes, bring me one. It will do me good."

César's view of things was almost identical with that of Don Emilio Santos: hate had laid hold on the city, and it was necessary to spread love on every side. Climb up to the housetops, the ancient walls, the Cathedral, and pour out love over the entire city!

He found an ally in Mosén Francisco. The priest told him: "Our mission is to carry on as though nothing were happening. If they forbid us to do one thing, we will do another or find the means of doing it a different way. If they forbid the people to attend Mass, we will celebrate Mass in the homes. There is one thing they can't take away from us." He touched his waist, which was girdled by a penitent's belt even sharper than César's.

Mosén Francisco had obtained permission from Julio to enter the jail! Don Jorge, Warning Voice, and the others held there on similar charges had asked to be allowed to make confession. Mosén Francisco went there, and when he came out he told César what he had seen: men who some day might return to their former selfishness, but who during those moments when they knelt before him had managed to divest themselves even of hate. They all repented of not having been better and of having contributed by their acts or omissions to the existing state of affairs. "If it were not for the secrecy of the confessional, I could tell you some heartwarming details," Mosén Francisco said. "You would see how quickly the hearts of men can change, and the paths by which love reaches them."

This was Mosén Francisco's hope, which César had difficulty sharing, for his ears rang with the phrases of his Latin professor: "Society is forsaking God.... Sin has taken possession of our land."

This was Mosén Francisco's hope, despite the fact that as he passed him on the way out of the jail, Teo spat on the floor, and despite the insults, which kept pace with the march of events, written all over the walls of the jail. Those arrested during the October episodes had begun the round of "*Mueras*." Warning Voice had reversed their intent the minute he entered the jail. Now Teo had taken pencil in hand, and his awkward but colossal scrawl was triumphing anew and eliciting raucous laughs from the gypsy, who had become Teo's faithful dog.

One thing had particularly affected the seminarian: the fact that it should have been Murillo who placed the bomb in the Museum and stole the image. Now he heard it said of him: "He's waiting for orders from the POUM in Barcelona. He may turn out to be Cosme Vila's biggest headache." Despite César's loving intentions, it was going to be hard for him to forgive Murillo—as hard as to believe that Warning Voice had truly rid himself of hatred.

César felt a little as Marta did: some things were simply too much for him. For that reason the seminarian and the girl hit it off at once, even though her actions at times disconcerted him. Marta disconcerted him because despite the circumstances—they hardly let her out of the house because of her father's situation, and she could not be seen in the streets with Ignacio because of Mateo—her animation and good humor never left her. Not that she did everything she wanted to do, but that when she felt something strongly she gave herself up to it completely. She gave the impression of being right at home in the thick of the conflict. Matías Alvear would shake his head and say: "She's a soldier's daughter, every inch a soldier's daughter." She had run off the flyers right under Major Campos's nose. She managed to meet El Rubio every day and give him the necessary messages for Mateo. She saw Padilla and Rodríguez with dangerous frequency and lectured them on the Falange, for the allegiance of the two Civil Guards was purely instinctive. "The error of both the capitalist and the Marxist system is in thinking that the interests of management and labor are opposed," she would read from one of the party pamphlets, while the audience of two twisted their lips, moving the butts hanging from their mouths. "In the new syndicalist order..."

Padilla and Rodríguez would scratch their heads. "That's good," they would say. "That's very good. But—" hitching their chairs closer to Marta's—"listen a minute. We can come back to that later. Why do we have to wait until November? What does your father say? Doesn't he realize that they are going to make mincemeat of us?"

Marta would repeat all this to the Alvears and tell them that she personally was not afraid of Julio. "He'll think twice before tangling with me." She would even take advantage of the slightest oversight on her father's part to slip out of the house, saddle her mare, and take a couple of turns around the Dehesa! The anarchists saw her one day and threw stones at her. She never batted an eye. Now, she said, she would go back some day when the Dehesa was filled with Cosme Vila's strikers. Ignacio told her he thought that would be a stupid taunt and César agreed. Marta accepted the truth of their view. "I didn't say it to show off, honestly," she explained. "It's just that it gets under my skin that because of those oafs we have to stop doing what we have been doing all our lives."

Marta told how the two sons of Don Santiago Estrada and two other members of the CEDA had come to see her. "You should have seen me! Giving the salute and saying: 'It all depends on your capacity for sacrifice.'" And another lesson from the pamphlets!

César didn't know whether to admire her or not. He liked her, but he wasn't sure her role was a fitting one for a woman. Carmen Elgazu, for example, had never read a pamphlet, even in Basque, and Pilar's reading was limited to going over the pages of her diary, to the days when Mateo had waited for her morning and evening at the entrance to the dress shop. Pilar wasn't a bit at home in the climate of the conflict. She bore her separation from Mateo bravely, but she grew visibly thinner by the day. Her love for Mateo revealed itself as something absolute, something that involved her whole being. They had even forbidden her to walk past the balcony on the Calle de Ballesterías where El Rubio stood guard chatting with the neighbors. One photograph, one photograph of Mateo on her night table at the feet of St. Francis of Assisi and St. Clara, was all she had. If Pilar looked to Heaven, it was to pray for Mateo, which was the extent of her selfishness. A picture of Mateo, an image in her memory…and every minute of the day brought some new fear. Every unfamiliar ring at the door seemed to herald bad news. She hesitated to open the newspaper for fear of the headlines. "Falange Leader Arrested in…" *El Demócrata* published a communiqué every day. "A clue has been turned up.… The trio that assaulted Dr. Relken is about to be arrested.…" Pilar would kneel in her room and pray: "Lord, why do they pursue him like a criminal? What has he done, what has Mateo done?" When she saw the doctor with his cropped head, she looked at him as though he were an ogre. The doctor answered her with a look that was different and much more complex than that which he had given César. "Pray for Mateo, César. The Lord will listen to a saint like you," she told her brother. At night she dreamed that she climbed up on the rooftops, that she bumped against a chimney in the form of a saxophone, down which she slid into El Rubio's kitchen, where she found Mateo mopping his forehead with his blue handkerchief, with one foot on the skull and the other on the turtle of the Chief of Police.

César felt much closer to everything going on around him than the year before, when he had felt strange among people. He would gladly have gone to see Julio and spoken his mind to him. His main preoccupation was the Christian Brothers, who did not have a roof over their head. He got Mosén Alberto to arrange for them to be decently lodged in private homes. He would have liked to have David and Olga removed as school inspectors. Unfortunately, Mosén Alberto discouraged him. "Nothing can be done. You see how things are," the priest said. "No one will be removed; there will be no religious statues, no catacombs, no nothing. And if they attempt a military uprising, we shall lose. Go, go to the Calle de la Barca and see how you are received! But I advise you to leave your razor home."

César did not share his view. Mosén Francisco went to the Calle de la Barca and nothing happened to him. Mosén Alberto had taken the death of his maid too hard. He did not believe that people like the owner of the Crocodile still existed.

The owner of the Crocodile! Why not pay him a visit, and through him find a good hiding place for Mateo? With El Rubio being Major Martínez de Soria's orderly, the apartment was a powder keg!

Act, act…as Mosén Francisco said. Monday afternoon, at the hour when the mountains of Rocacorba became ablaze, he went to the Calle de la Barca, with his skipping gait. He had no more than entered the Crocodile when he was struck dumb. There, leaning against the bar, was Canela, surrounded by soldiers. They were all drinking and the soldiers were throwing their caps in the air. Canela was drunk and on recognizing him she called out: "Well—is your little brother all well again?" César did not understand. He saw a flashy-looking woman get up from her seat in the corner. "Hey, this is the one who used to get around the kids with rosaries and catechisms!"

César went out. The street was a sea of faces. He thought he recognized some of his old students, boys and girls whose legs he had washed in the river. They had lost all their manners. He remembered them sitting on the ground with their legs crossed the way children should. Now they climbed up on the window grilles, whistled, pushed one another as they talked, eyed the light bulbs and laughed. And the cursing! No one greeted him. The silence was the worst. His influence on them had been that of water on marble. "Uncle César." It had all been useless.

César waited a little longer, waiting for the one soul, the one who surely existed and would come out to greet him saying: "Four times four, sixteen! How are you?"

But the owner of the Crocodile came to the entrance. "It would be better if you went," he told him. There were some gypsies around a hand organ grinding out *The Crime of Cuenca*. A man in a slaughterhouse worker's smock was trampling a pile of refuse and shouting: "The garbage collectors are on strike!"

César looked at the owner and, turning on his heel, started the trip back. "Hey, kid, hey!" César never turned around. In a shooting gallery the targets were Alfonso XIII, a Moor, a bishop, and an army officer covered with medals. "Step right up! Win a prize!"

On every corner stood men with slips of paper stuck in their caps. "Workers of the world, unite." They looked at him with suspicious interest as he walked by. "Where have we seen that face before?" they seemed to be asking themselves.

A ravenous dog followed at his heels, sniffing his pants. César stooped down and patted the dog on the ribs. "Good boy, good boy..." he murmured, just loud enough for the dog to hear. On the rear entrance of the Church of San Félix someone had written: "Long live Me!"

SEVENTY-NINE

THE strike spread relentlessly. Izquierda Republicana opened as many factories and workshops as it could, but without effect. The best intentions of the Costas were engulfed by the popular tide.

The strike mercilessly paralyzed the key points of commerce and industry and services as important as—the slaughterhouse worker was right!—garbage collection. The streets were filled with the strikers. Cosme Vila could have even suspended mail deliveries if he had wanted, for a number of postal workers were members, and they had offered to do the job; but Cosme Vila did not dare.

The businessmen of the city considered the whole affair a catastrophe without precedent. The traveling salesmen who arrived at the station with their sample cases took the first train out of town. Many owners of companies went over the books with their faithful bookkeepers and groaned in despair. Rats had appeared in several warehouses in the city. They scuttled warily over the boxes, making empty bottles tinkle.

The banks seemed more like funeral parlors. Mountains of outstanding drafts. All this cut the assistant manager to the quick, and he would sit disconsolate, examining his nails. Some uninformed client would arrive from out of town and ask: "What's going on?"

"Strike. There's a strike," the assistant manager would mumble.

Nevertheless, the first impression the city gave was of a holiday, to which the locked stores and the profusion of flags contributed. The real cause of it all was that Cosme Vila had put into practice his plan for the collection of foodstuffs and the establishment in the headquarters of the Centro Tradicionalista—it had not been possible to get the hall of the Marist Congregations—of the first People's Cooperative of Gerona.

Despite initial doubts and resistance that had had to be overcome, the plan for feeding the strikers from the products of the province was becoming a reality. The doubts had come mainly from the wives of the strikers, who, when the strike to the finish was ordered, foresaw hunger at the end of a week and told their husbands: "The same thing is going to happen to you as happened to El Responsable." Cosme Vila's radio broadcast announcing that a fleet of trucks would soon be traveling between the city and the province bringing in foodstuffs did little to dissipate their skepticism. When the first caravan of trucks was preparing to set out from the city to the four quarters of the province, they jeered at the party members mounted on the truck platforms: "We'll see! We'll be lucky if you come back with a couple of squashes! Don't forget the turnips!" They saw the problem in simple terms: the peasants of Catalonia were notoriously tightfisted; a likely chance of their giving away anything!

Nonetheless, everything turned out differently. The same trucks returned to the city at nightfall loaded with tons of food. The amazement and joy knew no limits. That accounted for the holiday air of the city. Everybody wandered about asking: "Where is all that going to be distributed, where are they going to hand it out?"

"In what used to be the Centro Tradicionalista."

The more impatient lost no time getting there with sacks, hampers, and every sort of utensil that would hold something to eat.

"Not so fast!" some said. "They'll give us instructions."

"Instructions, my foot!" came the reply. "You can't tell your stomach to wait." And off they went to the first People's Cooperative of Gerona, taking their children with them in case the load was too heavy.

Then came the disappointments. In the first place, the women all imagined that the whole thing would work on a first-come, first-served basis, with everyone grabbing what he wanted. Instead of this, they found the whole thing strictly and severely organized, with no chance of working any sleight of hand. Behind improvised counters stood a whole team of members to handle the distribution, with La Valenciana at their head.

"What the devil are you hanging around here for? Beat it! Scram!"

The women were flabbergasted. "What are you planning to do? Keep all that for yourselves?"

"Get out of here!" La Valenciana was on the point of tearing the hair off the head of one of the members from an outlying neighborhood.

The word finally went around. The distribution would begin Thursday morning at eight o'clock sharp. One had to have both a slip of paper made out at City Hall certifying the number of members of the family and a party membership card.

This gave rise to one of the largest feminine rallies ever seen in the Plaza Municipal. For twenty-four hours before the distribution was scheduled, City

Hall was besieged. The old porter rushed furiously out of the lost-and-found room. "Keep back, you witches, keep back!" They literally trampled him. Two Andalusian women locked him up in his cubbyhole. The janitor raised the roof, and two of the police set him free. Meanwhile the women had charged up to the Records office. A certificate, a certificate! There seemed to be not one family with less than six members. The arguments were interminable. The architect Massana, the Mayor pro tem, heard the uproar in his office and came out as mad as a wet hen. "Use your clubs if you have to, but get them in line," he ordered the police.

"Fascists!" the women howled. "You don't even want to certify the size of our families! Fascists, you'd like to see us all dead!"

It finally all worked out, and the certificates were granted, but not before the city had managed to collect one *real* each for them.

Thursday at the appointed hour the door of what had been the Centro Tradicionalista opened. At five minutes past eight the first woman—the wife of the gravedigger—walked out of the door with a basket heaped with food in her arms. A murmur of admiration went up from the interminable line that had formed. A moment later a second woman appeared—a distant cousin of Teo's—proudly balancing a monumental melon atop her head. Hurrahs for Cosme Vila and for the People's Cooperative began and they promised to go on indefinitely. "Long live the Communist Party! Viva Cosme Vila! Viva Russia!" More women came out with their baskets piled high.

Many husbands had lined up along the sidewalk, waiting. "What did they give you? What did you get?"

"Look! Potatoes, rice, flour, cherries. Here, just smell this watermelon!"

"And what about the—?" asked one, making a fist and rubbing his thumb and index finger together.

"Nothing, not a cent."

The resistance had been demolished. The strike could go on for weeks. Inside the depot, Victor checked the membership cards and certificates, Gorki handed down supplies, and La Valenciana kept watch over the scales.

"Open the sack, open the sack!"

"Take it easy! Did you think we were fooling?"

Some of the women complained about their ration. They claimed that the first on the line had been served more generously.

"Any more lip out of you and I'll pull off your you-know-what!" La Valenciana would scream, and, amidst the laughter, go on doling out potatoes, flour, and cherries. The cherries she would sometimes hang jokingly on the members' ears.

The women filed off toward their homes. The joy of cooking now! What a dish of rice they'd prepare! As the morning wore on, the husbands started drifting away. They sat on the curb and on the railing along the river wall. They pulled out the makings and began slowly to roll cigarettes or they opened up *El Proletario*, from which they learned that for the moment Ampurdán was the region heading the list of those providing foodstuffs; that Dr. Relken's shiner was not so purple as the day before; that the party was growing by leaps and bounds in the province of Madrid; and that in Russia during the first three months of the year the living standard of the workers had risen thirty-five percent.

The authorities, who had not taken either the radio talk or the family certificates very seriously, began to wear a worried look.

"Don't you realize?" Doña Amparo Campo asked Julio at noon. "Don't you see what's going to happen? The few stores that are still open say that there will be a shortage of everything in no time and that prices will go sky-high."

Julio didn't even hear her. With all this, the strike had taken a turn he hadn't foreseen. Damn that Cosme Vila! He thought about what Colonel Muñoz had said: "After fifteen days, then what?" He went to headquarters and called a meeting of the usual group: the Commissioner, the Mayor, the District Attorney, the Costas, Dr. Relken....

Meanwhile, Cosme Vila at his desk received reports on the day's activities. His motto was: "Never rest on your laurels." Comrade Morales appeared. "Now, about the print shop," Cosme Vila said. "*El Proletario* is as important as the food."

Morales explained that it was materially impossible to get out *El Proletario* every day. "We'd have to have a regular staff," he said.

"Very well," the leader replied, "I agree. But I would rather have a single sheet come out every day than four pages one day and none the next."

Cosme Vila dismissed Morales. He wanted to be alone. It was only alone that he could fully savor his triumph. It was not so much the cooperative—it was no trick to get "*vivas*" when you were giving away rice—as the country. The reports the party workers were bringing in from the province gave one a lift. They told Cosme Vila that they could never have imagined such willingness on the part of the comrades of the province to help. Several drivers described so vividly the unselfish and enthusiastic manner in which they had been received and given food by the peasants that Cosme Vila, for the first time in many years, felt his eyes grow moist.

"Then, they received you well?"

"Well? You have to see it to believe it!"

To see it, to see it with his own eyes. It was the invitation he had been waiting for. Cosme Vila dropped everything and set about deciding which convoy to accompany. He picked one with six trucks going to the town of Bisbal and climbed aboard the leader.

"When do we leave?"

"Right away."

The province was a radical change of scene from the city. The signs saying "Help the strikers in Gerona" flapped against the sides of the trucks as they sped along. Boys and girls stood along the roadside waving at them. Suddenly, not more than seven miles from the city, the first truck spied someone on the side of the road waving a flag.

"There, there's something ready for us!"

The convoy ground to a halt. "Comrades!" a peasant shouted. "We have some things for you."

June. The grain harvest was at its peak. The lead truck turned off into the fields. Reapers throughout the province were scything the ripe stalks. The workers jumped from the trucks to the ground. Cosme Vila imitated them. The workers raised their fist in greeting. The peasants returned the salute by crossing their scythes over their extended arms. Behind them stretched the golden fields of grain. The province must indeed be a garden, as Gorki said, Cosme Vila thought.

The peasants took them to a shed stacked with sacks. "For the Comrades of Gerona," said the label on each sack, scrawled in a hand like Teo's.

Some women who had been washing in a nearby irrigation ditch came up. "Here! Give them those figs in the basket there."

Cosme Vila's enormous head presided solemnly over the scene. He was wearing new rope sandals. Cosme Vila gave the peasants no clue as to his identity. He looked at their hard, hard, weatherbeaten faces with enormous noses, like Casal's. Their fanaticism shone in their small, restless eyes, glittering black dots. One truck loaded. "Here, let's have the rope." Everything was done with ease. There was almost no noise. They looked like smugglers, or the celebrants of some religious ritual. "Come back in fifteen days!" As the convoy pulled out, one of the peasants shouted: "Tell Gerona we're waiting for the land-reform program!"

Cosme Vila heard the shout. It seemed to come right up from the waving grain. The land-reform program. The women returned to their washing in the irrigation ditch. Land reform. It was evident that under all that he had witnessed throbbed the hope of land reform. The food that filled the trucks was the gift of sharecroppers; their backs had been bowed for generations with nothing to show for it.

The trip continued. They went almost to the seaside. The wind from the moving truck rushed past Cosme Vila's face, scattering his thoughts. Along the railroad track parallel to the road short, puffing trains were moving slowly toward the seashore, with the first of the summer vacationers in the windows. Not one responded to the clenched-fist salutes. "Fascists!" shouted the truck driver. They didn't hear him.

The unsolicited contributors—those who flagged the trucks down unexpectedly from the side of the road—filled Cosme Vila with a sense of joy. Nonetheless, he preferred the prearranged collections by the Communist cells. "Peasants of the world, unite!" At such meetings everything was carried out with an instinctive sense of organization. A local leader would hand the driver a list of what had been collected. The party seal on the paper was the guarantee that the amount indicated would not be one kilo short and that all the food was of the best quality. "We tried to get up to fifteen hundred pounds, but it was impossible." In many places they found announcements of the rally in Gerona still plastered on the walls.

"How many in Gerona have joined the revolutionary ranks?" Cosme Vila would be asked.

"About a thousand," he would say.

The chief and the local leaders would exchange a long look. It was clear that more help would be needed. The local leader would turn to the driver. "We'll see if we can send you something by train on Friday." Then they always asked for orders. "Don't you have any instructions for us?" In farewell, they raised their fists. "*Salud*, and at your orders!"

The return to Gerona was triumphal. The countryside was beautiful, but the land needed to be cultivated more productively and the river channeled into canals. In what was taking place Cosme Vila saw the union between the city and the land, the closing of the two arms of the tongs the German Communists talked about. The strike, which had occasioned this, had been a magnificent idea. The walls surrounding the great estates loomed up along the road here and there, their tops menacing with broken glass like the mailed fists of medieval knights.

When the first truck reached the grade crossing, Cosme Vila heard: "Cosme!" But the train was passing. Afterward the barrier went up. His in-laws waved to him, filled with emotion at seeing him seated atop the immense load of sacks on the first truck.

The outlying slums were filled with housewives awaiting the passing of the trucks. The atmosphere was one of well-being. From every side rose signs of appreciation and gratitude. The convoy slowed down as it entered the city limits. Cosme Vila rode through the streets at eye level with the balconies. Some, like the Inspector of Labor's, were shut tight, aggressively; others were crowded with families that clapped as the trucks went by.

When the convoy drew to a halt to unload in front of the Centro Tradicionalista, La Valenciana appeared in the doorway. She was dead on her feet, but she still had the strength to say: "We have made more converts today than with a year of speeches."

Don Pedro Oriol lived across from the Centro Tradicionalista. He witnessed the arrival of Cosme Vila. He pulled the shutter to. Don Pedro Oriol suffered. He was among those in the city who suffered the most. A good part of his life had been spent in that Center. It filled him with sorrow to see what it had become. He missed *El Tradicionalista.*

Moreover, he had been told that near the Hermitage of the Angels gasoline from one of the trucks had leaked out on the road, and that smoke had been sighted, smoke on the mountain.

"So much the worse for him!" Colonel Muñoz told Julio when the Police Chief filled him in on what Cosme was doing. "Those who are giving the food are the tenants, and what they are giving away is the owner's share. But when it comes to digging into their own share, it will be a different story! And then you will see what happens here, after they've got used to a full belly…

After eight days of strike and the People's Cooperative, the rest of the population was growing frightened. The Costas' in-laws had called them on the phone: "They are stealing our rice, they are stealing it!"

The Communist Party was giving every indication that it had decided to stake its very existence on an all-or-nothing bid for power. It was the subject of every conversation. But there was one thing that everybody was at a loss to explain. Cosme Vila's Communism could be justified in terms of his origins and the reflections to which his former employment might easily give rise. It seemed logical that Teo, Gorki, and La Valenciana should find themselves in the party. But how account for the sudden emergence as a comrade of Professor Morales? "What is that man doing rubbing elbows with the scum?" Everybody knew that he was on the executive committee. He would leave the Instituto after delivering a lecture on Cervantes or the theater of Racine, and go to the cooperative to measure out the cherries! And then off to the newspaper.

He was a great friend of David's and Olga's. Like them, he had started out as a schoolteacher. David and Olga had hoped to win him over to socialism. He had always stalled for time, saying: "Let me think it over. I'll have to think it over seriously." The result of all his thinking was that he joined the Communist Party. "I am aware of all the defects and all the cruelties," he told the teachers. "But I consider them symptomatic of a stage of development that must be endured because, unfortunately, it is inevitable. In retrospect it will be seen that it served a useful function." He was a great admirer of Russia, and he felt that it had made enormous strides since 1917, adapting itself to the modern world and infinitely multiplying its potential. "It is a new concept of man, which must be put into practice throughout the world." Some who knew him attributed the whole thing to a sexual origin: a bachelor schoolteacher embittered by his ugliness and lack of success with women. That was the reason he hated society, they said, and why he felt at home rubbing elbows with La Valenciana or hanging cherries on the ears of other hideous members.

His stand had caused amazement and a certain amount of uneasiness in the city. But from a practical point of view David and Olga could not bring themselves to regret his decision. Thanks to the interest he took in the matter, they finally succeeded in getting the pupils in a couple of dozen schools—though only a month of classes remained—to make kites, plant a piece of land, shampoo their hair, democratically take turns as monitors, give a scientific explanation of the cosmos, and listen attentively to the lectures on sexual hygiene!

Morales told them with a smile: "All I ask in return is that you turn over whatever your students raise to the cooperative."

Casal witnessed all this with some bewilderment. He finally asked David and Olga what they were up to. "What are you after, anyway?"

The teachers looked him squarely in the eye, as though they had finally decided that the time had come to give him a straight answer. "Casal, dear friend, we are going to lay the cards on the table," they said. "Don't get the idea that this has anything to do with getting our *Manual* put into use. What has happened is that we have received definite proof that the rumors about a military uprising are founded on absolute fact."

"What?"

"As truly as we're standing here," David continued. "Therefore we feel that we must all unite and avoid wrangling among ourselves."

Casal looked into their eyes. It was hard not to believe them. "Are you talking seriously?" he asked.

It was Olga who answered: "We are convinced that it is true."

She informed him that a mission of representatives of the Republic had gone from Barcelona to France to get guarantees of assistance from the French Popular Front when the time came.

Casal didn't know what to reply. He forgot the Workers' Cooperative, Cosme Vila's sophistries, and the difficulties he was encountering in drawing up a program that would satisfy everybody.

"So Julio was right..." he muttered. But the old doubts didn't die easily. Impossible, impossible! What could they hope to accomplish? A general here or there perhaps, but most of the military were openly in favor of the Republic.

"Don't kid yourself," David put in. "The trouble is that we are forgetting where the real danger lies."

Casal succumbed to the general state of nervousness. He got in touch immediately with the UGT leaders in Barcelona. The answer from Barcelona was: "It is true. Keep your eye on the military, the Carlists, and the Falange."

Casal's wife took a different view of the situation. "Does it surprise you that they should revolt?" she said. "What else can they do? Cosme Vila will kill off every last one of them."

Casal was suddenly filled with a blind fury. The major, Carlists, Falange. Where the devil was that Mateo that they couldn't lay hands on him?

Maybe Cosme Vila was right, after all. Would he go and talk to him or wouldn't he? He decided that he had already lowered himself too much. And besides, that dismal apartment! Casal decided that the comfortable bed he shared with his wife kept him from committing certain atrocities. But it was clear that the danger was serious. David's and Olga's tone of conviction did not lie. Casal thought he understood why the Socalist Party advised him not to get on the outs with Cosme Vila.

David and Olga told him about the attitude the in-laws of the Costas had taken. "They own half the town of Pals, and they are kicking because they were done out of eleven hundred pounds of rice."

IGNACIO did not miss a detail of what was happening. He recalled a conversation he had had with Professor Civil in which he said to his teacher: "When I see things clearly, I will fight."

Good God! Couldn't he see clearly yet? Wasn't it abundantly clear that to counteract the tons of venom that fell on the city every day what was proposed was to raise the salaries of the workers? Matías Alvear sensed that his son was being affected by the violence of what he saw going on about him. "Don't let yourself be taken in," he told him. "To be brave one doesn't need a rifle. If I were in your place, I would study harder than ever and come back from the examinations in Barcelona with honors."

These words, instead of having a calming effect on Ignacio, increased his state of ill-being. He was not thinking of himself, but of Mateo. It was just no go. Honors in the examinations, and Mateo not even there to take them! Professor Civil bemoaned the fact every day. "Tell me where he is, tell me where he is, and I will go and give him classes even if it means climbing down the chimney." Professor Civil, too, was a dreamer. But Ignacio never gave him the address.

Ignacio realized for the first time how much he cared for his friend. He was as jumpy as Pilar, or more so. He was as preoccupied as César about Mateo's hide-out. Any day now they would go up to El Rubio's to make a check. Mateo simply had to find a new place to stay. "We must have a talk with El Rubio. Perhaps he will think of the right place."

Ignacio wanted to leave the matter settled before going to Barcelona. He had bumped into Julio on the street, and Julio had said: "Ignacio, old boy! Perhaps you can give me a clue to where Mateo is hiding." Then the policeman had smiled and tried to pass it off as a joke with a slap on the back.

Ignacio had halted his arm midway. "It's all over between us, Julio," he had said.

Mateo let it be known that he didn't give a hang about the examinations. On the other hand, the idea of moving to a new hiding place seemed to him a good one, and he immediately suggested Pedro's house. "He will take me in," Mateo said. "I know he will. And besides, there at least I will have a radio!"

Pilar nearly fainted when she heard what Mateo proposed. "The home of a Communist?"

On the other hand, Ignacio approved of the plan. "What better place? Who would ever think of looking for him there?" Ignacio was sure that Pedro would never give Mateo away—unless under direct orders from Moscow.

It was decided that El Rubio should talk it over with Pedro. El Rubio had known him for years and he, too, trusted him. "Plow can he give Mateo away when he is a kid who never opens his mouth?" He also knew that Pedro hated Cosme Vila, Teo, Vasiliev, the whole lot of them, with all his soul. He considered them all traitors to Russia, and when he saw the special issue they had published he had exclaimed: "Trick photography! The real thing in Russia is twice as good!"

Marta had proposed, as a marginal note to the problem of Mateo, that Pilar accompany Ignacio to Barcelona. "A change of scene would do you good. Here you worry yourself to death," she told her friend.

Pilar flatly refused. "Suppose something happened while I was away...."

Ignacio was left with no choice but to go to Barcelona alone. He would be away at least three days. Many persons, including the assistant manager of the bank, gave him all kinds of advice. "Watch your step at the university. There are many students who belong to the Youth Freedom League. And, above all, be careful at the boarding house. Don't talk about politics or your beliefs with anybody."

Professor Civil went down to the station to say goodbye. "Brush up on lesson 43!"

Marta kissed Ignacio on the forehead. Just as the train began to move she ran up to the compartment window and put an envelope into his hands. "Deliver this in person!" she said. He glanced at the address: "J. Campistol, Balmes 110, Barcelona." Then she pulled out her handkerchief to wave goodbye. Ignacio saw that it was a blue handkerchief.

J. Campistol was the head of the Falange in Barcelona. Good God! The thing was clear enough. The girl wanted to confront him with a *fait accompli*. Why the devil was she waving that blue handkerchief? He had told her a thousand times not to look for trouble! Ignacio found himself mumbling a thousand oaths out the window.

"God keep you!" the girl shouted.

As soon as the train was out of sight, Marta put the handkerchief back in her sleeve. She suddenly felt utterly alone. She looked at Professor Civil. But in a minute she had recovered her self-possession. This was not the moment for tears, she told herself. On the contrary, it was her duty in those days to double her efforts. All the people at the station already had the latest newspapers and were reading them avidly. What had happened? The news was alarming. The parliamentary debates between the deputies were becoming increasingly violent. Calvo Sotelo's life had been threatened from the floor of the Chamber in no uncertain terms. José Antonio was still in jail; and Calvo Sotelo was the political leader by whom Major Martínez de Soria swore.

Marta went straight home, and from that moment she did not rest. In so far as she could she tried to imitate her father's vigorous approach to certain situations. Many of his observations on strategy were engraved on her memory. She felt that the time had come to put them into practice. Marta particularly recalled one of them: "In so far as possible, one must know one's collaborators."

Marta immediately thought of her comrades. Were they good or were they bad? They were a little bit of everything. By and large, she couldn't complain.

Jorge and Roca were her favorites. Don Jorge's son, despite his over-elegant appearance, was brave. He had spotted his father's two main tenants at the Communist rally, and he had waited for them afterwards in the Rambla. "My father is in jail," he told them, "and he has disinherited me. But if you attempt anything against him or against any other member of the family, you'll have to settle accounts with me. And you know that I rarely miss a partridge."

Marta also liked Roca. He was a little naïve. He felt sure that they would triumph "because Hitler started out the same way and he triumphed." He would have liked the comrades to meet in a beer hall, but there were no beer halls in Gerona, and they had to meet in Raimundo's barbershop or at Marta's house, which was still the safest place. But Marta liked him. She knew she could depend on him. His father had been fired from the municipal police. "All because I was driving on the wrong side of the road," the boy had explained jokingly.

On the other hand, Marta was not so keen about Benito Civil. She considered the professor's son a sad case. Maybe his wife was responsible, for she never left off complaining. When Benito had been sent to the cemetery to lay the red roses on the grave, his wife, clinging to his neck, had said to him: "You may never come back."

Marta did not care much for Octavio either. In fact, she liked him less than any of the others and could not understand what Mateo saw in him. "A hypocrite, and conceited to boot!" she thought. She was happy that it was Octavio who was in jail instead of Jorge or Roca, for example. She felt the absence of Rosselló because he was impulsive and had stood up to his father; she hardly knew Haro.

"It's a curious thing," Padilla would say to Marta. "When all is said and done, you're just a bunch of kids. Sometimes I ask myself if I haven't got mixed up in some kind of mess."

"Sit down and keep quiet," the girl would answer, and then she would rattle off another lesson from the party pamphlets.

Major Martínez de Soria, for his part, kept an eye on his daughter's activities. He had come to the conclusion that the Falange might prove useful to him the day of the uprising after all, though they were so few. "It's a pity that they are not about two hundred," he mused. In the final analysis, he felt he could count most on the "traditionalists." "The traditionalists have an advantage," he thought. "Almost all of them are hunters; on the other hand, among those kids Jorge is probably the only one who knows how to handle a gun." Besides, there were many more grown men among the traditionalists; people like Don Pedro Oriol, who, when they walked into the barracks, would be ready for all the consequences. The major was satisfied because after much deliberation he had finally decided to have a talk with the notary Noguer, and the notary had told him: "You can count on me." At the same time, Noguer had told him that he could not predict how many supporters would rally to the cause when the time came. "The situation is very grave. You know that," Noguer had said. "This Catalonian question is mixed up in it, too. But I think a lot of them will stick."

He thought it over for a moment, and then, placing his hand on the table as if witnessing a document, he said: "At any rate, you can count on thirty men."

Thirty men! Who were they, more or less? A lawyer, a doctor, three manufacturers, two commercial representatives... "Enough, enough," the major interrupted. That was all he wanted to know. He felt optimistic. *Renovación* had promised him ten men. Don Santiago Estrada had promised fifty. Perhaps the figures were a little high, perhaps not.

"What I regret," the major thought sometimes as he lost himself in the recesses of the house while his wife said her beads aloud, "is that the boy is not here. We will win in Valladolid hands down; but here the boy could be a big help to me." It also pained him that he could not discuss these matters with the man who courted his daughter, though he was sure that Ignacio would wind up in the Falange sooner or later.

The major sorely missed Warning Voice. "He would be the real bellwether." But he was beginning to doubt that Warning Voice would be released from jail. The fortnight had passed, and he was still behind bars. The major also missed Lieutenant Martín, "that imbecile who insults the dead," though he had found a capable substitute in the shavetail who had stood up to Teo, Second Lieutenant Romá, the son of a wealthy Barcelona family.

The major had no idea that El Rubio was harboring Mateo. He had picked him as an orderly with the knowledge that he had been an anarchist, thinking that this would disconcert certain officers. He would send him out on small errands, have him polish his puttees or rub down his horse; but he was careful not to give him an opportunity to rummage through his papers.

Marta was amused by these precautions, and made it a point to let her father see the friendship that existed between her and El Rubio.

"But—what makes you act that way with that clown?" the major would ask his daughter. "You ought to keep your distance."

"You have your little secrets, don't you? Well, so do I," Marta would say, drawing close to her father and pinching his florid cheeks.

COSME Vila did not rest on his laurels. He had foreseen from the very start the difficulties of which Colonel Muñoz spoke. The quantities of food he needed were fabulous. How long would the peasants put up with it? Besides, a number of basic foods—meat, milk, oil—were not included in the distribution.

The leader felt that it would be a mistake to bleed the province white, particularly as, for the time being, the city could in no way reciprocate. It was plain common sense to avoid even the possibility that the peasants might get it into their heads that their generosity was being taken advantage of. Another two weeks of contributions at the rate they were going and the first danger signals would begin to appear. A wife seeing her stock of chickpeas dwindling would look at her husband with ill-contained anger. Another seeing the party workers riding off happily in the laden trucks would say: "You know, those boys have found a system."

Cosme Vila was the only one aware of the danger. The others lived in blissful assurance. Who said the peasants would only give the landlord's share? They were already digging into their own, and there hadn't been any change of attitude.

This evidence of solidarity was widely commented on by the members in the city. Some of the workers even admitted that the peasants were more dedicated than themselves. "Don't kid yourself, they are, they are. Why, we don't even come up to their shoulders."

Comrade Morales explained this phenomenon in his conversations with David and Olga and, above all, with Victor, whom he was always trying to impress, unsuccessfully. "The peasants see in Communism an even more revolutionary solution to their problems than the workers," Morales would say. "The industrial workers know that what the factory produces is secondary, and that this condition will remain unchanged even if the day comes when they own all its wealth in common; on the other hand, the peasants can be sure that as soon as the land is divided up among them, they will have in their possession the means of providing themselves with all the necessities of life."

This, according to him, explained the fact that the cells in the villages were less spectacular than those in the city, but knew better what was at stake and were even more violent. Like Cosme Vila, Morales had made a tour through the province and had returned with new energies. He attended the daily meetings of the party workers, and there he had endless stories to tell. "The peasants meet in the sheds or threshing floors because the sergeant of the Civil Guard is always at the tavern or the tobacco shop. They don't talk much. The wineskin makes the rounds, and they are always looking out toward the fields and listening to the lowing of the cattle." Cosme Vila was looked upon as a father by those peasants who knew him and as a mythological being by those who did not. The former described him and spoke of the breadth of his forehead, to give an idea of which they had to raise the visor of their caps. Morales said some of them asked him: "And he's read even more than you, hasn't he?"

There was always one who spoke explaining the Communist doctrine. If he kept his explanations down to earth, his listeners' eyes glowed. If he got lost in fancy words and complicated ideas, the members of his audience would run their tongues over their teeth and say: "Yes, sure. I guess that's right."

They were convinced that the first steps on the road to happiness were to kill the priest and then the sergeant of the Civil Guard. With them out of the way, collectivization would follow. Their concept of collectivization was that all hands would pitch in together for the big jobs, with tractors to serve all, plenty of fertilizer, and airplanes to dust the crops and spray the olive trees. When the time for division of the crop came, each would contribute his assessment, but each would know he was his own boss. "They will contribute what they are called upon to give," Morales told Victor. "But each one wants to own his parcel of land and his animals."

That was why they filled the trucks, content to receive a copy of *El Proletario* in return.

"And the land program—how's it coming along?" they would always ask.

"Cosme Vila is working on it. The Fascists are making it tough going, but they'll lose out in the end."

"Good enough. Tell him we know how to wait."

But despite Morales's enthusiasm, Cosme Vila knew that they would not wait. The province would not put up forever with being the city's wet-nurse! Moreover, the number of beneficiaries at the cooperative was growing every day. Even some anarchists had turned up, hangdog fashion, for their mess of pottage. Cosme Vila realized that he had to lay his hands on some money so that the strikers could buy meat, milk, and oil, and in order to pay the peasants.

Money, money. He knew he should not let on to anyone about his problem, but he needed money. Morale in the city was at a peak. They were in control at practically every point, and the authorities were tottering. It would take just one more push. One push and the Mayor and the Commissioner would resign. If only the city government was in his hands! With the funds in the city treasury, his troubles would be over. There was still the problem of the fisherman. They had turned a deaf ear to his appeals. "We've already got our own Communism. If you want fish, cash on the barrelhead."

Money to buy fish, too, for the strikers.

There was no way out but to take it up with Barcelona. The one-armed comrade had promised him assistance whenever he wanted it, and Comrade Vasiliev had said the same thing. "If it becomes necessary, we can take up a subscription in Russia," Vasiliev had said. Cosme Vila decided that the moment had come to put these promises to the test, and he therefore decided on a trip to Barcelona, either in person or sending Morales and Gorki as delegates.

One thing was clear: Cosme Vila was not the only leader making decisions. At the time of Cosme Vila's soliloquies, interminable dialogues were going on at police headquarters. The Commissioner decided that things had gone far enough. This had led him to put things squarely up to Julio with an energy of which he had given little evidence previously. "You must send that fool an ultimatum!" he had said. Julio had taken the outburst in stride. Nevertheless, he felt that the Commissioner was right and that something had to be done.

The population of the city could not get food in the stores at any price, and the Communists were giving it away for nothing at the Centro Tradicionalista. At the railroad station they were refusing to unload shipments for some consignees. "Who is that stuff for? Costa, Corbera? Let it rot there!"

At the same time came the protest of the landowners, who had risen as one man to denounce the activities of the tenants. "You've wrung your last drop from this cow!" the tenants told them. "Ask the comrades in Gerona for your share." Some of the landowners let themselves be cowed by the threats, which generally came from the women. But most of them, following the example of the in-laws of the Costas, swore out summonses against the tenants and prepared to take the fight to court.

This was all of maximum importance, for the lawyers saw an opportunity to gain a platform from which to be heard. Moreover, the judge, who could not forget that Cosme Vila had demanded that he be replaced summarily, seemed predisposed to decide in favor of the landowners.

The consequences of such a decision might be extremely grave. *El Proletario* began printing black headlines: LANDOWNERS TRY TO BLOCK DISTRIBUTION OF FOODSTUFFS TO THE PEOPLE. JUDGE IN CONFERENCE WITH THE LANDOWNERS. DEFENSE OF THE TENANTS WITH EVERY MEANS AT OUR DISPOSAL.

That was how matters stood. Julio had no doubts about what Cosme Vila had in mind: he hoped that a legal battle would prove more trouble than it was worth, and that out of sheer exhaustion the landowners would abandon their claims. In that event, the peasants would have gained a more favorable position, for which they could thank the Communist Party.

"Of course, that's what he has in mind," the Commissioner agreed when he saw that Julio outdid even him in his accusations. "Let's see if we settle this business, once and for all!"

Rumors of the schemes that were being devised against him reached Cosme Vila. Whereupon he decided not to leave the city, and delegated Gorki and Morales to go to Barcelona. "I'll stay here to keep an eye on things."

The great mass of the members lived oblivious of these problems. In fact, there was no telling what they were thinking! Cosme Vila was constantly reminded of the admonition of Comrade Morales: "We must keep their minds occupied." It was perfectly evident that the members, idle hands without any work, were getting bored. Some had begun to drink. Others spoke of starting a theater group and a singing society.

The time had come, beyond a doubt, to set up the People's Militia. While the authorities were laying the groundwork for an offensive against the Communist Party, the party would take steps to defend itself. Point number nine on the program as it had been drawn up and approved by the committee. Some with rifles, the majority with wooden clubs. There wasn't a minute to lose! The chief missed Teo in the worst way. But he decided on reflection that the nature of the problem was such that he would have had to take personal charge of it under any circumstances. The thing, then, was to set up the People's Militia and—another key move—establish cells among the soldiers in the barracks.

The first steps had already been taken. For the barracks, he was counting on an artillery lieutenant, a sly one. As for the organization of the militia, the day after the executive committee had taken its decision, he had spoken with two old party members, a couple of retired soldiers—veterans of the African campaign—and both had enthusiastically accepted the task of whipping the raw material into shape. "Just say when, comrade," they had said. The party had uniforms, and caps as well. Provincial cells in the region of the Pyrenees had supplied the wooden staves, all of sturdy oak.

How many men would comprise the militia? Cosme Vila pulled out the party register. He thumbed through the pages, looking at the faces in the snapshots as Julio looked at the eyes of his suicides. He selected a total of two hundred and fifty men between the ages of eighteen and forty-five. He decided to notify them privately rather than risk the publicity that would stem from a public announcement in *El Proletario*. With each note delivered at their homes the militiamen received a small package containing a blue coverall and a blue cap.

"At the Dehesa at six o'clock tonight, with this uniform and rope-soled sandals," the note read.

The two hundred and fifty men received the order without knowing what it was about.

"Do you know anything about this?"

"Nothing! Not a thing. What do they expect us to do with this coverall?"

Curiosity made them punctual. Cosme Vila was there waiting with the two veterans. As the recruits arrived, Cosme Vila greeted them one by one.

"What's up?"

"The militia. The People's Militia!"

The men looked at one another, wide-eyed. At last! "What about arms?"

"That will all be taken care of."

Unconsciously the men assumed a martial air.

Cosme Vila delivered a harangue not unlike that of a squad sergeant. The faces before him were not those of the photographs in his file. They were less aggressive, less severe, weaker. Some real discipline would have to be knocked into them.

"Flop to it, boys. Buckle down!"

The two veterans stepped forward. The company was divided into sections and squads by alphabetical order. "How about letting us two stick together?" came the petition from among the ranks.

"Each man where he has been assigned. What are you—nuns?" Cosme Vila snapped.

"Appointment of sergeants and corporals!" a voice ordered.

The recruits chewed their nails. There was an air of great expectancy.

Cosme Vila rattled off the names. "I have been guided by services to the party, experience—some of you have already performed your military service—and by physical fitness."

The two veterans of the African war—one of them even had the waxed needle mustache—relived heroic days. The new sergeants and corporals were issued rifles; the rank and file received stout staves. The veteran with the mustache, Molina by name, said to Cosme Vila: "We like this. Here, at least, we know that everybody is a volunteer."

An unforeseen difficulty soon cropped up: the loudspeaker at the swimming pool, which poured out a constant stream of raucous dance music. And the spectators. They seemed to spring out of the ground, but particularly from the direction of the swimming pool, most of them anarchists wearing trunks. Future and the older daughter of El Responsable, who was wearing a white maillot that summer, stood out.

The two veterans proved themselves masters of the situation. "Open ranks—march!" The two hundred and fifty men obeyed, keeping an arm's length from one another. The platoons suddenly emerged, in perfect order. Cosme Vila took in the scene with his back against a venerable sycamore.

Soon, beneath the foliage, and during the infrequent moments of silence of the loudspeaker, the Dehesa rang with the martial voices of the veterans: "Hup, two, three, four!" For the time being, the uniformity of the ranks was haphazard, and the rope-soled sandals failed to produce the satisfying crunching on the sand the veterans would have desired. "To the rear—march!" Some continued forward, as though irresistibly drawn by the maillot of El Responsable's daughter; others headed in the opposite direction, toward Cosme Vila. The two veterans, also wearing blue coveralls so new and stiff that they stood away from their chests, looked at each other in despair.

Once again, from the beginning. The platoons regrouped. Each man in his place. "Hup, two! Your left, your right!"

And suddenly everything was coming out perfectly. "To your left—march!" The platoons turned smartly to the left. "To your right—march!" Everybody marched to the right. "To the rear—march!"

The militiamen about-faced and marched off as one man. And then, to the stupefaction of everyone, they found themselves face to face with a formation identical with their own, but made up of cavalry. The veterans' drill commands died in their throats. Nobody could fathom what had happened. Where had they come from? How? Who were these horsemen? The sun and sweat were blinding, and nobody could make out who they were.

Cosme Vila did not move a muscle. He had seen the horsemen enter the Dehesa at a trot even more aggressive than that at which Major Martínez de Soria took his turn around the circuit. "This bears Julio García's signature," he thought. And he had guessed right, for in another instant he recognized the caps of the Assault Guards.

The mounted police! The long-promised mounted police. The phone at police headquarters had rung, and a voice from the swimming pool at the other end of the line had delivered the spine-chilling news: the People's Militia! "This is the moment," the authorities had exclaimed. "Now we don't even have to send an ultimatum." And there were the animals now, whinnying restlessly, looking at the party members with glassy eyes, and being stared at in turn, as the militiamen took in the situation, with expressions that gradually changed from surprise to rage and the desire that lightning should strike them down.

It was a moment of great indecision. Two platoons of regular police had slipped in and now completely surrounded the militia. All eyes turned toward Cosme Vila, awaiting a sign. He continued leaning against the tree, his face an inscrutable mask. The militiamen felt foolish, standing there with the wooden staves on their shoulders. Those who had rifles knew that they were loaded; some of them were glad of this in view of the expression on the face of the officer of the guards as he dismounted and strode toward their ranks.

This officer was a giant, something like Teo, but with a beefier face. He wore the look of a man not disposed to waste any time. He addressed his first words to Cosme Vila: "By order of the Commissioner, you will hand over your rifles and come along with me. Order these men to disperse at once."

Cosme Vila listened to him. The loudspeaker at the swimming pool had become silent. "Comrades, don't hand over anything! Everybody, run for home!"

The militiamen were not prepared for that. Nonetheless, they tore off their caps and started off in every direction. But they got in one another's way, and the police on foot quickly managed to bottle them up. Those with the staves gave up almost without resistance, though the gesture of surrendering the weapon was accompanied by an ironic smile. Those with rifles put up a fight, but they were overpowered in no time.

The officer gave the command: "Start walking! Make it snappy and no talking!" Some obeyed. Others looked toward Cosme Vila and hung back. Still others pulled tobacco pouches out of their pockets with a frankly insolent air. "Start walking or there will be trouble!" the officer said, and pointed toward the clubs his men carried. Prudence won out. Little by little the militiamen began to break up. "Get going!" The police started after them, clubs on high, and the militiamen finally ran off as fast as their feet could take them.

Cosme Vila had remained behind, guarded by a cluster of policemen. "You are coming with me to headquarters," the officer said.

Cosme Vila did not move a muscle. "Are you taking me on foot or on horseback?"

"On foot," the officer said, returning his pistol to the holster. "March!"

The officer ordered the horsemen to return at a trot, and he sent nearly all the police on foot back to the station by another route. Only five remained to escort Cosme Vila.

They started walking, with Cosme Vila a few paces ahead. Someone among the bystanders shouted: "Lock him up!"

Cosme tried to size up the situation. The main avenue through the Dehesa was long. The boots of the guards resounded more emphatically than the sandals of the People's Militia. The Communist chief decided that Julio had made a mistake in ordering him brought in on foot. The route that they would have to take, once they got inside the walls of the city, would give the mass of the party members opportunity to realize what was happening and to take the necessary steps for his defense. If the police took the shortest route they would have to pass right in front of party headquarters!

For the moment, however, he was defenseless. The spectators trailing along behind him inclined to be hostile.

"Lock him up!" someone shouted again.

The Cathedral bell tolled the hour of seven as the afternoon shadows lengthened. The horsemen had passed out of sight. Cosme Vila strode out on the street leading to the Plaza de Telégrafos. As far as he could see, there was no sign of any gathering of his faithful.

"Farther along, perhaps," Cosme Vila thought. "The militiamen will have told somebody. It's still too soon."

Suddenly the whole scene changed. As they reached the bridge, where a number of roads leading into the city converged, they heard an ungodly racket from the rear. Shouts, grinding gears, roaring motors, auto horns.

Cosme Vila turned around, and the guards did the same. What was going on? One truck, another truck, and still another. Cosme Vila suddenly understood it all: the food convoy was returning to Gerona from Bañólas. "Food for the strikers of Gerona." The honking and the shouts were for the crowd to clear a path so that the trucks could get through. The trucks were loaded with great mounds of garlic, on top of which sat party workers.

Cosme Vila did not lose a second. He drew himself up to his full height, looked toward the trucks, and thrust his arm violently upward in a clenched-fist salute.

The members, from their garlic citadels, recognized him instantly. They saw the guards. Arrested! The chief was under arrest! Shouts broke from their throats. The horns blared in unbroken unison. The members leaped from the trucks to the ground and with apparent disregard for their safety rushed at the guards. Some, for lack of anything else, clutched handfuls of garlic.

The trucks came to a halt. There were women mingled with the workers. Balcony shutters flew open.

Two guards remained at Cosme Vila's side. The other three, clubs raised menacingly, prepared to stand off the workers. The officer sounded his whistle, but there was no sign of any more guards.

The sight of the clubs checked the workers. Suddenly, from the back of one of the trucks, someone threw a stone that struck one of the guards flush on the shoulder. The man dropped to the ground.

"You brutes!" shouted the officer, drawing his pistol.

The other guards also drew. Three shots were heard.

The panic was indescribable. Some of the workers took refuge behind the trucks. Others fled pell-mell. There was not a face to be seen on a single balcony.

Suddenly the first of the trucks started up and rolled rapidly toward the guards, forcing them to scatter. It came alongside Cosme Vila. The driver leaned out. "Climb in! Hurry up!" He had the door open.

Cosme Vila hesitated for a moment. "No!" he finally shouted. "But concentrate in front of police headquarters."

The guards, seeing Cosme Vila hesitate, thought he was going to climb aboard and fired at the tires.

Cosme Vila whirled around furious. "That's enough, now! That's enough!"

The truck roared away. Matías Alvear had appeared in the doorway of the Telegraph Building with his gray smock, and his pencil behind his ear. On hearing the shots, he had gone back inside.

Cosme Vila preferred being taken in on foot, now that everyone knew what was happening. In the distance he could see La Valenciana, easily recognizable by her open-necked blouse, at the head of a squad of party members. The injured guard had got to his feet. It was better that way, thought Cosme Vila.

"March!"

The pace was slow, for they had to be continually side-stepping piles of rubbish. The strike of the street cleaners and garbage collectors continued. The city stank, and it was becoming almost impossible to enter certain sections. There was talk of the soldiers taking over the sanitation services. Hungry curs, like the one that followed César in the Calle de la Barca, slunk through the streets.

EIGHTY

THERE was no Rightist newspaper to inform the public of what was happening. Nevertheless, the news filtered through in mysterious ways. Cosme Vila's attempt to set up the People's Militia heightened the tension everyone felt. What would happen now? Where would the intervention of the authorities lead?

Everything unfolded with implacable logic. Cosme Vila argued before Julio and the Commissioner that he had intended nothing more than to drill his members in marching. He submitted arguments that could not be wholly discounted: all but a few of the men were carrying wooden staves, and the rifles were unloaded. What possible threat could there be in empty rifles?

Julio called in the officer of the Assault Guards. "Show us those rifles." They were old, useless. Cosme Vila smiled.

Outside, the party members had gathered, shouting: "Long live Cosme Vila!"

Julio and the Commissioner went into a huddle. They decided to turn him loose.

"But forget about the militia!" Julio said in a tone that admitted of no contradiction. "If you try another drill, you will find yourself in jail sleeping alongside Don Jorge, and we will close down your headquarters."

"And you'll be hearing from us further," the Commissioner added, as a closing note.

Cosme Vila walked out, but he had stopped smiling. He was worried and tired. He ordered those who were waiting for him outside to disperse. He turned toward his home, where he could sleep. "Tomorrow we will talk, tomorrow."

To the many who felt that Julio had acted weakly, the Police Chief had a stock answer: "Everything will work out. You'll see. This, for Cosme, was vital. Now, you see, he can't take a step. He will burn himself out and have nothing to show for it."

The next day *El Proletario* attacked Julio bitterly. It published a picture showing the two guards firing at the fleeing truck. Events had brought the spirits of the party members to fever pitch, for the idea of having arms in their possession and lining up in military formation had filled them with enthusiasm.

Cosme Vila reached the office early. He was not sure that he had got the militia off on the right foot. Perhaps it had been a blunder. To hear the talk around town, one would have thought he had even mortars at his disposal. "No matter what you do, they will find some stick to beat you with, accusing you of scheming one thing or another," his wife had told him.

His mind was troubled, and those around him realized it right away. But there was no halting the march of events.

Victor approached him. "Listen a minute. I hate to bring this up now—but the people are kicking."

"What people?"

"The people who go to the cooperative."

"Well—what's the matter?"

"They always get the same things. They say they want some meat."

Cosme Vila gave Victor a long look. "We'll talk about that later."

Victor went out, and the driver of the lead truck the day before came in. "Listen, I couldn't tell you this yesterday with all the confusion, but out in the province they want to know what's happening with the land reform."

Cosme Vila finally blew up. "Leave me alone! Until Gorki and Morales get back from Barcelona I can't decide anything!"

This was his greatest worry. If the two delegates brought back the right news, everything would be taken care of, and the rifles, even if they were unloaded, would turn against Julio. Above all, what he needed was money!

"Go to the station and wait for them. When they arrive, bring them here without a minute's delay."

Gorki and Morales arrived by the morning train, on the same train as Ignacio. They had only to appear in the office door for Cosme Vila to know that the news they brought was only fair.

"Sit down. What news?"

The two delegates began talking at once, almost drowning each other out.

"They received us as though we were cabinet ministers."

"The big thing is to organize cells among the soldiers."

"They told us to—"

Cosme Vila cut them short. "Results! Results!" he snapped. "What about the money?"

It was Gorki who answered. "They will give some, but not much."

Cosme Vila's eyes went flat.

"The party doesn't have much money," the perfumer parroted. "And, naturally, all the provinces are asking for funds."

Cosme Vila sat numb. He did not hide the fact that he considered the news a severe blow, with grave consequences. "But Vasiliev?" he asked. "What did Vasiliev say?"

Seeing the state he was in, Morales tried to reason with Cosme Vila. "Vasiliev spoke very logically. He said he could ask for a subscription to be raised in Russia. He said that would take time, because he would have to draw up a report, send it off; they would have to go to work on it at the other end—and, as he said, we need help right away. Now, I have been thinking—"

Cosme Vila brought his fist down hard on the table. "Are they going to give anything or aren't they?"

Gorki pulled a chair over in front of the desk and sat down. "Vasiliev is coming himself on Saturday and he will bring something. But don't expect much."

The chief could not get it into his head that there was not going to be any money. How was he to cope with the offensive against the strike being organized on every side? It flashed across his mind that he should have gone to Barcelona himself. It was impossible for them not to have realized what was at stake. Two months more and they would be masters of the city and the province! Instead of that, they offered a lot of bureaucratic excuses. Cosme Vila sat thinking about the dedication of those who followed him and the sacrifices of the peasants on their behalf. He could not let them down! He was the chief, he was leading them along the road of the proletarian revolution. If he bungled things and the workers had to go crawling back to the owners asking for their old jobs, they would curse him until the day they died.

Morales read anger, not defeat, in Cosme's face. He decided to speak. "If I may, I should like to bring up a suggestion they made about our problem."

Cosme Vila looked at him. "What suggestion?"

"It might be the solution."

Cosme Vila shrugged his shoulders. "I'll tell you right now that some solution is going to be found," he said.

Morales continued, looking fixedly at Cosme as though he was not quite sure how his words would be received: "It involves the anarchists."

Cosme Vila frowned. "What do you mean, the anarchists?"

"Let me say two words without interrupting!" Morales said impatiently. "In Barcelona they think that we could parlay two things to our advantage: the fact that El Responsable is in a bad way here and that the peasants in the province of Barcelona are anarchists. Why don't we get El Responsable to ask them for help, for food? Vasiliev thinks they would probably be willing. Then we could make the cooperative a joint project. We would lend El Responsable the trucks. You get the idea! The membership would never even have to know. Or even if we told them about it, what's the harm?"

Cosme Vila heard him out in silence. At first sight, the suggestion struck him as absolutely grotesque. Join up with El Responsable! Who would keep all the food and the trucks to boot, if he could get away with it! But his practical sense soon began to assert itself. One thing was clear enough, whether he liked it or not: the support of the anarchists under the circumstances could be really effective. Why not think it over? There was no getting away from the fact that something had to be done! He saw Gorki and Morales searching his face for some clue to his thoughts.

"One way or another, tomorrow I will give you a solution," he finally said. He opened a drawer of his desk and pulled out a sandwich. A change of mood came over Cosme Vila. He was afraid that his reaction to the news from Barcelona might have weakened the feeling of unity in the delegates.

"Good, good!" he said, biting into the roll. "So you talked with Comrade Vasiliev in person."

"An hour and a half," Gorki said. "Not a minute less."

"And he was sorry not to be able to help you?"

"He was all apologies."

Cosme Vila assented with a nod. "Tell me how are things going in Barcelona."

Morales felt that this was his cue. "They are going well," he said. "The POUM is a tough proposition, but the party maintains an iron discipline. The Socialists are giving ground, and we even have some members in Izquierda Republicana. You know the score better than we do."

Cosme Vila asked about the leaders of Barcelona who had taken part in the rally in the Albéniz. "What about comrade Hernández?"

"He has sent his wife to Russia. She wants to learn Russian so she can translate Gorki."

Cosme smiled complacently. "And the one-armed man?"

"The one-armed man is in Barcelona for the time being. He said that our revolution in the province could serve as a model, and that it will be recognized as such in due time. He asked us to congratulate you."

Cosme Vila asked another question. "What about arms?"

"Vasiliev will talk to you about that."

The chief had no desire to prolong the conversation. He talked, but his mind was still impaled on the negative reply about the money. Something had to be done! He could see El Responsable's ironic eyes and Future's wavy head of hair before him.

He got up abruptly, as was his habit. "Very well, then. This afternoon we will hold a meeting of the whole committee. Now we must get to our work."

"What has to be done?"

"You get to your newspaper. Write up the trip to Barcelona. Give your impressions of what you saw and heard there. It should come out in tomorrow's edition."

"What about what happened at the Dehesa?" Gorki and Morales asked before leaving.

"Nothing. Just a few wild shots."

IGNACIO got back from Barcelona happy because of the grades he had tucked away in his pocket. The second year! Seated at the dinner table with his family and Marta, he told them how little trouble he had experienced in the examinations.

"I was afraid I would get tripped up on some tricky questions, but it was a snap. The professors were very decent. The whole thing went smoothly. I answered my questions and they passed me." He looked at his father. "I'm half a lawyer now!"

"Michelin tires," his father replied.

Ignacio's words made all their hearts lighter.

"How was the boarding house?" Carmen Elgazu asked.

"Everything was fine. I had a bed with two mattresses and a window that looked out on a garden—and what a chambermaid!"

Marta gave him an arch look. "How nice!"

Carmen Elgazu was sure that her son was keeping all the bad news from them. She loved him for it, but deep down she was uneasy. She asked him if everything he had seen in Barcelona was as pleasant as the maid.

Ignacio's expression changed. "To tell the truth, I stuck pretty much to my own affairs." Then he added: "Of course, there are things one can't explain."

"For example—" Marta said.

"For example—coming back on the train, a soldier wanted to climb out through the window, and he couldn't get the glass down. I think it was at the junction. Cool as you please, he stepped back and kicked out the glass. Of course, he couldn't get out then because of the pieces of broken glass that remained in the window. So he sat down without a word and without anybody saying a word to him."

The family was silent. So was Ignacio. He had moved over beside Marta and now and then he squeezed her hand under the table.

The anecdote had depressed Matías. "Which do you think is more dangerous," he asked his son, "Barcelona or here?"

"Barcelona, without a doubt."

"Why?" Marta said. "Things couldn't be worse than they are here."

Ignacio looked around the table at all of them. "Barcelona is more dangerous because it is bigger. There are more crosscurrents and all kinds of people mixed together. Here, if someone is killed, it doesn't go unnoticed. That is still an advantage."

Then he told how he had had to deliver a letter to a certain J. Campistol. On the way, he said, he had been caught in a crossfire and had had to duck into a café to seek refuge behind a counter.

Carmen Elgazu crossed herself. "Lord, son, how calmly you talk about shooting!"

Matías recalled that J. Campistol was the leader of the Falange in Barcelona, and he asked Ignacio about the letter. "It's pretty risky to be delivering little notes at this stage of the game, don't you think?"

He had forgotten that Pilar was sitting there. The girl's face had flushed at her father's words. They all looked at her. Her eyes were brimming with tears and they all thought of Mateo.

"Now, now, Pilar, don't take things that way," Matías said.

"We were talking about the Falangists in Barcelona," Ignacio put in.

Pilar had pulled out a handkerchief. She looked gratefully at them all for their kindness.

"Don't get yourself into a state, woman," Marta said. "Tonight Mateo is going to Pedro's house. He will be safe there, really. Besides, all this may not last long." Then she added, looking at Ignacio: "There are many of us who are fighting, so this won't last long."

Ignacio was on edge. "If you are referring to the Falange—"

"What's happening?"

Ignacio saw it was too late to withdraw his remark. "Nothing," he said. "I met a few of them at the university. That's all."

"What about them?"

"Well—how do I know? Show-offs. Bullies. In short, they struck me as first-class city smart-alecks."

Marta looked troubled. "But how did you know they belonged to the Falange?"

"By their blue shirts."

"It's strange that they should have been wearing them. It's forbidden in public, except on special occasions."

"In Barcelona apparently every day is a special occasion."

Marta did not look convinced.

"I'll tell you something else," Ignacio added. "They were forever looking at one another, saying CAFÉ, and laughing."

Marta turned red as a beet. The others looked perplexed.

"What does that mean?" César asked, touching his silver-rimmed glasses.

Marta flicked her bangs aside. "It's very simple," she explained. "CAFÉ are our initials: *Camaradas, Arriba Falange Española.*"

THE assistant manager of the bank had been assigned the mission of suggesting to the Costas that they transfer their money outside Spain. "Our bank can take care of all the details. We have already handled three similar accounts. I can very easily explain how it's done. You have your choice of Switzerland, England, or the United States...."

The assistant manager performed his task with a heavy heart. It hurt him to see capital fleeing Spain. But he preferred that to seeing it used for the purchase of arms for Cosme Vila.

The Costas replied with a brusqueness unusual in them: "As long as the Republic stands, we will not take out one penny."

They were at their wits' end with the strike, the militia, the assassinations, with everything, but they were prepared to defend the Republic to the last gasp. That was their guiding thought. On their last trip to Madrid they had been told that the Communists had the revolution planned for August, and that the military was planning its uprising for November. "The only thing we can do to ensure that both will fail is for all good republicans to join together in a bloc, for there are still quite a few of us."

The Costas felt that the sudden aggravation of the revolutionary tendency among parties, unions, and individuals was a result of the fear of a military coup. This made their father-in-law furious.

"You two are blind," he told them. "You are absolutely blind. That is the excuse they hide behind. They are heading toward revolution because that has been their plan from the first. Don't smile like that, for Heaven's sake! It has been the plan since 1931, not to mention since the beginning of your great Popular Front."

The Costas found themselves arguing with more and more people. Some of the old-timers around Izquierda Republicana ripped into Casal in a fashion they considered unfair.

The wives of the two industrialists, little accustomed to arguments, had reached a joint decision: they were going to Pals and taking the children with them.

The Costas had allowed them to go. Without them the house seemed empty. "When one has got used to a family..." But they felt their place was in Gerona, by the side of the people with common sense.

Lord save us, how few of those people there were! *El Demócrata* suddenly announced that Casal was going to present the Socialist program, with dark threats of what would happen if it was not accepted. "That's all we needed!" The Costas talked of resigning from the party. "You can all go fry asparagus!"

The opinion of the Costas did not dampen the enthusiasm Casal, David, and Olga felt with regard to the program. Not only had it been drawn up with all the latest Socialist experiments in all parts of the world in mind, but it had one feature that was truly original: it bore the seal of approval of the Labor Bureau. And the authorities were one hundred percent determined to see that it was carried out! It envisioned a glorious transformation of the province: increased rice production, garlic exports on a big scale, new markets for the cork industry, trade with Mexico.... The needs of every trade had been studied under a microscope, from slaughterhouse workers to the waiters, who had deserted the party.

A hundred pages, typed by Olga. It had been a tough job. The one thing the teachers could not understand was the attitude of Morales—with whom they talked frequently. Morales did not pay the slightest attention to their program, and *El Proletario* did not even mention it.

Professor Morales laughed at them. "Why are you surprised? Your Socialism is for children," he told them. "All over the world, intelligent people are beginning to realize that you Socialists get lost in a no-man's-land, and they are coming over to us. Don't think that all we count on are Teos and his like! Why don't you listen to Radio Moscow? Your favorite writer, Gide, has just been there and has spoken from the balcony on Red Square. We are going to run the text of his speech in tomorrow's *El Proletario*. He says that the West is counting on Russia to come to its rescue. What is the purpose of your scraps of paper? To raise the salaries of the teachers?"

Casal was furious. "They're going to have to swallow those scraps of paper!" he shouted. "We'll see who is the better tactician this time."

Unfortunately, it was not in the cards for the typographer to have his way. No sooner had the Labor Inspector put his signature at the end of the hundred-page document Olga handed him than a rumor began to circulate through the city which no one credited at first, but which was finally confirmed: Cosme Vila and El Responsable had reached an agreement, and from that moment on they were committed to assist each other in maintaining their respective strikes.

"Impossible!" shouted Casal. "How can that be?"

"Very simple," one of his members told him. "The peasants of Gerona will continue to turn over food to the Communist Party; at the same time the peasants of Barcelona will give El Responsable what they can. It will all go into a pool at Cosme Vila's cooperative, and both the Communists and anarchists will be supplied."

The news was soon officially confirmed. The pact had been made, "without this implying any ideological approximation. CNT-FAI and the Communist Party each continues to maintain its own positions, without yielding one inch."

Casal was amazed. "This can't work! They will be at each other's throats in a week!" He was mistaken. The Communists were kept in line by party discipline, the anarchists by their hunger and El Responsable's enigmatic smile, which seemed to say: "Let me handle this; you will not regret it."

Then Casal decided that the alliance actually didn't change matters at all and that his program would sound the clear note of common sense. Once again he was forced to recognize that such was not the case. When he went to see Julio, the Police Chief took the immense program in his hands, thumbed through it, and finally said: "Very nice! Very nice! Rice, agreements with Mexico...but for today, for now, what does it offer? Everybody out of work until God knows when. Those madmen can hold out for years."

Casal blew up. "All you have to do is publish the program, and everybody will come over to our side!"

"It will be published, my friend Casal, it will be published. But whether everybody will come over to our side remains to be seen."

David and Olga, with their characteristic pessimism, were convinced that the battle was lost. CNT-FAI and the Communist Party arm in arm represented an irresistible force. Even the general phoned police headquarters: "Jail those gangsters, lock up every one of them!"

El Demócrata published every word of the program.

"What's this about exporting garlic when there's not a clove to be found in the whole province?"

The members of UGT defended the program tooth and nail. "It's magnificent, it's just what we need." But how was it to be put into practice?

The trucks came and went. If one walked past the Centro Tradicionalista, one heard the sound of feet tramping on wood, and "Hup, two! Hup, your right!" They said that even women took part in the drills, which were now held upstairs behind closed doors, and that the use of arms was being taught. Every afternoon beneath the pleached foliage of the Dehesa, Victor and Professor Morales, whose classes at the Instituto had already come to an end, gave art instruction, brush in hand, to the young members of the party who showed aptitude and interest.

EIGHTY-ONE

THE jubilation of the anarchists at having regained a post of honor in the affairs of the city was so great that the bars and cafés that remained open saw their bottles emptied in less time than it takes to tell it. Even those who for days had been searching along the riverbank and in the nearby fields for something to eat managed to dig up from the depth of their pockets something with which to celebrate the occasion. Now anybody could jump on a truck covered with signs and flags, hum along the highway, and come back at nightfall with mountains of food! Their joy was as great as their misery had been. One had to have followed the life of El Cojo step by step from the day he was orphaned to understand why he shouted as he did. One had to know that Ideal's girl friend had told him: "Kid, why should I keep on going around with you if you haven't even got the price of a meal or a ticket to the movies?" to keep from smiling at the self-importance the boy radiated now.

Only a handful of the old-timers expressed the fear that Cosme Vila might be playing them a trick. The others would not hear of it. "What tricks? Tell that to the Bishop! His trucks get here, don't they? Well, that's all that matters."

El Responsable felt capable of hypnotizing the Commissioner himself. "You see now why I kept telling you to sit tight?" he told his followers. Many slapped him on the back. He had conducted the negotiations in Barcelona with consummate skill. His daughters had never lost confidence in him. "This seems like the moment to do something big," they told him.

Future, in a new suit, and with his hair carefully waved, resumed his strolls along the Rambla, just as in the good old days when he first had come to Gerona. Out came the hollow skull and the old repertoire of tricks. Once again he pulled coins out of the air whenever he came across a group of idlers.

"That's the way it is with anarchism," he held forth at the Café Gran Via. "Down one day, up the next, like the bookseller in Barcelona used to tell me. There were times when Bakunin had it pretty tough, but there were others when he had it very good. Now what? UGT, the republicans, the Catalanists, and the rest, taking a notch in their belts, while here we are, eating six-egg omelets. Eh, Santi! How do you like an omelet with six eggs? But we must not lose our heads. Omelets aren't everything. It is just a matter of time until everything, even the confiscation program, falls into our laps. We must not forget our program because we are well off."

El Responsable and Cosme Vila did not speak to each other. Their meeting, brief and to the point, had taken place on neutral ground: Raimundo's barbershop. Mutual interest had led them to agreement, but they left each other without shaking hands or a parting "*Salud.*" All negotiations were carried on through Future, who would speak to Gorki on the phone. Their last words were always: "Now each to his own business."

Conflicting emotions were at war in El Responsable's breast. On the one hand his enthusiasm grew, but so did his envy. Envy of Cosme Vila. What that man had accomplished in such a short space of time! He had snuffed out the servant at the Museum and Brother Alfredo. He had set fire to a convent and paralyzed the city. He published a newspaper and was organizing a People's Militia that could compete with the Foreign Legion.

El Responsable admitted that the CNT was a country mile behind the Communists when it came to results. "But we cut off the gas, light, and electricity!" Ideal protested. El Cojo recalled the explosion at the powder dump and the fright they gave the Inspector of Labor when the bomb went off in his office. El Responsable was not impressed. He knew all that had been well organized, but that it had not lasted long and that bad luck had prevented them from doing more.

Nonetheless, the fact that Cosme Vila had found no solution but to come to him proved to El Responsable that the Communist Party was off in the clouds. "I think we always strike closer to the heart of things," he said the day his executive committee held a full meeting for the first time since the resurrection.

Future gave him a challenging look, as if demanding proof. El Responsable, with all the naturalness in the world, continued: "I'm going to knock you all back a bit." (A moment's pause.) "Forget about killing off servants or monks!" (Another pause.) "Forget about blowing up this or that place! The way things stand, something decisive must be done, and CNT-FAI will take charge of carrying it off: Major Martínez de Soria must be eliminated."

The silence that followed his declaration was proof enough of the effect it produced. A hot-and-cold flash shot through all those in the gymnasium. Eliminate the...!

The tension slowly eased. One by one the anarchists began to ask themselves the same question, which emerged from the recesses of their consciousness: Why not?

Ideal was the first to speak. "He'd turn me into crow bait without batting an eye!"

El Cojo spoke from his perch in the window seat. "We should have done it when we had the chance in October."

"It's not that I take much stock in a fascist uprising now," El Responsable explained. "But if we let the military run around loose, they will let us have it in the neck some day, without a doubt. I think that if we put out the polestar's light the situation will clear up a bit."

Future agreed with El Responsable. "He is the number-one enemy in the city. I passed him the other day on the street and you'd have thought he was drunk. Whistling away! He is more of a monarchist than Romanones himself. He has a nose on him just like that of the ex-King, may he rest in peace.'

"What do you mean, rest in peace?"

"As far as I am concerned, an ex-King is a dead king." The atmosphere had become relaxed.

"What about the daughter?" El Cojo asked suddenly. "She makes quite a thing of always dressing in black."

The two daughters of El Responsable felt their hearts do a flip-flop. Future's girl, the younger one, was outraged.

"Don't be an idiot! She has nothing to do with it!"

"Nothing to do with it, eh? What about riding horseback?"

"Come on, don't be a pain in the neck! Stick to the father, fine; but let the family be."

El Responsable made an effort to dominate the situation. He resumed the tone in which he had opened the meeting. "Why have I proposed this? For one simple reason," he explained. "I consider that the danger always comes from the army. It keeps thousands of men garrisoned, eating soldier's fare, and losing the best years of their lives. I have often thought that there can be no progress until the army is done away with." Then he added: "Nobody likes the idea of killing a man less than I do. But I'll be hanged if I can see any other solution."

El Cojo suddenly slid down from the window. "Something has occurred to me," he said. "Are we sure that the major is the number-one man?"

"Who else, then?"

It was evident that El Cojo had a fixed idea. "What's a major, after all?" he said. "There are even generals to reckon with. I would rather storm the jail and settle the score with Warning Voice and that Don Jorge, the son of a..."

Future's girl seemed to like the plan. Ever since the day when the dentist had looked at her in a certain way as she left the swimming pool, she never thought of him but a surge of violence swept over her. "It's an idea worth keeping in mind," she said.

Blasco voted against it. "Those two are already in the bag. It's those on the outside who need the treatment. If not the major, Noguer the notary will do very nicely, or one of the others. There is no shortage of talent."

Future mulled it over. Sometimes he felt envious of El Responsable, who had the edge on him in experience. He had managed to get the CNT in Barcelona to listen to him and to mobilize the peasants. "I don't know if I could have pulled that one off," Future admitted to himself.

"El Cojo is right," he finally said. "Who can say for sure that the major is the biggest fish, and not just a tool? What about the Bishop, or His Slipperiness the priest of the Museum there, who confesses him every day? His Slipperiness, above all, for my money..."

El Cojo disagreed, with energetic shakes of his head. "Copying, always copying others," he said. "Hasn't a bomb been tossed into the Museum already? I tell you the jail is the thing. We have to make an example of Warning Voice and that owner of four hundred farms."

"Forty."

"All right, forty."

Santi was living the most exciting moments of his life. He was sure that the thing to do was to please all of them! But he did not speak. El Responsable had forbidden him to take a voice in the official meetings until he was seventeen.

El Responsable listened with his head bowed and his eyes fixed on the dumbbells on the gymnasium floor. He pressed his lips together so tightly that his oldest daughter was afraid that any minute he would grab the dumbbells and fling them at the heads of his associates.

"That's enough!" he finally burst out, lifting his head and looking daggers. He yanked his cap down to his eyebrows. "Why all these plans and all this talking?" Nobody spoke up. "The only number one here is the army. Priests, dentists, landowners... Who is it that has the guns?" He looked at El Cojo. "What would you rather have pointed at you, a machine gun or a forceps?" He looked around the room. "Sometimes I think you are all idiots. The number-one man here is Major Martínez de Soria."

Nobody replied.

"That doesn't mean," El Responsable continued, breaking the silence, "that it has to be done tomorrow."

The sergeant, the boy friend of El Responsable's older daughter, had not opened his mouth. But he had it in for the major more than any of them. He was happy over the decision that had been reached, but, knowing his comrades, he was afraid that it would never get beyond the project stage. "The big question," he said, "is how this mission is to be accomplished."

This military language made Future nervous.

"One catch is that the major never goes out alone," Ideal observed.

That was true. Blasco, who hung around the café frequented by the officers, confirmed it. "He always has two or three young officers at his side."

"And if not, he is with his wife and daughter," El Cojo said.

El Responsable's older daughter raised another point. "Before going into how it is to be done, perhaps we should discuss what the authorities are going to do."

El Responsable replied with a negative gesture of great conviction. "Nothing," he said abruptly, repeating the gesture as if flicking something away. "Nothing. They will be delighted."

"Delighted?"

He pulled off his cap. "They will play it dumb." His tone left no grounds for doubts. "Let's see if just once we can do things using our heads," he said. "The first thing we have to do is tail him and find out everything about his habits: what time he leaves the house, what route he takes to get to the barracks, and so on."

The others all said they thought the best time would be when the major rode horseback in the Dehesa. Why talk about it any more? The only thing to do was select the weapon. Future was in favor of the pistol, El Cojo of a hand grenade.

"Shut up, all of you! We'll decide that later," El Responsable said, furious once again. "For the time being, you three will watch," he ordered, pointing to Blasco, Ideal, and Santi.

"And what do I do? Dance the rumba?" El Cojo asked indignantly.

El Responsable fixed him with a look. "You take up a post in front of the Museum and observe the schedule of His Reverence."

EIGHTY-TWO

MATEO'S long reclusion in El Rubio's house had not brought the two of them to a closer understanding. Every time Mateo tried to talk to him about the "vertical syndicate" and "sea routes," El Rubio tapped his helmet or, in its absence, the cap that went with his Pizarro Jazz uniform and replied: "Let me tell you something. With the girl you've got, I don't know why you want to get mixed up in these things."

Mateo felt discouraged. Pacing about the room, circling the figure of Rubio's almost blind mother, he asked himself how these solitary souls could live without some great ideal throbbing in their breasts. "You'd think they would die of boredom and disgust," he mused.

Mateo wore his blue shirt constantly. One of the good things about having to remain in hiding was that he could wear it. There were times when he felt himself a figure of great importance, voluntarily withdrawn into the shadows, from which he directed the destinies of millions. At other moments he recognized that in reality he had launched only a half dozen upon the combat, but that thought was enough to make his heart skip a beat. It seemed to him that in the *Confessions* of St. Augustine, which Pilar had sent him, he had learned to assay the real value of a single soul, a soul disembodied, with all the depths and heights of which it is capable. The more he read, the more convinced he became that St. Augustine, had he lived at that moment and in Spain, would have been a member of the Falange.

The day El Rubio told him: "You can move to Pedro's house now," Mateo didn't know whether to be happy or sad. He had begun to feel at home among the household objects, the orchestra programs on the walls, had even become accustomed to the light. On the other hand, he was also attracted by the idea of the dissident, solitary Communist's flat.

Rodríguez lent him his uniform. When he clamped the tricorne on his head and looked in the mirror, Mateo did not recognize himself. El Rubio laughed. Mateo was having his troubles with the belts and straps. It was night now, and just before stepping into the street, Mateo commended himself to the patroness of the corps.

Everything went off as smooth as silk. Nobody gave him a second look. He turned into the Calle de la Barca and noticed that the garbage El Rubio had spoken of had been collected. He climbed up to Pedro's flat. He knocked in the manner agreed upon, and the door opened.

Pedro received him with his usual seriousness. Mateo wanted to express his appreciation for the generous action, but at the same time to make sure that Pedro had no hidden intentions. With these thoughts in mind, he thrust out his hand and held Pedro's eyes with his. Pedro looked as though he felt intimidated. He shook hands with Mateo and then leaned back against the skeleton of a sewing machine standing in a corner.

Mateo was the first to speak. "Look here. I don't want to seem insolent or anything like it. And don't think there is anything behind what I am going to ask you. But I should like to know why you agreed to hide me."

"Well—why not?" Pedro replied in a natural tone. Mateo felt relieved.

Pedro had lost weight during the strike. Now he was back at work in the quarry as usual, and the pitiless sun had turned his skin almost black.

"All right, I'm here now," Mateo said. "But I don't want you to worry about me; you go on about your business as usual. I will stay where you tell me, and you won't hear a peep out of me."

"I've thought about that. You see the setup," Pedro said, pointing to the balcony. "You can see everything from the outside, so I think you had better plan to stay in the kitchen."

"All right, the kitchen it is."

"Take the radio in there with you if you'd like," Pedro added.

Mateo's face lit up in a smile. "Thank you. I appreciate that a lot."

It was apparent that Pedro had made up a list of things to tell him. "In case of emergency, the key to the trapdoor to the roof is hanging there," he said, pointing to the back of the door. "If you go from roof to roof you come out at San Félix Church."

Pedro's words jerked Mateo back to reality. At any moment Julio could pounce on him. He asked permission to go into the kitchen.

"Whenever you like," Pedro said.

Mateo entered. The first thing he saw was a hanging roll of sticky flypaper. Then a rope stretched from one side of the room to the other. A dripping faucet. A small, dirty window.

Next to the door, tipped against the wall, was a short-legged wicker chair.

"Was that your father's chair?"

"Yes."

On the wall was a greasy spot left by some human head that had habitually rested there.

Mateo approached the window instinctively. The Cathedral! That lifted his spirits. It was a little window, but big enough to allow a good view of the Cathedral. The belfry, looming gigantic, seemed close enough to touch.

"I suppose you can hear the striking of the hours."

"What do you think!"

Everything was settled. Mateo gave Pedro the money for his board. He would do the cooking for both of them. When Pedro got back from work he would find supper waiting for him.

"You tell me what you like."

"I like everything."

Mateo remained pensive for a moment. There was still a delicate point to be ironed out. "I'm going to have to be in contact with some one of my comrades," he said.

Pedro looked at him. Now it was his turn to think. "Is there anyone the police haven't got a file on?"

"Yes, there are several...."

"Well, let it be one of those. But only one."

"Good enough. Only one.... Let me think a minute. One about my height and build. He will be wearing a Civil Guard uniform, too."

There was nothing more to discuss. A mattress and blanket for the kitchen; a cot for Pedro in the dining room. Mateo got up at seven o'clock and boiled milk for Pedro, who went off to work under the broiling sun in the quarry.

As soon as he was alone in the flat, Mateo thought immediately of Pilar. If only she could come to see him! It was hard, this separation. Why couldn't the dress shop have been right across the street? He might have seen her that way, if only with one eye peering through the balcony shutter.

Before noon there came a knock at the door. Pam, pam, pam! Then a fourth knock. It was Rodríguez. Mateo fumbled impatiently with the latch. "Come in, come in!"

Rodríguez could not stay long. "I will be back tomorrow. I have to meet Marta. Let me have the uniform."

"But what's happening?"

"Nothing. Everything's going smoothly. Here is *El Proletario* so you can catch up on the news."

Mateo asked him to bring a world history the next day. "Ask Marta or Ignacio for one. What time are you coming?"

"The same as today. Eleven o'clock."

The world history proved his salvation. Rodríguez brought it to him the next day, and he no sooner saw the book than he thought he recognized it. Sure enough! It was the history Pilar had used when she studied with the nuns.

Mateo took it in his hands with emotion. Knights on horseback on the cover. *A Compendium of World History*. He opened to the first page; there, in a childish scrawl, he read:

Blessed Virgin, Virgin pure,
Make them pass me
In this course.

What a source of consolation for Mateo! When the heat of the day, or despair, entered the kitchen through the little window, Pilar's childish lines would restore his spirits. A muffled cry of joy escaped Mateo's lips. Rodríguez looked at him closely. "What's the matter with you? Are you losing your wits?" Mateo tried to hide his emotion.

Rodríguez lived in a more realistic world. He did not find it difficult to bring Mateo into it.

"Pardon me, Rodríguez. Let's get down to business."

Rodríguez filled him in from A to Z on the progress of the cooperative, the militia, and Cosme Vila's tie-up with the anarchists; he gave him a copy of *El Demócrata* containing Casal's program. Mateo read it through carefully. "Not one word about man, the bearer of eternal values," he said when he had finished.

Rodríguez went to see him every day at a different hour. On July 1 Mateo could tell by the way he knocked on the door that something extraordinary had happened. The news he heard confirmed his guess: three workers, still wearing their coveralls, had approached Benito Civil as he left the offices of Massana and Ribas, the architects.

Mateo stood up.

"I'm not fooling," Rodríguez said. "They want to join."

Mateo's eyes were suddenly damp. "But who are they? Go on!"

"Two masons and an electrician."

Rodríguez told him the details, and it was apparent that the men were in earnest. All three belonged to UGT. Casal's program had left them cold. "Nobody fights for a swimming pool." One of the leaflets that had fluttered down from the housetops had reached the hands of one of the three. They had discussed it. The electrician was a sort of romantic kid who "writes poetry and things like that." The two masons were tired of so much confusion and so much blaspheming.

Mateo pulled out his lighter. If only Ignacio were there so he could grab him by the lapels! He had made a bet with him. Ignacio had said: "Workers, never." Now he had three; two fed up with blasphemy and one who wrote poetry and things like that.

"The major must be told that he can count on three more rifles," Mateo said.

"He already knows," Rodríguez said. "With those from CEDA who joined we are now fifteen."

"Sixteen!" Mateo corrected him.

"Yes, counting yourself, of course," Rodríguez agreed. "And if you count Marta, seventeen."

Mateo shook his head firmly. "Marta has nothing to do with arms. If anything, she can take care of first aid."

Mateo asked Rodríguez for the latest word on the uprising. "It's a funny thing. I'm supposed to be the leader and now I am the one who receives instructions."

Rodríguez gave him the latest list. "CEDA can count on fifty men. Renovación a dozen, Liga Catalana thirty-five. And the traditionalists are many; I don't know the exact number."

"Thirty-five from Liga Catalana!" Mateo considered that a triumph. "You see that if you talk to the Catalanists the right way, they too can see the light!"

Rodríguez would not give in. "Sure, but let's see what happens the day the shooting starts."

"Is there anything new on the generals?" Mateo asked.

"Not in the peninsula; but there is news from the Balearic and Canary Islands."

"Who are in command?"

"General Goded in the Balearics; Franco in the Canaries."

Mateo was all keyed up with the news about the three workers. His curiosity that day was insatiable. "Why do you think the government has left Mola in Navarre? That is the stronghold of the Carlists."

"To cover up what they are doing elsewhere. It's a blind, but so much the better for us."

"When did you last see the major?"

"Yesterday."

"What does he say?"

"Well—we talked about the garrisons that are considered a sure thing, the ones we can count on without fail."

"Which are those?"

"The major says Alicante, San Sebastián, Oviedo, and Santander."

"Alicante!" Mateo echoed enthusiastically, remembering that José Antonio was there. "What about Barcelona and Madrid?" he asked.

"Doubtful. In Barcelona everything may depend on the Civil Guard."

Mateo suddenly found himself wishing the uprising was to be the very next day. Solitude and confinement and his desire to go into the street and breathe fresh air again were responsible for his impatience. "Where are we supposed to report? At the artillery or the infantry barracks?"

"Keep your shirt on! Nobody knows yet, not even the major."

"All right, all right, enough of that. Look—what about the officers here?"

"The same as before, half and half," Rodríguez said. "But the major is sure we've got enough to win."

Mateo shifted in his chair. "One last question. What are they planning to do with the general?"

"Well—if he is stubborn—" Rodríguez made a gesture with his forefinger circling his throat.

The door opened and Pedro entered, the yellow dust caked on his lashes. He always carried *El Demócrata*, never *El Proletario*. Rodríguez got up. Mateo asked Pedro: "Why don't you ever buy *El Proletario*?"

Pedro snapped on the radio. "I wouldn't give those traitors a plugged penny."

MOSÉN Alberto became aware that a man was following him. He could not go out without bumping into him. Whenever he looked out the Museum windows, there the man was, limping along under the arches, talking with the taxi drivers and bootblacks, now and then glancing up at the balconies.

"Who is he?" Mosén Alberto asked César. "Do you know him?"

César nodded his head. "They call him El Cojo. He is the nephew of El Responsable."

"Of the FAI?"

"Yes."

El Cojo's error consisted in not disguising his vigilance, in proposing to carry it out openly, almost flaunting his activity, as he thought an anarchist should.

The reports he gave El Responsable bore a deadly similarity. "He goes out at eight o'clock and heads right for the Jesuit's pow-wow. He goes into the sacristy and comes out all done up. He is always assisted during the Mass by that bald fellow from the Arús Bank. At nine o'clock he goes home. He must breakfast like God Almighty, for he comes out with more bounce to him than you and me together. He goes to the palace. At eleven o'clock, straight to see the notary Noguer. They conspire until one o'clock. Then lunch. He hardly leaves the Museum during the afternoon. Sometimes, around seven o'clock, he goes back to the notary's. He's back by nine o'clock. There are days when he visits the biggest fascists on the Rambla, that family related to the comrade from Madrid who visited here."

"The Alvears?"

"Yes; the father works in the Telegraph office."

El Responsable nodded. "And who visits him?"

"Very few people. You can tell that Museum would not interest anybody but a mummy."

"But who are they, I'm asking you."

"Well—the most frequent visitor is the sister of the Costas. What a scarecrow! Then, of course, the servant goes in and out. And some nuns. And every afternoon, without fail, the seminarian with the cropped head and the ears."

"What about the major? Does he ever visit the Museum?"

"Never." El Cojo, too, was impatient. "Now you know the whole setup," he told El Responsable. "When do we go into action? I think the best time is when he comes out of the palace. There is never anyone around up there; it is deserted."

El Responsable's prudence allowed Mosén Alberto to go on living. Living with fear in his bones, but still living. The feeling of being constantly observed put him beside himself. In his dreams he encountered El Cojo, with his red handkerchief. On more than one occasion he had been on the point of stopping him on the street and asking him: "What is it you want with me, anyway?"

But César had advised him to be patient, and not give them any further cause for resentment. "Maybe this will all come to an end sooner than we think," he told Mosén Alberto.

Mosén Alberto had changed. He talked with less assurance and he celebrated Mass with more fervor. He was even ready to admit that during that argument with Ignacio the boy had spoken some true words! For that reason he now went frequently to visit the Alvears. Aside from Carmen Elgazu's loyalty, he knew that he had only to mention Marta's name to assure himself a pleasant session.

One thing bothered him. Not even Carmen Elgazu ever mentioned in his presence the uprising that was in preparation, despite the first-hand information on the subject which the Alvears surely had. Matías Alvear always played dumb, as though the military didn't exist or spent their time reading magazines in the barracks or playing dominoes. Pilar had been drawn in like a snail for days; now she pressed her lips together in a tight line to give herself a determined appearance. Not even César gave rein to his tongue! The seminarian limited himself to repeating from time to time his phrase: "Maybe this will all come to an end sooner than we think."

To keep abreast of developments, step by step, Mosén Alberto therefore had no recourse but to pay the daily visits El Cojo described: the visit to the notary Noguer. The women who visited him at the Museum, even Laura, never had any precise information. "How am I to know?" Laura asked. "Nobody tells me anything. The major himself gave me the politest brush-off you ever saw." Her brothers, she said, were completely off the track and always found out about things twenty-four hours after everybody else.

The notary Noguer satisfied the priest's thirst for information, however. The ex-Mayor was in on all the preparations down to the smallest details. He had completely won the confidence of Major Martínez de Soria. "The same old story," he said with a smile, "when the going gets rough, Liga Catalana is called on for advice."

The priest wished with all his soul that the uprising would come as soon as possible. He was awaited in the bishop's palace every day as the fountainhead of credible information. Opinion in the episcopal council was divided. Some thought the uprising held out hope for a change for the better; others didn't. Many believed that in the event the uprising was successful, the military would save the churches and monasteries from the danger of the torch, but that they would present their bill and deal with the Church in a high-handed manner. The older clerics insisted that the majority of the military leaders were doubtful Christians, given to drink and other vices. The reputation that attached to Major Martínez de Soria confirmed them in these views.

Mosén Alberto held more practical views: "For the time being, let's recognize that they defend the possibility of our continuing to exercise our ministry. Afterwards we shall see. I suppose that in the army, as everywhere, there are all kinds."

But the clerics were hard to convince, and when they sang together in the Cathedral choir they kept timorous eyes on the main entrance.

Mosén Alberto continued in his role as the principal counselor of the city's entire female religious family. The Mothers Superior of all the convents visited him. Mosén Alberto's advice was that they should find places of safekeeping for all the valuables in the convents. "Have the pianos sent to some private home. All linens of any value should be hidden."

Some Mothers Superior paid attention to him; the majority, however, said: "But for goodness' sake! Why should they bother us? What have we done?"

The notary Noguer was more than ever concerned about Mosén Alberto: he considered the priest to be the man in most danger after the Bishop. The news that El Cojo was watching Mosén Alberto kept him preoccupied. He did not know what to do. "For to warn the authorities would be to waste time," he said.

Mosén Alberto asked him in the name of all the saints not to worry so much about him. "What God wills will happen. Don't worry. Tell me the latest gossip."

A great change had come over the notary Noguer. From a naturally peaceful soul, he had turned into a tactician who manipulated imaginary bands of armed men with real pleasure. All the objects on his desk in a twinkling became symbolic instruments of aggression. "The nerve centers of the city will be swiftly occupied. One cannon in front of the post office. Here, in front of City Hall, another. In front of the radio station—I can't remember now. The major thinks a squad will be sufficient for the Telephone Building. Three squads at least for the police station. Provisional headquarters will be set up where Cosme Vila now has the coop."

The notary Noguer claimed to know that the Falange had asked to be assigned to the most dangerous stations. "The major considers them too young, however. Besides, his plan is to mix us all up, the civilians and the troops."

Mosén Alberto became silent whenever the Falangists were mentioned. He still considered them irresponsible, and pagans to boot. But he recognized that they were brave. Their thrashing of Dr. Relken had warmed the cockles of his heart.

They often discussed the general situation. The notary always referred to the "enemies of society"; Mosén Alberto said the "enemies of the Church." The notary had witnessed a Socialist parade in Baracelona, and it had given him gooseflesh. "With shock troops, if you please, and red flags! 'Long live the People's Militia!' And raising their fists as they went past the barracks! The assistant manager at the bank is right," he said. "The Masons have the reins of the whole business in their hands. Barcia has gone to Geneva for the meeting of the Grand Orient. God knows the orders he will come back with."

The names of Julio and Olga often came up. The notary considered them the two most criminally responsible characters in the city. "Don't you see what Julio is doing? He is just sitting back and waiting to see which way the cat jumps. As for Olga, she has a mind of the first order, unfortunately employed for bad ends. She observes what's taking place completely unperturbed."

Mosén Alberto listened to him without so much as a blink. He shared the notary's opinion, and saw yet another character as nefarious as the two first mentioned: Colonel Muñoz. "He's an armchair admiral, that one! He'd see the city razed and never move a muscle."

"The major is more afraid of Colonel Muñoz than of the general himself," Notary Noguer said. "He thinks the first step must be—"

The notary had got that far with the sentence several times before, and never finished it, to the point where it had aroused Mosén Alberto's curiosity. What ailed him? What step was this, the mere thought of which deprived him of his faculty of speech?

It was indeed a curious thing, and Mosén Alberto felt certain that the day would come when the notary would explain himself without having to be questioned. One morning particularly charged with news, the notary appeared to have made up his mind.

"Mosén," he said, "I have been on the point of talking over a certain matter with you for some time." He took off his glasses and continued: "You know that I have pledged myself to take my place with a rifle wherever I am ordered the day of the uprising. The problem is this: what if I have to make use of my weapon?"

Mosén Alberto passed his cape from one arm to the other. The notary's wife was not present, which made the conversation easier.

"In other words," the priest said, after reflecting on the question, "what you are asking me is if, under given circumstances, it is right to kill?"

"Exactly."

The priest remained silent for a moment, his head bent low. Then he spoke. "It seems to me that, for reasons which you and I analyze here every day, the military uprising is justified from a moral point of view. Therefore, to take part in it is in itself just. Now, at the same time, each individual has his own soul to reckon with. In the last analysis, it is the individual intent that matters. If on that given day you go into the street and kill out of hatred, you will sin.... If you kill in self-defense, you will not sin."

The notary Noguer seemed to be wrestling with the priest's words. "You know," he said, "that distinction is valid when made here abstractly, over a couple of biscuits and a cup of chocolate. But—it is another thing when it comes time to pull the trigger."

Mosén Alberto had a feeling that they were getting into deep water. "The important thing is the initial act, the act of going into the street with the conviction that one is acting in self-defense or performing a duty. In the heat of the fight—what is a man to do?"

The notary looked at him fixedly. "Conclusion—I can go out at peace with myself."

Mosén Alberto bit his lips. "I think you can." Then he ran his hand over his face. "At any rate," he added, "I should like it if you took the problem up with another priest, too. Mosén Francisco, for example."

"I can ask him," the notary replied. "But I already know what the answer will be."

"What do you mean?"

"He'll look at the benches of the catechism class and say: 'Go out freely—don't be afraid.'"

Mosén Alberto went home preoccupied that day. He felt that advice such as he had been asked to give was not of man's province. Fortunately the notary had said: "I'm going to talk to you as a priest."

Priest! Mosén Alberto thought about the verb "to kill." As he walked toward the Museum his mind went over "the reasons one may. . . ." Everywhere along the streets he saw signs of violence and danger. Groups clustered on street corners; a flag of the FAI rising unexpectedly above a newspaper stand.

Priest. . . . He found himself confronted with a deep moral problem: many people like the notary Noguer were prepared to take up arms to defend him—that is to say, the Church—rather than to defend themselves. Mosén Alberto felt that a few months earlier that thought would have brought him to the verge of vanity. He would have said that it was no small thing to be the minister of an institution in whose defense so many souls were glad to give up their lives. Now the responsibility compelled his thoughts. He was a better man. He had only to cross the threshold of the episcopal palace to feel it. In the presence of those golden tapestries hanging from the ceilings, he recalled his visit to Rome in the company of the notary Noguer on the occasion of the jubilee.

"Why so much wealth?" his companion had asked when they left the Vatican. The image of the first Christians, poor and barefoot, rose up before the notary.

Mosén Alberto had answered him then: "How would you expect the Church to defend itself if it continued in the Catacombs and the Holy Father lived in a garage? The Church now has millions of faithful whom it must be prepared to receive, whom it must protect from persecutions, and whom it must look after in those places where they suffer. Nazareth was logical when there were only twelve fishermen who believed in Christ. Those twelve fishermen have triumphed now, and the Vatican symbolizes that triumph."

Mosén Alberto still felt that all this was true. Nevertheless, on that day when he had given a man sanction to take up arms, he felt that something had to be added: the minister of that triumphant Church should continue living in private like the twelve fishermen. He should tread the rugs of the palace, however thick they might be, with a complete absence of pride or pleasure. Were it possible, he should put sand in his shoes!

Mosén Alberto longed to be good, to divest himself of all that was superfluous. He often stopped in his solitary walks through the halls of the Museum and thought of the bomb that had exploded there. What a warning from the Lord! In an instant a being like Murillo, with his walrus mustache and dirty raincoat, could put an end to one's faculties of judging others and bring him face to face with the Supreme Judge, who would ask: "What have you done with the talent I gave you?"

"Lord," he would have to answer, "I employed it in setting myself up in my pride as an expert in ancient altar paintings, and in dazzling simple souls like Carmen Elgazu with quotations from the Bible." Until one day, in the eternal wheel of time, he would see Carmen Elgazu occupying in heaven one of the golden chairs he now enjoyed in the bishop's palace. Sand in one's shoes, a bomb in the Museum! Those were the two threads of remorse which drew his soul upward. In the last analysis, César and the dead servant....

Especially César. Ever since the boy's return from Collell, Mosén Alberto had been obsessed by him. What was there about him that made his words superior to those of the canons of the Cathedral? He was obsessed with César, for he had discovered something about him more important than his work in the Calle de la Barca: he had discovered that César wanted to die.

It was evident. It was reflected in his eyes and in every word he spoke. One phrase was constantly on César's lips: "Sin has taken possession of the city." Not the flags had mastered the city, nor the militiamen: it was sin, the collective sin of all, including César. Feeling himself impotent to atone for all this with little acts like going without dessert or wearing his penitent's belt, César wanted to carry out the supreme act: he wanted to give his life. The true meaning of that phrase the seminarian so often repeated: "This all may end sooner than we think," dawned on Mosén Alberto. Good God! It was clear that he could not be referring to the union of CNT and the Communist Party or to the car in which Doña Amparo Campo rode here and there buying what she chose. It was evident that, without knowing it, he was referring to himself, to his own spare, fine-drawn flesh, already appearing to be reaching toward heaven. César wanted to offer up his insignificant self for the spiritual restoration of Gerona, and, above all, for the salvation of "the enemies." César, in fact, was asking God's permission not to kill, but to die. It was perfectly clear to Mosén Alberto. Above all, César wanted to save Teo! He continually spoke of him. He wanted to go to the jail to see him, to take him tobacco. It seemed to César that Teo, with the size of him, was the representation of what one day perforce would become very small before the judgment seat of God.

Mosén Alberto reflected on all this. As a result he felt himself a better man and a better priest. It was only when he saw El Cojo spying on him under the arches that he felt his heart still very much of this world, and that it was not as easy for him as for César to transform his hate into love.

EIGHTY-THREE

DON Emilio Santos, Don Pedro Oriol, Professor Civil, Matías Alvear, and, in general, all the people their age and older could not sleep. They spent practically half the night awake. Matías Alvear would hear the Cathedral bells toll three o'clock, four, five. Toward dawn he would manage to doze off, the same as Carmen Elgazu.

The conversations between husbands and wives sharing the same pillow gave the measure of what was happening, of the pervading anxiety. The sensation was that every home lived under a hanging sword that at any moment might describe its fatal arc.

Each person thought how best to protect what was dearest to him; if the nuns transferred their pianos to places of safekeeping, and Pilar sewed Mateo's picture inside her dress, the architect Ribas, head of Estat Català, sensed that trying days were ahead for Catalonia and sought, above everything else, to keep alive the sacred flame. He feared that other concerns might banish from the minds of the people what he considered the prime consideration: the well-being and prosperity of Catalonia. If a church was burned down, it was for him one more monument lost to Catalonia. If a section of track was blown up, he said to his fellow members: "That is a section of track Catalonia has lost." Ribas, the architect, was sure that the principal objective of Major Martínez de Soria was to clamp the four Catalonian provinces under lock and key. So he was on the alert to salvage whatever he could. He had said to the architect Massana: "We should get permission from the Cultural Department of the Generalidad to take over whatever we consider of value if it looks as though there is going to be trouble."

The architect Massana approved of the plan, and with the aid of Julio they received permission without too much difficulty.

Cosme Vila, too, defended what lay closest to his heart: the prestige of the party. He was fearful that public opinion would look askance at the pact with the anarchists and he sought ways to divert attention from it, much the same as with the burning of the Christian Brothers' School. He decided it would be a good move to attack the Trotskyite cell. *El Proletario* launched the campaign with a series of virulent articles against Murillo, Salvio, and their cohorts. The charges that the Trotskyites drew up against Cosme Vila and the Communist Party were concrete and just the opposite of Pedro's: they had betrayed the world proletariat, sacrificing its interests to those of Moscow. "Vasiliev is the absolute ruler! If he orders a pact with El Responsable, it is made; if he orders the resources of the province depleted, he is obeyed!" Murillo bolstered his arguments with facts recalled from the days when, "walking in darkness," he had formed part of the executive committee.

Cosme Vila countered by affirming in *El Proletario* that Murillo, resentful over his expulsion, planned to send his followers out into the roads to attack the trucks still supplying the city with food. "Stand guard on the roads!" In the villages the peasants themselves stood around-the-clock watches.

But Murillo and his band were not the only ones to be feared. "Where are Mateo and the others who attacked Dr. Relken? It is impossible to find them, despite a house-to-house check. Without a doubt they are hidden somewhere in the country, and hunger and hate will surely lead them to some desperate act."

A period of watchfulness began. Watches were set up along the roads and at the railroad crossings. The press and the cooperative were guarded. The sickle hung over each household, for men began spying on one another. Assault Guards patrolled the city: "Your papers!" There was a search for pistols and revolvers. For these reasons people of Matías Alvear's age could not sleep. For these reasons Cosme Vila was more careful than ever of his personal security and prestige.

Some of the smaller businessmen went to see him. "Listen," they said, "what is it you really want?"

Cosme Vila showed himself adamant. "Our program is clear. Ownership should be in the hands of the community."

When Vasiliev made his visit to Gerona, he brought with him the promised check, insignificant in amount, but he made up for it by touring the streets escorted by the whole executive committee. He put in an appearance at the co-op, where he was cheered by the women; he climbed into one of the trucks and visited the province, which in truth was a garden. "Possibly the most varied and beautiful province in Spain," Vasiliev said.

Yet at the station, as he said goodbye to Cosme Vila, Vasiliev told him: "Everything looks fine; you are handling things as you should, and giving us grounds for satisfaction in every respect. But there is one thing I did find lacking—something fundamental, which a party leader should never overlook."

Cosme Vila's eyes opened wide with infinite curiosity, and he was glad that Vasiliev was telling him this alone, where the others could not hear.

"I noticed," Vasiliev continued, "that your wife was not drilling with the militia."

The train pulled out, and Cosme Vila stood for a moment rooted to the platform. His wife! Vasiliev was right. A surge of admiration for the sagacity of the man and the revolution he represented filled his breast. He felt small, a mere apprentice....

His wife was flabbergasted. "Me with a rifle? But why? Don't you realize that the baby—" Cosme Vila searched his wife's eyes with his own, waiting, waiting, not saying a word. By that silence the wife of the leader understood that Cosme Vila must be right, that if he felt she should attend drill, he had his reasons. So she left the baby's bottles and went to the first floor of the Traditionalist Center, where her appearance left the two veterans of the African war, all the militiamen, La Valenciana, and the rest of the women who were learning to march and to handle a gun, overcome with emotion.

Cosme Vila did not stop there. He ordered his father-in-law to attend the drill sessions, too. "Your wife can watch the grade crossing," he told him.

His father-in-law looked at him perplexedly, but got up, put on his vest, and said: "Let's go!"

Cosme Vila now supervised the drill sessions personally. His wife's clumsiness got on his nerves, and when he got home he would say: "I don't want any supper." This was her punishment: no supper for him, and being forbidden to kiss her sleeping son. The baby no longer put his foot in his mouth. Now he pointed to the colored pictures of horses, cows, and giraffes in a book his grandfather had brought him. Sometimes he got his fat little hands on a copy of *El Proletario* and tore it to shreds, stuffing pieces in his mouth. Cosme Vila would stand looking at him, at a loss as to what he should do. It seemed strange to him that this tiny being seated on the floor, with his small, flat head, should indeed be his son. He did not want to give rein to his emotions. If he could only take him along to the drill sessions! When he was old enough to stand the trip, he would send him to Russia.

The atmosphere of vigilance hung over the city. Fathers watched sons and neighbors watched neighbors. The strike continued. Dr. Relken offered his services to the architects Massana and Ribas: "If I can be of any help in guarding the monuments and works of art, feel free to call on me."

Professor Morales said to David and Olga: "What do you think of the changes in such a short span? My grandfather was rich. He died without having been aware for one quarter of an hour in his whole life that such a word as 'people' existed. Now this word has become the most important. It is the main concern of everybody. I think that to have achieved this more than makes up for the closing down of a few factories."

"But, in the final analysis, what is it you people hope to accomplish?" the couple asked.

"Our objectives here are to force the resignation of the Mayor, and to have the name of the Municipal Theater changed to the 'People's Theater.' From there on, up the ladder rung by rung. For Spain as a whole we plan to do what has been done in Russia. With the permission of the UGT...."

Ignacio had been told at the bank that he could take his annual vacation whenever he felt like it. "Vacation? What for?" He couldn't leave the city, even to go to Puigcerdá or the shore. He couldn't even leave his own house after eight o'clock in the evening. His father had forbidden him to do so. His only walks in the city were those to Marta's house, where he went every day. "I'll take my vacation later—around Christmas, or some other time."

At Marta's house it seemed as though nothing was happening. The fact that both father and daughter dissembled their activities reduced dinner table conversation to generalities and gave a fictitious air of tranquility. Nevertheless, they kept watch over each other like hawks, and the major's wife watched them both.

"There is one thing I don't understand," Ignacio said to Marta. "With the hodge-podge you are assembling—Renovación, CEDA, Falange, and so on—what is going to happen if you win? The Republic, I suppose, is out...."

Marta thought for a minute. "Would you believe it," she finally said, "I never once thought of that! I've never given a thought to what will come afterwards. I don't know why I assumed that we would put the program of the Falange into practice."

Ignacio wagged his head. "That proves a lot of things, but then—I suppose the big shots know exactly what they are about."

Marta again was silent for a moment. "Well—to tell you the truth, I'm not sure they know much more than I do," she said.

Ignacio made a gesture of amazement.

"Yes, man, don't act so surprised! I suppose that for the moment what they want is to restore order to the nation. Afterwards—I don't know," she continued. "For example, my father would like to restore the monarchy, but I understand that many of the generals who are taking part are republicans and want to maintain the Republic."

Ignacio heard her out thoughtfully. Then he said: "Of course, it's clear enough. It all depends on how the thing comes off—whether it turns out to be difficult or easy...."

On hearing that, Marta, for the first time, seized him by the wrists and looked deeply into his eyes. "Tell me, Ignacio," she said, her voice filled with sweetness. "What do you hope, that it will be easy or difficult?"

Ignacio returned her searching gaze. "I hate to disappoint you. But I can't give you the answer you would like."

"Why not?"

"No. Don't misunderstand. I don't look lightly on the fact that La Valenciana has a rifle pointed at your father, at you, and at everyone who doesn't wear a blue coverall. I don't like any part of that business. But at the same time I don't see clearly what is to come afterwards. I have no choice but to sit on my hands like a fool."

Marta let go his wrists and lowered her eyes. "So you are still convinced that Spain has no salvation? That there is nothing that will lift up the sentiments of the people, awaken them?"

Ignacio shrugged. "I can't see it, that's the truth. Warning Voice, the notary Noguer—what will make them change? If they win, they will be right back at the old stand. Even heavier-handed than before because their consciences will bother them less after what they've been through. But I don't want to talk about the others; I'll speak for myself. I don't know what's the matter with us in this country, Marta. We are—I think we are crazy. You think that I live a nice, calm life, isn't that right? That I use my head, that I've got a grip on myself. Why not? I passed my second-year exams, I don't go to UGT any more. Well, I can assure you that I am more unstable than ever and that I am the same old Ignacio as before, or worse. I sway with every passing wind. You, I respect, but it's because of you, I think, not me. Do you understand? I think that I'm afraid of losing you. Around the house I keep my nerves under control because my mother deserves at least that. But if I had been brought up in the streets, I'd be on one of those trucks now, or maybe blowing them up on the highways. What hope is there, Marta? We are—I don't know! Professor Civil talks his head off about Mediterranean culture. Why are we always tilting at windmills? Oh, sure, they say we are more sensitive than others, that we are the advance guard. I should like to be convinced that all this business of yours is a crusade, do you understand? How can it be a crusade if the majority of those carrying it out are—? Oh, I know, the idea is superior to the man, and so forth. Great oaks from little acorns grow. I don't know, I just don't know. 'By their works you shall know them.' When I think about the works of Don Jorge…"

Marta listened to him deeply moved. She looked at the young man standing before her, dark-haired, with his energetic, clean-cut face, with an expression very much like that of Matías Alvear, except for his eyes, which were his mother's, and something of the air of Madrid about him though he had never lived there, and she felt that she admired him. She admired his inner struggle, and his frankness. He needed only a push and... He had only to realize that it was precisely in his hands, in the hands of people like himself and his father, the eternal, solid middle class, to give character and an elevated tone to the mission of reconquering Spain.

"Your error consists in seeing only Warning Voice and the notary Noguer—and people like my father," she said. "But rest assured there are lots of others, lads like Roca and Haro, like Padilla and Rodríguez, and men like the assistant manager of your bank. There are two masons and an electrician—many, many middle-class people. They will be the bedrock of the nation. I understand what you are saying, and I am not going to try to convince you right now. You will see it with your own two eyes. Look: I can save a lot of words. Do you want to know something? It will serve you as a point of reference. Do you know who went to offer to take over a post of duty with a rifle? Just guess."

"I don't know."

"Professor Civil."

THE first to catch on to the fact that Major Martínez de Soria was under surveillance was El Rubio. The major thought his orderly was useful only to keep his puttees shined and his horse well curried; the fact was that El Rubio had taken a liking to him, mainly because he was Marta's father.

El Rubio knew the ways of his old comrades. Therefore he had only to see Ideal peering at the balcony with his face shielded to know that something was up. Then he saw Blasco in front of the barracks lighting a cigarette with his face turned to the wall; a little later it was Santi seated on the curb with a bored look on his face.

The thing was as clear as the nose on your face. How clumsy they were at covering up their game! If the thing hadn't been so tragic, for pulling a trigger is both the easiest and the hardest thing in this world to do, it would have made him laugh. As it was, he felt a twitching in his heart. He stood for a while with his nose pressed against the windowpane, and then called to Marta: "I hate to tell you this, Marta, but I think it's my duty: look who is out there."

Marta looked out the window and saw Ideal loitering in front of a stationery store. "It's Ideal. What of it?"

"They want to kill your father."

The girl's face flushed and she turned toward El Rubio with a terror-stricken expression. The memory of her brother shot down in Valladolid flashed across her mind. She didn't know what to say. "Do you think they—"

"I know them. That's why I'm telling you."

El Rubio told her everything he had observed during the week. "Tell your father without delay," he concluded. "My advice is that he go out as little as possible—and never alone. And another thing, tell him to find a new orderly."

"But why?"

"If I am with him it will only make matters worse. They wouldn't mind letting me have it, too."

Marta realized that what he was saying was perfectly true. She felt a great wave of gratitude toward this boy whom Mateo considered frivolous. She was sure that Ignacio had been right when he said: "Nuts! He's got more to him than he knows himself and than you'd ever guess from hearing him play the saxophone."

Marta wasted no time in getting to the barracks. On the way, when she was nearly there, she saw Blasco light up a cigarette. She breezed past the sentinels, who knew her. She reached her father's office and found him at his desk. It took her only a few words to convey El Rubio's warning.

Major Martínez de Soria was visibly shocked. He ran his hand over his hair. Marta had an urge to throw her arms around his neck, but she contained herself.

"Of course, of course. I'll be careful," the major said, gazing out the window.

Suddenly his face went red. An uncontrollable fury seized him. He cut loose with a string of oaths that in their incoherence sounded like the general's. Marta was shocked as she listened to him. She had never seen him in such a state, and this brought home to her the danger really involved in the situation. In the barracks patio a few soldiers strolled back and forth with a defiantly bored look about them. "There'll be an end to this soon enough, there'll be an end to this!" the major shouted.

The truth of the matter was that the news had taken the major by surprise. He had been expecting an attack from the Communists, but never from El Responsable. His first reaction was to blame Colonel Muñoz and Julio for instigating the plot; then, lowering his tone of voice to soothe Marta, he murmured: "No, no, forget that. It's that herd of swine themselves."

Her father's reaction revealed an important thing to Marta: he was not immune to fear. For a few moments she noticed an unmistakable slump to his shoulders. Then he gave the impression of struggling to regain his self-possession, and finally of having done so.

For if it was true that the fear of receiving a bullet in the temple suddenly paralyzed the major, it was equally true that the next minute the man felt more strongly than ever the responsibility resting on his shoulders. He alone directed the uprising in Gerona: if something happened to him, the chain would be broken, and others would have to start again from the beginning.

He reflected that the fact that his attackers were utterly irresponsible put two faces on the matter. On the one hand, it seemed likely that it would be easy to escape them because their plans had not been systematically thought out; on the other, escape seemed more difficult in that any one of them was capable of giving his life to accomplish the objective of killing him.

He came to grips with the problem in its immediate terms. The first thing was to get Marta home safely. He called two soldiers and ordered them to see her to the house. He summoned to his office Romá, the shavetail, and two other lieutenants he trusted completely.

The young officers became furious when he told them the news. Their youth moved them to conceive spectacular plans. The major masked his feelings and told them: "Careful, careful, we must move very carefully."

When he decided that Marta must be home, he ordered his lieutenants to accompany him, and they left the barracks together. They went down the Seminary steps, walking as though nothing was amiss, but the four of them kept a sharp watch on doorways, balconies, and corners. They saw no one who looked suspicious, and reached the major's house without incident. They had no more than entered when Marta said: "Look. There is one of them."

Ideal was still absorbed in studying the fountain pens behind the plate-glass window of the stationery store.

Lieutenant Romá looked at him with infinite contempt. "Who? That dung beetle?"

At the sight of Ideal, the major's face flushed anew. "To think that those creatures can checkmate the army!"

Major Martínez de Soria followed developments in Spain like everybody else. The thing that annoyed him most was the "outrages against the army." According to him, the War Ministry stood back and never raised a finger to halt a series of transfers and shifts which invariably affected the officers who were the pride of the corps. Many promotions and many responsible assignments went to those whom their fellow officers considered the most incompetent. "It is more important to be a supporter of the Popular Front than to have fought for Spain and have an unblemished service record."

He still held his post by sheer good fortune. His friendship with Goicoechea had stood him in good stead. "People like him, if they can keep from stopping a bullet, still have some influence," he said. For that reason he did not intend to let vermin like Ideal fell him with one swing of the ax. After discussing a number of projects, which ranged from rounding up all the anarchists and throwing them into a dungeon filled with boa constrictors, to the major's not setting foot outside the house, they settled on something that struck them as more effective: they would inform Julio of what was going on, making it clear that he would answer with his head for anything that happened to the major.

It was the major's own idea. He entrusted delivery of the message to Second Lieutenant Romá and the older of the two lieutenants, by name Delgado. "You know what to do. Go to police headquarters. Put it up to him in such a way as to leave no room for doubt."

The young officers hung back for a moment. They liked the plan, but anything short of wiping out all the parties to the plot seemed side-stepping the issue.

"Take it easy, take it easy," the major said. "This doesn't mean that I'm going to go riding in the Dehesa and make a target of myself." A smile creased his face. "Officially, as of this moment, I have a heavy cold." He gave them each a slap on the back and saw them to the door.

Marta was consumed with curiosity to know what had been decided. Her father's only words to her as she burst out of her room were: "I'll tell you in good time, little one, I'll tell you."

The officers went straight to police headquarters. None of them had ever spoken to Julio before. They recognized him because his hat at a slant, his cigarette-holder, and his dark complexion were unmistakable. Who was there that did not know about him? After all, he had become the most important person in the city, with Cosme Vila and Doña Amparo Campo as runners-up. Julio's wife was not hiding her light under a bushel. The automobile that was at Julio's disposal as Chief of Police was rarely available for his use. Doña Amparo Campo recalled trudging through the fields of La Mancha as a girl, and she now wanted to make up for it. She barely greeted her old friends like Carmen Elgazu. She lived in a world of pure fantasy in which she dazzled the maid, tried on new housecoats all day before the looking-glass, and filled the house with every kind of gadget. To Julio she would say: "I don't know why you put up with that oaf of a Commissioner. Why don't you take over that job, too?" The only people she thought her social equals were Dr. Relken and Colonel Muñoz. "Doctor, come and have dinner with us."

Dr. Relken almost invariably accepted. "But, Doña Amparo—easy on the oil, eh?"

The entry of the two officers into Julio's office left Officer Antonio Sánchez agape. Lieutenant Romá could not restrain a glance at the door on the left, behind which he knew that Octavio, Haro, and Rosselló kept up their singing of subversive anthems. Then he told Julio they wanted to speak to him alone.

Antonio Sanchez withdrew. Julio kept Berta and the snow-scene paperweight with him.

The interview was brief and to the point.

"Señor García, the anarchists are planning an attempt on Major Martínez de Soria's life. El Responsable, his nephew, Future, the bootblack, and the rest of them are involved. We and a group of officers for whom we are authorized to speak are particularly anxious to see that this shall not be carried out. This is our proposal: you see to it that the thing is cut short. You are the Chief of Police, and it is a matter that concerns you. If nothing happens, that's that, and everybody will be happy. If something happens to the major—even though not at the hands of the anarchists—we shall not be able to answer for the consequences."

"Answer to whom?"

"To you, sir. *¡Viva España!*" The officers turned on their heels and left the office.

Julio sat motionless behind his desk. One thing seemed clear to him beyond a shadow of a doubt: those officers, if the occasion arose, would be as good as their word. For that reason the matter required thought. Julio had reached a peak in his career, and it would hardly do to have the whole thing come down around his ears at this point. His waiting room was filled with people who had things to take up with him. Architect Massana, the Mayor, was waiting to see him! He had come to ask authorization to levy a tax on the trucks that brought the food to the city when they entered the city precincts. Most of Julio's mail from Barcelona and Madrid was marked "Personal." The world was his oyster, and the Madrid days when he had filled himself up on crullers, a nobody without a cent in his pocket, were a thing of the past. As Dr. Rosselló told him: "Wagner is better for home consumption than Andalusian folklore."

It was impossible, therefore, to permit all this to be cut short by two young officers in an instant. It was a strange situation. The life of Major Martínez de Soria had suddenly become precious to him. It was almost as precious to him as the life of Doña Amparo Campo. For behind the officers who visited him there were surely others, and behind them others....

It was essential that the major's life be respected. At the same time the officers had to recognize that he could not be hanging forever on the heartbeat of their commander. For the time being, yes. They could lay aside their fears! He would call in El Responsable and all his sidekicks and lay down the law, and no two ways about it. He knew how to handle the matter: he would couple his order with some promise or concession.

But this alone would not be enough. That shavetail had said: "Even though not at the hands of the anarchists...." Was he insinuating that it was not the anarchists alone who had passed the death sentence on the major?

Julio, pushing his hat back, asked himself how the devil they had got wind of it. For he knew the plot to be a fact. He had been informed personally by Murillo, who had become one of his best sources of information, thanks to the fear inspired in him by Cosme Vila's threats. Murillo had communicated to him that the Communist Party was preparing to liquidate various figures of the community, including Major Martínez de Soria and some doctors.

"Why doctors?" Julio had asked the Trotskyite leader.

"It's the Russian tactics," Murillo answered. "Liquidate doctors. I don't know why." In any case, what mattered was that the major headed Cosme Vila's black list, too.

Julio stroked Berta. The voice of Lieutenant Romá echoed in his ears. The hatred it betrayed! "After all," he thought, "I pay them in the same coin."

MOSÉN Alberto was being watched; Major Martínez de Soria was being watched; Julio was answering for the major's safety with his head. *El Proletario* repeated over and over: "Murillo and the Falange are planning to blow up the food trucks."

One thing perplexed Gerona: Cosme Vila's insistence that the Mayor be removed from office. The architect Massana met comments with a shrug: "Does that surprise you? He wants to turn the job over to Professor Morales."

Perhaps he was right. The professor had rapidly become the man of the hour, pushed into the limelight by the praise the newspaper showered on him and by the conviction among the strikers that a man like him enhanced the prestige of the party.

Cosme Vila did everything he could to build up the popularity of his future mayor. There was no lack of opportunities. Cosme Vila sent him off on a tour of the province to speak to the peasants on the land-reform program. In every corner of the province his voice was heard announcing to the tenant farmers that the channeling of the Ter River was under study, along with the creation of a number of reservoirs that would convert the whole province into irrigated land. The only stumbling-block, it seemed, was the question of expropriations. The proprietors refused to give up one foot of land, just as the factory owners refused to turn over to the workers one share in their enterprises. "This will delay the reform, but it is bound to come! If we stick together, we will triumph together!"

Professor Morales carried out every assignment he was given with an air of bliss written all over his face. La Valenciana, every now and then, would pull him by the coat-tails and say: "So, Lope de Vega, you are becoming the big cheese, eh?" Morales would laugh, for it never would have occurred to him that La Valenciana had ever heard of Lope de Vega.

The state of panic in which the city lived, the profusion of revolutionary flags, the absence of laughter, the sudden silences that fell upon the streets, gave Morales food for thought. "The necessary phase," he repeated to himself. He looked at himself in the mirror. What did his ugliness have to do with all that, with his blind obedience to Cosme Vila, despite the fact that, compared with him, Cosme was a primal being, or at best a diamond in the rough? Nothing. Nothing at all. The only cause he recognized was his conviction that the hour had struck, the hour of the rebellion of the masses. Up to the present the masses had always lagged a century or two in assimilating the ideas that the elite elaborated for themselves. So that by the time the many Valencianas of the world began to make these ideas their own, the elite had taken off in new directions or returned to ancient molds. Now, for the first time, masses and elite would fuse, creating a single organism. That justified telling the peasants that the rivers would be channeled, and putting up with the famished dogs roaming the streets. Men of property were being ruined by the strike; the rats of fear gnawed away the black of their hair. An undercurrent of protest swelled and swelled: groups formed on street corners. There was talk of machine guns at the Chamber of Commerce! For the first time men whose one thought before had been how to sell canned goods or cloth at the highest possible price went to the walls of Montjuich and clenched their fists, without raising them, toward where they supposed Cosme Vila's mongoloid head might be, or the cap of El Responsable, or Julio's hat at a slant.

Now they talked about Professor Morales; especially the elite, with its advantage of a century or two. Morales read in the eyes of old friends—other professors, lawyers, Dr. Rosselló himself—a boundless fear. It was as if these men supposed that he was pointing them out with his finger, giving their names, uncovering their faults, the discrepancy between their beliefs and their acts, the indifference with which they heard out their poor clients, and their horror of Marx, not because, having localized the cancer, he proposed inhuman remedies, but because his prophecies were relentlessly coming true.

The professor had eyes that looked store-bought, removable, separated from his soul by a metallic foil. With them he constantly observed how his greatest enemies, women, reacted to him. He would have loved to crush them all. As he saw it, it was they who filled their husbands with alarm to permit themselves the subsequent luxury of inspiring them with courage. He asserted that the big names who headed the black lists went in fear because of their women. It was

Mosén Alberto's maid who cautioned him regularly: "Be careful, Mosén, they are still watching you." It was the wife of Don Santiago Estrada who never stopped saying to the head of the CEDA: "Who are those two following us? Can you see the button in their lapels?" It was the wife of Major Martínez de Soria who went to and from church with the grave mien of a warrior's widow, which gave the major the chills. It was Laura who would have been capable of overthrowing the jail; it was the wives of the merchants who protested: "We'll have to go begging any day now!" And among themselves it was they who cried and ranted, cursing the deep pulsation of the masses on the march.

It was Professor Morales who had suggested the extermination of the doctors. Except for Dr. Rosselló, the rest had more faith in morals than in science. Bedside medicine-men, with not a little of the priest about them, they slipped the thermometer into the armpit with a smile on their lips. Then they prescribed doses of resignation to the families. They were free to act in that manner, and perhaps it was not a bad thing. But for the purposes of a revolution they served as shock absorbers, as the great mitigators of human suffering, and they were just as likely to cure a member of the masses as an exploiter. Even Cosme Vila had been taken aback at hearing Professor Morales declare: "The scream of a man when there is no one to amputate his leg serves revolutionary ends better than giving thanks to the Virgin because an operation has turned out well."

The city responded to Professor Morales with clenched fists beside the walls and in the homes. Every day trains from France passed through the city filled with travelers on their way to Barcelona for the heralded People's Olympiad. These travelers, rather than sports fans, seemed, from their appearance and baggage, more like the members of a phantom army. They saluted with clenched fists from the windows of the cars, and wore handkerchiefs around their necks exactly like El Cojo and Ideal. Professor Morales went down to the station to wave flags as they passed through. Many people insisted that the trains that stopped delivered mysterious boxes for the Communist Party.

Every day people opened their newspapers expecting the drop that would make the glass overflow, the match that would touch off the tinder. Not even the rivers of Gerona could get together. The Oñar was down to a trickle, and its stagnant pools had their same old stench. The Ter, on the other hand, was swollen with roiled waters, as if fearful of being channeled any day. The month of July poured down its incandescent heat on the people's heads, making them throb. The sun never rested from morning till night. There was a moment at noon, when its rays fell plumb, that people stood motionless in the streets, as if desiccated, their last energies sucked from them by the sun's rays. Souls trembled within cages of bone.

Many people went down to the railroad station every day to wait for the arrival of the out-of-town newspapers. Among them was Matías Alvear, who took *La Vanguardia*, the only newspaper in which he had any confidence.

One day the train was late. Matías Alvear had time to smoke several cigarettes as he paced back and forth on the platform. *La Vanguardia* did not arrive until noon, at the very moment when the sun's rays fell plumb. Matías Alvear noted that the headlines were much bigger than those of *El Proletario*. People swarmed around the newsboys. He managed to get a copy. He saw a squad of Assault Guards and decided to go home without opening his paper. He would read it in peace when he got to the dining room.

He climbed the stairs slowly, opened the front door, and settled himself in his armchair. Carmen Elgazu noted that something special had happened and she passed behind him frequently to see if she could get a clue from the headlines.

Once glance and Matías realized that the match had been put to the tinder. Events of unprecedented seriousness were taking place in the nation's capital, to judge from the reports of what was happening in Parliament. Matías did not smile as he had once done when he read: "Uproar in the Chamber." On the contrary, from the first word his face took on an expression of the deepest preoccupation.

Calvo Sotelo had described the situation in Spain in gloomy terms. Apparently it was not the River Ter alone whose waters were roiled and swollen. Calvo Sotelo gave the official figures on events since February 16: 400 bombs set off in different places; 330 killed, and 1,511 wounded; 170 churches totally destroyed, 295 partially destroyed; 485 strikes; some 12,000 persons of Rightist affiliation in jail....

The words of Calvo Sotelo had made a tremendous impression in the Cortes, and the President of the Council, Casares Quiroga, warned him for the fourth time. Calvo Sotelo shrugged his shoulders. "Good, Señor Casares Quiroga! I'm on record as taking notice of Your Excellency's threat. And before all the world I will answer you as St. Domingo de Silos replied to a king of Castile: 'Your Majesty, you can take my life, but that's all you can do.' That's all that is lacking! I've got broad shoulders."

As the chamber emptied, in the corridors, La Pasionaria said in a voice that everyone could hear: "That man has spoken for the last time."

Matías Alvear's brows knit. Carmen Elgazu, passing behind him, had managed to read only "St. Domingo de Silos." "Why can't they leave the saints alone?"

Matías Alvear felt almost ill because from the first instant his intuition told him that the threat would not end in words, but would be carried out, leading to a situation beyond repair.

The Christian Brother hidden in the home of the assistant manager of the bank asked him: "But can these figures be true?"

"They don't even have the nerve to deny them," the assistant manager replied.

When Ignacio read: "You can take my life, but that's all you can do," he recalled that his mother had used almost the same words the day Julio came to visit them, in referring to the death of Mosén Alberto's maid.

Cosme Vila thought to himself: "It's the necessary phase." Major Martínez de Soria accepted the idea that Ideal was capable of shooting him, but he could not believe the government of the Republic capable of ordering the same thing done to Calvo Sotelo.

Matías Alvear found everyone in the Neutral at a great pitch of excitement. Don Emilio Santos was in the best humor of anyone, for he had received news from Cartagena: "My son is still alive!"

The hours passed slowly. Professor Morales wrote in his diary: "Elite and masses begin to fuse: the President of the Council and El Cojo pass sentence on people for the same reasons."

THERE was no rest, for there could be none. And this was because everyone was as good as his word. When Santi promised that he would eat an omelet with six eggs, he ate it.

For that reason, when the 13th of July came, everyone understood. It did not surprise Matías Alvear; neither did it surprise Major Martínez de Soria. When the radio, *La Vanguardia*, and *El Proletario* all carried the news that the President of the Council had fulfilled his promise, everyone understood that it had to be that way, and that there was no rest, for there could be none. "The authorities of the East Cemetery of Madrid have reported to the City Council that at about five o'clock this morning a body was left there which has been identified as that of Señor Calvo Sotelo."

Surprise was in store for the wife of the major as she saw the blotches on her husband's face take on a violet hue. And for Carmen Elgazu on seeing her husband, unable to go on reading his paper, get up and go downstairs into the street.

There was also a surprise for Lieutenant Romá on seeing the major stride into the barracks, despite the decision not to set foot outside his house. "What's happened?"

The major did not answer him. "What day of the month is today?"

"The 13th."

The 13th of July. The radios blared out all the details. Assault Guards had turned up at Calvo Sotelo's house and asked him to come with them. In the pickup truck they put a bullet through the back of his neck. David and Olga deplored the fact. Casal chalked it up to an act of reprisal by the guards: "The Falange killed Lieutenant Castillo of their company, and this was their revenge.'"

The major was not interested in reasons. For the first time the: cry "Assassins!" had escaped his lips. The newspapers published pictures of the endless line of mourners passing before the bier in the funeral home in Madrid. Major Martínez de Soria was the first from Gerona to manifest his solidarity. He sent a telegram to the family of Calvo Sotelo conveying his regrets. Don Pedro. Orioli and Don Santiago Estrada soon followed. Then the line began to form. Matías Alvear, with the pencil stuck behind his ear, said to Jaime: "This reminds me of those days in October."

Carmen Elgazu lived somewhat on the margin of the actual events, and she was unaware of the real importance of Calvo Sotelo. She became more mistrustful every day of the women who said to defend themselves or their husbands: "Haven't you read...?" It seemed to Carmen Elgazu that there was a clear dividing line between the good and the bad in each soul; and when doubts arose, there were the Ten Commandments.

For that reason at that particular moment she had no idea of the course political events might take. But she was sure that the fact that a man was President of the Council did not alter the basic principle that he had no right to threaten a fellow man's life. "Was Calvo Sotelo Catholic?" she asked Ignacio.

"Yes," the boy replied.

That was all she needed to know. She felt that everything became clear. For an instant she had a glimpse of a tragedy that cast its shadow over the entire country. But its dimensions suddenly made her dizzy. Something instinctive forced her to circumscribe the problem to what was bound up with the fibers of her own being. It was as if her heart told her: "What do you understand of all the rest?"

She had a presentiment that a catastrophe was approaching, not in the East Cemetery of Madrid, but within the circle of her own family. Perhaps it was because she was alone in the flat, because none of her children were there, and because of the way Matías had gone out.

She did not know what to do. She could have read the newspaper to learn more fully what had happened; she did not want to. She looked outside. A wonderful play of shadows was settling over the housetops. Lights were going on across the way. Women could be seen setting the table. The table. The eternal table. She would have given anything to see her own family sitting around the table at that moment. What time was it? She went into Ignacio's room and lit a candle in front of the image on the night table.

The doorbell rang. It was Pilar. Carmen Elgazu smiled when she saw her. She kissed her harder than usual.

"Is something the matter?" the girl asked.

"Nothing, daughter, nothing. There's nothing the matter."

Ignacio rang. Carmen Elgazu kissed him as usual. "Has Marta been by?" the boy asked.

"No, son."

Matías returned. He had probably been at the Neutral. He looked out from the balcony at the river. "They are all arriving," Carmen Elgazu thought. She took the newspaper off the table and spread the tablecloth. It was a yellow one, with flowers in the corners.

César was still missing. He was probably walking around the parish. He would call the children together and play with them. Sometimes he would stop in the middle of the game and give them a graphic description of the death of Christ. He would press his back against the wall and spread his arms in the form of the cross. It was so dramatic that the children held their breath.

The bell rang. Pilar went to the door, sliding across the tiles of the corridor. Carmen Elgazu heaved a sigh at the sight of César. She came up to him and gave him a kiss, which the seminarian returned. "Harder, harder!" she demanded.

César gave her a quizzical look. "Didn't I kiss you hard?" he asked.

Matías put on his earphones.

Ignacio noticed shadows flickering on the walls. "What's that?"

"I lit the candle in your room."

"It's not very cheery."

PART V

July 18 to July 30, 1936

EIGHTY-FOUR

JULIO understood that the die was cast. It was not likely that the military would wait until November. To launch the coup they would take advantage of the climate the recent events had created. The policeman regretted the fact that Gerona was so small. It was impossible for one group to avoid the others. He knew that if he walked along the Rambla he would run into Second Lieutenant Romá; if he turned around and walked in the other direction he would meet up with Lieutenant Delgado. It seemed to him that an ironic expression played over their faces, and that they looked pointedly at his head. But Julio reassured himself: "They'd better not be fools. For home consumption, Wagner, not Andalusian folklore...." He had a talk with the general and with Colonel Muñoz in which he set forth his misgivings. There was going to be no choice but to give the people arms.

The general asked himself if Julio had lost his mind. He refuted his arguments one by one for the hundredth time. Sanjurjo, Franco? What could they do, the one in Portugal, the other in the Canary Islands? Giving arms to the people was, under the circumstances, the most harebrained idea he had ever heard of. "I understand that the peasants are organizing a rally here. Maybe we should offer them a few field guns."

Julio answered: "You two are living in a limbo, and one fine day you're going to find yourselves in jail. Major Martínez de Soria will read a proclamation to his men and send them out to take over the city. He will probably have the support of two hundred civilians, perhaps three hundred. He will shoot us all. The whole lot of us."

Just then the three daughters of the general telephoned him, and this interruption saved Julio from finding himself in the barracks basement keeping Lieutenant Martín company. Lieutenant Martín had confided to the sentries that the worst thing about being under arrest was the lack of women.

Julio was not cowed. He had his plan and he was going to put it in practice.

No general was going to throw a monkey wrench in the works! There was no one he could trust. "I'll have to save the city by myself."

He realized that he represented the only possible liaison with Cosme Vila, with El Responsable, with Casal, with all of them. He ran the men over in his mind. He thought of Mateo. "Mateo thinks they're the only ones who're willing to give their lives. He's going to see how many there are on the other side. What a pleasure it will be to give that whippersnapper a lesson!"

Doña Amparo Campo was impressed by her husband's poise. With all he had on his mind, he followed his normal routine as though nothing were happening: his bath every morning, listening to his records, reading Voltaire. There were evenings when he sat up talking philosophy with Dr. Relken until three in the morning. "The two ideas, the two ideas I was talking about," said the policeman. "The world is splitting up into two camps."

Dr. Relken found the problem more complex. He laughed at Julio, saying: "So the world is no longer divided into five parts, but fivo." Dr. Relken, too, was in favor of giving arms to the people. "And you ought to throw the remaining Falangists into jail."

Julio shook his head negatively at this suggestion. "Many more have joined up. Their families would become even more exasperated. Their fathers would offer their services to the army."

Julio did not lose his head even though he was convinced that the uprising was doomed to failure. Perhaps momentarily, and by surprise, the military might successfully seize some garrison; but in most of them they would be routed. Therefore he was concerned only with his immediate problem, which was saving Gerona. For it would take the major or that shavetail only twenty-four hours to put an end to his bath and his record collection.

He advised Dr. Relken to leave. "Go to Barcelona, as a favor to me, until all this is over. You were lucky the first time; there's no sense to tempting Providence...."

The doctor thought Julio's advice was sensible. "But don't you think I might be useful here?"

"I don't see how. You accomplished your mission at election time."

The doctor meditated. "I hate to leave, because the mines really interested me," he concluded.

"What would you like to do? Take a hand in the game?"

"And why not? It means a lot to all of us."

"Don't be a fool," Julio said to him. "You come back later, after the atmosphere has cleared. Then we can look even for platinum in the Pyrenees if you want to."

Cosme Vila and El Responsable answered Julio's summons. And the policeman was amazed at the naturalness with which both of them replied: "We'd give our lives without a minute's hesitation."

Julio asked them if their fellow members would be willing to do the same. El Responsable took offense, because he felt that the mere question was insulting. Cosme Vila, on the other hand, found the problem interesting, but one that he could not answer offhand. "Why not ask?"

Cosme Vila never thought about death. Death could paralyze his activities, but the doctrine for which he was fighting was so great that it would perpetuate him in time. What more could he ask? He might be dissolved in earth, but his work would have been accomplished.

Julio's question, however, reminded him that the danger was one that threatened them all, and that his personal decision was not enough. It was necessary to know the strength of each grain of sand to calculate the total resistance. The card index in his office bore witness that certain men were willing to live, and wanted this living to be effected under a new order; but there was no evidence on the cards that they were willing to die.

What a smart devil Julio was! Cosme Vila thought the problem over and discussed it with Professor Morales. The idea filled the professor with enthusiasm. The entries on the card index would have to be completed. But this could not be done in a hurry. The truth would have to be painlessly arrived at, by the searching of eyes in the course of a conversation.

"Whom shall we ask?"

"The members. The men over twenty."

Cosme Vila turned this over. It seemed a little spectacular, and yet... As he understood it, it was not enough to know that the members would obey an order. The potentiality that mattered depended on a blind willingness that did not count the costs. Cosme Vila stepped out of his office and ran his glance over the members. Gorki and Morales could try the idea out. What difference did it make? The conscience should not be a secret.

Morales began the next day when he had finished with the newspaper. Headquarters was full at any hour of the day because of the strike. All the comrades greeted him as he came in: "Hello, Lope de Vega!"

He talked with a man about forty years old who had been lamed in an accident in the quarries. They carried on their conversation in a corner. The man was in a rage over the threat of a military uprising and swore that he had seen it coming for a long time.

Morales nodded his head. Suddenly he shot a question at him: "Would you be ready to give your life to defeat them?"

The man did not hesitate for a second: "Of course."

Morales's face revealed his satisfaction. "What you have said fills me with pride. I am really a newcomer to the party, and your example gives me great courage."

"I hold membership card 120," the man told him.

Morales watched him steadily. "These are difficult moments," he went on. "I sometimes ask myself, what would we do if the party demanded the maximum sacrifice of us? For instance," and here he paused, "if it were to ask us to give our life, not for this affair of the military, but—without telling us the reason. What would we do?"

The man stood perplexed. He ran his hand over his head. "What's this leading to?"

"Nothing. I just wondered."

The man in turn marked a pause. Then he said: "That's something nobody can ever tell. I—think I would give it."

Professor Morales seemed moved. "Are you married or single?"

"Single."

Gorki had not heard that conversation. The mission he had been assigned pleased but at the same time frightened him. "To ask a man if he is willing to die is an awfully big order...." Cosme Vila, however, had said to him: "What's the difference? After all, the conscience should not be a secret."

Without quite knowing how, Gorki found himself on the balcony talking with membership card 171. A young fellow about thirty, who worked at a dry cleaning establishment. He had been studying Russian for a long time without making any headway.

"Would you give your life for the party?"

"Of course."

"Are you married or single?"

"Married."

Gorki offered his interlocutor a cigarette. He was following the line Cosme Vila had suggested. "And suppose the party asked something harder of us," Gorki went on in an offhand tone.

The party member smiled. "I can't think of anything harder than giving one's life."

Gorki blew a smoke ring. "Well, there is something harder. To give another's life."

"Another's?"

"Yes, another's."

The member looked puzzled. "I don't follow you."

"Anybody's," Gorki went on. "One of the comrades—Victor." He leaned back on the railing. "Or your wife's," he went on in the same tone.

The member gave a start. "What's my wife done?" he inquired. For a moment he had thought Gorki was in earnest.

Gorki soothed him. "No, don't be afraid. It's not a question of her having done anything. We're just talking, don't you sec?"

Cosme Vila strolled over to them.

The member was still twirling his cap in one hand. The idea of his wife obsessed him. "Well—if it was my wife," he said, looking suddenly at Cosme Vila, "I'd want to know what for."

Cosme Vila gave a gesture indicating that he had no idea what they were talking about. Yet the shadow of a frown drew his brows together. When he had suggested the question to Gorki and Morales, he had done it almost exclusively as an intellectual sport. Now, with a man of flesh and blood before him, a married man, he realized that the matter had real importance. To the point where he asked himself if he would sacrifice his wife. He recalled her features, her pallor after the baby was born, her clumsiness in handling the rifle at drill. It seemed to him that he would sacrifice her. He leaned on the railing. The examinee had gone away nervous. Cosme Vila thought about his son, the youngster who already pointed with his finger to cows and horses in the picture book. "Not the baby. Not the baby," he said to himself. "I'd want to know what for, too."

He muttered this last phrase almost aloud. "What did you say?" Gorki asked him.

"Nothing," Cosme Vila answered.

Morales went on with his investigations. He sat down in front of those he was questioning, and it brought back to him examination days at the Instituto when he asked the students: "Who founded Rome?" Now his questions were addressed to men and were of far greater import.

WITHOUT knowing it, Major Martínez de Soria had been carrying on a similar poll. The fact was that every officer who, in the armory, had given him his word of honor had by that act offered his life. The same was true of the two hundred and thirty-five men who made up the lists—the definitive list—furnished by the four parties the major called national parties.

A few hours after the news of the death of Calvo Sotelo he received the order to make ready. In view of the dramatic turn of events, the uprising had been pushed four months ahead of the scheduled date. Any moment the order would be flashed to assemble the forces that could be depended on and declare the city under martial law. "You are empowered to take such measures as you deem advisable."

The major walked about the dirty, forbidding barracks. He read the obscene remarks that had been chalked on the walls by the soldiers, who, their term of service over, wanted to register their nonconformity. They signed such remarks with their name and the date, which was really brave of them.

Lieutenants Romá and Delgado never left his side. The telegram finally arrived, in code. It said laconically: "The 19th."

EIGHTY-FIVE

MATEO received the order as he was getting Pedro's supper ready. A thing had happened to him which he could not explain. The hours dragged so that he was always going over to the kitchen window and looking at the great stone mass of the Cathedral bell tower. And it suddenly seemed to him that this bell tower, under the full blaze of the sun, was beginning to bend over, to bend over, that its base was giving way, and that any moment it would fall on his head. Mateo shrank back in the kitchen, stumbling over the chair with its short legs. He rubbed his eyes. That was a nightmare. He tried to get himself in hand and went back to the window. Then he went over to the stove to get Pedro's supper ready.

Pedro had noticed how nervous he was, and had said to him: "Just say the word and I'll go find you a woman. We can put out the lights."

Try as he would, Mateo could not be angry. He realized that possibly Pedro might be right. However, he controlled himself. Not only because of the danger and his promise to lead a chaste life, but because of Pilar. Her *World History* still offered him its touching plea:

Blessed Virgin, Virgin pure,
Make them pass me
In this course.

Rodríguez called and told him: "The 19th, at six thirty a.m." Mateo's worry was whether to go to see Pilar before presenting himself at barracks. Half past six in the morning seemed an awkward hour. There were moments when he said to himself: "It seems to me it's my duty to go and see my father. He certainly deserves it."

He had been able to wrest only a single confidence from Pedro. The latter was convinced that in Russia man was happy. "In Russia my father would not have committed suicide."

Mateo looked at him sympathetically. "Why not?" he asked.

"Because he wouldn't have, because he would have been happy there."

Mateo tried to explain to him that in Russia happiness was impossible because believers suffered persecution and non-believers bore within their souls, there as everywhere, the suffering of being incomplete.

But Pedro shook his head as he ate sardines, which was the thing he liked best. "If only things here were the way they are there! My father wouldn't have committed suicide."

The wall Pedro threw up between them discouraged Mateo at times. He asked himself if after victory they would be able to convince anyone. Thinking of the masons and the electrician, he took heart. But he told himself that every soul about him was searching for the absolute, and that the absolute—St. Augustine made it very clear—could not be supplied here below not even by the Falange. At this point Rodríguez arrived, and the enthusiasm of the Civil Guard revived his spirits.

Another thing Mateo was concerned about was whether Major Martínez de Soria would allow them to guard the general, the Commissioner, and Julio García until their fate was decided. Mateo felt nobody so deserved to be entrusted with this mission as the Falange.

Rodríguez asked him: "Have you done much shooting?"

Mateo smiled. "In Madrid."

"Jesus, what a lot of things you did in Madrid!"

Warning Voice and Don Jorge learned through Laura that the hour of their liberation was approaching, but they did not know the exact date. From that moment they lived with their ear keyed to every step on the stairs. They recognized the walk of everybody

in the jail, and in a little while they looked at each other disheartened. Only the gypsy at times gave them a little hope, for the rhythm of his steps varied. As a rule he dragged his feet sleepily; but occasionally it seemed as though he was dancing. The dance steps called up to them the image of a messenger jingling keys—and carrying armloads of guns for them.

Laura had managed to slip a revolver between the bars. Don Jorge wanted it. So did Warning Voice. Sometimes when Teo strolled around the patio, Warning Voice took aim at him in his imagination. But on several occasions he had felt sorry for the giant. Teo did not seem the same person since his jailing. The shock he had undergone over the fact that Cosme Vila had not released him was indescribable. The whole world had tumbled down about his ears, his whole set of values had been shattered. "And to think I would have given my life for him!" Nor could he understand why La Valenciana had not come to his rescue.

Don Jorge had noticed that Teo, removed from the contagion of the mob and without his dray, was a child. The gigantic platform of his wagon and the mob turned him into something he was not, a brute, a madman.

One of the lawyers pointed out to Don Jorge and Warning Voice that they had probably changed, too. Outside jail, it would have been inconceivable that they would have discovered a single human trait in Teo. When they heard this, they both recalled the admonitions of Mosén Francisco the day he had heard their confession, and, by association, the danger that still hung over their heads. "We are making great plans for when we are free, and who knows whether we will come out of here alive?"

The city realized that the crucial hour was at hand, for suddenly train service was halted. It seemed that a special state of alarm existed in Barcelona; several strikes had broken out, and communications had been interrupted. Those with relatives in that city were uneasy.

El Responsable realized that the deferment granted Major Martínez de Soria could not be extended. The uprising was imminent, there was no time to be lost. His habits were well known. The plan was to "shoot him in the back as he turned the corner of the Municipal Plaza, under the arcade, on his way to barracks between three and four in the afternoon." There was a stairway there that led to a roof. The assassin would drop through a skylight into a garret where a friend of Blasco's, a bootblack, lived.

Future had been chosen for the work. El Cojo was considered too impulsive. A clean shot in the back of the neck was called for, like that the Assault Guards had used on Calvo Sotelo.

It could be assumed that Lieutenant Romá and the other two would vacillate for a moment, and that their first impulse would be to succor the major when they saw him fall. Those seconds would be enough for Future—who, besides, would be disguised—to rush into the hallway and lock the door. Future said to Blasco: "Tell your pal the bootblack to have a bottle of rum waiting for me."

El Responsable's daughter asked him: "Are you sure your hand won't shake? When all's said and done, the major is a man."

Future shook his head. "If it was his daughter, I couldn't. But to hell with him."

Doubts had arisen with regard to Mosén Alberto. In any case, he could be attended to later. The business on hand was the major, in view of the fact that the trains had stopped running, and news was expected every minute.

But, in spite of everything, Future spent three days disguised, with beard and mustache, on the stairway on the corner of the Municipal Plaza without catching a glimpse of the major.

The major had not forgotten El Rubio's warning. The disappearance of Ideal, Blasco, and the others led him to assume that the period of vigilance was over; the last time he had gone out was the day he received the telegram. On his return home he decided to stay in the house until the morning of the 19th, with a machine gun within reach.

El Cojo was in a frenzy. "We're getting just what we deserve for waiting so long."

El Responsable was in a cold fury. Ideal suggested assaulting the house. "They'd mow us down," the leader pointed out.

Cosme Vila had given up his plan. He assumed that the major would have a substitute who had been completely briefed, and nothing annoyed the Communist leader so much as an act that made enemies and effected nothing else. His one concern was to learn the exact date, the date of the uprising. He discussed the matter with Julio, but neither of them could hit upon a clue. Julio was inclined to think it would be the 1st of August; Cosme Vila thought it would be sooner. Dr. Relken before leaving said to them: "Gerona in itself is of slight importance. In the long run, as Barcelona goes, so goes Gerona."

El Responsable, in view of the turn things were taking, altered his plans. He ordered Future to hide in an outside room rented from an old woman in a flat across the street from the major's apartment. From this room they could watch the stair door. Ideal and Santi took turns watching; the minute the major showed himself, Future would go after him and trust to luck.

The major imagined, more or less, that this was what they would be doing, and he lived anxious hours, as did everybody. Unbeknown to his wife, Professor Civil had come to offer to take up arms. It was the first thing he had hidden from her since the Cuban war! And he felt the gnawing of remorse. Notary Noguer, however, had said to him: "We appreciate it deeply, professor. For a person like you to have made up his mind to join us proves to us that we are doing our duty. But possibly we won't need so many men. In any case, you be ready; if we need you, we'll let you know."

The professor felt a little humiliated. He supposed they did not want him because of his age. He, like Matías Alvear, heard the Cathedral bell chime four, five. There were moments when he asked himself: "Have I caught the fever from that Mateo?" For the professor's pronouncements against the use of violence had been as frequent as his commendation of the concept of a legally constituted government and similar ideas. These concepts had provoked Mateo to laughter; his invariable answer was that it was stupid and suicidal to make the future of the country hang on a juridical abstraction.

And despite all this, Professor Civil had made up his mind. He reached his decision the day he saw Vasiliev parading between a double line of women in front of the cooperative. He seemed to discern in the Russian's eyes an irony beyond words. "Spanish women!" Professor Civil burst out. He thought of his wife. Ignacio pointed out to him that his remark was worthy of Mateo. Moreover, Ignacio had been noticing that many people, without realizing it, were employing the language of the Falange. Prieto himself in his speeches talked about "national concepts," "spiritual values," "historic adventures." The assistant manager alluded to "the inalienable birthright of the race."

But Professor Civil realized that, as far as he was concerned, the explanation was simpler. He had caught the fever not from Mateo, but from his son Benito. He had renounced his earlier ideas because of him. The professor loved his children too much not to find grounds to justify their follies—and even follow them. His mental clarity and his command of theoretical concepts collapsed in the face of his family feelings. All his life he had realized this was true on occasions of minor importance; now a major issue was involved. As he himself put it: "If one of my grandsons, with his top in his hand, were to ask me to forgive the Jews, I do believe I would."

The conclusion Ignacio drew from all this was that the prevailing atmosphere had addled people's brains. A great transformation was taking place. It could be seen even in people's faces. Tower of Babel's nose was sharper than before, with a hint of cruelty about the tip; Carmen Elgazu was being swallowed up in the circles under her eyes, which gave her a dramatic air. Marta's bangs had become shorter, and her face was now all eyes. Calm, determined, black eyes of compelling intenseness, which gazed with all their youthful ardor upon Ignacio, César, Pilar, all of them, Major Martínez de Soria, Padilla and Rodríguez, the city. And at times, without her mentioning it, at the balcony behind which Ideal and Santi were looking after Future as though he was an opera star on the eve of his debut.

On the 17th a tocsin sounded its warning: several garrisons in Africa had revolted. Major Martínez de Soria was nonplussed, for the date that had been set was the 19th. He assumed that fear that the government might take measures in that zone, which was considered vital, had forced the leaders to push the program for the peninsula forward by forty-eight hours.

But he had no definite information. The name of General Franco was frequently mentioned. This name reassured the major, for he knew the prestige of the general among the troops in Morocco. The corps on everyone's lips, was, however, the Foreign Legion. "In that case, it's Lieutenant-Colonel Yagüe," the major pointed out.

It was impossible to get the facts of the situation. "How can it be Franco, when he's in the Canary Islands?" Colonel Muñoz had objected. The colonel claimed to know who the leaders were, and he was certain that Sanjurjo had been in Spain for some time, and that the guiding spirit of the whole movement was General Mola.

It was not until the following day, the 18th, that the radio reports began to grow less confused. The rumors about Africa were true, and not only the Foreign Legion was involved, but all the Moroccan troops and all the garrisons: Melilla, Ceuta, Tetuán, Larache. At the bank they worked only a half day on Saturday, and the assistant manager sat at home glued to his short-wave radio. The brother of the Christian Doctrine sat beside him. The radio exploded into cries of "*¡Viva España!*" The Caid had assembled the warriors of Beni-Urriaguel on the plains of Axdir and had said to them: "For the glory of God, for the strength and power that reside in Him! To the glorious hero, so fortunate of hand, soul, and heart, to General Franco! May the divine blessing be upon you and those who fight with you in the good cause. We will not return from Spain until each and every one enjoys your peace. Because God helps His servant as long as the servant helps his brother. You will see that our heroic men are not afraid to die!"

Julio was carefully following events, and it seemed clear to him that the plan of those who were beginning to be called "rebels" would be to use Moroccan troops. "Divine blessing," he repeated sarcastically. "The same old story. Mohammedans defending Catholicism." What was not clear to him was how they were going to transport the troops to the peninsula, for Julio was convinced that the navy would remain loyal to the government and would blockade the Strait of Gibraltar.

"Maybe they'll transport them by air," suggested Officer Sánchez.

"I don't know where they're going to get the planes."

The last news bulletin stated that the government was in complete control of the situation. This set off an explosion of happiness among all who opposed the uprising. Casal and David and Olga did not leave UGT headquarters, where the radio was on all the time. The Costas had received a telephone call from their wives in Pals. "What's happening? What's happening? Come back here with us. We're frightened." The Costas promised to come home, but they had not the faintest intention of going. The uprising had awakened all their old democratic fervor. They forgot about the strike, about the illegal closing down of the Rightist centers. They were giving serious thought once more to the problem of Catalonia. Architect Ribas was right. That would spell the end of Catalonia. This was the anxious word that was spreading through the city. "We'd see the Moors invading Catalonia!"

Someone claimed to have heard that the idea was to transfer the population of Catalonia en masse. Fortunately the news about Africa was encouraging. "And if they can't make a go of it in Africa, they won't dare to try it anywhere else!"

When one of the jail guards indignantly told of the uprising against the Republic, Warning Voice smiled and remarked: "You call that a republic? It's a bunch of gangsters."

Major Martínez de Soria kept cool. He understood that the movement had been victorious in Africa, as in the Canary Islands. This was the first phase. The next day, the 19th, would be the day of decision for the peninsula.

What the major was afraid of was that during the night the general and Julio might order the city occupied, with the Assault Guards as the hard core. It did not occur to him that they would dare to give arms to the people.

He lay down, without taking off his uniform, to catch a few winks of sleep. He was up frequently and looking out of the window. Seeing everything quiet and the streets still unoccupied, he said to his wife: "It doesn't seem possible they could be so naïve! I can't figure out how they can't see that today is the day."

Day was beginning to break. Major Martínez de Soria leaped out of bed. The moment had come! His wife got up too and, taking advantage of the fact that the major had left the room, knelt before the crucifix. He surprised her in this attitude, but said nothing. He walked over to her and kissed her hair. Marta was dressing in her room. She had a first-aid kit on her night table marked with the initials: CAFÉ.

Marta had told her father that the anarchists were keeping watch on him from one of the balconies across the way, and for that reason the major had ordered Lieutenant Delgado to come for him with a car. In this way Future, or whoever they were, would not have time to carry out their plan.

El Rubio arrived at six fifteen. At six seventeen, three trusted soldiers. The four were to remain in the apartment with the major's wife.

At six twenty a car rolled quietly up and stopped at the door. "There they are." The major and Marta ran down the stairs. The door of the car opened, and they slipped in. "*¡Viva España!*" Lieutenant Delgado was at the wheel, and he stepped on the accelerator. The major asked him: "Is everyone at his post?"

"Everyone, major."

On the way to the barracks, men could be seen hugging the walls or walking down the middle of the streets. These were the volunteers, the ones who had taken an oath to support the uprising.

An hour later the city was in the hands of the military. Everything had been carried out with mathematical precision. Troops, Civil Guards, civilians.

The general, in pajamas, was pacing his room, horrified. Lieutenant Romá, Benito Civil, and a young chap from CEDA sat there, gun in hand, watching him. The lad from CEDA had asked one of the general's daughters for a cup of coffee. Colonel Muñoz was locked in his office, together with Major Campos, in the custody of a captain, Padilla, and Don Jorge's son. The Commissioner was under house arrest, as were Cosme Vila, El Responsable, and Casal. The only ones who had not allowed themselves to be taken by surprise were Julio and Dr. Relken. Dr. Relken had left for Barcelona by car the evening before. Julio was not at his home. When Rodríguez, under the orders of a lieutenant, knocked at the door, Doña Amparo appeared, with her eyes starting from her head, and asked: "What do you want? He's not here; he's not here." They searched the apartment but did not find him. Doña Amparo refused to give any information concerning his whereabouts.

"We'll wait for him," said the lieutenant, as he put a record on the phonograph.

As the city came awake, it began to realize what was happening. It was Sunday. Many people, coming out of their houses with prayer books under their arms, shrank back for a moment. Armed men! When they recognized the persons carrying arms, they felt their hearts start throbbing with mixed emotions. The die was now cast! Some openly rejoiced; others considered it a dastardly business. More than a dozen, looking at the civilian volunteers, said to themselves: "I ought to be doing the same thing."

In the other camp the reaction was wordless and of an inner violence that was beyond words. The strikers went into the streets, and the hatred of centuries was concentrated in their glances. But orders were drastic. Break it up! No gatherings of more than four persons. The moment anyone showed signs of resisting, the rifle butts prepared to swing into action. There was a hint of reluctance about some of the soldiers, but the officers kept a close watch near by. The civilian volunteers carried out their assignment with an alacrity that warmed the major's heart.

Astride his horse, the major proclaimed martial law. The memory of the Chief of Staff who fell in October in the same posture crossed his mind fora second.

Warning Voice, Don Jorge, and the other landowners had been released from prison. Teo, as he saw them leave, clenched his fist, even though he assumed that their sentence was up. "Tell Cosme Vila he is a s—!" All Warning Voice's humanitarian sentiments had disappeared.

Octavio, Haro, and Rosselló, too, were set free. They emerged as pale as from a sickbed. When they saw the faces of two Civil Guards at their cell door at that hour of the morning, they had looked at each other uneasily. At the sound of "*¡Viva España!*" they leaped to their feet. And when a rifle was held out to each of them, they understood. They emerged shouting, and when they got into the street, looked up at the cloudless sky, and then spied Mateo, who was waiting for them with a smile on his face. "*¡Arriba España!*" he shouted.

The three Falangists threw their arms around him "*¡Arriba!*" they answered.

Mateo said to them: "Your post is at the Military Hospital. Hop to it. Report to Sergeant Hurtado."

Mateo had set out at six fifteen. Pedro, who got up late on Sundays, when he saw him come into the dining room and start for the door, was frightened at the thought that he might be planning suicide like his father. "Where are you going?" he asked.

Mateo answered: "To defend Spain."

Pedro sat up in bed. He did not understand what he meant. He thought Mateo had lost his mind.

"The news about Africa is true," Mateo informed him. "It's our turn today."

Pedro quickly took it in, and he glared at Mateo with sudden anger. Mateo went over to him resolutely. "I'm very grateful for what you have done. And don't forget that there are ten thousand Falangists in Spain who are ready to do the same for you whenever you need us."

He gave no further explanation. He realized that it would be impossible for him to convince Pedro. He went out in the street, and he did not stop to see either his father or Pilar. He went straight to the barracks. But he walked through the Rambla and his eyes went instinctively to the Alvears' balcony.

He had not yet met the two masons and the electrician, who were on guard duty at the station.

Toward noon the streets had filled with spectators. The truth of the matter was that the forces were few, considering the size of the city. There were sections where nobody would have thought the matter was serious. And the spirit of criticism began to manifest itself, for there were persons like the assistant manager who looked as out of place with a rifle as a cat with a flag. Don Jorge, however, carried his with complete ease, as did Don Pedro Oriol.

There was talk of the uprising in Barcelona, in Madrid, everywhere. Some said it had triumphed everywhere. On the contrary, news came of street fighting in Barcelona. The revolt of certain garrisons, like that of Zaragoza, had left the general confounded. "How could it have happened? Cabanellas is in Zaragoza, and he's as good a republican as I am!"

The boy from CEDA who was guarding him shrugged his shoulders ironically. "That's the way it goes, general. Maybe Cabanellas didn't wear an apron."

Lieutenant Romá gave the boy a good dressing down. His military code could not tolerate making fun of the garrison commander. Nothing would have given him greater pleasure than to shoot the general, but he was not going to stand by and see him humiliated.

In front of union headquarters there was a heavy guard. No one was allowed to go in. This prevented gatherings of any sort. The followers of Cosme Vila, El Responsable, Casal, and the members of Izquierda Republicana and Estat Català talked to one another furtively on street corners or at their homes. "This is intolerable. What can we do?"

Some said: "I've got arms. I've got a rifle. I've got a pistol." But how were they to organize? When they learned that their several leaders were under arrest, their fury grew. "We've got to do something." Professor Morales was afraid they would shoot Cosme Vila. Olga was convinced that the same thing would happen to Casal. "We've got to do something!" But, few though they were, machine guns had been set up at strategic points, and a couple of cannon. All had the sensation that they had been blind idiots. "Why, they were telling us themselves what they were going to do!"

In the face of the common enemy, a sense of solidarity was springing up among the members of all these groups. Many of them moved about the city, taking a deliberately provocative attitude. They would stop in front of one of the places being guarded by boys of CEDA and the Falange, and pull out a cigarette case.

Rosselló and Don Santiago Estrada's older son would listen to no explanations, and would come toward them with rifles cocked. In front of the city slaughterhouse Mateo stopped several of them and ordered them to put up their hands. He proceeded to search them. He found a strange protuberance on one of them. It was his pipe. The worker smiled slyly. On another he found a revolver. He arrested him, and was leading him away when a second lieutenant came over. "What's going on here? Don't do anything without consulting me." And it was the lieutenant who led the prisoner away.

Many families had forbidden their children to leave the house. Some refused even to let them attend Mass. A large number of people felt that the uprising was justified; but, on the one hand, ignorance of the military's real intentions, and, on the other, fear that the whole thing might be a failure, with the terrible reprisals this would occasion, kept everyone plunged in torturing anxiety.

Matías Alvear had forbidden his children to go out. It was only toward eleven, when he became convinced that there was really nothing to fear in the streets, that he yielded to Ignacio's and Pilar's pleas and allowed them to go out to take a look around, with orders not to separate. Ignacio wanted to see what the city looked like, with the rebels in action—and Marta. Pilar wanted to see Marta with her first-aid kit, and, above all, Mateo. The four hours of waiting, from seven to eleven, had seemed interminable. She had been keeping an eye all that time on the Rambla from the balcony window. She had seen many soldiers, the notary Noguer, and Warning Voice, but not Mateo. When she and Ignacio went out, they crossed street after street, but all in vain. They did not see either Marta or Mateo, until finally, in front of the slaughterhouse, they saw Mateo.

Pilar could hardly breathe. There stood her sweetheart in his blue shirt with the arrows embroidered on the front, armed with a rifle. Confinement had made him pale; his long hair was badly in need of scissors. Mateo did not see her. It was Padilla who said to him: "There comes a suspicious-looking character."

Mateo whirled around. When he saw Pilar, his first instinct was to go toward her. But the second lieutenant was watching him. The girl saw Mateo look toward her without moving from his post and bow his head, and she realized that that was the most he was allowed to do. She clenched her teeth, and it was all she could do to keep from stamping her foot with rage. She happened to notice just then that not more than five yards from where she was standing was a machine gun, and a group of soldiers was motioning her back. Pilar gazed at that diabolical contrivance, and it made her want to cry. She would have called out: "Mateo!" but he had already turned away, carrying out some order. The sight of his friend armed had made the strongest kind of impression on Ignacio, and all their conversations about the "dialectics of pistols" came to his mind. In 1935 Mateo had already offered his services for a projected march on Madrid from the frontier of Portugal! Now Ignacio watched him, following his every gesture. When he saw him go over to a group of men and search them, it gave him a feeling of discomfort he could not define, in spite of the fact that there was nothing of the braggart or bully in Mateo's behavior. Then, like Pilar, he turned his eyes toward the machine gun, and his distress grew. The muzzle, unbelievably narrow and thin, was pointed at the Postal Building, toward the door by which Matías Alvear entered and left every day.

Ignacio took Pilar by the arm. "Let's get out of here. When all this is over, he'll come to the house." They passed Communist headquarters. It was deserted. The sign across the balcony looked as though it had never been in use. The Cathedral chimed the hour. The light shimmered on Montjuich as if the walls sensed that they were reliving important events.

It was impossible to find Marta. Please God, nothing had happened to her! On the bridge Warning Voice was shouting: "Disperse!" Men one would never have dreamed of were carrying arms. Under the arcades several employees of the bank were prophesying in football language the defeat of the military.

Suddenly Ignacio caught sight of the major. He was driving slowly past in a car with Lieutenant Delgado. The major waved at him and Pilar through the open window. Pilar, without stopping to think what she was doing, raised her hand to her lips and blew him a kiss. She was very fond of Marta's father, whom she considered a brave man. And the major still offered her cocktails when no one was looking.

Ignacio merely bowed.

The sight of the major made a great change in Pilar. She thought she, too, should have been out with a first-aid kit. She realized it now. What if the Communists began sniping from the windows? There must be very few nurses. To be sure, she did not know how to give injections.... She would have given anything to meet Marta and ask her what she should do. Ignacio said to her: "Come on, let's get home. They're probably worried about us." The assistant manager was coming along the Rambla, and he managed to get to Ignacio. He was in despair. It had seemed to him that the most important thing to do was to go to the Lodge on the Calle del Pavo and uncover everything that went on there, and the major had refused. A lieutenant came up and said: "That's enough conversation."

Ignacio and Pilar went upstairs. The table was set, and Don Emilio Santos was seated in the dining room. He got up when he saw them. He had been unable to endure his loneliness, there in his flat, with the maid, who was so nervous that she had broken a plate and a cup at breakfast. He'd stay and have lunch with them. "Have you seen Mateo?" he inquired.

"Yes. He's in front of the slaughterhouse."

Don Emilio Santos had been all over the city without finding him. "He might have come to see me!" he complained.

"If he didn't," Ignacio answered, "it's because he had orders not to. There's a second lieutenant in command who doesn't let them call their soul their own."

Don Emilio Santos had been listening to different radio stations. Bitter fighting was going on in many cities. "What a lot of people are dying at this very minute!" In several provinces the uprising seemed to have been a failure. The government stations were issuing reports that boded ill for the rebels. The authorities had not hesitated to give arms to the people. Most of the coast of the Mediterranean apparently had proclaimed its loyalty to the government.

Don Emilio's words turned the rice into a cold, unpalatable dish. Everyone felt a lump come into his throat. The coast! That meant Cartagena.... But Don Emilio Santos was sure it was a lie. Ignacio was thinking of Alicante, too, where José Antonio was being held. "Probably when the thing started they set him free." What a lot of people were dying at this very minute! The words kept throbbing in their brains, as the forks rose slowly to their lips. Carmen Elgazu was thinking: "We must light the candle again." Instead of lighting it to St. Ignatius, however, for some reason she could not explain to herself it seemed more fitting to light it to St. Francis of Assisi.

Don Emilio Santos said: "To St. Ignatius, to St. Ignatius, who was a soldier."

"St. Ignatius a soldier?" asked Pilar in surprise.

Carmen Elgazu yielded to the guest's wishes. Matías Alvear was nervous. He was one of those who realized most clearly the issues at stake. He knew that no matter what the outcome, events would continue on their mad course. He thought of his relatives, his brother Santiago in Madrid, his nephew José. His brother in Burgos would probably be a prisoner of the military. The Falange was powerful all over Castile, even though the peasants—What would the military do with his brother, the head of the UGT in Burgos? In Gerona the word was that Casal was going to be shot. And what if the miners of Asturias came down to attack Castile?

Carmen Elgazu asked him if he had heard anything about the north. Don Emilio knew nothing. "There's no word. The north is Catholic. It's probably with the military. But there's no word."

César listened to first one and then another without uttering a word. He had been deeply stirred by the address of the Caid, which Don Emilio Santos, too, had heard. "May the divine blessing be upon you.... God helps His servant as long as the servant helps his brother." What did these last words mean? It was the vague Moslem poetry. The Caid had also said: "You will see that our heroic men are not afraid to die!"

"Nor I," thought César. Then he repented of his vanity. And yet it was true. Or rather he longed to die. He did not understand one word of what was taking place. He did not know whether the severity of the major's glance was commendable; whether the figures given by Calvo Sotelo were accurate; whether one thing justified the other. What was evident was that Spain had not had charity, and that someone must give his life to expiate this evil. He offered his. He was not Cosme Vila, nor a soldier, nor did he belong to the Falange. He was a seminarian; that is to say, he represented the Church, with its eternal power to renew itself; but he also represented the sinner. He had gone to Mass at half past six that morning, and his return had coincided with the calling out of the troops. He was one of the few citizens who heard the first proclamation of a state of martial law. At Mass it had seemed to him that at the moment of the Elevation, Mosén Francisco had gazed with infinite supplication upon the consecrated Host. As though he knew that many men would perish in that day. As Don Emilio Santos was talking, César was thinking of Mosén Francisco. He was sure that dying would not matter to Mosén Francisco, either.

"What ails you, son? Why don't you eat?" Carmen Elgazu said to César.

The city was bathed in a flood of sunshine.

EIGHTY-SIX

HOUR by hour the news grew more alarming. The Movement was bogged down in many places. The Basque country was remaining loyal to the government. Major Martínez de Soria was baffled. San Sebastián had been considered absolutely certain. Nationalism had prevailed over every other consideration among the Basques.

Savage fighting was going on in Madrid. Valencia was loyal. In Barcelona, General Aranguren of the Civil Guard had placed himself at the orders of the government. This was another blow for the major. Captain Roberto, of the Civil Guard of Gerona, and Padilla and Rodríguez were almost crying with rage. "The Civil Guard backing those filthy scoundrels! It can't be." And yet it was, and very possibly this was going to tip the balance in that city in favor of the government, and carry with it all Catalonia, the frontier, the seaports.

The only good news continued to be that arriving from Africa, Castile, Navarre, Oviedo—of all places!—and a few scattered spots in the south, Cádiz, Granada. In Seville, General Oueipo de Llano was using to the best advantage the men he had and the reinforcements arriving from Morocco by some mysterious route.

Most of the air bases having planes were in the hands of the government. The navy, too, as Julio had predicted. The destroyer *Churruca*, after landing a division of legionnaires in Cádiz, had headed for a government port.

Major Martínez de Soria said: "Madrid was always considered hopeless, and the plans from the first moment were to send four columns against the capital, two from the north and two from the south. But the defection of the Basque country changes everything!"

It became known that in Castile volunteers by the hundred were flocking to the Falange, and that in Navarre the Carlists were responding en masse to General Mola's appeal. "There are families where grandfather, father, and all the sons, wearing the red beret, report for duty," Don Emilio Santos stated.

"The Navarrese are half Basques," said Carmen Elgazu.

"Don't mention the Basques to me," Pilar grumbled. But in other places "the people" had stormed into the street with utter disregard of danger.

Late that night came the final, the fatal news that put an end to all hope: the forces that had revolted in Barcelona had surrendered. General Goded himself—General Goded!—had appealed over the radio to avoid unnecessary bloodshed. This implied that the rest of the garrisons of Catalonia should follow his example.

Surrender! Major Martínez de Soria blenched. Second Lieutenant Romá and the other two lieutenants riveted a gaze of superhuman intensity upon him. Lieutenant Martín, who had been released, thought: "Surrender? Never." Many of the volunteers on patrol duty in the streets had not heard a single word of what had happened, and were under the impression that everything was going according to schedule.

Major Martínez de Soria weighed the possibilities of holding out. It was his belief that half the city was behind him. He had asked for flowers for the grave of the major killed in October, and all day long there had been a procession of people carrying wreaths to the cemetery. He held stout buildings, the city walls, Montjuich.... He thought of the War of Independence. On the pinnacle of the monument a lion roared.

But then he realized that resistance would be madness. It had always been held a foregone conclusion that the labor unions in Barcelona could organize an army of eighty thousand men in a few hours. These, supported by the Civil Guard, spelled certain defeat. They would descend on Gerona with an impetus not to be withstood. Not to mention the peasants of the province. Nor the internal enemies, most of them armed.

It was impossible to resist. Gerona was lost. The major calculated that Castile, Navarre, Galicia—apparently the movement had triumphed in Galicia—Seville, and Africa would provide vantage points from which to organize the reconquest of the rest of Spain. These regions and some miracle... But Gerona was lost, and there was no choice but to capitulate. The strikers and other people who were talking about "Loyalists" and "Rebels"—"Loyal to whom?" the major asked. "To Casares Quiroga or Vasiliev?"—were already showing signs of restlessness, as though getting ready to fall upon their prey.

Major Martínez de Soria, who was at the barracks, asked for cognac. He thought of his wife, of the plea he had read in her eyes. He thought of Marta, with her first-aid kit waiting at the Military Hospital for the wounded who fortunately were not arriving. He thought of the two hundred and thirty-five civilians he had dragged into the venture with him. And of the other two hundred, like Professor Civil, whose services had not been utilized, but whose names were on the lists.

The major knew that the time had come for him to die. He could take a car and try to make it to the border. The mere thought made his flesh crawl with self-contempt. He would go on shouting: "*¡Viva España!*" until lead silenced his heart. It was better to die this way than at the hands of El Cojo a few days earlier. At least, now he had sowed the seed. And he would be united with his son. Where was his son? Mateo would say: "Above the stars." The major smiled. The other, Fernando, was in Valladolid, and Valladolid was Spain.

Barcelona has surrendered, Barcelona has surrendered! The shouts seemed to come from the very walls. The major stood up. The first thing to do was to order the volunteers to retire, telling them that the movement had failed and that they were free to go to their homes or do whatever they thought best. "They must be warned that the reprisals will probably be terrible." In the end the Movement would triumph, but for the moment there was no hope for Gerona. The soldiers should be ordered back to barracks. The officers should follow his example, and he planned to hand himself over to the authorities. And let each of them know how to die with honor, like gentlemen and officers of the Spanish Army!

It was a hot night. It seemed that all the mysteries of the ancient city had come to life. A shower of shooting stars fell over the Cathedral, and Professor Civil, looking at them, told his wife that this foreboded war. Hollow steps echoed over the cobblestones of empty streets. Rodríguez, who was on patrol duty, told his comrades that these were the footsteps of the troops that fought against Napoleon. "In those days, even the women took up arms. Now there's only one, Marta."

"If there's a war," Rosselló answered, "you'll see Martas by the dozen."

Those guarding the railroad could hear the murmur of the roiled waters of the Ter. From the depths of the cistern in Pilón's house strange birds flew out, croaking. Beyond the city walls the Stations of the Cross, painted white, ascended the hill under the kiss of the moon. It was a wondrous city where one would have said love should rule. Beneath its arches psalm after psalm could be chanted in an ineffable litany.

The orders that began to circulate, however, recalled rather the *Dies Irae*. Surrender, we have failed; the reprisals will be horrible. In less than an hour the two hundred and thirty-five volunteers had learned the truth. How was it possible? Now they began to understand the sarcastic smiles they had been noticing, the covert remarks. Blasco had yelled out impudently: "You'll all be bald tomorrow." Under the shower of stars the volunteers looked at one another, their faces revealing utter dismay. The differences of age made the situation even more poignant. Surrender! Each man for himself now! Goded had surrendered. What about Major Martínez de Soria?

"It's Major Martínez de Soria who has issued the order."

"The farce is over," a soldier spoke up.

At this point the electrician, the last of the Falange volunteers, showed the stuff he was made of. Shifting his rifle to his left hand, he went up to the soldier, snatched the cap off his head, and struck him across the face with it, as though it were a gauntlet. There was a terrible fight, the first since martial law had been declared. The soldier was foaming at the mouth. "We'll meet again, big boy."

Mateo came over. He had been introduced to the electrician that afternoon. "Good for you!" he said to him. And then to the soldier. "What do you call a farce? The capitulation of Spain?"

The soldier, with a knowing smile, was walking off. One of the officers ordered him to stand at attention and slapped him across the face with all his strength.

Each man was making his plans. Some thought nothing would happen to them, and they went off home, intending to remain there. Others were seized by the wildest fear and were thinking of the most unbelievable places in which to hide. Still others said stoically: "It's useless. They'll find us wherever we go." Someone timidly remarked that the military had been overhasty and deserved no thanks for the mess it had got others into.

Orders were: "Return all arms to barracks." Some obeyed, others held on to theirs. All were thinking about their families and how they would be received when they returned vanquished, and the fear that would come over them. Voices of serene counsel made themselves heard: "What difference does it make? We've done our duty. *¡Viva España! ¡Arriba España!*" Eyes grew damp at the sound of "*¡Viva España!*"

Day was dawning when the streets began to empty. The machine gun in front of the Postal Building had disappeared, as had the cannon. The only people left were the Civil Guards, some soldiers, a few officers, and the members of the Falange. The other men had left.

Warning Voice was trembling from head to foot when he reached home and told Laura what had happened. "I've got to get away! I've got to get away!" He realized that there would be no salvation for him. He thought of the Costas. "You must get word to your brothers immediately."

Laura was crying. "What do you want them to do? You know they were furious about the uprising. Besides, I don't know if they'd be able to do anything. Oh, God, what are we going to do?"

There were two taps on the bedroom door. It was the maid, Dolores. "Sir, I know what has happened. I was thinking about you all day yesterday. Let's take the car and go to my village. You know how much we all love you there. We'll all protect you, every one of us."

Her words fell on Warning Voice's ears like a message from heaven. "Pack the suitcases. Put this in, put that in..."

Noguer the notary went up to see Mosén Alberto, who had not gone to bed that night. The notary said to him: "We have to get across the border without a moment's delay. We'll have to go as far as we can by car and then hire a guide. You're coming with us."

Mosén Alberto hesitated. He said he could take no steps without consulting the Bishop first. "Then go to the palace and be at my house before eight. The major is not going to send word to the authorities until the middle of the morning. There's not a minute to lose."

Don Pedro Oriol was unwilling to leave his apartment. "I'm tired. Besides, what can they do to me? I suppose there are other victims they will be more interested in."

Mateo called together all the Falangists and said to them: "Comrades, you know that the Movement has not failed in Gerona. Anyone who says the contrary lies. We have triumphed here—and without opposition. Our work has been fruitful. Now we must withdraw, because there has been treachery in Barcelona. But it doesn't matter. Perhaps we shall all die, but Spain will be saved. If only a single redoubt had remained to us, that would have been enough, and there are not only redoubts, but whole provinces. May God watch over us! *¡Arriba España!*"

All of them surrounded him with wild enthusiasm. "You, at least, find yourself some safe place," Rosselló said to him.

"I'm going to see my father," Mateo answered. "We may meet again. I give you my word of honor that I will do whatever I think best for the service of Spain. If I could give my life to save José Antonio's, or that of any one of you, I would."

EIGHTY-SEVEN

AT exactly nine o'clock the major ran up the white flag over the barracks and sent a note to the general stating that he was surrendering with all his men and equipment "to avoid bloodshed." The note concluded: "I believe that I have served Spain. A thousand and one times I would do what I have done."

This was the signal. All who had been guarding the prisoners withdrew to the barracks and then to their homes. The general went out in the street, and there he met Colonel Muñoz, who had gone out to look for him. Both made their way to police headquarters. The Commissioner was in his place, mopping his forehead. Officer Antonio Sánchez, too. Julio had not arrived yet. "The first thing to do," said the general, "is to arrest these traitors. Let's go to the barracks."

The Commissioner suggested the advisability of waiting a few minutes. He had notified all the heads of the unions and political parties that had remained faithful to the government of the Republic, and courtesy seemed to demand that they should form part of the delegation to the barracks. "We must not forget that it was the people who carried the day in Barcelona and many other places."

The general was of the opinion that this was strictly a military and police affair, and Colonel Muñoz shared his view. "We'll go, you in your capacity as Commissioner, and Julio as Chief of Police. What's become of Julio?" A squad of Assault Guards would accompany them.

The Commissioner reluctantly yielded. Cosme Vila, El Responsable, and Casal would be furious when they learned about it. Possibly they were still being held. "One of them may even have been shot."

They set out on foot, a compact group that aroused breathless expectation as it walked down the Rambla. People were timidly beginning to appear on the streets. When they recognized the general and his party, all understood what had happened. Surrender, then, was a fact. "They're on their way to the barracks to arrest Major Martínez de Soria."

The delegation crossed the Piedra Bridge. A strange silence hung over that section of the city. They followed the avenue running parallel to the river. In the distance, across from the barracks, dark blotches could be discerned. There seemed to be some kind of disturbance going on. As they approached, they heard shouts and noises. "What's happening?" They had assumed they would find the barracks silent as a tomb, with the officers lined up to await their arrival. Instead, there was evidence of great agitation. Suddenly it flashed across the general's mind that the note the major had sent might be a trap, that the officers might be waiting to fire on them point-blank. Small in the distance, the white flag fluttered. And the shouting continued. The general ordered several of the Assault Guards to advance and find out what was happening. They returned in a few moments with news that the people gathered there were members of the Communist Party and the CNT-FAI. As soon as they had seen the white flag go up, they had rushed there to demand justice. The general ripped out a string of oaths. "Are there a lot of them?"

"There are more arriving every minute. If you don't hurry up, they'll storm the barracks."

The delegation moved forward, and when they came within five hundred yards of the building, they were greeted by a sight that strained their credulity. Soldiers began to pour out of the barracks, throwing their caps in the air and stamping on them. "Discharged! Discharged!" they shouted. They tore off their jackets, and some of the civilians, laughing, gave them their vests, shirts, or caps, putting on instead the discarded military garments. Some women took off their blouses and put them on the soldiers' heads like shawls.

"Who has ordered them discharged?" roared the general in baffled exasperation.

Nobody answered. When the soldiers caught sight of him, some of them started to run; others made no move. Someone suddenly shouted: "Major Campos!"

Future was standing near by, and he remarked in a loud voice: "We're not going to keep on having an army, are we?"

Colonel Muñoz pointed out to the general the urgency of putting under arrest the officers who had revolted. Everything else could be straightened out later. "Make way, make way!" The growing crowd was enormous. The news of the surrender had by this time spread all over the city. "And where is Major Campos?"

At that moment the major appeared in the barracks door, flanked by two sergeants who had kept to their houses during the uprising. He explained to the general that when he had seen the mob gathering outside the barracks, he had feared the worst. The only feasible plan that had occurred to him to prevent the soldiers' lynching the officers was to discharge them. "The order for them to return to duty can be issued at any moment," he added.

His words infuriated the general, who had to admit to himself that what the major said made sense. He strode into the barracks. "Where are those morons?"

"In the officers' lounge."

They walked over to it, and the general himself threw open the door.

Major Martínez de Soria was standing in the middle of the group that had supported the revolt. Some twenty of them. The general looked them over one by one, with a special pause for Second Lieutenant Romá, who had kept him shut up in his room in his pajamas for four hours. The officers were standing, their arms at their sides. Not one of them stepped forward or saluted the general. Their intention was clear. The general could not utter one word; he was speechless with indignation. He went over to Major Martínez de Soria and, first making an obscene gesture, with one jerk stripped off his star. Then he did the same to the others, with staccato rhythm and lightning speed, always leaving them their decorations. Meanwhile Colonel Muñoz was disarming them. As he took the major's sword, he said: "I am sorry...." After handing over his sword, the major took off his white gloves, too, and laid them on the table beside the bottle of cognac.

The general addressed them briefly, informing them that they were charged with armed revolt against the government to which they had sworn allegiance, and that they would be tried by a summary court martial. Major Martínez de Soria pointed out that they had sworn allegiance to Spain, not to a government that was bringing about its ruin. The general replied that it was not the moment to quibble about words.

"Where are they to be held?" asked Colonel Muñoz.

"In—in the guardhouse. Any guardhouse!" the general answered.

Major Campos approached the general to suggest that the crowd gathered outside would undoubtedly prefer to see them held in a civilian prison, in the city jail. "Don't forget, general, that it was the people that—"

"To hell with the people!" The general was sick and tired of the word. Unfortunately, the only guardhouse in a suitable state was the one at the infantry barracks. "We'll have to take them there at once. Get going!"

Major Martínez de Soria blenched. He had heard the noise of the mob outside, and he knew only Major Campos and fear of the bullets had held back that landslide. And to go out now, and cross the city on foot! He knew the general too well to suppose that he was acting in bad faith. But he had a reckless streak in him; he acted by instinct.

"General," said the major, "my daughter is here in the office. I would appreciate it if you would see that she is escorted home."

The general blinked at him. "Your daughter? What is your daughter doing here?"

The major paused for a moment. "Well—there she is."

Colonel Muñoz spoke up: "Don't worry. She will be escorted home."

The Assault Guards surrounded the prisoners. The general, Colonel Muñoz, and the Commissioner came out first, the others following. It seemed to Major Campos a very unwise move, but he knew that the general was completely self-assured and firmly believed that he could cow the crowd with a shout.

When the figure of Major Martínez de Soria appeared in the doorway of the barracks, a blood-curdling howl burst from the mob. "Murderers, murderers!" For the first time Communists and anarchists were really joined without distinction. The Socialists were fewer, but there were some. And soldiers, wearing berets or women's blouses on their heads. And the Murcians in the front row. The whole colony of Murcians was there, with a few of the children. "Murderers, murderers!" Many were armed and were waving pistols. When Lieutenant Martín emerged, the intensity of the uproar doubled. "The graves of Joaquín Santaló and Jaime Arias!" They had almost forgotten them.

The lieutenant had lighted a cigarette, and one of the officers of the Assault Guard struck it out of his hand. "Don't try to show how tough you are, you damned fool."

The delegation moved off. The guard was so close that it would have been impossible to break through. Suddenly a shout came from the roof of an army truck parked near by. "Let's get arms!" The general did not quite understand, but he wheeled around. "Let's get arms!" The crowd immediately broke into two groups. One consisted of those who preferred to see Major Martínez de Soria without his star, his sword, his white gloves, his eyes and soul exhaling sorrow; Second Lieutenant Romá, assuming an attitude of Olympian indifference; Lieutenant Delgado pale as a corpse; Lieutenant Martín, and the others of those who preferred to wait for a moment when they could break through the guard and throw the officers into the river. The other group consisted of those who at the cry of "Arms!" were fired by the word, recalling those they had seen the night before in the hands of the rebels, the machine gun by the Postal Building, and the cannon. The first group followed the officers; the second stormed into the barracks.

The general realized that it was too late to do anything about it, and that the half-dozen sergeants he had left in the barracks would be powerless to hold back the avalanche. Major Martínez de Soria called out to Colonel Muñoz: "You promised to look after my daughter."

"Don't be afraid. I've taken care of that," the colonel answered.

The discharged soldiers acted as guides for those who preferred arms, leading them through the long corridors toward the depot of rifles and hand grenades. Two cannon were standing in the courtyard. Members of the People's Militia climbed on them and would have liked to touch them off. They wanted to make off with all the arms they could carry. Some of the hand grenades were too large to fit in their pockets, so they stuck them in their shirtfronts. They buried their hands in the boxes of bullets, tossing them into the air or letting them cascade through their fingers. Many put a bullet in their mouth. The cold metallic contact refreshed them. The shrewdest found themselves submachine guns and hurried out with them. Others strapped on belts with two revolvers. Pieces of flag made handkerchiefs to tie around the neck after the fashion set by El Cojo. Some tied them around their head, like pirates. "There are lots more arms at the infantry barracks," the soldiers told them. The truck parked outside was loaded with arms, and someone drove it off at breakneck pace to Communist Party headquarters.

While this had been going on, the other group had been advancing across the Piedra Bridge. The sidewalks were filled with people watching the passage of the arrested officers. "Murderers, murderers! Three thousand comrades have died in Barcelona! Two thousand in Madrid." The general was moved by those figures. The Assault Guards doubled their vigilance to make sure that none of the officers should offer an easy target for the mob.

There was an unexpected clash as they entered the Rambla. From the opposite direction came Cosme Vila, El Responsable, La Valenciana, Professor Morales, and Julio, Indian file. The first of them had just been liberated. Julio had decided to emerge from his hiding place in Dr. Rossclló's house.

"There they are," shouted the Commissioner when he saw them. The general ordered his men to advance without taking notice. But the crowd had spied it leaders and rushed forward to meet them, clenched fists high, shouting: "Long live Cosme Vila! Long live the Communist Party! Long live the CNT! Long live Russia!"

"Not a single 'Long live the Republic,'" remarked Lieutenant Romá to Lieutenant Delgado.

The latter was unable to restrain himself. "Long live Spain!" he shouted. Only a few overheard him. For the first time Colonel Muñoz looked at him menacingly. "Does it scare a colonel to hear 'Long live Spain'?" Lieutenant Delgado asked him.

Cosme Vila looked like a corpse. In twenty-four hours his eyes had become so incredibly sunken that one would have said the sentinels guarding him had been pushing them in with their fingers. Considerable hair still fringed his head, but the top was utterly bare and glistened in the sun. He was in shirt-sleeves, wearing loosely tied sandals and the broad belt his father-in-law had given him. He answered the cheers of the crowd with his fist raised in his own unique manner. Everyone could see the butt of an enormous pistol sticking out of the holster on his right hip.

El Responsable was wearing two pistols. His cap, clamped down on his head, and its aggressive visor, could not quite conceal the gray of his eyes. He was shorter than Cosme Vila, but as he walked, his feet seemed to cling closer to the ground. Cosme Vila's walk betrayed his bureaucratic origin, his bank employee background. He had worn shoes for many years. El Responsable hardly lifted his feet. And he advanced, advanced with a rhythm not to be halted. He gave the impression that he could have walked through the bodies of Major Martínez de Soria, the general, the multitude, and gone right on. He was surrounded by his followers. Santi, with a flying leap, had thrown his arms around El Responsable's neck and given him a kiss. Then he looked at the two revolvers and ran his hand caressingly over them.

"To think we can't kill them!" El Cojo said, looking at Lieutenant Martín.

La Valenciana's neckline was suitable to a festive occasion. The sight of the Murcians' children stirred her maternal instincts. "Five children, five children," she shouted, pointing to her breasts.

"Come, now, stop talking nonsense," Julio said to her.

Professor Morales was carrying a book under his arm, and his air was very dignified. He seemed the theorist of what was taking place, arriving at profound conclusions regarding mass psychology.

As for Julio, he looked glum. He liked none of all this. The sight of the arrested officers and the crowd following them told him clearly what had happened. When he had come out of hiding, his first impulse had been to go to the barracks and take charge; but he had realized that this was the moment either to win over or to lose Cosme Vila and El Responsable. And he had preferred to win them over. "If we all line up against them, nobody will have any control over them."

He was pleased that the crowd should see him with them, between its two leaders, identified with them. That was enough. Now he was free to hamstring the plans of both of them, which he imagined must be cataclysmic.

When the Commissioner saw Julio, he approached him. "Thank God," he exclaimed. The phrase seemed incongruous in that atmosphere.

La Valenciana let out of a roar of laughter. "You're a bigger fascist than Lope de Vega!"

As Vila and El Responsable came abreast of the prisoners and their escort, the two men looked at each other with a tacit understanding. The ever-present Assault Guards! Not to let the people take justice into their own hands in this business of the military! El Cojo was right.

Colonel Muñoz spoke to Cosme Vila. "I want you to distract these people's attention. The officers have to receive an official trial. That is law the world over."

Cosme Vila stared back at the colonel. Julio upheld the same thesis as Colonel Muñoz—even Professor Morales agreed with it. "It's law the world over." It was a psychological victory for the colonel. Cosme Vila thought how the news would look in the press of the whole world.

"Distract these people's attention."

Cosme Vila looked at El Responsable. The latter was furious; his people were milling about, waiting for orders. While this had been going on, the general had not halted. The officers and their escort were now some two hundred yards off.

"We're not interested in those laws," said El Responsable. "Who passed them? Alfonso XIII?"

Cosme Vila shrugged his shoulders. "You do as you please with your people. I think the military must be tried."

The colonel sighed with relief. He turned and walked off. El Responsable bit his lips. His self-esteem was at stake. His daughters came over to stand beside him.

At this point Professor Morales spoke up: "But we must demand that they be tried before a popular tribunal, by the people."

Those words aroused a wild enthusiasm. A Tribunal of the People! La Valenciana saw herself in robes of justice, wielding a gavel, pronouncing sentence right and left.

Even El Responsable was carried away by the idea. "But it's got to be soon," he added.

The nervousness of the crowd, which could not hear the dialogue, was mounting by the minute as the distance between it and the prisoners increased. The officers and the guards had already turned the corner of the Municipal Plaza. "Now what do we do, now what do we do?" The reserves of available energy were inexhaustible.

Just then honkings were heard. The truck that had gone to deposit the arms at Communist Party headquarters was coming back jammed with members, those wearing handkerchiefs around their heads like pirates. Every one of them had a submachine gun. Gorki rode in the middle. Cosme Vila recognized among them the man who worked in the dry cleaning establishment who had said: "If it was my wife, I'd want to know what for."

In spite of his potbelly, Gorki gave a flying leap from the truck and rushed over to Cosme Vila. "Our people are dying by the hundreds in Madrid. The army and the priests have barricaded themselves in the Montaña Barracks."

The priests, the priests—it was the magic word. This was Gorki's psychological triumph.

"Comrades, the people are giving their blood. In Gerona the people have been victorious. Let's clean out the lairs of the opposition!"

Cosme Vila, in shirtsleeves, with his wide belt and sandals, set off in the direction opposite to that taken by the officers. He had reached a decision. The thing to do was to level every church in the city. No more weighing pros and cons. No more delay!

He was making for the Church of the Sacred Heart, the church of the Jesuits. It was the nearest. The crowd caught on at once and with amazing ease forgot about Major Martínez de Soria. Julio caught on, too, and inconspicuously detached himself, making his way to police headquarters. Amid shouts, cheers, *vivas*, and *mueras*, Cosme Vila drew the thousand fanatics after him. The church loomed up before them. The sight of its serene gray towers and, above all, its huge locked door threw them into a frenzy. "They've locked up; they knew what to expect!" Beside the church was the deserted rectory. Someone knew that there was a passageway between it and the temple.

The leaders of the mob broke into the house. Nobody there. Empty. In the waiting room there was a table and a huge chronological album of the popes. Santi was among the first in, and he rang every bell his fingers could find. Down a gloomy corridor they came to the communicating door. They entered the church. Those who had remained outside were waiting for the immense door of the church to be thrown wide.

When they heard the first blows, they rushed up the stairs, unable to restrain themselves, and, as one man, flung themselves against the doors, trying to help those struggling with them on the inside. At the sixth try, the doors gave way. And at that moment all the lights went on. Santi had discovered the switches in the sacristy and had illuminated the festival. The temple was incapable of holding them all. Shots rang out. El Responsable was firing his revolver at the Sacred Heart on the main altar. He did not miss a shot, and yet the image did not fall. Most of the times he hit it in the mouth, so that with each shot the expression of the image changed, which aroused the crowd more and more. The side altars and benches were broken up by others of the raiders. La Valenciana had drenched her face in holy water. Gorki had climbed up on one of the pulpits, and with a long stick someone handed him was trying to reach the great central chandelier with its tinkling prisms.

The obsession of most of the mob was the confessionals. On each of them was a card with the name of the confessor. "If only a few of them were inside!" The wood was hard and unyielding. The rifle butts hardly made a dent on it. Some of the crowd sat inside the stalls, others knelt beside them. "The things that have gone on here!"

Future was the athlete. He was the first to approach the immense crucifix at the entrance. Taking hold of its base, he called for aid. "Into the river with it, into the river!" he shouted. Dozens of willing hands were raised. "Gangway, gangway!" The caravan set out. Christ lay flat, his feet higher than his head, for those bringing up the rear were taller than Future. When they came to the river embankment, the Oñar spread out muddy before them. To throw the cross over, they had to rest it on the railing, and raise it by a superhuman effort. "Heave-ho!" Christ fell, describing a complete half-turn. He fell, and stood cleaving the mud like an arrow. The wooden arms of the cross pointed pathetically in all directions. The image rested head-down, like St. Peter.

Inside the church the struggle of man against matter was at its height. Everything was of such good quality that there was no choice but to employ fire. Cosme Vila put the first match to the high altar. He decided on this because he calculated that, in view of the thickness of the stones, the building would not burn, so there would be no danger to the neighborhood. Only the altars would go. All the hangings took fire. A confessional burned, then several benches. El Responsable was firing at the chandelier, and he had many imitators. Seeing Gorki in the pulpit, Cosme Vila suddenly thought: "No question about it. He's the one for mayor."

Professor Morales had not realized that it was so easy to destroy things that were centuries old. And what most impressed him was that everything was being done almost without the intervention of the human voice. Everyone was using hands and feet, pushing obstacles out of the way with his stomach, shooting. Some were laughing. Others were remembering that they had been married here. A tray gave an echo like a gong, arousing superstitious fears lest something fall and crush them. There was the legend *Ave Maria Gratia Plena Dominus Tecum* following the concavity of the crypt; colors; tactile surprises; but almost no intervention of the human voice. Professor Morales smiled as he watched the activity of Raimundo, the barber. Why were hypocrites taking part in this work?

Suddenly the flames shot up. The smoke was growing thick. All, including Cosme Vila, realized that it had been a mistake to set off the blaze so fast. Now they would have to get out. With all the games they could have made up in there! Nobody was satisfied with his achievements. Except Future. Future was smashing the organ pipes.

"Everybody out! Out!"

They obeyed reluctantly. The fire was so aromatic. The whole temple gave off exciting smells—wood, incense. A good smell. At that moment the main chandelier crashed to the floor, and by a miracle the child of one of the Murcians was not brained.

When Cosme Vila came out of the door, he had a great surprise. He had imagined that those of the crowd who had not been able to get into the church would be waiting outside, but they were not. "Where are they?" he asked. Aside from those who had been inside, there was almost no one.

"They've gone," someone informed him, "to the other churches."

That was what had happened. They had been unable to endure the torment of doing nothing, and another column had quickly formed, headed by Blasco, with the Church of the Carmen as its objective.

Cosme Vila was enraged. He had wanted to organize everything methodically, but that had not been possible. It was then that El Responsable realized that Cosme Vila was directing the orchestra. With all there was to do in the city! He made a sign to his followers and without saying a word set off in a different direction, as though he had just had an inspiration. Before leaving the street, he looked back and saw the first gigantic flame shooting out of the main entrance. Odd that one should not even care to see the crowning of one's labors, that one should the so quickly of operating in the same spot! An embarrassment of riches. All the lairs of the opposition that were just waiting for his purifying touch!

While the Jesuit church was being gutted by the flames, the same scenes, but perfected by experience, were being repeated in the Church of the Carmen, which Blasco and his gang had taken over. El Cojo, who hated to imitate—and especially to imitate Cosme Vila or Gorki—instead of mounting the pulpit and performing other cheap tricks, had made straight for the ciborium, smashing it with the butt of his rifle. His idea was to get at the chalice. He took it in his hands and turned around. "*Fratres, fratres!*" he shouted, raising it as high as he could. He called to all to gather around him. The militiamen drew near, though for the moment they did not know what El Cojo was up to. Suddenly it flashed into their minds. Communion! El Cojo was calling them for that. Some of them knelt, others remained standing. El Cojo assumed a solemn air and came limping over to the communion rail. He began handing out a communion wafer to each of them, murmuring as he did so: "*Miserere nobis.*" When he reached the twelfth, he could not restrain himself any longer. He let out a roar of laughter and, ripping open the shirt of Blasco, who was acting as his acolyte, emptied the remaining wafers between his shirt and skin. Blasco writhed like a dancer. The bootblack took one of the wafers and tried to stick it on his forehead. It seemed to him that the most fun would be when he started to run and the white disks began falling through his pants' legs.

El Cojo then climbed the steps of the high altar. With a push he threw down the image of the Virgin of the Carmen. Then he climbed into the niche it had occupied and stretched out his arms like a preacher. Someone had turned on the lights, which threw into relief the livid scabs on El Cojo's lips. Veritable volleys of shots rang out, their targets the images. El Cojo began to fear he might be mistaken for a saint. "Hey, be careful!" and he gave a leap. The wood of the altar gave way under his feet, and he found himself buried up to his waist, bleeding from deep scratches. Several comrades had to help him get loose. He was furious. On the floor gleamed a frame and glass. He stamped them to pieces with his heel. It was the Gospel according to St. John.

This group of vandals seemed to have more imagination. It was gold that had dazzled Cosme Vila's contingent. The gold of the candelabra, of the crowns, of the monstrance. To move about among gold objects they could destroy! El Cojo and his hordes were more given to horseplay. Thus, instead of dragging the main crucifix into the streets, they dragged out two confessionals. And a Communist came out of one of them with a collection of dirty postcards in his hand, saying he had found them in the confessional. Another claimed to have found a wine flask. "Sure, sure, to wash away the sins." And he raised it to his lips. They all wanted to share in the fun. Some of the passersby laughed.

The wife of Casal, whose flat was close by, came to the window and called out: "Do any of you know where Casal is? Do you know where Casal is?" Nobody paid any attention to her. Flames were beginning to lick out of the temple. Huge flames, monsters' tongues of different colors. The building materials here seemed more inflammable than those of the Sacred Heart, the odors less pungent.

A kind of contest had developed all over the city. What had begun as a multitude had now broken up into groups of from fifty to one hundred. The sense of being free had aroused in many the idea of making themselves leaders. They were not content to help Future throw Christ into the river. They wanted to operate on their own.

As a result, in less than two hours eight churches in the city had been set afire and three convents had been destroyed. The desk at which Pilar had studied had been smashed to splinters, and the nuns' beds and pianos urinated upon, the pianos of those convents whose Mothers Superior had not followed Mosén Alberto's advice. Where had the nuns got to? The militiamen did not find a single one, but they did find out their secrets. At the Congregation of Mary, food supplies for five years; in the Convent of the Heart of Mary, an underground passage.

"The catacombs, the catacombs they were talking about!"

"Catacombs my ass. I'll bet this communicates with the sacristy of San Félix, with the priests. Did you think they slept by themselves?" The leader of that group was Ideal. With a flashlight he groped along the dark passage. The others followed him, convinced that at last they were going to come upon the secret center where the ecclesiastical orgies and tortures took place. But they began to notice that it was growing damp and that water was seeping in. "How is this possible when it's much higher than the river here?"

"They've probably flooded it, they've flooded it so we can't see anything!" They turned back angrily. But they soon discovered a side passage. Following this a few steps, they came to a kind of rectangular court with flagstones set into the wall, and mounds of loose earth. Ideal stopped. He was accompanied by Sergeant Molina of the People's Militia. "What's here?" Someone brought a pick and hammer, and they easily pried loose one of the flagstones. "Skeletons!" There they were. "The beasts! That's where they hid the bodies!"

"The corpses of babies they got caught with," someone said. No question about it. They were rickety skeletons, as though shriveled up. One after another the stones were loosened. Ideal buried his hands in the bones of one of the skeletons, and it crumbled away. Others, however, were whole in their wooden coffins. "Get this outside, get it outside." They pulled out the coffins and carried them up to the convent. "Where shall we put them?"

"Out there on the sidewalk so everybody can see them!"

"The dirty sows!"

"Bring that little one, the one of the baby!"

The exhibit of skeletons on the sidewalk fired the imagination of all. Murillo, who had led his Trotskyite cell into the convent across the way, the rich Convent of the Congregation of Mary, was informed of the discovery made in the Heart of Mary. It seemed to him that his cohorts would look very silly if all they did was to break everything they could get their hands on and eat up a five years' food supply. The dissenter must always go his adversaries one better in everything. His second in command was Salvio, the sweetheart of Don

Emilio Santos's maid. Murillo had seen too much broken plaster of Paris in his decorator days for smashing or even shooting images to make any impression on him. Besides, from that part of the city four other burning churches could be seen, the nearest that of San Félix. He had to do better than that. The convent square opened on the stairway to the Cathedral. The setting was therefore grandiose. Murillo and several others went into the sacristy, where they all put on religious vestments. Murillo pulled on an alb that came halfway up his leg, then a chasuble with gold embroidery and an old biretta he found on a hatrack. Salvio put on a surplice, which he tied around his waist with a red sash. And then a chasuble. Not one of them but found himself a chasuble. They took the aspergillum, two censers, and the missals. And then the pallium. Someone came upon a small pallium the nuns used when the Bishop visited their chapel. And then the monstrance, which Murillo took in his two hands. Thus attired, they went outside.

On the sidewalk on the other side of the street, the skeletons. On this side, the improvised procession, chanting "*Miserere nobis.*" All of them were singing "*Miserere nobis.*" In the center the sweeping stairway to the Cathedral, then the soaring, majestic facade, and then the bell tower, which went on telling the hours the same as always, the same as when Matías Alvear listened sleepless at night.

The news of what was taking place reached Ideal's ears. He came out to watch the show with the others. Under the canopy Murillo was ascending the Cathedral stairway. The censers bobbed in the air. Those carrying them were unskilled in their use and banged themselves on the knees, giving rise to great hilarity. Suddenly Murillo turned around. His walrus mustache gave him a ferocious air. At that moment he became bored with the whole business. To tell the truth, he felt that none of all that was a patch on the skeletons Ideal had stumbled upon. He tossed the monstrance into the air and started quickly down the stairs as though a wonderful idea had just come to him. But the chasuble interfered with his movements, making everybody laugh. Those holding the pallium were left deserted. Fortunately, someone was passing around a chalice filled with wine. This cheered everyone, though in a few minutes both groups were looking around, as though admiring what they had done and seeking new things to do.

It didn't seem possible that one could get so little fun out of a monstrance. Ideal had thought it would afford jokes for a lifetime; but once it was broken, it was nothing but a piece of junk like any old thing Blasco had in his room.

The four fires, however, were growing and kept spirits high. "Let's go see what's happened in San Félix!" All together, Murillo and his group, the anarchists, and the others rushed down the street. Only two or three women stayed with the skeletons, standing guard over the bones, and repeating: "Did you ever see such a thing! The sows!"

The Church of San Félix smelled of blood. The flames were bursting from crevices everywhere, and there was a crowd in the square looking on. The bell tower was as beautiful as when in other days, on St. John's Eve, it had been illuminated by lights from below.

In the center of the crowd a man stood out above all the others, a giant: Teo. He had been set free at nine o'clock that morning along with the gypsy and the boy who had tried to kill his brother with a sickle. Teo knew that Cosme Vila had issued the order for his release, but felt no gratitude toward him. Left forgotten for days and days! He did not want to go near Cosme Vila. He had watched the passing of the officers from the window of a friend's house. And then he saw the crowd setting out for the Church of the Sacred Heart without even a thought for him. Not once had Cosme Vila stopped to ask: "Where's Teo?"

Whereupon Teo went into action on his own. He came down to the street just as El Responsable was leading his column to the Dominican convent. Teo's impressive bulk lured away some fifty of these followers, and they set out for San Félix. "It's the next most important after the Cathedral." Teo would have liked to go first to the home of Warning Voice and Don Jorge, but he realized that the people were demanding mighty deeds.

This was why San Félix now smelled of blood. Because those who had followed Teo were Murcians almost to the last man. Cosme Vila overawed them, but not Teo. So when they made their way into the temple and discovered that, contrary to what had happened in the Sacred Heart, the benches were not empty, all the sun that had blazed down on their heads on the sands of S'Agaró, all their pleas to the architect for water that was fit to drink, and all the scenes of their childhood in Murcia blinded them, and they hardly knew what they were doing.

Before setting anything afire they went over to the benches. Each of them was carrying a submachine gun; they had been the foresighted at the barracks arsenal. And when they got to the benches they made another discovery: the persons kneeling there were not people as they understood the term. They were not like their mothers or their sisters; they were nuns. And unlike Ideal, who accused the nuns of having babies in the underground passageways, the Murcians accused them of not having them, of not wanting to be mothers, of betraying mankind. For that reason, and because of the way they wore their hair, and their long garments, and their mealy-mouthed airs, and because of the terror in their eyes when they turned and saw those men with the red handkerchiefs around their heads, and because of the tiny beads of the rosaries that shone in their hands, the Murcians mowed them down with bullets. They did not know how many there were; five or six. Some of them fell forward, leaning against the benches in front of them as though still praying. Others fell sidewise across the legs of the first. One, the youngest, fell backwards, her arms flung wide at her sides, and her flat, terror-distorted face fixed on the vault of the church.

Teo could not say whether this was good or bad. It had this in its favor, however: it had been done without orders from Cosme Vila. Besides, what difference did it make? Didn't they believe in heaven? They would meet Brother Alfredo there. Though it had been said he didn't care much for women....

But Teo found the whole spectacle not to his liking. It was days now since he had seen the gigantic platform of his dray, and he no longer believed in a discipline under which a leader left a faithful member like himself to rot in jail. His individual soul had recovered itself. He could not bear the sight of the Murcians shoving their hands inside the nuns' habits to see what was there, jewels or flesh different from that of other women, so he decided to burn down the church. He decided this without its having been his intention when he set out at the head of the column. His intention had been simply to find out something that had troubled him ever since he was a child: the truth about the incorruptibility of the body of San Narciso, the patron saint of the city, who was preserved in a glass urn in that church, behind the altar that bore the saint's name. Teo remembered that his mother, at fair-time, had taken him and his brother there and had made them kiss the shrine. He wanted to learn the truth. For he was sure that the body was made of wood. He had no choice but to burn down the church so that the sight of the dead nuns would not haunt him, and so as not to see the foolery of the Murcians. However—why not first remove the urn with the saint's body, and then set fire to the church? "Come here," he called to the strongest of his followers. They all wanted to help. It was hard work, for the urn was mortised in. But they managed it. Teo was a giant. "Take this to my house!" Teo lived close by, at the beginning of the Calle de la Barca. They went up to his flat and dumped the relic there. And when they returned to the church, it was already burning inside, and the flames were licking out from crevices everywhere.

It smelled of blood, not of wood or incense. It smelled of blood to Teo and to the Murcians, the only ones who knew the truth. When Murillo saw the giant, he dodged back. He recalled that when he had been expelled from the assembly Teo had tried to trip him as he ran off the stage. Yet everything went differently on this occasion. Teo had seen him too, and when he saw the chasuble, the alb halfway to his knee, and the biretta on his head, all his resentments disappeared, and even his remorse over the five—or six—murders. Teo let out a roar of laughter. "The bishop! The bishop!" And he walked over to Murillo. Everyone followed him. Teo recalled that Murillo hated Cosme Vila. To Murillo's surprise, Teo threw his arms around him. Behind them Ideal with his aspergillum was blessing the scene.

The whole city seemed a volcano out of which the final grandiose, definitive flame might suddenly spurt. Dozens of hearts felt in their centers, in that tiny exact center perceptible only on special occasions, that man's human condition had died and that in its stead something base and alien had filtered into his bones, compounded of a reversion to the primeval and of what may prevail in the world's last moments, making of him a being deranged, seeking to slake his thirst by hurling into the void the water of all the springs.

Mosén Francisco, from a kitchen window similar to the one in Pedro's house from which Mateo had so often peered, had seen Teo carrying out on his back the urn holding the body of San Narciso, and then the flames bursting from the church. He knelt on the kitchen floor, covering his face with his hands, and his sobs echoed through the house. A cat lying beside the stove looked at him as though startled and finally went over and rubbed its soft fur against his cassock. Suddenly Mosén Francisco got to his feet and was about to rush down the stairs, but the other people in the flat held him back. They told him he was too young to die. Mosén Francisco wanted to save the monstrance, the chalice, the body of San Narciso, Teo—everybody. The master of the house called to his wife to bring a rope, and he tied the priest to a chair. He tied his hands and his feet and put him in a corner. Mosén Francisco understood that it was God's will that he should go on living, and he left off straining against the ropes. He smiled. "Thy will be done," he murmured. And he asked his protector to release one of his hands, just one, so he could stroke the cat.

Dozens of persons had watched with anxiety the fanning out of the columns all over the city, and they knew that El Responsable had set fire not only to the chapel of the Dominicans, but to the entire convent. As Ignacio rushed away from the bank—business as usual at the bank, in spite of everything—he saw Cosme Vila in person, with an escort of six militiamen, go up to Don Jorge's house, another group to that of Warning Voice, and another to Don Santiago Estrada's. Then a music store, which suddenly began to vomit forth guitars, violins—and pianos!—whose destination was the river, where some sank from sight in the mud and others remained stuck in it like the Christ of the Sacred Heart.

Everybody knew that the general and the twenty officers had reached the infantry barracks, and that the twenty under arrest had been locked up in the guardhouse without their insignia, without their white gloves. Everybody knew that Julio had rushed out in search of Cosme Vila to get him to bring his work of destruction within bounds. Everybody knew that in many cities of Spain fighting was still going on, that in Barcelona the anarchists had born the brunt of the battle, that counterparts of Cosme Vila and El Responsable were achieving their revolutionary transfiguration. Mysterious radios were broadcasting the news that in the port of Cartagena the sailors had mutinied and had thrown their officers, with stones and iron weights tied to their necks and feet, into the ocean—that Mediterranean which Professor Civil loved so well—one after another. This news had paralyzed the heart of Don Emilio Santos with the thought that his elder son was there, while, on the other hand, it had rejoiced the heart of his maid, who for the first time since she had been in his employ told Don Emilio she hated him "for a fascist."

Cosme Vila and El Responsable knew all this and more. They knew now about the sensational discovery that had been made in the vicinity of the Cathedral—food stores for five years and skeletons. Skeletons of the nuns' babies. They were said to be exposed at the foot of the Cathedral stairs. This they must see! This had to be confirmed, photographs taken, Vasiliev notified, and the anarchists of Barcelona, Russia, the whole world. "Victor, bring your camera!" El Responsable was to assemble all his men and lead them to the skeletons at the foot of the Cathedral stairs.

This was done. The word spread and brought all the people together again. Suddenly, without knowing how, the thousand men and women—two thousand, perhaps—who had gathered in front of the barracks when the officers surrendered, now met again, every last one of them, in the Cathedral Square, ready to view the skeletons.

But they all suffered a disappointment. What they saw was bones, just a pitiful pile of bones. All of them realized that a skeleton, whether of a nun or an illegitimate child, was made up of the same bones each of them carried about under his skin. Besides, who said those were babies' bones? They were not the right size unless by a divine dispensation the nuns had brought them forth full grown.

This letdown over the dead turned the gaze and thought of all toward the living. They exchanged glances of interrogation. What was at hand which was the essence of living, the very symbol of life, of strength, of that which endured to the end of time? The Cathedral! The shout arose from some parched throat that had not shared in the round of the wine flask in the Church of the Carmen or that of the chalice Murillo had passed out. The Cathedral! All eyes turned to the great stairway, on one of whose steps a castoff chasuble gleamed. And then to the facade and to the bell tower above it. Its spire was the spire of the city. It was the peak, the presiding principle, the beginning of life. No man its height, not even Teo. Only the mountains of the Pyrenees, visible beyond the windings of the Ter.

Cosme Vila and El Responsable looked at each other. To the Cathedral! Santi was carrying a red flag. It might have been made from his own flesh or from the blood that had gushed from El Cojo when he leaped from the niche of the Virgin of the Carmen. All together they began to ascend the stairs in close rank. Cosme Vila had a presentiment that they would not reach the top without something happening. How many stairs were there? The boys at the Institute said there were ninety, others a hundred. Be that as it may, there were a lot of them, and the sun was blazing on them and on Cosme Vila's bald spot.

Cosme Vila had a presentiment that this something which was going to happen would be the appearance of the Bishop. The Bishop had undoubtedly been informed of the burning of the churches, of the Jesuits' convent, the Dominicans'. It was to be expected that the Bishop would stand for everything except this: the burning of the Cathedral. To him the Cathedral was undoubtedly what the Kremlin would be to Cosme Vila under similar circumstances. What wouldn't Cosme Vila do to save the Kremlin?

The thousand men and women—perhaps two thousand—slowly climbed the stairs unaware of what Cosme Vila was thinking. And yet, as always, he was right. Before they reached the top someone did appear. It was not the Bishop; it was the architects Massana and Ribas, the cultural delegates of the Generalidad. And beside them another man with a book in his hand: Professor Morales.

What had happened? The three men raised their arms to indicate that they wished to address the crowd. Everybody halted, and the three began to speak. They understood the feeling that moved the people, their desire for vengeance, but this would be a fatal error. The revolution must be constructive and not destructive. What would it benefit them to burn down the Cathedral?

The whole world would be shocked. If, as a church, it deserved to be burned, as an architectural monument, particularly for the width of its nave, which was unique in the world, it must be preserved and converted into a Museum of the People. Everything in it that had a religious connotation would be burned: altars, images, missals; even the bells would be melted down to make arms, arms to assist the people wherever they needed them, in Zaragoza, Castile, or Madrid, in the Montaña Barracks. But the building must be spared and turned into a Museum of the People, to house the trophies and the living history of the revolution. All Catalonia would be grateful to Gerona. It would be an honor for Catalonia. "Long live the Revolution, long live Catalonia, long live the Museum of the People!"

The voice of the architect Ribas worked the miracle. Even Cosme Vila was thrilled. He realized that the architect was right, and Professor Morales's endorsement confirmed him in his belief. Museum of the People! It was a wonderful idea. They would put Don Jorge's genealogical tree there, Warning Voice's dental chair, which looked like an instrument of torture, the "incorruptible" body of San Narciso....

Cosme Vila turned to the crowd. "Comrades! Comrade Ribas is right. Break it up. That's enough for today. He and architect Massana and representatives of the people will organize this museum. For this reason architect Massana is going to resign as Mayor so he can take charge of this museum. For that reason he proposes as his successor Comrade Gorki, and the latter accepts. Comrades, at six o'clock all of you are to be in the Municipal Plaza."

Cosme Vila felt it the part of policy to say a few words as a sop to El Responsable and the anarchists. "We have all joined forces to present a united front to the enemy. The cooperative will continue operating for the benefit of all. The women can go there to get what they need. Those in charge are going to open the doors right away. *¡Salud!* Long live the Revolution!"

EIGHTY-SEVEN

THERE was no rest for the city, none for the two hundred and thirty-five men who had revolted or their families, for priests, nuns, and officers, for anyone with uncalloused hands or wearing a gold bracelet or a hat.

Such a change had taken place in a few hours that everyone, defenders and attackers alike, felt as though the ground had given way under his feet and he was floating in the air. Everyone, that is, except Cosme Vila, El Responsable, Casal, David and Olga, and the men who, suddenly, in the various districts of Gerona and the neighboring towns, assumed leadership, seated themselves in the town halls, and appointed revolutionary committees.

Possibly this development most clearly gave Cosme Vila the feeling that the hour had come: the simultaneity with which these little committees sprang up on the periphery of the city, revolutionary committees, which, as they spread countryward, adorned their headquarters with agricultural symbols, committees that were winning over the provinces, the farms, the fields, the telegraph poles. In the twinkling of an eye each Communist cell of peasants was converted into a joint committee with the anarchists. From shed or threshing floor they moved to a central meeting place; from spade to machine gun, from cart to commandeered car, from anonymity to open control of the village.

And the radios were relentless. The manager of the Gerona station had gone over to Cosme Vila as the latter was descending the Cathedral steps, saying: "Comrade, we will broadcast the reports you give us. Professor Morales could join our staff." Professor Morales, long before the crowd on the stroke of six had proclaimed Gorki mayor, informed the radio audience of Gerona that Barcelona was completely in the hands of the people, that in Madrid the military had surrendered at the Montaña Barracks, that the government could count on the gold, the power, the moral support, and the sympathy of Russia, France, England, and all the great democracies of the world, and that in all the history of military uprisings there had never been such a fiasco as this one.

Professor Morales had concluded: "In a week there will not be one focus of fascist infection in the whole country."

For that reason the eight fires in the city and the news that Cosme Vila, El Responsable, and Casal were that night setting up a local revolutionary committee in imitation of the various districts and villages filled households with an anxiety beyond their powers to cope with. This was why Laura was rushing in despair to the home of her brothers; why the cloistered nuns of San Daniel were groping for refuge somewhere; why Corbera, the sandal factory owner, was slipping into the episcopal palace with a blue coverall for the Bishop so that he could take him home with him till some better hiding place could be found; why Don Pedro Oriol was refusing to leave his home in spite of the pleas of his wife; why Mosén Alberto and the Noguers were stopping their taxi twenty kilometers from the frontier and talking with a man who was asking two thousand pesetas apiece to guide them across the border; why the owners of the Soler factory were making arrangements to take ship in Palamós; and why Matías Alvear was receiving communications of this sort in the Telegraph office: "Congratulations on triumph of proletariat. Vasiliev" and "Arriving tomorrow incognito. Vasiliev."

Everyone had the feeling that the time-honored table with its embroidered cloth, around which the loved ones, the better and the worse, the more and less devoted, had been wont to sit, was now going to become just a flat surface, with an empty place or two, and the dining room a room with one or two chairs calling in vain for their human complement, their accustomed number.

In many families the absences were already a fact: in Major Martínez de Soria's house, in Mateo's, in Don Jorge's, Dr. Rosselló's, the mason's, the electrician's....

These families, and many more, were torn between wanting their members both near and far away. As near as possible to their hearts, as far as possible from the machine guns of the Murcians, of the Revolutionary Committee to be made up of Cosme Vila, El Responsable, Casal.

Even Doña Amparo Campo had an absence to mourn—that of Julio. Julio had not yet returned. He had been away for forty-eight hours. On the eve of the uprising he had hidden in Dr. Rosselló's house. When he learned that the military had surrendered, he appeared in the Rambla with Cosme Vila and El Responsable; later he went to headquarters, and he had not yet come home. Doña Amparo Campo said to Colonel Muñoz: "Naturally, he wants to see if he can bring things under control."

Colonel Muñoz answered: "The battle has been too bitter everywhere. Too much blood of the people has been shed."

The general had a simple solution for everything: "Throw them in jail!" But Doña Amparo Campo was afraid, and the Commissioner confessed to himself that he was losing weight by the minute.

Julio had kept his composure, though there had been moments when he was on the point of losing it, and he had never denied the gravity of the situation. Certainly he did not think that either jail or losing weight was going to solve anything. The facts were bitter—why deny it?—less for their effects than for their causes. For the thing that really frightened Julio was the complete, the absolute, transmutation of values, of the symbols of authority. In a word, the offices of the Commissioner and Chief of Police had, as though by magic, become paralyzed, while in other parts of the city, organizations taking over their prerogatives were springing up like weeds, without asking permission or even notifying them. The power of authority was completely in the hands of the political parties and the labor organizations.

All this was very serious. Julio knew that he was the only hope of the families around the embroidered tablecloths with the empty plates. The eight fires and the rest were a lesser evil. But the question was what was going to happen now. His suicide file had taught him many things. He knew that suicides, when they became fed up with destroying their possessions, their home, and their ambitions, destroyed themselves. Just so, when the revolutionary committees got tired of tearing down stones, they would begin to tear down men. He already had an anonymous note on his desk, saying: "For God's sake, we don't know the whereabouts of six nuns of the Heart of Mary!"

Six nuns. Where could they be hiding? Behind the stone slabs Ideal had pried loose in the underground passage? And where could the Bishop be? And Warning Voice? And Noguer the notary? And Mosén Alberto? They had all disappeared. And, above all, Mateo and his group. It was as though not a single Falangist lived in the city. Either the stars their hymn spoke of had drawn them as the noon draws the tide, or they had taken to the mountains; they might even be hiding near at hand, closing breaches with pieces of blue shirt.

Julio had received an order from Colonel Muñoz: to look after the wife and daughter of Major Martínez de Soria, to be responsible for their lives. Julio had carried out the order with regard to the wife, who was in her apartment under the protection of a squad of Assault Guards; he had done his duty by Marta, sending her out under guard to the destination of her choice when she left the barracks.

Julio was prepared to do everything in his power to arrest the march of the forces that called themselves revolutionary and he called blind. It was imperative to appeal to the good sense of Catalonia, to talk about the Generalidad and not about Russia, about the Costas and not about El Responsable. Massana and Ribas had saved the Cathedral. The city and its art owed their very existence to them. It was an encouraging example. It was a great pity that Gorki, an Aragonese, should have been named Mayor, and that an Andalusian should now be driving Don Pedro Oriol's car. Why was that allowed? This was the occasion for Catalonia to reveal its personality. He would have to talk with Cosme Vila, with El Responsable, and especially with Casal and David and Olga.

One thing worried him: Officer Antonio Sánchez had seen Pilar blowing Major Martínez de Soria a kiss as he drove past her. Officer Sánchez knew that the Alvear family was something sacred to Julio, but in spite of that he had mentioned the incident to the other Assault Guards. And according to Colonel Muñoz, if it had not been for the fact that he and the general had been in charge of the arrested officers, most of the Assault Guards would have looked the other way and allowed the thousand clenched fists to descend on the prisoners, particularly when they were crossing the river.

Julio, he could not say why, had the Alvear family very much in his thoughts. The games of dominoes he had played with Matías, the cups of coffee Carmen Elgazu had served him, always saying: "I'm going to bring it right in. I like to let it settle." Why had the kids had to fall in love with Mateo and the daughter of the major? It was one fine mess now, with this Revolutionary Committee. And then César, whom nobody would be able to stop from trying to save—God only knew what, possibly the Diocesan Museum.

"Sánchez, turn off that radio!" Professor Morales's voice was hurting Julio's eardrums.

EIGHTY-NINE

THE two hundred and thirty-five men who had gone into the streets bearing arms and had retired on orders from Major Martínez de Soria had disappeared from the streets. Very few of them failed to realize clearly how things stood; most of them, even before the arrest of the officers and the fires, knew, as Warning Voice knew, that their only salvation lay in hiding or flight.

Mateo decided on flight. Before the white flag had been run up over the barracks, and as soon as he had said goodbye to his comrades, he went to his house. Don Emilio Santos opened the door. They locked it from the inside. Don Emilio Santos took him in his arms.

"Father, I can do nothing for my comrades. I have to get away."

"Get away to where, son? And how?"

"I have to get across the border."

"On foot?"

"On foot, naturally. You can see the mountains up there."

Father and son would have wished to prolong the scene, the embrace, to say many things to each other. But both realized that there was no time to lose. They looked out the window. The city was still quiet. The white flag had not yet been raised.

Don Emilio finally let Mateo out of his arms and said to him: "You must find yourself a guide. I'll give you money."

"Give me a little money, but I have no confidence in any guide." Mateo told his father that he had complete faith in the final triumph, and that they would be together again. He advised Don Emilio to go into hiding, too. "You must find some safe place away from Gerona." Then he added: "Promise me you will."

Don Emilio Santos repeated over and over again: "You're not to worry about me." He talked on, and yet he could not grasp the fact that he was saying goodbye to his son. It was all happening so fast! Until suddenly Mateo felt his eyes swimming in tears. He threw his arms around his father once more, and Don Emilio Santos said: "May God bless and keep you." He held the boy tight, breathing deeply, for he had forgotten to breathe for moments past. He had the feeling that his son was entering upon an even more trying period than the preceding and he wanted to give him courage, to hearten him.

The scene could not be prolonged. Time was of the essence. On a sudden impulse Mateo pushed open the door of his sealed study and looked at it for the last time. There were his books. Dust, dust everywhere. Then he looked around the dining room and went into his bedroom. Finally, without looking at his father, he pressed his hand and set out toward the home of the Alvears.

He hurried up the stairs and rang the bell. At first there was no answer. Then a voice asked: "Who is it?"

"Mateo."

The door was flung open and Mateo stood face to face with Pilar, who threw her arms around him—for the first time. Her hand caressed the long hair on his neck. She kept stammering: "Mateo, Mateo...."

The boy walked into the flat, toward the dining room. Ignacio was at the bank, César at the Museum helping Mosén Alberto pack his bags and hide the bed of the Blessed Father Claret somewhere.

Carmen Elgazu served him coffee. Matías Alvear told him that all that had been a rash act, that the military should have waited another month and made sure of success in Barcelona and Madrid.

Mateo replied: "There wouldn't have been time." Then he outlined his plans. "The minute they run up the white flag, the mob will invade the city. I have to get away to France."

This announcement left them in a state of consternation. The thought of Mateo's setting out on foot toward the mountains utterly terrified Pilar. Besides, she realized that this meant complete separation. She still felt that he ought to go to some big city. Madrid, perhaps.

"Madrid?" Mateo was of the opinion that in Madrid the reprisals would take on a resemblance to the *Inferno*.

Matías approved of the boy's getting away, but he turned thumbs down on the plan of setting out blindly, without knowing the terrain. "It's a good forty miles. You'll arouse suspicion. And the mountains can be very treacherous.... Aren't there any of your Falangists who know the Pyrenees? But of course there is—Jorge. Jorge has hunted there."

Mateo raised his eyebrows. That was true. It might be an idea. Don Jorge had holdings in the vicinity of the Pyrenees. "And I'd like to take Rosselló along, too."

The problem was how to locate them.

"Jorge has probably gone home. His father—I would think—has forgiven him. I doubt that Rosselló has wanted to see his family. He's probably at the boarding house with Octavio."

Pilar kept Mateo's hand in hers. Everybody's eyes were on him, in spite of the fact that they realized that it was a mistake to waste time, and that those few hours had to be used to the best advantage. Finally Matías Alvear told Pilar to go out and see if she could pick up the trail of the two Falangists.

She left, and before long was back with Jorge and Rosselló, and with Octavio as well. Octavio, too, wanted to get away, even though his sweetheart assured him that she could find him a safe hiding place.

Matías Alvear looked at them, his face clearly revealing the fact that he thought they were crazy. "You're out of your mind. How far do you think the four of you together are going to get? Not half a dozen miles from the city."

"He's right. There are too many of us."

"Split up in two groups—two and two."

This was the arrangement. Rosselló knew something about the roads, or at least that was what he said. He and Octavio would go together.

"What about Roca and the two masons, and—?"

"I think they've all got the same idea. Maybe we'll all meet in Perpignan."

Pilar was in despair over the speed with which the arrangements were being made and the thought that she would have to part from Mateo in front of all those people. She could not show him what she felt. She put her arms around him again, and he kissed her on the forehead. In that second they lived again all the months they had spent together, the vows of fidelity their hearts had taken.

"I'll be back."

"No, no, you won't come back!"

Finally Mateo drew away from Pilar and went over to Carmen Elgazu, asking her to give him a kiss. As she did so, she hung a medal about his neck. Moved though she was, while they talked she had been preparing a lunch for them to take along: four packages.

"Are any of you short of money?" Matías asked them.

Rosselló. Rosselló did not have a cent.

"Wait a minute." Matías went into his bedroom and came out with one hundred pesetas. "That's all I can give you."

Rosselló thanked him.

The boys left one by one, at ten-minute intervals. The first to leave was Jorge. Each would meet his traveling companion at the city gate. They went by the Dehesa, following the highway. Pilar murmured from the balcony: "God bless you all," and then she went to her room and threw herself upon the bed.

IGNACIO had been unable to say goodbye to Mateo. He had left for the bank just as the troops were withdrawing and the news of the surrender was spreading. His first concern had been for Marta, of whom, as yet, he had had no word.

At the door of the bank he was informed that the anarchists and Communists had gathered around the barracks. Ignacio did not even go in. He made straight for Marta's house. Her mother said to him: "She went with her father to the barracks."

Jesus! A wave of panic swept over Ignacio, but he managed to control it, for Marta's mother's eyes were fixed on him in supplication. "Don't you worry," he said to her, "I'll bring her here, somehow." He was just leaving when the telephone rang. It was Colonel Muñoz informing the major's wife that a squad of Assault Guards was on its way to safeguard her. He assured her she had nothing to worry about.

Ignacio went bounding down the stairs. His first impulse was to go to the barracks, but he quickly realized that if they saw him it would be worse. Then he said to himself: "The only thing to do is to talk with David and Olga...."

He set out for the UGT. What a long time since he had mounted those stairs! He asked for the teachers. They came out. They could not conceal a start of surprise when they saw him. "You here?"

Ignacio realized instantly how incongruous the situation was, and that he had acted without stopping to wonder whether it was the logical thing to do. The surprises life held! Here were David and Olga, who had nothing to do with the case, dragged away from their revolutionary plans to take a hand in the affairs of Major Martínez de Soria's daughter. But Ignacio did not flinch. He still believed in miracles. He looked steadily at the teachers and told them his story.

The shoulders of David and Olga drew together as though seeking each other, as always happened when they were confronted with the unexpected. "Do you realize what you are asking of us?"

"I do."

Olga needed only a second to get her surprise under control. She reacted immediately. Perhaps, she thought, life is not the hard and fast thing we at times believe it. "All right. Let her go to our house."

"But," said Ignacio, "she's at the barracks."

"The barracks!" The teachers looked at each other. There was not a minute to lose. Olga went out, with Ignacio following a short distance behind her.

When they reached the Piedra Bridge, they saw the crowd approaching, escorting the officers toward the infantry guardhouse.

Olga went over to one of the officers of the Assault Guards. He answered: "The girl asked to be taken to the barracks of the Civil Guard. She must be there."

Ignacio caught up with Olga and suggested that they take a taxi and go for her at once. They found one quickly, and got off at the corner nearest the barracks. Inside they found Marta sitting between Padilla and Rodríguez.

At sight of Ignacio, Marta got to her feet, an expression of hope on her face. But as soon as she saw Olga, her expression changed. She was about to say something, but Ignacio went up to her and took her wrist with a restraining gesture. Olga took no notice, saying: "She will have to be disguised." Padilla, completely unruffled, asked them to wait a minute. He went out and came back with two braids he had just cut off his daughter's head. Olga fastened the braids on Marta, tying them with ribbons. Then a green flowered skirt, and Olga took her by taxi to the school.

And Ignacio was left alone, wandering about the city at the very moment the fires began.

Olga's generous act and Padilla's composure had exhausted his capacity for wonder. He was an eyewitness to everything that happened. He saw the cross in the river, he saw El Responsable's column line up, the other columns, he saw the flames breaking out everywhere, he saw the skeletons lying at the base of the Cathedral. His sorrow was complete, and he realized that the tumor had finally come to a head. What came over him at this point was a sense of responsibility. He had got Marta to safety. Now he had to look after his family—and Mateo. He started for home. Mateo was already making for the Pyrenees, his lunch and his sandals under his arm. César had to be saved. He went to the Museum. Mosén Alberto was already gone, and Ignacio took César home. The maid had to be saved. He went back to the Museum and took her, without asking permission, to Julio's house, saying to Doña Amparo: "I don't suppose there'll be any objections." Don Emilio Santos had to be saved. He went to the flat near the station and took Don Emilio home with him.

He thought of the assistant manager, whose chair he had noticed was empty when he went by the bank that morning. He went to his house. He knocked, and a voice inquired: "Who is it?"

"Ignacio, from the bank."

In thirty seconds the door opened, and there stood the assistant manager, with an air of surprising dignity. He led Ignacio into the dining room, where he introduced him to Brother Juan, one of the friars of the Christian Doctrine, who was sitting glued to the radio.

The assistant manager did not let Ignacio talk. It was as though he refused to understand that Ignacio had come to warn him that he had to leave the flat and hide somewhere. The assistant manager was thinking of nothing but the radio and the short-wave broadcasts. He made Ignacio sit down and listen to a speaker who said he was talking from Jaca. The voice said that the victory of the military was indubitable in spite of the fact that the uprising had failed in certain garrisons because of treachery. It repeated time and time again that all Castile was in the hands of the military, all Galicia, and part of the south. The remarks were punctuated with shouts of "*¡Viva España!*" the music of the Foreign Legion hymn, and that of the Falange.

Ignacio became impatient, and said to the assistant manager: "This is all fine. But you have to find yourself some safe place."

There was no response from the assistant manager. He was obsessed by the radio. Brother Juan sat with his eyes on the ground, waiting to see what the assistant manager planned to do.

Ignacio grabbed his superior by the lapels. "Disguise yourselves and we'll go to Tower of Babel's house. I'll go out first and see that the coast is clear. You'll be safe there."

The assistant manager smiled. "I'm not moving from here," he said firmly.

"But don't you realize that this is absolutely crazy?"

It seemed to the assistant manager that to leave his home was an act of desertion.

"Don't be a fool. Everybody is taking cover. God only knows where Don Santiago Estrada is by this time."

The assistant manager looked at him for the last time. "The rest can do as they please. I'm not leaving here."

Ignacio replied in a fury: "Then we'll come and take you away."

He left the house. He did not know what had come over him. He had a foreboding that something horrible was going to happen, and every person, even those with whom he had no close ties, seemed to him a sacred thing because he realized that life was hanging by a thread. He entered the bank just as the employees were leaving by the rear entrance, after the morning's work.

They were all surprised to see him in such a hurry and sweating. Ignacio wondered: "Can it be that they don't know about the fires?"

On the contrary, they were talking about them with complete indifference. He managed to get Tower of Babel aside and to tell him how things stood with the assistant manager and the danger he was running. "Take him to your house."

Tower of Babel looked down at him from his towering height. "Who? Me?"

"Yes, he'll be safe in your house."

Tower of Babel looked at Ignacio as though he had gone crazy. "But why? What danger is he running?"

"What danger? Don't you know that he was carrying arms?"

"What's that got to do with it?"

"They're going to kill all of them."

"They're going to kill—?" Tower of Babel walked on. "Come off it, Ignacio. You're getting the people mixed up in your mind with the military."

There was no way of convincing him. For a moment Ignacio was disconcerted. He was figuring out another plan when he suddenly saw Blasco go by, followed by a group of bootblacks. Their faces were the faces of strangers, and their waists were girdled with pistols and daggers. They looked at him in a strange manner. Ignacio thought they were probably worrying about him at home, and he turned toward the Rambla. The hymns of the Jaca radio station were buzzing in his ears.

MEANWHILE Mateo and Jorge, their pants already badly torn, were looking down on the distant towers of Gerona and the smoke, smoke rising from the heart of the city.

"Yes, I know, Spain is on fire," Mateo said to Jorge. "But Spain, see here—" and he showed him a map sewed inside his shirt. "Spain is a destiny in—"

Jorge cut him short: "Save it, Mateo. The Pyrenees are more vertical than your Syndicate."

NINETY

At six o'clock Gorki was named Mayor. The mob burst into the City Hall and pitched out into the street the pictures of distinguished men whom they happened not to know. The perfumer saw, in the office that had been made ready for him, the immense armchair, and the walls covered with tapestries depicting historic events. He was in the seventh heaven. Turning to all who had followed him to his office, he said: "Comrades, you anti-fascists of Gerona are going to get free water, gas, and electricity. The city is at the service of the citizens, not the citizens at the service of the city!" As Gorki's aides, Cosme Vila appointed Professor Morales and Sergeant Molina. Gorki discovered a package of English cigarettes in a drawer of the desk. He held it up, showing it to everyone: "English cigarettes, English cigarettes!" A roar of laughter went up at the expense of the former Mayor, architect Massana.

At the same time another ceremony was going on outside which the instinct of the crowd sensed as being of supreme importance: the commandeering of cars. Two hours sufficed for the mob to take over nearly every car in the city. The first to possess himself of one had been Alfredo, an Andalusian, whose choice had fallen on that of Don Pedro Oriol. The next step was to strip all the garages in the city. Future took over a truck that delivered coffee. Cosme Vila had given orders that at least three cars were to be put at the service of the Communist Party. El Responsable for his part envisaged many trips. Murillo, whose cell was displaying great activity, got himself two Buicks, that of Noguer the notary and another. By right of office, the City Hall Ford belonged to Gorki. La Valenciana was fed up with riding in trucks that reeked of garlic, and she hoped Teo would stop his nonsense and provide her with something better. Don Santiago Estrada's Balilla was taken over by the UGT.

There were altercations at the garages. "By whose authority?"

"The Anti-Fascist Revolutionary Committee."

"What committee is that?"

"You'll soon find out."

Certain garage owners refused to comply in spite of everything. Whereupon the members of the militia asked them: "Were you one of those who were bearing arms or something?"

It was a persuasive argument. The garages, public as well as private, which had been closed because of the strike, were forced open. When the new driver showed as he drove off that he knew how to handle a car, the garage owners gave a small sigh of hope. But the opposite often happened.

By seven in the afternoon the city was a speedway. Cars of every make and size were coming and going at breakneck speed. The panic of the pedestrians grew by the minute, for in no time the appearance of the cars had completely changed. Flags flapped over the hood, and the bodies were covered with signs, most of them macabre. Future had tied a shinbone to his truck and it went banging against the tailboard. The bootblacks were in the limelight once more, and one of them had drawn a skull on the windshield of his Renault. But, above all, guns. Gun muzzles were sticking out of the lowered windows. Every car bristled with rifles. It was impossible to step onto the balcony without feeling oneself the target of the dozens of guns whizzing by. Suddenly there was a squealing of brakes, and a group of militiamen dismounted. What for? Nobody knew. Something important.

The possession of the cars gave the new owners a great sense of assurance. The gasoline stations were ordered not to run out of gasoline, the wives of the soldiers of the people's army began to admire their men and to believe that the revolution was in earnest. But many of the men answered: "You are very much mistaken if you think I have requisitioned this car to have fun. There's lots to do, lots." That was what Julio had feared, and in this he coincided with Professor Civil: the need to justify the car would lead to the wildest projects....

Cosme Vila would have liked to organize everything systematically, and to that end he had named the Anti-Fascist Revolutionary Committee of Gerona, with himself and Gorki as chairmen, El Responsable and Future representing the CNT-FAI, Casal and David representing the UGT, and Alfredo, the Andalusian, as the direct representative of the people. This committee was to be empowered both to give orders and to punish violations. All systematization, however, proved impossible. The meeting was called for seven o'clock, in what that morning had been the headquarters of Liga Catalana. All the committee members except David were present, and the Anti-Fascist Revolutionary Committee drew up a message to be read over the radio. But one needed only to step out on the balcony to see that the mob did not give a hoot about messages and that the members of the people's army could do their own planning and carry out their own revolutionary operations. The news arriving from the rest of the country was contradictory; some reports said there was fierce resistance on the part of the fascists, and this raised feeling still higher. Eight more churches were burning, in some cases the whole structure, in others just the altars. The Revolutionary Committees of the outlying areas traveled back and forth from their villages to the center of the city, reporting on the measures they had taken. The committee of the village of Salt quickly attracted attention because of its two cars, one always close behind the other, which soon came to be known as the death cars, for they carried a flag with black letters saying: "Death to the Fascists." The members of the committee of Salt were a thorn in the flesh to those of Gerona. In Salt they had not only burned the church, but cut off what made the priest a man and then had hanged him in the fountain in the square, with his feet in the water. They could go and see it if they didn't believe it! He was still there. And they had cleaned up the insane asylum, carrying off the nuns in a wagon. They only made the inmates still crazier with their praying!

Now they were doing something useful. Some of them were cleaning the water closets of the movies, the cafés, the headquarters of the Revolutionary Committee. Others were scrubbing the floors in the homes of the workers, and of course all of them would have to go to the fountain in the square every day and do a little dance in front of the priest.

Some of the members of the people's army of Gerona shrugged their shoulders. "What's so great about that? Wait and see what happens here tonight." It annoyed them that the committee of Salt should think itself so smart because its cars had been named death cars. Wait till they saw the names they were going to give theirs! The first thing to do was to complete the lists, which had not been done yet. How many had been carrying arms? Four hundred, five hundred? What about Liga Catalana? And the members of the Civil Guard who were still in the barracks? There was no call to be putting on so many airs about wetting the feet of one priest!

Others thought all the talk about lists very funny. As though they didn't know all the names by heart, or as though one couldn't tell a fascist by his smell!

Opinion was still fluid, and a phrase had only to be pronounced emphatically for the whole crowd to repeat it and consider it an order. Rumors of every description were rife. "They say all radios have to be turned in. They are asking for empty bottles, nobody knows what for. Employers will have to appear before the Revolutionary Committee for trial!" Many of these rumors were later denied, but some of them died hard.

One of these orders was put into effect, for it did not come from just any group, but from the one headed by El Cojo, composed of a considerable number of anarchists. This had to do with the religious images in private houses. The families were given until midnight to bring the images to the Rambla, where on the stroke of twelve they would become the fuel for a big bonfire. And to this end El Cojo and Santi, who were directing operations, had drawn a huge circle with chalk in the middle of the Rambla.

There were discussions and struggles in the families. Many women considered it a mortal sin to hand over the images. They left the houses with their baskets as though going to market, carrying in them a St. Anthony or a St. Teresa of the Infant Jesus, which they buried on the outskirts of the city, taking careful note of the spot. Others disguised the images, and many an infant Jesus became a plump doll with curling eyelashes. Virgins looked on while sandals were laced up their legs. The foot crushing the head of the serpent was an excellent imitation of a dance step.

Matías Alvear came home from the Telegraph office with the news that the arrests had begun and that the committee had decided to use the Seminary as a jail and had emptied it of its contents, leaving only the halls and the bare cells.

The searches had begun, too. Along the Calle del Progreso the militiamen were going from floor to floor, and Matías, with his own eyes, had seen Future throwing the volumes of the *Espasa Encyclopedia* out of the window of a lawyer's apartment one by one. Dozens of people were standing around watching, as though in the hope that any minute he would toss out the lawyer in person.

Pilar stepped out for a minute to buy Don Emilio Santos tobacco, and she heard the loudspeaker of the Café Cataluña repeating incessantly: "The whereabouts of the members of Falange must be discovered! Hear this! Hear this!" And it gave the address of the members one after another.

Late that night Ignacio went out again. He made his way between the rushing cars to the UGT headquarters with the idea of waiting till David and Olga came out to ask them if he could go home with them to see Marta.

After a long wait, David came out, and he made no objection. Everyone knew that he and Ignacio had continued friends. On the way David told him that he had refused to form a part of the Anti-Fascist Committee of Gerona because he did not like the turn things were taking.

Ignacio hardly answered him. He felt that David's responsibility in what was happening had been very great, and he did not want to talk about it. He had accepted from them the favor of hiding Marta, but he felt this laid no obligations on him beyond politeness. If they began talking, he might say over-harsh things.

But it was as though David sensed none of this, as though he was thinking aloud. He was obsessed by the cars bristling with guns which rushed by, and fearful of the coming of night.

"They are going to commit some atrocity tonight," he said. "Casal is going to try to prevent it, but I have my doubts. I have my doubts."

Ignacio was walking along the riverbank, recalling the days when he was being tutored at the school. A thousand thoughts were churning in his mind. He thought of Mateo in the mountains. He thought of the Church of San Félix—where he had made his confession to Mosén Francisco—a charred ruin now. What had happened in the world? "When I see clearly, I will fight!" He recalled that in the Calle de Rutila he himself had forgathered with El Responsable and El Cojo, in the dining room around a red-hot stove. Anxiety clutched at his heart, and the need to redeem himself, to redeem all this madness. To save. He must try to see the assistant manager again! He would go to Professor Civil's house and take him somewhere, for as the father of a Falangist he was in danger. Those two colossal ideas Julio talked about—face to face! The trouble was that they were not face to face, but one on top of the other. When Major Martínez de Soria had read the proclamation declaring martial law, Cosme Vila had been under arrest in his home; now that Cosme Vila was the big shot of the city, Major Martínez de Soria lay on a straw pallet in jail. Was all this going to be of long or short duration? By some miracle, might Spain be restored to peace? Poor Spain! What was happening in Málaga, what would his cousin José be doing in Madrid, what position would the family in Bilbao have adopted?

Imprinted on his eyeballs was the expression on those faces framed in red kerchiefs. All that was subhuman; man had renounced his human estate. Ignacio felt himself possessed of an indomitable will. He was neither confused by the fires and the pistols nor afraid of them. He would stand up to them and save what he could for those who in one way or another had put their trust in him. His father was too downcast, and his mother might perhaps do something rash. Poor Pilar, crying her heart out on her pillow! Feverish plans began to form in his mind. He thought about Cosme Vila, seeing him in the Arús Bank pounding away at the typewriter, and asked himself if it would not be licit to put a bullet through him...and another through El Responsable...and one through this one and that one.... He wondered that he could be thinking such things without a shudder. Where was his gun? And what about the childhood of those men? The hunger they had suffered? Would killing them serve any useful purpose? For one Cosme Vila or one El Responsable dead, how many new ones would crop up? Was he going to kill off the whole mob?

David, beside him, was repeating: "Cosme Vila and El Responsable, unfortunately, will suffice."

NINETY-ONE

THE CNT-FAI and the Communist Party sufficed. Once the stars had become the absolute monarchs of the firmament, undimmed by clouds or even a moon; once the heap of images in the Rambla had become charred embers, still oozing paint; once all the men of Matías Alvear's age had heard, from their homes, the Cathedral bells chime the hour of three, the CNT-FAI and the Communist Party threw open the wide gates of the cemetery.

All the efforts of Julio, who, like David, had feared that night like no other in his whole life; all the optimism of the general, who was convinced that a prompt trial of the officers would take care of everything; all Casal's cross-questioning of himself, putting in one balance-plate his indignation at the uprising against the Republic and in the other the value of a human life—none of this prevented the opening of the wide gate of the cemetery. Nor the efforts of the Costas or the whole governing body of Izquierda Republicana, who went first to the Commissioner and then to the headquarters of the Anti-Fascist Revolutionary Committee, pointing out that all that was going on had nothing to do with the defense of the Republic. All in vain. The architects Massana and Ribas had saved the Cathedral, but they were unable to save the people, the bodies. The bodies of Don Santiago Estrada and his wife; those of the assistant manager of the bank and Brother Juan; that of Don Pedro Oriol; those of Don Jorge, his wife, his maids, and all his children except Jorge, who was in the Pyrenees; of Captain Roberto of the Civil Guard; of Padilla and Rodríguez, who were recognized by a waiter as the assailants of Dr. Relken; of the parish priest of San Félix and the three priests of the city; of the three doctors and the lawyer who had owned the *Espasa Encyclopedia*; of Benito, Professor Civil's son, and of Roca and Haro—a total of thirty-six bodies turned into food for the worms because they could not be utilized, like the Cathedral, as a museum or serve any utilitarian need of the people.

It was the cars bristling with guns, the members of the Communist party and the CNT-FAI riding inside them. Cosme Vila and El Responsable had planned the operation sitting in the president's office of the Liga Catalana, in the chair the notary Noguer had occupied. At three on the dot the first car stopped before the home of Don Santiago Estrada. Its occupants went up to the flat and knocked; as nobody answered, they knocked again. The head of the CEDA finally opened the door and was instantly informed that he, his wife and children were under arrest.

"By whose authority?"

"By the authority of the Anti-Fascist Revolutionary Committee."

The children were not at home. Don Santiago Estrada realized how things stood. His wife was in bed; she was not given time to dress. She felt a pair of sinewy arms, those of Blasco, pushing her into the hall, down the stairs, and into a car beside her husband. Don Santiago Estrada and she looked at one another and each read in the other's face unmitigated fear. Everything took place with frightening ease in the silence of the night: the squealing of the tires as the car braked, the chill of the night air, the shoves toward a wall where the niches could be sensed, the faint stir of the cypresses, footsteps, the snick of breech-bolts, the embrace, a burst of gunfire, and death.

Don Pedro Oriol's wife begged them to take her with him. Future said: "Nope, not you. You haven't done anything."

Don Pedro said to her: "You stay here and pray for me."

Don Jorge received them ceremoniously. Nobody had gone to bed that night. One of the maids opened the door when she heard the pounding and asked: "What do you wish?"

"To talk with your employer for a moment." Four Murcians and Cosme Vila himself followed the maid in. Cosme Vila was suspicious of all this formality, and he pushed the Murcians ahead of him. The maid opened a door. A shot rang out, and another, and then another. Three of the Murcians fell screaming. Cosme Vila saw Don Jorge with a gun in his hand, gloves, spats, perfectly self-possessed. Beside him stood his whole family, his wife holding a rosary in her fingers. Cosme Vila flattened himself against a wall and pressed the trigger of his submachine gun. "Rat-ta-ta-ta." The family dropped one after another. The maids made a move as though to kneel or run, and they were mowed down in turn. Cosme Vila stepped into the room, and the Murcian administered the *coup de grâce* to the bodies that had fallen on one another. Cosme Vila ordered: "You stay here on guard. I am going to find someone to take these fellows to the hospital." Two of the Murcians were groaning on the floor; the third lay still.

Thirty-six bodies were dragged from their houses and driven to the cemetery. Some died in terror, others bravely—Roca and Haro shouting: "*¡Arriba*

España!" Benito Civil calling his wife's name; the three doctors with utter amazement painted on their faces; the priest of San Félix wanting to forgive his enemies, but without achieving it; the lawyer of the *Espasa Encyclopedia* begging them on his knees to spare his life; Padilla taking leave of his wife with these words: "See that the little one lets her braids grow out again"; Rodríguez saying to the militiamen: "But Spain will win, don't make any mistake"; the assistant manager firmly convinced that his death had been decreed by the Lodge of the Calle del Pavo.

Half of the city learned during the night what was going on. The neighbors of those who were taken from their homes; those who peered fearfully out of windows when they heard the cars stop; those who heard the screams of the victims on the stairs; those who sensed something strange and menacing in the slamming of the doors; those who without stirring from bed recognized in the steps on the sidewalk something hard and belligerent from which there was no appeal. The other half knew nothing. They assumed that the searches were going on, that the militiamen were getting drunk on the pleasure of driving a Fiat or a Cadillac, and that women were mixed up in the business.

Most of the militiamen were amazed to see how easy it was to kill a man or five men. One had only to think the word "fascist," take aim at the heart or the head, and fire—and that was all there was to it. Besides, in spite of the stars, the night hid many things in the cemetery. One could not see the eyes of the condemned person; that was the most important. One could see a blurred outline against the niches, and certain objects that gleamed, a button, a wrist watch, a fountain pen. But the main thing was not to see the eyes, the eyes of Don Pedro Oriol, for instance.

What the dark could not manage to hide, though, were the words. Words came through with perfect clarity. Supplications to God—who had seen God?—defiance like that of Rodríguez, shouts of "*¡Viva España!*"—appeals for mercy. But, above all, the tone of the voices. Certain voices had sounded strangely amidst the niches and the cypresses. That of Brother Juan, for instance. Brother Juan was French and he had cried out: "*Mon Seigneur et mon Dieu.*" Ideal did not understand the meaning of the words, but the timbre of the voice made him shiver for a moment. Because it seemed to him that Brother Juan had spoken after he was dead, when Ideal himself and Santi had gone over and finished him off, holding the pistol muzzle against his head. A long while later, when they stopped the car on the Piedra Bridge and Santi said: "I'm thirsty," Ideal could still hear: "*Mon Seigneur et mon Dieu,*" and he told himself that he must ask the daughters of El Responsable what that meant. He was not going to ask them right away; he'd wait a few days.

The one who had no fear was El Responsable. El Responsable, on the contrary, wished it had been light and not dark. It annoyed him not to be able to see the eyes, though he was sure that the men lined up along the wall were seeing his. On his third trip, as he went over to three men of the Tradicionalista Party to give them the *coup de grâce*, he felt a desire to plunge his hands into their blood.

Those who became most excited were those who carried out their missions after daybreak. There was no faking then, no diffuse outlines, no vagueness. The thing in front of them was not a mass of shadow; it was a person. In all its insignificance and grandeur. The imminence of death gave the gestures of those about to die an unwonted relief, a strange importance. Some of them who dragged themselves along like lizards were revolting. Others, on the contrary, displayed a boundless calm, a rare precision in every movement. As though each of their gestures had been the object of thought for years. Especially the way of moving their feet as they approached the ordained spot, and the lowering of the head. It was like a moment of absolute concentration.

Dawn revealed all those details, heightened by the fact that the setting, too, was different. For with the coming of daylight nobody could bear to stay on in the cemetery. The paths to the left, to the right, were so clogged that the sight was nauseating. Besides, the gravedigger kept saying: "That will do, that will do."

For that reason they decided—Blasco was the first to think of it—not to stop there, but to follow the highway and carry out their missions by the gullies along the road or by a tree unexpectedly appearing around a bend, suitably situated on an embankment.

All this gave a new turn to the significance of the act. There was a glimmer of logic about scything down lives in the cemetery. It was already impregnated with the odor of death, with the sap of the dead; Joaquín Santaló and Jaime Arias were there. But in the open country, by a tree or in a grove...

Farther along the highway they found groves winged and poetic in the light of dawn. There the steps of the condemned took on even more solemnity as they approached the appointed tree. All nature was coming awake with the day, beginning to live, and, lo, here were these men to be killed! It was a little harder to squeeze the trigger except when aiming at those who dragged themselves like lizards and gnawed their fists.

There were instances in which the setting proved so overwhelming that a kind of terror which they were powerless to control seized the militiamen. This happened to Blasco and Future when, on their last trip, they stopped the car and ordered out the lawyer of the *Espasa Encyclopedia* and two priests they had surprised in the home of a devout old woman. Something in the surroundings made the two anarchists lose their heads, and they could not wait the necessary seconds for their victims to cross the gully to the other side. They began to shoot them in the back from inside the car, without getting out. Then they frantically turned the car in two hair-raising reverses, and shot off without even remembering the *coup de grâce.*

And so it went. From daybreak all the rest, to the total of thirty-six, were assassinated along the roadside or beside the trees, and left there unburied. Which was not pleasant, for on the farms life went on as usual and girls passed near by, carrying jars of milk, or a little herdboy walked along with his cows or goats. The discovery of the corpses so horrified some of them that they began to run, driving the animals before them, to tell of their find. The grown people had heard the shots. Some of them had thought they were those of hunters; others had guessed the truth. In any case, nobody ventured to go near the spot, for the cars were still arriving.

No two of the militiamen experienced the same sensations. There were those like El Cojo, who at the same time that he felt an acrid taste in his mouth was annoyed because the bodies fell to the ground. He would have wished them to remain upright so that he could go on firing, as in a shooting gallery at the fair. Others tried to remember why they were doing what they were doing. It was no use. They could recall only the most trivial reasons, as happened to Future when he took aim at Don Pedro Oriol. All he could remember was that one day he had seen Don Pedro stooping over to pick up a piece of paper he had dropped on the sidewalk. It was impossible for him to recall another thing, either *El Tradicionalista* or the timberland Don Pedro owned. The same thing had happened to Cosme Vila in Don Jorge's house. When he saw Don Jorge standing there unperturbed, with gloves, spats, and a shotgun in his hand, despite the rage the gun aroused in him, and the lordly, self-assured air the whole house emanated, one image slashed across his mind as he squeezed the machine-gun trigger: that of Don Jorge asking him one day at the Arús Bank where the men's room was.

There were kaleidoscopic impressions succeeding one another like waves of the sea. Murillo suffered this phenomenon in a strange form. Murillo, on his own responsibility, in the company of Salvio and other comrades, had lined up along the road a stockbroker and two lawyers, the three of them members of the CEDA. And just as he fired he made the discovery that the stockbroker looked amazingly like Cosme Vila. The same huge head, prematurely bald, the same thin, straight mouth. Without knowing why, instead of aiming at the man's heart, he aimed at his head.

The only woman who took part in all this was La Valenciana. Only on two trips. Before going for Don Jorge, Cosme Vila had ordered two squads of the People's Militia to take charge of the three doctors. La Valenciana had insisted on going with them because she hated doctors. They had never given her help when she needed it; in her five deliveries she had had to make shift as best she could, without benefit of doctors.

La Valenciana did not shoot because, contrary to Gorki's and Teo's belief, she did not know how to handle a gun. But on both trips she had opened the door for the doctors and politely invited them to step out. She treated them with all courtesy, partly to seem refined, and on the last trip because she recognized the fact that two of them were men of venerable appearance, men of the sort she might have liked to marry when she was young.

Afterwards she laughed, and had the audacity to strip off their wrist watches and rings, something Blasco was incapable of doing, or Gorki either, in his single intervention. As a matter of fact, the only ones who looted personal possessions were La Valenciana, Future, El Cojo, Santi, the Murcians, and Cosme Vila. Cosme Vila, before leaving Don Jorge's home, just as he stepped across the doorsill, turned back and took the family tree from the wall, for he recalled that he had promised it to the People's Museum.

The Murcians were probably the most spontaneous and natural of all. They carried out their work with a kind of primitive, animal happiness. They were convinced that they were performing a duty, an important surgical operation for the good of the worker and society. The skulls drawn on the windshields seemed to them to symbolize future well-being, the end of poverty. Words, eyes, French phrases, changes of light and setting, meant nothing to them. They would have done the same thing in the same way at any hour or in any place. And it seemed logical to them to take not only wallets, but gold teeth, too.

For that reason they greatly regretted not finding Warning Voice in his house. This was the great failure of the starry, revolutionary, unclouded night. They had all had visions of the death of Warning Voice, with his gold-rimmed glasses, his tight gold smile, his gold watch. It would have been the big number, and here was the house empty! It was a great disappointment. They all felt the same way—Cosme Vila, El Responsable, El Cojo. All the search parties called at Warning Voice's house, one after the other, and it was always the same story. The open door, the dental office with its instruments of torture. The Murcians found a portrait of a Carlist general on the wall; subsequent searchers found it broken in a corner.

The case of Mosén Alberto was different because they all were hopeful that the quarry had not escaped. The Museum had been under the vigilance of the Assault Guards, reinforced by the architects Massana and Ribas, as cultural delegates of the Generalidad. Not a single search party believed the officer when he said: "Mosén Alberto is not here." But they could not very well shoot it out with him. Mosén Alberto would not get away; all they needed to do was to station sentinels behind the arcades in the plaza.

As was to be expected, there were those who took no part in the killings. Victor worked all night on *El Proletario*; Professor Morales, worn out with so much broadcasting, went to bed.

Like Casal. Casal knew what was going on, but there was nothing he could do. Moreover, his inner conflict still tormented him. On the one hand the measure seemed monstrous; on the other, he sad to himself: "Perhaps it's necessary." In any case, he confessed to his wife that for the first time in his life he had heard figures that made his head swim. What he was alluding to by figures was "what remained to be done." Because it was evident that this night was only the beginning, and that its victors, its undisputed victors—Cosme Vila and El Responsable—had in mind further plans to be carried out in successive stages. The difference between the two leaders lay in the fact that Cosme Vila willingly accepted these stages. He realized that nothing in the world, not even a bullet fired in cold blood, can penetrate more than one heart or at most two at a time. Therefore he accepted as an incontrovertible fact, in view of the number of hearts, the need of many nights and many bullets. But El Responsable felt the hours slipping between his fingers, and he rebelled against this. Here it was morning, and they had made so little progress in their labors! Now the city was awakening, and they would have to wait until night again. Why could not time stop?

His daughters repeated the words of the gravedigger: "That will do, that will do."

El Responsable realized that they were right. He had triumphed. The defeated was the sergeant, the friend of his older daughter. Three times his rifle had jammed, as though it had been bewitched to keep him from firing. The defeated was his wife, who kept on saying the rosary in the insane asylum until finally the Revolutionary Committee of Salt wrested the beads from her hands. The defeated were the thirty-six who had experienced in their flesh the justice of the people.

El Responsable spoke of the dead, of his wife, of the sergeant, because he did not know about the real defeated of the night, the one who felt himself the most pusillanimous, the most mean-spirited, the most abject, the least worthy to call himself a man: Teo.

Teo was the great failure of the night. Because, when all is said and done, those who died were not rejected by the fact of dying, but took from the living, and left among the living, something consubstantial. Nor had a single one of the thirty-six died alone, with the sole exception of Don Pedro Oriol.

Whereas Teo was alone, absolutely alone. Without a car, without a party, without a fixed objective.

Teo had made a thousand calculations, and every one had gone wrong. He had believed that he had only to crook his finger and La Valenciana would come running. This had not been the case. He saw her for a minute, but she looked away coquettishly and kept on her way. He had also believed that the Murcians would ask him to act as their leader, as when they set fire to San Félix. This had not happened, either. There had been a big change in the Murcians since the requisitioning of the cars, and they seemed to want to run things by themselves.

The result was that Teo found himself alone. He had gone home to get a bite of supper, thinking that perhaps at the last minute, when operations got under way, he would have the company of somebody, perhaps a taxi driver. So he kept telling himself: "Of course. Naturally." But he had reckoned without San Narciso. When he opened the door of his flat, he was unexpectedly confronted with the urn holding the body of San Narciso. It gave him a terrible shock because the posture of the saint, with his hands crossed on his breast, was strangely pathetic in spite of the fact that as a child Teo had heard his mother say: "He looks as though he was sleeping."

Teo still tried to master himself, to overcome his fear by a frontal attack, to approach the saint and look him straight in the eye, man to man, thus proving to himself that it was nothing but a piece of wood, and then all that would vanish. But what happened when he did this was doubly strange. It seemed to him not only that the face was not of wood, but really of flesh, but also that the flesh was not dead. It seemed to him that it was a living countenance, that the lips were murmuring something, something that sounded like "Bo, bo..." He felt his muscles turn numb, and only the fact that he was wearing a cap kept his hair from rising on his head. He could not eat. He went out slamming the door. It seemed to him that he was dreaming. And he spent the night wandering alone, without venturing to speak to a taxi driver or to take part in any of the operations. This allowed him to witness and evaluate many things. The constant twinkling of the stars, the solidity of the stones, the last flickering flames of all the burned buildings, now heaps of rubble on empty lots. Teo made the complete rounds of the city. He saw the cars stop, and recognized the occupants by their silhouettes. "That's Blasco. That's Santi." He recognized Santi by the way he took the stairs at a bound; El Cojo by his limp; La Valenciana by the gleam of her bare bosom. He hid in the doorways, peered around the corners. He saw them taking someone from Don Jorge's house to the hospital. This puzzled him. He saw the skeletons in front of the Convent of the Heart of Mary. And suddenly, in the river, a figure erect, arms stretched wide. It was the Christ of the Church of the Jesuits, still standing head down. The loneliness of Christ in the muddy waters of the river was beyond description. Teo leaned on the railing of the bridge and observed Him. It seemed to him that He too was saying something. It was then Teo was afraid he might be going mad. He spat. Finally, exhausted, he went to the stable where his two horses and his dray dozed. There he found the breath of friendship; there he managed to fall asleep.

NINETY-TWO

BY midmorning the phantom of death stalked the city. A collective sense of responsibility floated at head-level. In reality the thirty-six were not gone; they were present, all the more so because of the ease with which their departure had taken place.

People realized the role enemies played in the city and in the life of each of them. Severed, a void remained. The wives of the militiamen felt diminished without Don Santiago Estrada.

It was a tedious morning, with the wounds of the night before unfolding in the grayish light. The blackened buildings, the pianos in the river, a fish on the keyboard of one of them, the horrible black char of the images on the Rambla in the rough circle described by Santi, the red flag floating over the Cathedral, and, near the station, two new cars converted into scrap.

Around eleven came a shift of scene. The militiamen made their appearance once more. They had got a few hours' sleep and were ready for another day's work. With them the cars reappeared, and in them many excited, voluble women dressed in blue coveralls. All of a sudden the women got out of the cars and stopped pedestrians, pinning an emblem marked "International Red Cross" or "For the People's Militia" on them. The two confessionals of the Church of the Carmen had been set up on either side of the Piedra Bridge like collectors' booths, and two militiamen sitting inside them were receiving contributions.

Once more noise was rife in the city, and people went quickly about their business, except those persons who were finding delectation in what had occurred or took it for granted. Among these were many one would never have expected. One of the postmen, a friend of Matías Alvear, completely knocked the wind out of the latter's sails when he said to him: "Well, at last there'll be apartments to let!" Others had bought *El Proletario* and were reading with unconcealed satisfaction the lists of the city's presumptive fascists.

The cafés and barbershops had opened and were full of militiamen, some of whom insisted that the military had not been defeated everywhere, nor anything like it, that they were in full control in many parts of Spain, and that in others the people were still fighting. This aroused the fury of their listeners at the thought that Major Martínez de Soria and the rest of the officers were being safeguarded by the authorities. And not only they, but their families enjoyed official protection. The wife of Major Martínez de Soria, Marta—everybody firmly believed that Marta was calmly staying on in her own house.

One fact was evident: people tried to think of the familiar faces they would never see again, and could not. The sovereign law of self-defense left no room for any other thought. The cars once more became an obsession—many of them now bore names similar to those of the vehicles of Salt. And even more than the cars, the steady stream of orders issued by the Anti-Fascist Revolutionary Committee. It was forbidden to wear mourning, forbidden to ask a missing person's whereabouts, forbidden to make an investigation of the highways, forbidden to leave Gerona without a safe-conduct stamped by the committee. Controls had just been set up. Armed guards would be stationed at every exit from the city to check the movements of vehicles and persons. Signs pasted on the walls bore the information that the Anti-Fascist Revolutionary Committee had set up the necessary offices to ensure the proper functioning of this service.

"Do you know if it is permissible to go to such and such a quarter?"

"I don't think so."

Everybody, instinctively, had stopped wearing a hat. A hat clashed with the blue coveralls of the militiamen. Possibly the only hats remaining in the city were those of Julio García, rakishly aslant, and of Matías Alvear.

One great source of danger was quickly localized: the maids. It was they who informed about who was hiding whom. They went out of their employers' houses, stopped the first militiamen they met, and said: "They're hiding a priest on the third floor."

This gave rise to indescribable panic. The homeless, those seeking haven, were numbered in the dozens. Nuns appeared from distant towns, disguised as best they could, to knock at the door of a relative. "Dear God, you here!" The maids, the maids had seen them arrive.

Don Emilio Santos's maid informed to Salvio on three factory owners from Barcelona, who, wearing false mustaches and leather windbreakers, had hidden in the house next door.

There was a steady stream of militiamen through the streets taking those under arrest to the Seminary, which had been turned into a jail. For this reason many apartments were vacated, to be occupied by the militia or to house some revolutionary service. Blasco and El Cojo installed themselves in the home of Noguer the notary, where, to their utter stupefaction, they learned from some papers in the desk that Don Jorge had disinherited his son Jorge for having joined the Falange.

Everyone was convinced that those under arrest would be shot at night. So the members of the family, as soon as father or brother had been led away, realized that the only possibility of saving him was for one of the militiamen to take his part, alleging that he owed him a favor.

This gave rise to a great commotion. Everyone racked his memory to see if on some occasion he might have done this one or that one a favor, a workman, El Cojo, some poor person.... Many times the search ended in complete despair, for the probing turned up nothing. In other cases there came a cry of hope: "One day I gave Blasco a big tip.... I arranged for the wife of Alfredo, the Andalusian, to have an operation free of charge."

The militiamen receiving such visits dropped their cigarette stubs on the floor and rubbed them out. Some of them took a deep breath, meditating, and then answered: "All right. Don't worry. Don't go out any more than you have to." Others flashed back with incredible violence: "You've got your nerve! If you did anyone a favor, that's your business." Alfredo, the Andalusian, had the same answer for all: "I'm sorry, but one half has to take it on the chin for what the other half does."

Doña Amparo Campo received many visits. Her reply to all appeals was: "My dear, we'll see what can be done. Julio will do his best. If it depended on us..." Olga, too, was swamped by people of every sort who supposed that David had agreed to serve on the committee, which was not so. Olga disabused them. "However," she concluded, "there is no reason to be so alarmed. The first moments of all revolutions are disagreeable. But this will all clear up soon." Olga's great worry was that someone might suspect Marta's presence in the kitchen. Marta was quiet, absolutely motionless; but a cough, some unforeseeable accident... For this reason Olga said to everyone: "When you want to see me, the best place is the UGT, not here."

THE Alvear family was among those seeking a protector. Julio had sent them a message: "Be on guard. They are looking for Mateo and Marta, and your house will be searched. Be careful with Ignacio and César."

It was to be expected. Carmen Elgazu felt in her heart that the danger was approaching, and she made ready to defend her own with her nails. This was no time for tears. She was determined to save her children, and she made up her mind to go in person to see Julio and say to him: "Here is your chance to rid your soul of some of its spots. You yourself guard them here in police headquarters." She was completely indifferent to the humiliation this represented. The life of Ignacio and César was all that mattered to her. Besides, Don Emilio Santos was staying with them. He kept repeating: "I'll go away, I'll go away. I don't want to get you folks into trouble."

Carmen Elgazu was just getting ready to go when Matías Alvear stopped her. When he had received Julio's note, he had thought so hard that it seemed to him he had hit upon their salvation. A gleam of light shone out of the depths of memory. Ignacio had given blood at the hospital. Matías could not recall to whom. But he knew it was someone—strange—someone who he'd be willing to bet now...

"Wait a minute," he said to his wife. "Ignacio, what was the name of that man you gave blood to at the hospital?"

Ignacio was not missing a single one of his parents' gestures, waiting for them to put their plan into practice, for he had his own. "Dimas," he answered. "His name was Dimas."

"Where was he from?"

"From Salt."

Dimas, and from Salt! From the town whose committee—! "Don't move from here," Matías said to them. "Wait for a quarter of an hour. Let's see if we can settle everything at the same time. They haven't started searching along the Rambla yet, and I'll have time."

His enthusiasm and determination were so great that they all prepared to obey him.

Matías was back in exactly half an hour. His return was dramatic. His heart was going like a triphammer. He still could not explain how the idea had come to him. It must have been the hand of Providence. When he received Julio's note, his desire to save his children was so great that he had hit upon the solution.

The fact of the matter is that he returned with a tall, unshaved man armed with two huge revolvers: Dimas, of Salt. And accompanying Dimas, another militiaman, short, whose gleaming white teeth gave him a pleasing expression. Dimas was growling: "You should have said so, you should have said so. Not even God is coming in here."

Carmen Elgazu and César were struck dumb at his words, but they understood their meaning, as did Ignacio, as did Pilar. Such a weight had rolled off Matías's shoulders that Dimas's language amused him.

The presence of Don Emilio Santos disconcerted the two men. When Dimas learned who he was, he looked at his secretary. "Now, this is too—" But the memory of what Ignacio had done effaced everything. "It's all right. I'm not going to argue. Not even God is coming in here."

Dimas had been conducting searches for more than thirty hours, and it was hard for him to accept the fact that in this house he could not pull out the drawers and knock things about. For this reason, without meaning to, his eyes kept roving from left to right. Carmen Elgazu, looking at him in profile, was horrified. It was the profile of a sick man or a criminal. In one of these sweeping glances he spied a tiny figure wearing a Catalan stocking cap standing on the sideboard. Dimas walked over to it and gave a whistle. "Well, will you look at that?" he said. "The Virgin." But he did not knock it off.

The man filled César with infinite pity. Why did he talk that way? Why did he wear those sideburns and those revolvers? How did he think he, poor devil, could stop God from coming in? Suppose God had come in through him?

Carmen Elgazu overcame her disgust and took the floor. She asked Dimas to guarantee the lives of her children and of Don Emilio Santos. She told him that he would never regret a good deed, and that he would know he could count on their friendship. "You see now that in this life we need one another."

Dimas agreed without any objections. His secretary smiled. He kept looking and looking at Pilar. Carmen Elgazu's assurance won her Dimas's respect; besides, she was the only person in the world who had ever used the formal "*Usted*" when speaking to him.

Matías inquired what he planned to do to make good his guarantee.

Dimas looked at him as though his dignity had been offended. "You have the word of the Revolutionary Committee of Salt."

Matías assured him that he did not doubt it, but he still wanted to know what he planned to do. Dimas's secretary answered: "Well—one of us will stay here on guard all the time."

Carmen Elgazu went pale. "Only one?"

Dimas asked if she wanted a battalion.

Matías said to her: "Don't be silly, woman. One is enough. It's the presence."

The phrase caught Dimas's fancy. "You said it. It's the presence."

Dimas left, and his secretary, who said his name was Agustín, remained. Carmen Elgazu made him coffee. It would be horrible to have a militiaman in the house all the time; but—it was the presence.

Agustín gave them all such a sense of security that the family at once stopped thinking about themselves. Their thoughts turned to all that was happening outside, to those who had died, to those fleeing across the Pyrenees, to Marta, motionless beside the aquarium.

They were all thinking how to be of use and help to the others. Matías went out for a moment, to the Telegraph Building, thinking to whom he could give asylum. He hid two images in his office, St. Francis of Assisi and St. Clara. He put them in an iron box that had been standing in a corner for months.

When he returned to the apartment, he got a great surprise. Ignacio and César were gone. Ignacio had acquired such confidence—besides Agustín had assured him that the "rides" would be given only at night—that he made up his mind to go and see Marta again, for he could not live without news of her. As for César, for the first time he had committed a serious fault: he had run away in spite of orders not to stir from the flat. Carmen Elgazu was unable to account for it. Neither could Pilar. Even Agustín, with his rifle over his arm, asked himself why the hell César had done that.

"He was looking at the newspaper, and then he rushed out," the militiaman kept repeating.

"The newspaper?" It was Matías who asked the question, and he began to understand what had happened. Matías had noticed that César was deeply affected by the list of the churches that had been set afire. He probably wanted to go and see them. Dear God! What if he had tried to save something the fire had not destroyed?

Matías left the house again in search of his son. "With his cropped head!" Since Dr. Relken's departure, César's was the only such head in the city. Besides, everybody knew him. Matías, panting along the streets, felt once again, for the second time in a few hours, a deep sense of paternity.

Of course, there was no danger. Agustín was right, the "rides" took place only at night. There were so many people in the streets that they were just about the safest place there was. One pedestrian more or less did not matter, provided he wasn't wearing a hat.... It was at Matías, who was wearing his, that they looked much more closely than they would at Ignacio or César.

He returned without finding his son. There was nothing to do but wait. Of all the crazy things! Neither César nor Ignacio should have gone out. Matías could not restrain a supplicating glance in the direction of the peasant girl in the stocking cap who presided over the dining room.

Ignacio reached the school without any difficulty. When Marta saw him, she threw herself into his arms. All the coolness and self-possession she displayed in the presence of the teachers or when she was alone deserted her, and she began to cry: "Ignacio, Ignacio..." She stayed in the kitchen, she did not move from there, she slept there. At night the cockroaches frightened her.... "Tell me, what has happened in the city?"

Ignacio realized that Marta knew absolutely nothing about the dead. Not even about the fires. The window of the kitchen did not look toward the city.

It faced the country, the river—the cemetery. But nobody could have noticed anything in the cemetery. The wall was as impenetrable as ever.

"It seemed to me last night I heard—"

"It was nothing," Ignacio quieted her. He was going to ask the teachers to be sure not to let her get hold of a newspaper. He would have to keep her from finding out.

"How is my mother? And my father? And Padilla and Rodríguez?"

"Fine, fine. They're all fine. Your mother is calm, she gets along very well with the guards. Your father is in the infantry barracks, that you know. Things are quiet for the time being. Mateo by this time is probably in Perpignan. Padilla and Rodríguez are fine. They managed to get away in a car. I don't know where they got hold of it."

"Where did they go?"

"I don't know. Barcelona, I think."

Marta could not take her eyes off him. She was ashamed of wearing those braids of Padilla's daughter, and the flowered skirt. "I must look a sight." Ignacio recognized her only by her voice. By her voice and her look and the soul she put into each word.

"And how are you?" Marta asked, clasping her hands behind Ignacio's neck.

"Calm, as you can see. Waiting. Waiting," Ignacio repeated.

Then Marta talked about the teachers. "They are trash, just as I told you! Disgruntled, full of resentment. You only have to watch them eat! Besides, they sleep here in the next room, and I swear to you they are pigs."

Ignacio gave a gesture of displeasure, and Marta did not pursue the subject.

"You know," she said, "the same thing happens to me as to Pedro: my only consolation—aside from the aquarium, of course—is the radio."

Olga had brought a small radio into the kitchen. And with patience, Marta occasionally managed to pick up distant stations, even Africa.

"We haven't lost, Ignacio. Not at all. To be sure, we have lost the places that matter most, but do you know how many capitals of provinces are in our hands?"

"No, I don't."

"Twenty-three, counting Mallorca. And there are other isolated points of resistance, such as the Alcázar in Toledo."

Ignacio did not share her optimism, but the last thing in the world he wanted was to disillusion her. Ignacio had paid close attention to Prieto's latest statements: "What can the military hope to do? We have everything. We have the gold. . . ."

Ignacio stayed with Marta until David came home. He wanted to wait for

David to thank him once more, and to ask him to walk along with him for a block or so. "So they won't see me leave alone."

David became furious at the sight of him. On the way he said: "Don't come here anymore. Can't you understand that they will get suspicious?" At the gloomy expression that came over Ignacio's face, he added: "I'll arrange to meet you from time to time and take you with me."

Ignacio noticed that David had come by car, in the UGT Balilla.

When Ignacio got home, he found everyone in a panic. Night was coming on, the jail was filling up, and César had not returned.

"Agustín, for God's sake, go out and see if you can find him," Carmen Elgazu implored the militiaman. But he tried to persuade her that it would be dangerous to leave them alone in the house.

"The boy is one, and you here are five."

It seemed to Carmen Elgazu that each of the parts was equal to the whole.

Ignacio wanted to set out to look for César, but Agustín stood at the door with his gun and refused to let him pass.

NINETY-THREE

WHEN the shadows invaded the city, the death cars turned on their headlights once more. With anxiety at their hearts, the families watched the hour advance. When would the raid begin? Whose turn would it be? The one hundred and sixty prisoners in the Seminary and the twenty-two women held in the jail repeated the rosary.

It had been necessary to requisition more cars, for several of them had been smashed up during the day. Julio, accompanied by the Costas, had gone to see the general, for they found what was happening frightening; but Cosme Vila had said to him: "If you try anything, we'll use the machine guns."

Julio quickly realized that he was in danger himself if he did not come to some decision. The Assault Guards assigned to headquarters were on edge, complaining about having to guard the wife of Major Martínez de Soria and the Diocesan Museum. It was perfectly clear that they would never turn their weapons on the people. The majority of them were of humble origin, and they were all itching to join up with their own.

Julio stroked Berta as he watched the death cars' lights go on. The Costas were desperate, too. They had gone to the Anti-Fascist Revolutionary Committee to protest once more. The only member they were able to see was Casal, who, though the figures he heard still made him dizzy and he was doing what he could to restrain Cosme Vila and El Responsable, never for a moment lost sight of the casualties the military uprising had occasioned among the people.

Casal said to the Costas: "Don't be naïve! Protests at this stage of the game! Go to Barcelona and find out how many workers were killed in the clashes. And in Madrid, and in Oviedo." And he concluded: "The best thing you can do is to stay home as much as you can...."

The militiamen dined well and drank to match. They had a hard night's work ahead of them. It was common knowledge that many people were concealed in unbelievable hide-outs. "They have walled themselves in behind secret doors." With all the secret doors there were in Gerona!

By midnight their patience was exhausted. They could wait no longer. The streets were deserted. Alfredo the Andalusian went up to the apartment of the Treasury Department representative, drove him to the cemetery, cut off his ears, and killed him.

At one o'clock Gorki and three militiamen went up to the apartment of the Judge of First Instance, who had tried to keep his job at the time the program was formulated. He was transported to the cemetery in pajamas. The Treasury Department representative had been his best friend. He recognized him, let out a scream, and fell beside him.

At half past one, the presiding judge of the Circuit Court. El Responsable and Future, who had decided to work together that night, took care of him. El Responsable's daughters had said to them: "We want you two to stay together. Something might happen."

The manager of the Telegraph Department, of the Telephone Company, the stationmaster, and two more doctors.

Professor Morales knew that all this was just a curtain-raiser, and that the big show was set for four a.m., and he had told himself that stout-hearted men were needed. In general he did not have much confidence in the militiamen. They were drunk. They had been drinking all day with the committees of the neighboring villages, and they all were carrying jugs of wine in the cars. It was the women who kept egging them on to drink.

For that reason he had got hold of a splendid reinforcement for the selected squads: Teo. He told himself that Teo's help would be invaluable, with his strength, his enthusiasm, his experience. Besides, it was a pitiful sight to see the giant wandering about alone. During the day he had started out with his dray and had made a trip to the station as though to advertise the fact that he was taking no part in anything. But for a week the station had seen no train, and he came back with an empty cart.

Morales went to see him. He said to him: "Cosme Vila sent me here. He admits that you are right, but you know that discipline—"

Teo's eyes became slits. "Cosme Vila sent you here?"

"He ordered me to come in person and say that we are waiting for you. Besides, he wants to organize an act of homage to the memory of your brother in the cemetery."

These last words were too much for Teo. All his resistance melted. He muttered something, undoubtedly some word of satisfaction. He began to believe that Cosme Vila had sent for him. He began to suspect that this was logical, that they needed him. Professor Morales added: "If you don't come, we'll have to take La Valenciana to the insane asylum."

Teo brought his fist down so hard on the urn of San Narciso that he almost broke the glass. "Come on, let's go," Morales said to him. "I'll come back for the saint." And he took Teo's arm. He took him to the Anti-Fascist Revolutionary Committee.

When Cosme Vila saw Teo and caught the knowing look Professor Morales threw him, he smiled. "*¡Salud!*" he said, raising his fist.

La Valenciana stretched her legs. "*¡Salud*, fascist!"

Teo squeezed his cap between his fingers. He looked around the office that had belonged to the head of Liga Catalana. On the wall he saw a sheet of paper: "Instructions for the act of homage to Teo's brother."

It did not say "Jaime Arias"; it said "Teo's brother." His enthusiasm was so unbounded that he took charge of the major operation, the one Professor Morales knew was planned for four a.m. El Responsable and Alfredo the Andalusian looked upon him as a serious rival. So did Future. However, they all thought: "There'll be work enough for everybody."

Never again would Teo wander alone about the city exposed to sentimentalism and madness. Professor Morales said to him: "Listen to the radio."

Ten minutes later he heard: "The Communist Party salutes Teo." The giant picked up the seal of the Anti-Fascist Revolutionary Committee, blew on it, and, unbuttoning his shirt, stamped the seal on his breast. But his chest was too hairy to take it.

La Valenciana said to him, roaring with laughter: "I'll tattoo you later on, handsome."

The cars dashed back and forth, slamming on their brakes in front of the houses. The panic was absolute, and each person gave the best or the worst of himself. Teo was to give the worst, as Professor Morales and Julio were doing, as Pedro, the dissenter, was preparing to do. Others gave the best, and among these were Dimas the militiaman, Agustín his secretary, Mosén Francisco, and César.

Mosén Francisco had not accepted Laura's suggestion that he take refuge in the Costas' house. Mosén Francisco had only a single idea, especially since his parish priest had died: to carry on his cure. The occupants of the flat where he lived had given up tying him to a chair as they had done at the time San Félix was put to the torch. "If you do that, you will be responsible for many things," he said to them. Mosén Francisco had disguised himself as a militiaman in a blue coverall, cap, bandolier; red handkerchief, gold wrist watch. All this had been supplied by La Andaluza, for whom he had sent. Now he was waiting for dawn to come to put his plan into practice, even though La Andaluza said to him: "It's madness, it's madness."

Something totally unforeseen had happened to Pedro the dissenter: Radio Moscow had approved the Anti-Fascist Revolutionary Committee. The boy realized that it was his duty to cooperate, and he felt grave remorse at having harbored Mateo. Radio Moscow had not mentioned the Revolutionary Committee of Gerona specifically, but it had referred to all of them when it spoke of the Spanish Communist Party. Pedro ate two sardines, drank a glass of wine, and presented himself at committee headquarters half an hour before Teo got there.

Cosme Vila frowned. "What do you want, kid?"

"I've come to offer my services."

Cosme Vila bit his lips. "All right. Report to Comrade Molina."

Sergeant Molina asked Pedro: "You got a gun?"

"No."

"Go in there and get one of those rifles. And be here at half past three."

Pedro was to give the worst of himself that night. On the other hand, Dimas and Agustín honored their word. César had not returned. The Alvear family was in utter despair, but the fact was that César had looked at the newspaper, had gone out, and had not returned. The whole family had gathered in the dining room around a candle lighted to the only image in the house, the Virgin of the Pillar disguised as a Catalan peasant girl. They wept as they prayed, and Don Emilio Santos was weeping, too. Carmen Elgazu riveted on the little image all the force of her eyes of a mother. Her strong arms had dropped to her sides; imploring protection, imploring the return of her son. Contrary to his custom, Matías had knelt and answered in a louder voice than usual the prayers of his wife. Pilar was sobbing, recalling César. She saw him there still, in the dining room, with his innocent face, his big ears, wrinkling his forehead in perplexity as he listened to one and then another. How much she loved her brother! Mateo had always said of him: "He's a saint loose in the world."

Ignacio had difficulty breathing. They had had to hold him to keep him from going out. Of them all, he was the most convinced that something bad had happened to César. César had not hidden his desire from Ignacio. "I feel that the Lord is calling me." God, what had he done, where had he gone? Ignacio too prayed aloud: "Remember, Blessed Virgin Mary..."

Dimas and Agustín had ordered them not to go out. They had brought another militiaman from Salt to guard them, a silent man who sat in the hall, rifle in hand, as though performing a routine duty. And Dimas and Agustín had set out in search of César, to give the best of themselves.

Acting upon Matías Alvear's suggestion, they had made the rounds of the burned churches one by one. They picked their way through the ashes, entered the smoke-blackened sacristies, looked under the benches. César was capable of kneeling there, hugging some holy object to his breast. In San Félix it seemed to them they heard a noise behind San Narciso's altar, and they shouted: "Who's there?" They walked forward, and just as they looked around the altar, they saw a wall collapse.

Then they visited the three chapels that had not been touched, whose altars still gleamed with gold. And in one of them they found traces of him: a broken window. They crawled through it, went over to the main altar, and opened the tabernacle. Not a thing there. The ciborium was gone. Ignacio had said to them: "He is probably trying to save the ciborium with the consecrated wafers."

They went out again, through the window, first taking a shot at the image on the altar. In the second chapel the same thing had happened: the ciborium was gone. In the third, that of the Home for Aged Priests at the other end of the city—the ground the boy had covered!—a woman said to them: "Oh, I know who you're looking for. They caught him in there swallowing the communion wafers. They took him away."

"Where?" asked Dimas, looking down the cemetery road.

"No, to jail, to jail. Or at least they went that way."

"Swallowing the communion wafers." Dimas did not understand it. His secretary said to him: "Yes, I've heard they do it."

It was then eleven at night. Straight as an arrow, they made their way to the Seminary, which had been turned into a jail. If they were only in time! Three militiamen were standing guard at the door.

"We're members of the Committee of Salt. We've come to see if you've got somebody by the name of César here. César Alvear."

One of the militiamen blocked the entrance. "Let's see your papers."

Dimas touched his pistol belt. "Isn't this enough for you?"

Agustín pulled out a paper and handed it to the man. "Head of the Committee of Salt."

The man said to Dimas: "Wait a minute, comrade."

They all stepped into the vestibule together. The bells on the wall still had signs reading: "Director's Office, Sacristy, Library." The militiaman looked at a list a page long.

"Have you got them all listed?"

"Lord, no. Just the first batch."

Dimas was outraged. The Committee of Salt was handling such matters much more efficiently.

Cars kept pulling up with new prisoners. The militiaman said to Dimas: "Look, the best thing is for you to go up and look for him yourself. I haven't got the time to take care of you."

Dimas and Agustín flew up the stairway. Both of them tried to remember what César looked like. Agustín, particularly, recalled him well. "He had great big ears," he said.

When they got to the first floor, they began to stumble over prisoners. The halls and cells were crowded with them. There was very little light. Agustín pulled out a flashlight and shone it along the faces. It was a ghoulish review. The presence of the two militiamen, and, above all, Dimas's gruesome aspect sowed dread among the prisoners. Each felt that the slaughter was about to begin, and as the light blinded him, said to himself: "This is it." The review was a review of terrorized eyes, sweat-beaded foreheads.

Dimas went along spewing oaths. "What a bunch of rabbits! Wetting their pants!"

They could not find César. They visited the cells one by one. He was not there. They went up to the next floor. Agustín said: "The best thing would be to call his name."

Dimas took the suggestion. "Silence," he roared. The hearts of the prisoners skipped a beat. "César Alvear! César Alvear, step forward!"

Nobody answered. Against the back wall of a huge room, without light, which had once been the main dormitory, the room where Ignacio had slept when he was a seminarian, César had heard his name and had started to get up to answer the call. But two hands held him in his place. One clutched him firmly by the arm, the other covered his mouth so he should not give himself away.

"César Alvear, seminarian!"

The person who was holding César back and silencing him was Professor Civil. The professor had been arrested at ten o'clock at night, and when he saw César brought in he went over to him because he felt sorry for him. The countersign of the prisoners was: "Don't identify yourself." The militiamen sometimes got tired, and that might save one's life.

"César Alvear!"

"He must be in one of the cells," said Agustín.

Dimas ripped out another oath, and they went out. They shouted César's name down all the corridors, they opened all the doors. The flashlight came into play again. Nobody had seen him.

They went down to the vestibule, where they talked with the militiaman. "Don't you remember whether—"

"How do you expect me to remember? There are over three hundred."

Dimas felt utterly frustrated. With fanatical tenacity he and Agustín set out for the headquarters of the Anti-Fascist Revolutionary Committee, which had been meeting in plenary session. It was midnight. Casal had left, but Cosme Vila and El Responsable were smoking, and Teo was there, as were Sergeant Molina, La Valenciana, and about twenty militiamen.

Dimas went up to Cosme Vila, who had known him for a long time. "Greetings to the Committee of Salt!" said Cosme.

Dimas told him what had happened—in part. He supposed that if he talked about sparing César, Cosme Vila would not hand him over—that is, if the boy was still alive. The best plan would be to say that the Committee of Salt was "demanding him because it has some accounts to settle with him."

Cosme Vila looked at him. "The seminarian from Collell?"

"I don't know where he's from. He's the seminarian who lives on the Rambla."

"What does the Committee of Salt want with him?" Cosme Vila asked himself. He said aloud: "Wait a minute." He pulled a paper out of his pocket. He looked at it and said, raising his head: "I'm sorry, comrade. You're too late."

Dimas let out a horrible oath, stamping his foot like a child.

La Valenciana went over to him. "Were you that fond of him?"

Agustín had caught hold of Dimas by his bandolier and was pulling him out of the room. "Sons-of-bitches!" screamed Dimas. "He was nothing but a kid. We'll settle this man to man."

Teo got up and started toward him. Gorki pushed Dimas and Agustín out of the room and slammed the door.

Dimas did not have the heart to go back to the Alvears and tell them the news. "I had given them my word. The other kid gave me his blood!"

"It was his own fault," Agustín answered. "He was crazy to go out."

Dimas kept repeating: "To eat communion wafers!" He hadn't the heart to go. He set out on foot for Salt in the darkness of the night. The street lights picked out his sick or criminal profile as he passed beneath them. He had ordered Agustín: "You go."

It was Agustín's job to bear the news. He could feel the thudding of his heart as he set out for the Rambla. He knew that when he opened his mouth to talk, his teeth shone so that it looked as though he was smiling. How could he tell them the news without their thinking he was smiling?

When he knocked, the militiaman on guard opened the door. Agustín walked toward the dining room and found the whole family standing in the hall, waiting.

AGUSTÍN said: "We were too late."

The big operation was carried out on the dot of four. Independent squads had been at work on their own since twelve, when Alfredo had gone for the Treasury Department representative. The committee had been waiting in the office Dimas and Agustín had gone into, talking and listening to the radio. Cosme Vila had refused to drink, as had El Responsable. But not Future, who was joking with La Valenciana. Teo had told them: "You know, that old San Narciso isn't made of wood; he's just sawdust."

An unidentified station worked them up to fever pitch about three o'clock. It was a "fascist station" that had been set up somewhere in the south of Spain. They heard a voice which claimed to be that of General Queipo de Llano, the general who had risen in Seville. He said that his troops were spreading out across the province, heading for Huelva and Badajoz. He said that his plan was to make contact with the army, which had consolidated all its bases and positions in the north, in Galicia, Castile, Navarre, and Aragón. He said that when the forces of the south made junction with these others to the west of Madrid, they would form a solid front that would march against the Basque country, against Madrid, and then toward the Mediterranean. He praised the fighting spirit of the Moors, the Foreign Legion, the Mehalla, the Falange. He wound up addressing himself to all those hidden "in the Red zone," those who were suffering persecution and torture, telling them to trust in the triumph of the Army of Salvation. "For if the Reds have the gold, the others have the military experience and the moral support of thousands of volunteers flocking to their side as they extend the area of their occupation."

El Responsable had made a move to turn off the radio several times, but Cosme Vila had shaken his head. He wanted to hear it all, and as he listened, he tapped the desk with a pencil. He laughed, commenting on the general's whisky-hoarse voice.

The excitement of the committee and of the special squads waiting in the adjoining rooms was indescribable. As it struck four, Cosme Vila got to his feet. "Comrades! To the Revolution!"

EVERYBODY stood up. Almost everybody took a submachine gun; some of the militiamen, like Pedro, a rifle. Everything was done with precision speed; everyone knew his place. Cosme Vila told them goodbye, and with a gesture confirmed the leadership of El Responsable and Teo in the job on hand. He told them goodbye from the head of the stairs. The noise of the descending squads was deafening. Only Cosme Vila, Professor Morales, and a couple of militiamen standing guard remained at committee headquarters.

The column moved toward the Seminary. The sky was starred as it had been the night before. The militiamen on guard at the door heard them coming. They had been notified. "Open the doors!" There was only one, and they threw that open. Six trucks were waiting in line.

El Responsable and Teo went up the steps of Santo Domingo to the esplanade of the building. "*¡Salud*, comrades. *Salud!*" they greeted those in the vestibule.

Some fifty men went up to the first floor. The prisoners heard the steps on the stairs, and their prayers, thoughts, or sleep were cut short. They looked at one another. "This is it."

"Bring them all into the library."

The largest room was the library. With the books gone, the real size of the room could be seen. El Responsable's voice was heard by all the prisoners in the corridors and adjoining cells. The militiamen moved forward, pushing the prisoners ahead of them with their gun butts. The lights had all been turned on. They went into the cells and kicked the sleepers awake. "All of you to the library!"

In five minutes the occupants of the whole first floor were assembled there: one hundred and forty-seven men lined up along the rear and the right-hand wall.

El Responsable pulled out a list. "As I call out the names, line up along the left wall."

And he began the list. The first name thundered in the air: "Juan Ferrer."

Nobody moved. This was the countersign. Nobody was to come forward.

But Juan Ferrer was in the first row, and Future said to him: "Hey, you, don't pretend to be deaf!"

Juan Ferrer lowered his head and stepped over to the left wall.

The names dropped, one by one, to the number of one hundred, the figure that had been agreed upon. It was impossible to escape. There was always a militiaman who recognized them. Those who really were not in the group were on the second floor. As the prisoners lined up against the wall, Teo tied them together by their wrists. He had begun with the left wrist, but many of them were wearing wrist watches, which got in the way, so he fastened the rope around their right wrists. He had made up three groups, two of fifteen, and one of sixteen men.

The forty-six men were led away. Then El Responsable addressed the others: "Now, don't be afraid. This place is getting too crowded. You are to be transferred to the Cárcel Modelo in Barcelona."

The prisoners looked at one another. Nobody believed what he said, and yet…

"Are the trucks downstairs?" Teo asked Future.

Future looked at him with surprise. "Didn't you see them?"

The prisoners were led downstairs and loaded into three trucks heavily guarded by militiamen. The trucks drove off.

El Responsable and his aides went up to the second floor, where the operation was repeated, this time in the main dormitory. "Everybody in the dormitory!"

One hundred and twelve men lined up against the back wall. El Responsable had observed that there was only one priest on the first floor. He knew this because on the list the priests' names were marked with a cross. "Those whose names I read step over to the left wall."

His task this time was more difficult. There were a number of priests whom nobody knew, not even the militiamen. In lay clothes the priests looked completely different. Nearly all of them, however, answered to their names in spite of the countersign. They did this because when silence followed the name called out by El Responsable, his eyes took on such a sinister glow that the priests were afraid that this might mean new names on the list. At times El Responsable and Teo went over to the line and questioned the prisoners directly, making them turn around to see if they had tonsures.

"Aren't you the priest Morató? Aren't you the priest Morató? Aren't you the parish priest of the Cathedral?"

They identified the priest Morató because they demanded that all the prisoners show their papers, and among them they found an identification card in the name of "Jaime Morató, priest." It was not necessary to ask the parish priest of the Cathedral for his papers. He had not answered when his name, Eusebio Turón, was called out; but when he heard: "Aren't you the parish priest of the Cathedral?" he raised his head and took a step forward. "Yes, I am."

"Over there to the left." And he was tied to the others.

Professor Civil's name was not read out, but that of César was. "César Alvear." He was number seventy-eight on the list, and there was a cross alongside his name, too.

César took a step forward. Professor Civil held on to his hand, but César said: "Let me go, they are calling me."

César had recognized several of those whose names had been read out. One was a man who was always coming to the Museum and asking: "Could I see the picture of the martyrdom of St. Stephen?" Another was always in the Café Neutral working crossword puzzles. And Corbera, the owner of the sandal factory. His name had caused a stir, for everybody knew that he had been El Responsable's boss. Señor Corbera took his place in the line, looking at his former employee with an enigmatic smile. When he was in his place, he said: "Responsable—"

"What do you want?"

"May God damn you."

That wounded César to the depths of his soul. Up to that moment he had been most distressed when the names of the priests were read out. He knew how much they were needed in the diocese, where some of them had to look after the needs of two parishes. If so many departed… He was deeply moved, too, by the presence of another seminarian whom he knew only by sight, who was two years ahead of him; but Señor Corbera's words…

César hoped they might tie them together, his wrist linked to that of Señor Corbera on one side, and on the other to that of the parish priest of the Cathedral, for example. In this way he could manage to do two things: ask the blessing of the priest at the last moment, and say to Señor Corbera: "Sir, don't curse anyone when you are so close to death…."

But it was not to be. Neither the one nor the other. Teo tied him to two silently weeping strangers. Each of them was whispering: "Criminals, criminals!"

This was the word César heard when, on an order from El Responsable, the three groups marched away; when he saw the lights being turned off behind him and knew that he was leaving Professor Civil and the others "not called up" with the blood frozen in their veins; when he descended the steps and into the street; when he got into the truck to which he was assigned and into which he had to be helped because the step was too high.

The Seminary! It seemed to him a very special act of grace that his last abode had been the Seminary. He thought of Dimas's words: "Not even God is coming in here." And then he had been arrested and taken to the Seminary. The Lord led each one to the place He had assigned him.

He would have liked to ask the driver to go down the Rambla so that he might send the balcony of his house his final greeting; but beside him he was hearing: "Criminals, criminals!" The truck—the last of the three—moved along the Calle de Ciudadanos—past the Arús Bank—into the Municipal Plaza—the Diocesan Museum!—turned by the river—the crucifix of the Sacred Heart!—finally taking the road to the cemetery.

The wind was blowing in their faces, and César, suddenly, without knowing why, looked at the stars, which were growing dim, and then thought of his age: exactly sixteen years, three months, and two days. Then he thought of the ciboria he had hidden in the walls. "I have taken communion sixty times today," he said to himself.

As they rounded the last curve before the cemetery, he thought of his family, of his mother, Carmen Elgazu, his father, Matías, of Pilar and Ignacio. And of José in Madrid, and his uncle Santiago, and the cousins in Burgos, and all those of Bilbao. "So many souls, Lord, so many souls!" And then he thought of Dimas and Agustín. How was it possible that Dimas and Agustín, who had pledged their word, should have gone to the prison to kill him? He forgave them. He regretted that his prayers for them would have to be brief, for he had so few minutes of life left.

The gate was wide open. As they drove up, the three trucks that had preceded them—carrying those from the first floor—were turning around to leave. The militiamen greeted one another: "*¡Salud*, comrade!" "*¡Salud!*"

César had hidden one Host, just one, in his vest. As the prisoners were being lined up against the niches, and the firing squads readied, he took it out with his free hand. He was getting ready to put it into his mouth and swallow it slowly, forgiving the militiamen. At his side he heard the sobbing and the uninterrupted murmur: "Criminals, criminals!" He turned and said to the priest nearest to him: "I repent of my sins, Father. Will you give me absolution?" Then he looked at Señor Corbera, whose eyes glittered with rage. "Take this," he said to him suddenly. And he elevated the Sacred Species, holding it between his thumb and index finger. Señor Corbera blinked three times and suddenly, understanding, took communion.

A volley rang out, and César felt something gently pierce his skin.

Moments later he heard a voice saying: "I absolve you in the name of the Father, the Son, and the Holy Spirit," a voice coming nearer and repeating: "I absolve you in the name of the Father, the Son, and the Holy Spirit." And he also heard groans. He opened his eyes for a moment. He saw a militiaman kneeling and taking tiny communion wafers from his wrist watch and putting them into the mouths of his fallen neighbors. In the militiaman he recognized Mosén Francisco. César's eyes closed. He felt a kiss on his forehead. Then his heart closed.

GLOSSARY ONE

Persons Appearing in the Novel

1. *Fictional Characters*

Agustín	An anarchist
Alfredo, Brother	A teacher at the Christian Brothers School
Alvear, Carmen Elgazu de	Wife of Matías Alvear; mother of César, Ignacio, Pilar
Alvear, César	Son of Carmen Elgazu and Matías Alvear
Alvear, Ignacio	Son of Carmen Elgazu and Matías Alvear
Alvear, José	Son of Santiago Alvear; nephew of Matías Alvear
Alvear, Matías	Husband of Carmen Elgazu; father of César, Ignacio, Pilar
Alvear, Pilar	Daughter of Carmen Elgazu and Matías Alvear
Alvear, Santiago	Brother of Matías Alvear
Ana María	First sweetheart of Ignacio Alvear
Andaluza, La	Brothel-keeper
Batlle, Jorge de	(father). Wealthy Catalan landowner
Batlle, Jorge de	(son). Member of the Falange
Blasco	Bootblack, anarchist

Campistol, J.	Member of the Falange
Campo, Amparo	*See* García, Amparo Campo de
Campos, Major	Army officer, Mason
Canela	Prostitute
Cervera, Julián	Commissioner of Gerona
Civil, Benito	Son of Professor José Civil; architect; member of the Falange
Civil, José	Professor of Law
Cojo, El	Nephew of El Responsable; anarchist
Costa brothers	Industrialists; leaders of Izquierda Republicana
Costa, Laura	Sister of the Costa brothers
David	Schoolteacher; Socialist
Dimas	Anarchist
Elgazu, Carmen	*See* Alvear, Carmen Elgazu de
Estrada, Santiago	Leader of the CEDA in Gerona
Future	Anarchist
García, Julio	Childhood friend of Matías Alvear; policeman; later Chief of Police
García, Amparo Campo de	Wife of Julio García
Gorki	Communist
Grandullón, El	Anarchist
Flaro	Falangist
Ideal	Anarchist
Jaime	Fellow worker of Matías Alvear; poet
Martín, Lieutenant	Military man refused admission to the Falange
Martínez de Soria, Major	Leader of military uprising

Martínez de Soria, Fernando	Son of Major Martínez de Soria; Falangist
Martínez de Soria, José Luis	Son of Major Martínez de Soria; Falangist
Martínez de Soria, Marta	Daughter of Major Martínez de Soria; sweetheart of Ignacio Alvear
Massana	Leader of Estat Català; architect
Morales	Professor; Communist
Mosén Alberto	Priest; director of the Diocesan Museum
Mosén Francisco	Priest
Muñoz, Colonel	Military man; Mason
Murillo	Image maker; Trotskyite
Noguer	Notary; later Mayor of Gerona
Octavio	Falangist
Olga	Schoolteacher; wife of David
Orencia	Servant of Emilio Santos
Oriol, Ernesto	Son of Pedro Oriol; friend of Ignacio Alvear
Oriol, Pedro	Lumber dealer; owner of *El Traditionalista*
Padilla	Civil Guard; Falangist
Padrosa	Fellow worker of Ignacio Alvear in the Arús Bank
Pedro	Stone cutter; Communist
Relken, Dr.	German archaeologist
Responsable, El	Anarchist leader
Ribas	Architect
Rodríguez	Civil Guard
Rosselló, Dr.	Physician; Mason
Rubio, El	Anarchist; orderly to Major Martínez de Soria

Sánchez, Antonio	Assistant to Julio García
Santaló, Joaquín	Izquierda Republicana deputy
Santi	Pupil of David and Olga; anarchist
Santillana, Agustín	Friend of Matías Alvcar
Santos, Emilio	Friend of Matías Alvear; father of Mateo Santos
Santos, Mateo	Organizer of the Falange in Gerona; sweetheart of Pilar Alvear
Senilloso, Carlos ("*Warning Voice*")	Dentist; journalist; husband of Laura Costa
Teo	Carter; Communist
Tower of Babel	Fellow worker of Ignacio Alvear in the Arús Bank
Valenciana, La	Communist
Vasiliev	Russian Communist
Victor	Typesetter; Communist
Vila, Cosme	Communist leader; fellow worker of Ignacio Alvear in the Arús Bank
Warning Voice	*See* Senilloso, Carlos
Zurita Belaustegui, Carlos	General; military commander of Gerona

2. *Historical Characters*

Alfonso XIII	(1886–1941). Last King of Spain; dethroned in April 1931.
Aranguren Roldán, José	(1875–1939). General; commander of the Civil Guard in Barcelona at the time of the military uprising of July 1936; put down revolt in that city; commander of Valencia when Franco's troops entered in 1939 and was shot shortly afterwards.
Azaña, Manuel	(1880–1940). Member of the revolutionary

	committee that brought about the overthrow of the monarchy and the establishment of the Republic; headed several cabinets between 1931 and 1933; in 1934, accused of having taken part in revolutionary uprising, was imprisoned; in 1936, elected President of the Spanish Republic; held office for the two and one-half years of the Civil War; died in France.
Bakunin, Michael	(1814–1876). Russian revolutionary and writer; challenged the position of Marx at the First International; organized Anarchist International.
Baroja, Pío	(1872–1956). Novelist.
Batet, Domingo	(1872–1936). General; military commander of Barcelona who put down the Catalan uprising of October 1934; military governor of Burgos in 1936; refused to support military uprising, and was shot.
Besteiro, Julián	(1870–1940). Socialist leader; Professor of Philosophy at the University of Madrid; President of the Cortes Constituyentes from 1931 to 1933; remained in Madrid throughout the Civil War, endeavored unsuccessfully to arrange an honorable peace; condemned to death, died in prison several months later.
Botella y Pérez, Alvaro	(d. 1939). Politician and journalist; owner and managing editor of *El Luchador,* republican newspaper of Alicante.
Cabanellas Ferrer, Miguel	(1872–1932). General; conspired in favor of the Republic in 1931; prominent in military uprising; president of the Burgos *Junta.*
Calvo Sotelo, José	(1893–1936). Lawyer; politician; held important posts under Primo de Rivera; monarchist; active in opposition to the Republic; leader of Renovación Española; his assassination on July 13, 1936, by a group of Assault Guards to avenge the shooting of one of their number—Lieutenant Castillo—precipitated the Civil War.
Casares Quiroga, Santiago	(1884–1950). Lawyer; politician; member of the revolutionary committee that paved the way in 1931 for the Republic; held various cabinet posts under Azafia.

Castillo, Lieutenant	*See* Calvo Sotelo, José
Cid, El (Rodrigo Diaz de Bivarv)	(1043?–1099). National hero.
Claret, Father	(1807–1870). Priest; Archbishop of Santiago de Cuba; confessor of Isabel II; beatified in 1934, canonized in 1950.
Companys, Luis	(1883–1940). Catalan lawyer and politician; appointed civilian governor of Barcelona under the Republic; at time of uprising of October 1934 was tried by court martial and sentenced to life imprisonment; freed on triumph of the Popular Front in February 1936; restored to post; remained in office during the Civil War; took refuge in France; was returned to Spain in 1940; condemned to death; executed.
Costa, Joaquín	(1846–1911). Jurist; politician; sociologist.
Franco Bahamonde, Francisco	(1892–1975). Head of the Spanish State since 1939; collaborated with General Millan Astray in forming the Spanish Foreign Legion, which he commanded in 1921; appointed military commander of the Balearic Islands by the Republic in 1933; made brigadier general in 1934; chief of staff the same year; after triumph of the Popular Front, named military commander of the Canary Islands; when military uprising began, he flew to Morocco and took command of the troops.
Galán Rodríguez, Fermín	(1894–1930). Army captain who took part in army revolt in 1926; sentenced to military prison for two years; revolted against the monarchy on December 12, 1930; tried and executed two days later.
Ganivet, Angel	(1865–1898). Writer and diplomat; precursor of the "generation of 1898."
García Hernández, Angel	(1900–1930). Army captain associated with Captain Galán (q.v.) in uprising that prepared the way for the Republic; tried and executed on December 14, 1930.
Gil Robles, José María	(1898–1980). Professor; politician; head of Acción Popular and the CEDA; Minister of War in the Lerroux Cabinet, 1934–1935; shortly before outbreak of the Civil War went to Portugal, where he resided.

Giner de los Ríos, Francisco	(1839–1915). Professor, educator, and philosopher; founded the Institución Libre de Enseñanza, a school where liberal professors expelled from the universities could carry on their teaching, and which later continued as a liberal school.
Goded, Manuel	(1882–1936). General; chief of staff, 1931; military commander of the Balearic Islands, 1936; in military uprising of 1936, took command of garrison in Barcelona; surrendered to triumphant republican forces; tried by court martial; executed.
Giocoechea, Antonio	(1876–1953). Lawyer and politician; member of monarchist party, Renovación Española; collaborated with Franco.
Granada, Fray Luis de	(1504–1588). Mystic and preacher of the Dominican Order.
Hernández, Jesús	Communist; Minister of Education, 1936–1938.
Isidore of Seville, St.	(560?–636). Bishop of Seville; famous for his learning; author of *Etymologies*, well known in the Middle Ages.
Kautsky, Karl	(1854–1938). German Socialist; important theoretician of Marxism.
Kun, Béla	(1886–1938). Hungarian Communist leader; Premier of Hungary in 1919.
Largo Caballero, Francisco	(1869–1946). Labor leader and politician; president of Socialist Party and the UGT; head of Spanish Government from September 1936 to May 1937.
Lerroux, Alejandro	(1864–1949). Journalist and politician; founder of Radical Party; joined forces with the CEDA in 1934; fled to Portugal on outbreak of the Civil War.
Llull, Ramón	(1235–1315). Catalan mystic and philosopher.
López Ochoa, Eduardo	(1877–1936). General; Captain General of Catalonia after proclamation of the Republic; under Gil Robles government, was entrusted with putting down revolutionary uprising in Asturias; killed by mob while patient in a Madrid hospital at outbreak of Civil War.

Lozovsky	(1878–1952). Soviet leader.
Maciá y Llusá, Francisco	(1859–1933). Catalan leader; on proclamation of the Republic, was appointed President of the Generalidad of Catalonia; when region was declared autonomous, was elected President of the Generalidad (1932).
Malatesta, Enrico	(1835–1932). Italian anarchist writer.
Maragall y Gorina, Juan	(1860–1911). Outstanding Catalan poet.
March, Ausías	(1397?–1460). Famous Catalan poet.
Martínez Barrios, Diego	(1853–1958). Politician; member of revolutionary committee responsible for bringing in the Republic; held various cabinet posts; after triumph of the Popular Front, became President of the Cortes; after Franco's triumph, an exile in Mexico.
Martínez Campos, Arsenio	(1831–1900). General and statesman.
Metge, Bernat	(1350–1413). Catalan writer and humanist.
Miaja Menant, José	(1878–1958). General; military commander of Madrid at outbreak of the Civil War; commanded republican troops.
Mola Vidal, Emilio	(1887–1937). General; military commander of Pamplona at outbreak of the Civil War; took command of nationalist forces advancing on Madrid; coined phrase "fifth column"; killed in airplane accident.
Nelken, Margarita	(1898–1968). Writer, art critic, politician; first Socialist, then Communist; later broke with Communism.
Pasionaria, La (Dolores Ibárruri)	(1885–1989). Labor leader; Communist deputy to 1936 Cortes; General Secretary of the Spanish Communist Party since 1942; resided in the Soviet Union.
Prieto y Tuero, Indalecio	(1883–1962). Politician and journalist; Socialist; held various cabinet posts under the Republic; Minister of Defense, 1937–1938; resided in Mexico.
Primo de Rivera, José Antonio	(1903–1936). Political leader, son of General Primo de Rivera; founded the Falange Espanola

	in 1933; after Popular Front triumph in 1936, was arrested; accused of having inspired and incited military uprising, he was tried, condemned to death, and executed on November 20, 1936.
Primo de Rivera y Orbaneja, Miguel	(1870–1930). General; in 1923 set up Military Directory; governed as dictator of Spain from 1923 to 1929.
Queipo de Llano y Sierra, Gonzalo	(1875–1951). General; conspired against Primo de Rivera; fled to France; when the Republic was proclaimed, returned to Spain and was named Captain General of Madrid; on outbreak of the Civil War, supported the nationalist movement; Captain General of Seville throughout the war; became famous for his radio broadcasts.
Rafols, María	(1781–1853). Nun; heroine of the War of Independence.
Ramón y Cajal, Santiago	(1852–1934). Biologist; winner of a Nobel Prize.
Riquelme y López Bago, José	(1880–1972). General; on outbreak of the Civil War remained loyal to the Republic; fought on the Guadarrama front and in Extremadura; commanding general in Catalonia; resided in France.
Romanones, Count (Alvaro Figueroa y Torres)	(1863–1950). Politician and writer; leader of Liberal Party under the monarchy.
Salazar, Antonio de Oliveira	(1889–1970). Portuguese professor and politician; reorganized Portuguese Government into corporate state, which he has directed since 1933.
Sanjurjo y Sacanell, José	(1872–1936). General; at first favorable to the Republic, he headed a revolt against it in August 1932; tried and condemned to death; sentence commuted to life imprisonment: pardoned in 1934; from Portugal, he conspired in the nationalist uprising; killed in airplane accident as he prepared to leave Portugal for Spain.
Teresa, St.	(1512–1582). Nun; founder of discalced order of Carmelites; author of powerful mystical writings.
Unamuno y Jugo, Miguel de	(1864–1936). Writer and philosopher.
Yagüe Blanco, Juan	(1892–1952). General and politician; commanded the Foreign Legion on outbreak of the Civil War; at close of the war was made member of the National Council and Air Minister.

GLOSSARY TWO

Glossary of Organizations, Periodicals, and Spanish Terms

Acción Católica — Catholic organization represented politically by Acción Popular; founded in 1931; bore some resemblance to the German Catholic Party.

Alianza Obrera — Workers' Alliance organized by the Unión General de Trabajadores; intended as a sort of popular front confined to working-class parties.

Anarchists — The Anarchist Party of Spain was founded in 1872; it spread in both rural and industrial areas; through the Confederación Nacional del Trabajo, or CNT (q.v.), the federation of craft unions founded in 1910, a great number of Spanish workers, not necessarily anarchists, were impregnated with the anarchist spirit.

Arriba — Falangist newspaper of Madrid.

Casas Viejas — Andalusian village where small anarchist uprising occurred in 1933; its harsh repression by the Azafia government caused widespread indignation among working classes.

Carlists — Party that supported the claim of Don Carlos, brother of Ferdinand VII, and his descendants, to the Spanish throne; three civil wars were fought over this claim; reactionary Catholic movement opposed to liberalism; largely confined to the Basque Provinces, Catalonia, and Castile.

CEDA (*Confederación Española de Derechos Autónomos*) — Coalition of right-wing parties under the leadership of Gil Robles; its objective was organization

	of Spain along the lines of the Austrian Corporate State.
Claridad	Largo Caballero's left-wing Socialist newspaper.
CNT (*Confederación Nacional del Trabajo*)	Founded in 1910 by the Syndicalists, whose objective was the establishment of anarchism; opposed to the UGT, founded by the Socialists.
Congregation of María	Religious society.
Debate, El	Jesuit-controlled newspaper of Madrid.
Estat Català	Catalan youth movement founded by Maciá; violently antagonistic to the Anarcho-Syndicalists.
Estraperto	(literally Contraband). Name given to scandal that wrecked the CEDA-Radical coalition in 1935; several Radical ministers were accused of having taken bribes from a Dutch adventurer wishing to set up illegal gambling establishments in Spain.
FAI (*Federación Anarquista Ibérica*)	Semi-secret society of anarchists founded in 1927; members of the FAI had to be members of the CNT, though not all members of the CNT were in the FAI; designed to prevent Communist infiltration into anarchist groups.
Falange Española	Fascist organization founded in 1932 by José Antonio Primo de Rivera.
Generalidad	Government of autonomous Catalonia.
Izquierda Republicana	The Left republican party; formed largest group in the Cortes; represented active, progressive elements of middle and lower middle class; hoped to carry out a reform program that would arrest revolutionary tendency that had been growing since 1917 among workers.
JONS (*Juntas de Ofensiva Nacional Syndical*)	Several small fascist groups that merged with the Falange Española in 1934.
Liga Catalana	Catalan bourgeois party; Catholic, conservative.
Monarchists	Supporters of Alfonso XIII and his heirs.
Radical Party	Right-wing republican party led by Lerroux.

Radical Socialist Party	Left-wing republican party. *See* Izquierda Republicana.
POUM (*Partido Obrero de Unificación Marxista*)	Rigidly Marxist group organized in 1936, uniting two small dissident groups, the Bloque Obrero y Campesino and the Federación Comunista Ibérica; especially hated and persecuted by the Communists.
Renovación Española	Monarchist party headed by Calvo Sotelo.
Sardana	Catalan folk dance.
Socialist Party (*Partido Democrático Socialista Obrero*)	Founded in 1879; its first leader was Pablo Iglesias; grew very slowly at first; by bringing together various unions, in 1888 organized the UGT, trade union of ordinary social-democratic type directed toward improving workers' conditions; grew most rapidly from 1910 to 1917.
Traca, La	Satirical anticlerical newspaper of Valencia.
UGT (*Unión General de Trabajadores*)	*See* Socialist Party.

CLUNY MEDIA

Designed by Fiona Cecile Clarke, the CLUNY MEDIA *logo depicts a monk at work in the scriptorium, with a cat sitting at his feet.*

The monk represents our mission to emulate the invaluable contributions of the monks of Cluny in preserving the libraries of the West, our strivings to know and love the truth.

The cat at the monk's feet is Pangur Bán, from the eponymous Irish poem of the 9th century. The anonymous poet compares his scholarly pursuit of truth with the cat's happy hunting of mice. The depiction of Pangur Bán is an homage to the work of the monks of Irish monasteries and a sign of the joy we at Cluny take in our trade.

"Messe ocus Pangur Bán,
cechtar nathar fria saindan:
bíth a menmasam fri seilgg,
mu memna céin im saincheirdd."

Made in the USA
Las Vegas, NV
15 November 2021

34525377R00246